Praise for THE DEVIL'S COMPANY

"*The Devil's Company,* a treat for lovers of historical fiction, sees the return of Benjamin Weaver in his third exciting romp through the varied and sometimes surreal landscape of eighteenth-century London. [Weaver's] underlying humanity saves him from the macho posturing that ultimately undermines the moral authority of most action-adventure heroes. . . . The narrative keeps us fully engaged with phaeton and boat chases, explosions, seductions and a colorful visit to a brothel. . . . Liss's eighteenth-century London is one that James Bond would have felt at home in. The action is fast and full of surprises. . . . Another virtue of *The Devil's Company* is its timely subtext, which explores the beginnings of corporate culture and globalization. . . . The success of [historical fiction] depends largely on creating a convincing illusion. In this respect, the novelist's principal tool is language, which must sound authentic but never drag or test the reader's patience. Liss rises to this challenge with great skill in this accomplished, atmospheric and thoughtful novel." —*The Washington Post*

"Creepily prescient . . . Liss is a standout in his ability to bring a period to life, and to find parallels between past and present. . . . Conspiracies and corporate corruption are common fodder for thrillers, but Liss's take is unique in both setting and detail. . . . *The Devil's Company* is as distinguished by the compelling voice of its narrator as it is by its vibrant detail. . . . A great story." —*The Denver Post*

"[Liss] sustains the action and suspense with sharp pace and uncluttered prose. . . . The historical frame is well constructed, and op-ed writers could do worse than study some of the back-and-forth given here on free trade. . . . Liss has done his work well." —*Bloomberg*

THE DEVIL'S COMPANY

THE DEVIL'S COMPANY

A Novel

DAVID LISS

BALLANTINE BOOKS
TRADE PAPERBACKS
NEW YORK

2010 Ballantine Books Trade Paperback Edition

Copyright © 2009 by David Liss
Random House reading group guide copyright © 2010 by
Random House, Inc.

Published in the United States by Ballantine Books,
an imprint of The Random House Publishing Group,
a division of Random House, Inc., New York.

BALLANTINE and colophon are registered trademarks
of Random House, Inc.
RANDOM HOUSE READER'S CIRCLE & Design is a registered
trademark of Random House, Inc.

Originally published in hardcover in the United States by Random House,
an imprint of The Random House Publishing Group,
a division of Random House, Inc., in 2009.

LIBRARY OF CONGRESS CATALOGING-IN-PUBLICATION DATA
Liss, David
The Devil's company: a novel / David Liss.
p. cm.
ISBN 978-0-8129-7452-2
eBook ISBN 978-1-5883-6911-6
1. Weaver, Benjamin (Fictitious character)—Fiction. 2. London (England)—
History—18th century—Fiction. 3. Private investigators—England—London—
Fiction. 4. Jews—England—London—Fiction. 5. East India
Company—Fiction. I. Title

PS3562.I7814D472007   813'.6—dc22   2006045129

Printed in the United States of America

www.randomhousereaderscircle.com

2 4 6 8 9 7 5 3 1

Book design by Barbara M. Bachman

THE DEVIL'S COMPANY

CHAPTER ONE

—

*I*N MY YOUTH I SUFFERED FROM TOO CLOSE A PROXIMITY TO GAMING tables of all descriptions, and I watched in horror as Lady Fortune delivered money, sometimes not precisely my own, into another's hands. As a man of more seasoned years, one poised to enter his third decade of life, I knew far better than to let myself loose among such dangerous tools as dice and cards, engines of mischief good for nothing but giving a man false hope before dashing his dreams. However, I found it no difficult thing to make an exception on those rare occasions when it was another man's silver that filled my purse. And if that other man had engaged in machination that would guarantee that the dice should roll or the cards turn in my favor, so much the better. Those of overly scrupulous morals might suggest that to alter the odds in one's favor so illicitly is the lowest depth to which a soul can sink. Better a sneak thief, a murderer, even a traitor to his country, these men will argue, than a cheat at the gaming table. Perhaps it is so, but I was a cheat in the service of a generous patron, and that, to my mind, quieted the echoes of doubt.

I begin this tale in November of 1722, some eight months after the events of the general election of which I have previously written. The rancid waters of politics had washed over London, and indeed the nation, earlier that year, but once more the tide had receded, leaving us none the cleaner. In the spring, men had fought like gladiators in the service of this candidate or that party, but in the autumn matters sat as though nothing of moment had transpired, and the connivances of

Parliament and Whitehall galloped along as had ever been their custom. The kingdom would not face another general election for seven years, and in retrospect people could not quite recollect what had engendered the fuss of the last.

I had suffered many injuries in the events of the political turmoil, but my reputation as a thieftaker had ultimately enjoyed some benefits. I received no little notoriety in the newspapers, and though much of what the Grub Street hacks had to say of me was utterly scurrilous, my name had emerged somehow augmented, and since that time I had suffered no shortage of knocks upon my door. There were certainly those who might now stay away, fearing that my exploits had an unpleasant habit of attracting attention, but many more gazed with favor upon the idea of hiring a man such as myself, one who had fought pitched battles as a pugilist, escaped from Newgate Prison, and shown his mettle in resisting the mightiest political powers in the kingdom. A fellow who can do such things, these men reasoned, can certainly find that scoundrel who owes thirty pounds; he can find the name of the villain who plots to run off with a high-spirited daughter; he can bring to justice the rascal who stole a watch.

Such was the beer and meat of my trade, but, too, there were those who made more uncommon uses of my talents, which was why I found myself that November night in Kingsley's Coffeehouse, once a place of little reputation but now something far more vivacious. Kingsley's had been for the past season a gaming house of considerable fashion among the bon ton, and perhaps it would continue to enjoy this position for another season or two. The wits of London could not embrace this amusement or that for too long before they grew weary, but for the nonce Mr. Kingsley had taken full advantage of the good fortune granted him.

While during daylight hours a man might still come in for a dish of coffee or chocolate and enjoy reading a newspaper or hearing one read to him, come sundown he would need a constitution of iron to attend to dry words. Here now were nearly as many whores as there were gamers, and fine-looking whores at that. Search not at Kingsley's for diseased or half-starved doxies from Covent Garden or St. Giles. Indeed, the paragraph writers reported that Mrs. Kingsley herself inspected the jades to ensure they met her exacting standards. On hand as well were musicians who played lively ditties while an unnaturally slender posturer contorted his death's head of a face and skeletal body into the most unlikely shapes and attitudes—all while the crowd duly ignored him. Here were middling bottles of claret and port and Madeira to please discriminating men too distracted to discriminate. And here, most importantly, were the causes of the distraction: the gaming tables.

I could not have said what made Kingsley's tables rise from obscurity to glory. They looked much like any other, and yet the finest people of London directed their coachmen to this temple of fortune. After the play, after the opera, after the rout and the assembly, Kingsley's was the very place. Playing at faro were several well-situated gentlemen of the ministry, as well as a member of the House of Commons, more famous for his lavish parties than for his skills as a legislator. Losing at piquet was the son of the duke of Norwich. Several sprightly beaux tried to teach the celebrated comedienne Nance Oldfield to master the rules of hazard—and good luck to them, for it was a perplexing game. The great brought low and the low raised high—it all amused and entertained me, but my disposition mattered little. The silver in my purse and the banknotes in my pocket were not mine to wager according to my own inclinations. They were marked for the shame of a particular gentleman, one who had previously humiliated the man on whose behalf I now entered a contest of guile and deceit.

I spent a quarter of an hour walking through Kingsley's, enjoying the light of countless chandeliers and the warmth of their fires, for winter had come hard and early that year, and outside all was ice and bitter cold. At last, grown warm and eager, with the music and laughter and the enticements of whores buzzing in my head, I began to formulate my plan. I sipped at thinned Madeira and sought out my man without seeming to seek out anyone. Such was an easy task, for I had dressed myself as a beau of the most foppish sort, and if the nearby revelers took notice of me they saw only a man who wished to be noticed, and what can be more invisible than that?

I wore an emerald-and-gold outer coat, embroidered almost beyond endurance, a waistcoat of the same color but opposing design, bright with brass buttons of some four inches in diameter. My breeches were of the finest velvet, my shoes more silver buckle than shiny leather, and the lace of my sleeves blossomed like frilly blunderbusses. That I might go unrecognized should anyone there know my face, I also wore a massive wig of the wiry sort that was fashionable that year among the more peacockish sort of man.

When the time and the circumstances seemed to me as I wished them, I approached the cacho table and came upon my man. He was a fellow my own age or thereabouts, dressed very expensively but without the frills and bright colors in which I'd costumed myself. His suit was of a sedate and dark blue with red trim, embroidered tastefully with gold thread, and he looked quite well in it. In truth, he had a handsome face beneath his short bob wig. At his table, he contemplated with the seriousness of a scholar the three cards in his hand and said something in the general direction of the ample breasts belonging to the whore upon his lap. She laughed, which I suspected was in no small degree how she earned her master's favor.

This man was Robert Bailor. I had been hired by a Mr. Jerome Cobb, whom it seemed Bailor had humiliated in a game of chance, the outcome of which, my patron believed, owed more to chicanery than fortune. The tale I had been told unfolded accordingly: Subsequent to losing a great deal of money, my patron had discovered that Bailor possessed the reputation of a gamer who misliked the randomness of chance as much as he misliked duels. Mr. Cobb, acting upon his prerogative as a gentleman, challenged this Bailor, but Bailor had insolently excused himself, leaving the injured gentleman with no option but perfidy of his own.

Needing a man to act as his agent in these matters, he had sought me out and addressed his needs to me. I was, according to Mr. Cobb's instruction, to manufacture a battle of cards with Bailor. Mr. Cobb had employed me to that end, but I was not the only one in his pay. So, too, was a particular card dealer at Kingsley's, who was to make certain I lost when I wished to lose and, more importantly, won when I wished to win. Once I had succeeded in humiliating Mr. Bailor before as large a crowd as I could muster, I was to whisper to him, so that no other ears might hear, that he had felt the long reach of Mr. Cobb.

I approached the red velvet cacho table and stared for a moment at Bailor's whore and then for another moment at Bailor himself. Mr. Cobb had informed me of every known particularity of his enemy's character, among them that Bailor had no love for the gaze of strangers and loathed a fop above all things. A staring fop could not fail to attract his notice.

Bailor set down his three cards upon the table and the other two players did as well. After a smirk, he gathered the pile of money to himself. He slowly raised to me a pair of narrow eyes. The light was such that I could observe their dull gray color and that they were well lined with red, sure signs of a man who has been at play too long, has enjoyed his spirits overmuch, and is vastly in need of sleep.

Though somewhat hampered by bushy brows and a flattened nose with wide and flaring nostrils, he also possessed strong cheekbones and a square chin, and he was built like a man who enjoyed riding more than beef or beer. He therefore had something commanding about him.

"Direct your eyes elsewhere, sir," he told me, "or I shall teach you the manners your education has sadly omitted."

"Och, you're a rude one, ain't you, laddie?" I said, affecting the accent of a Scotsman, for in addition to fops, I had been made to understand that Bailor detested North Britons, and I was fully outfitted to attract his ire. "I was only having a wee peek at the lassie you've got 'pon you. Perhaps, as you're not using her for aught but a lap warmer, you might lend her to me for a spell."

His eyes narrowed. "I hardly think you would know what to do with a woman, Sawny," he answered, using that name so insulting to Scotsmen.

For my part, I pretended to hold myself above such abuse. "I ken I wouldn't let her turn stale while I sat playing at card games. I ken as much as that."

"You offend me, sir," he said. "Not only with your odious words but with your very being, which is an affront to this city and this country."

"I canna answer for that. Your offense is your own. Will you lend me the lassie or no?"

"No," he said quietly. "I shan't. What I shall do is challenge you to a duel."

This drew a gasp, and I saw that a crowd had gathered to watch us. Some twenty or thirty spectators—sharply dressed beaux with cynical laughs and their painted ladies—pulled in close now, whispering excitedly among themselves, fans flapping like a great mass of butterflies.

"A duel, you say?" I let out a laugh. I knew what he meant but pretended to ignorance. "If your honor is so delicate a thing, then I'll help you see who is the man of the two of us. Have ye in mind blades or pistols, then? I promise ye, I am equally partial to both."

He answered with a derisive bark and a toss of the head, as though he could not believe there was still a backwards creature who dueled with instruments of violence. "I have no time for such rude displays of barbarism. A duel of the cards, Sawny, if you are willing. Do you know cacho?"

"Aye, I ken it. 'Tis an amusement for lassies and ladies and little boys who haven't yet the hair on their chests, but if it is your amusement too I'll not shrink from your wee challenge."

The two gentlemen who had previously sat at his table now vacated, standing back that I might take one of the seats. I did so and, with the greatest degree of subtlety, glanced at the dealer of cards. He was a squat man with a red birthmark on his nose—just the fellow my employer, Mr. Cobb, had described to me. We exchanged the most fleeting of glances. All progressed in accordance with the plan.

"Another glass of this Madeira," I called out, to whatever servant might hear me. I removed from my coat an elaborately carved ivory snuffbox and with all deliberate slowness and delicacy took a pinch of the loathsome stuff. Then, to Mr. Bailor, I said, "What have ye in mind then, laddie? Five pounds? Is ten too much for ye?"

His friends laughed. He sneered. "Ten pounds? You must be mad. Have you never been to Kingsley's before?"

"It's me first time in London, for all it matters. What of it? I can assure ye that my reputation is secure in my native land."

"I know not what back alley of Edinburgh from which you come—"

I interrupted him. "'Tis not right you address me so. Ken ye I'm the Laird of Kyleakin?" I boomed, having only a poor notion of where Kyleakin was or if it was a significant enough place to have a laird at all. I did know that half the North Britons in the metropolis claimed to be laird of something, and the title earned the claimant more derision than respect.

"I have no concern for what bog you call home," Bailor said. "Know you that at Kingsley's no one plays for less than fifty pounds. If you cannot wager such an amount, get out and cease corrupting the air I breathe."

"Fie on your fifty pounds. 'Tis no more than a farthing to me." I produced a pocketbook, from which I retrieved two banknotes of twenty-five pounds each.

Bailor inspected them to ascertain their legitimacy, for neither counterfeit notes nor the promise of a dissolute laird of Kyleakin would answer his purposes. These, however, came from a local gold-smith of some reputation, and my adversary was satisfied. He threw in two banknotes of his own, which I picked up and proceeded to study, though I had no reason to believe—or to care—if they were not good. I merely wished to antagonize him. Accordingly, I peered at them from all angles, held them up to the burning candles, moved my eyes in to study the print most minutely.

"Put them down," he said, after a moment. "If you haven't yet reached a conclusion, you never will unless you summon one of your highland seers. More to the point, my reputation is known here, yours is not. Now, we begin with a fifty-pound bet, but each additional wager must be no less than ten pounds. Do you understand?"

"Aye. Now let us duel." I placed my left hand on the table with my index finger extended. It was the agreed-upon signal to the dealer that I wished to lose the hand.

Even in such times when I often played at cards, I never much relished cacho, in which a man must make too many decisions based entirely on unknown factors. It is, in other words, a contest of chance rather than skill, and I have little interest in such. The game is played with a shortened deck—only the ace through the six of each suit in-cluded. Each player is dealt a card, he makes his wager, and then the circle is repeated twice more until each player possesses in his hand three cards. With the ace counting as a low card, whichever man has the best hand—or, in this case, the better hand—is declared winner.

I received an ace of hearts. A poor start as, in this simple game, hands were often won simply by a high card. I grinned as though I had received the very card I most desired and threw ten pounds into the center of the table. Bailor matched my bet, and my confederate dealer presented to me another card. The three of diamonds. Again, a poor showing. I added another ten, as did Bailor. My final card was the four of spades; a losing hand if I ever saw one. We both put in our ten pounds and then Bailor called me to lay my hand flat. I had nothing of value; He, however, presented a cacho, three cards of the same suit. In a single hand he had unburdened me of eighty pounds—approximately half as much as I might hope to earn in a year's time. However, as it was not my money and I had been instructed to lose it, I could not much lament its passing.

Bailor laughed as rudely as a puppet-show villain and asked if I wished to further mortify myself by playing another hand. I told him I would not shrink from his base challenge, and once more I signaled the dealer that I wished to lose. Accordingly, I soon lost another eighty pounds. I now began to affect the countenance of a man agitated by these events, and I grumbled and muttered and gulped angrily at my wine.

"I would say," Bailor told me, "that you have lost this duel. Now be gone with you. Go back north, paint yourself blue, and trouble no more our civilized climes."

"I've not lost yet," I told him. "Unless you are such a coward that you would run from me."

"I should be a strange sort of coward who would run from taking your money. Let us play another hand, then."

Though I may have had some initial reservations about my involvement in this deception, I began now to develop a genuine loathing of Bailor, and I looked to his defeat with great anticipation. "No more of these lassie wagers," I said, opening my notebook and taking out three hundred pounds' worth of notes, which I slapped down on the table.

Bailor gave the matter a moment's consideration and then matched my wager. I placed my right hand on the table with the index finger out—the signal that I would now win, for it was time to present this man with his unhappy deserts.

I received my first card, the six of clubs. A fine start, I thought, and added another two hundred pounds to the pile. I feared for a moment that Bailor would grow either suspicious or afraid of my bold maneuver, but he had offered the challenge himself and could not back down without appearing a poltroon. Indeed, he met my two hundred and raised me another hundred. I matched the bet quite happily.

The dealer presented our next cards, and I received the six of spades. I attempted to hide my pleasure. In cacho, the highest hand possible is that of three sixes. My employer's man meant to assure my victory. I therefore put in another two hundred pounds. Bailor met the wager but did not raise it. I could not be surprised that he grew uneasy. We had now both committed to eight hundred pounds, and its loss would surely hurt him a great deal. He was a man of some means, I had been told, but not infinite ones, and none but the wealthiest of lords and merchants can relinquish such sums without some distress.

"You're not raising this time, laddie?" I asked. "Are ye beginning to quake?"

"Shut your Scots mouth," he said.

I grinned, for I knew he had nothing, and my Scots persona would know it too.

And then I received my third card. The two of diamonds.

I strained against the urge to tell the dealer he had made a mistake. He had meant to give me a third six, surely. With so much of my patron's money on the table, I felt a tremor of fear at the prospect of losing. I quickly calmed myself, however, recognizing that I had been merely anticipating something far more theatrical than what the dealer had planned. A victory of three sixes might look too much like the deception that we, indeed, perpetrated. My collaborator would merely give Bailor a less distinguished hand, and our contest would be determined by a high card. The loss for my opponent would be no less bitter for its being accomplished by unremarkable means.

All about us the crowd had grown thick with spectators, and the air was warm with the heat of their bodies and breath. It was all as my patron would have wished. I glanced at the dealer, who gave me the most abbreviated of nods. He had seen my doubt and answered it. "Another hundred," I said, not wishing to wager more as my store of Cobb's money grew thin. I wished to have something left should Bailor raise the bet. He did so by another fifty pounds, leaving me with fewer than a hundred pounds of Mr. Cobb's money on my person.

Bailor grinned at me. "Now we shall see, Sawny, who is the better man."

I returned the grin and set forth my cards. "Not so bonny as I would like, but I've won with less."

"Perhaps," he said, "but this time you would have lost with more." He laid down his own cards: a cacho—and not only a cacho, but one with a six, five, and four. This was the second highest hand in the game, one I could have bested only with three sixes. I had lost, and lost soundly.

I felt a dizziness pass over me. Something had gone wrong, horribly wrong. I had done everything Mr. Cobb had said. The dealer had shown every sign of being Cobb's man. I had delivered the signals as planned. Yet I must now return to the man who hired me and report that I'd lost more than eleven hundred pounds of his money.

I glanced over at the dealer, but he would not meet my eye. Bailor, however, leered at me so lasciviously that I thought for a moment that he wished for me, and not his whore, to return with him to his rooms.

I rose from the table.

"Going somewhere, Sawny?" one of Bailor's friends asked.

"All hail the Laird of Kyleakin," another called out.

"Another hand!" Bailor himself shouted. "Or shall we call this duel concluded, and you the loser?" He then turned to his friends. "Perhaps I should take my winnings and buy all of Kyleakin and cast out its current master. I suspect I have quite a bit more than I should need upon this very table."

I said nothing, only wanting to escape from the coffeehouse, which now smelled to me intolerably of spilled wine and sweat and civet perfume. I wanted the shocking cold of the winter night air to wash over my face, that I might think of what to do next, contemplate how things had gone wrong and what I might say to the man who had entrusted me with his wealth.

I must have been walking far more slowly than I realized, for Bailor had come up behind me before I had reached the door. His friends were in tow, and his face was bright, flushed with victory. For a moment I thought he meant to challenge me to a duel of another sort, and in truth I would have welcomed such a thing, for it would have eased my mind some to have the opportunity to redeem myself in a contest of violence.

"What is it?" I asked of him. I would rather let him gloat than appear to run. Though I was in disguise and any behavior I might indulge would not tarnish my reputation, I was still a man and could not stomach flight.

He said nothing for a moment, but only gazed upon me. Then he leaned forward as if to salute my cheek, but instead he whispered some words in my ear. "I believe, Mr. Weaver," he said, addressing me by my true name, "that you have now felt the long reach of Jerome Cobb."

—

CHAPTER TWO

*A*T FIRST LIGHT I ROSE FROM MY BED, NEITHER RESTED NOR REFRESHED, for I had not slept as I turned over in my mind the events of the previous night. I made every effort to understand what had happened, as I anticipated the unpleasant meeting in which I would inform Mr. Cobb that, rather than delivering him his revenge, I had made him a staggering eleven hundred pounds the poorer. More than that, his intended victim had anticipated the ruse, and Bailor had offered yet another humiliation to Mr. Cobb. I had given serious consideration to at least a dozen possibilities to explain how I had come to such a turn, but none made sense save one. To understand why I reached such a conclusion, however, I should retreat a step and inform my readers of how I came to such a pass.

I had been in Mr. Cobb's employ for less than two days before my unfortunate encounter at Kingsley's Coffeehouse. I received his summons on a cold but pleasantly bright afternoon, and having nothing to prevent me from answering him, I attended his call at once at his house on Swallow Street, not far from St. James's Square. A fine house it was too, in one of the newer parts of the metropolis. The streets were wide and clean compared to much of London, and they were said to be, at least for the moment, comparatively free of beggars and thieves, though I was about to observe a change in that happy state.

The day was clear and a welcome winter sun shone upon me, but this was nevertheless London in the cold months, and the streets were slick with ice and packed snow, turned to shades of gray and brown and black. The city was thick and heavy with coal smoke. I could not be outside but five minutes before my lungs felt heavy with the stuff, and not much longer than that before I felt a coat of grime upon my skin. Come the first break of warm weather, I would always venture outside the metropolis for a day or two that I might repair my lungs with clean country air.

As I approached the house I observed a manservant on the street not half a block before me, walking with a large package under one arm. He wore a red and gold and pale green livery and held himself with a haughty bearing that bespoke a particular pride in his station.

I reflected that nothing attracts the resentment of the poor with greater rapidity than a proud servant, and as though the world itself responded to my thoughts, the fellow was now set upon by a crowd of a dozen or more ragged urchins, who appeared to materialize from the cracks between the buildings themselves. These unfortunates, full of grotesque glee, proceeded to dance about and tease him like demons of hell. They had nothing more original to say than *'Tis the popinjay* or *Look at him—he thinks he's a lord, he does.* Nevertheless, even from my rear vantage point I could see the manservant stiffening with what I thought was fear, though I soon realized my mistake. The urchins continued their harassment not half a minute before the servant lashed out like a viper with his free hand and grabbed one of the boys by the collar of his ragged coat.

He was a well-appointed servant, there could be no doubt of it, for his livery was crisp and clean—almost a martial style to it. For all that, he was also an odd-looking fellow, with eyes far apart and a disproportionately small nose set over comically protruding lips, so he resembled nothing so much as a confused duck—or, at this moment, an angry and confused duck.

The boy he grabbed could not have been more than eight years of age, and his clothes were so ragged I believed nothing but soil and crust held them together. His coat was torn, and I could see he wore no shirt beneath it, and his pants exposed his arse in a way that would have been comical upon the stage or revolting in an adult mendicant. In a child, it merely summoned feelings of deep melancholy. The boy's boots were the most pathetic thing of all, for they only covered the tops of his feet, and once the monstrous servant elevated the child, I could see his filthy, calloused, and bloodied soles.

The other children, equally tattered and filthy, shouted and danced about, calling names and now pelting the man with rocks, which the servant ignored like a great sea monster whose thick skin repelled assaulting harpoons. The boy in his clutches, meanwhile, turned a bright purple in the face and twitched this way and that like a hanged man at Tyburn thrashing the morris dance.

The manservant might have killed him. And why not? Who would prosecute a man for killing a thieving orphan, the sort of pest that hardly merited more concern than a rat? Though, as my reader will learn in the pages to follow, I am, when circumstances dictate, able to adopt the most plastic of morals, the strangulation of children rests firmly in the category of things I will not tolerate.

"Set the boy down," I called. Neither the urchins nor the footman had seen me, and now all turned to look as I approached the scene. I held myself erect and walked purposefully, for I had long since learned that an air of authority carries far more weight than any actual rights of office. "Set the child down, man."

The servant only sneered at me. He could perhaps tell from the simplicity of my clothing, and from observing that I wore my natural hair and no wig, that I was of the middling ranks only and no gentleman to be obeyed without question. Nevertheless, he heard the tone in my voice, and I trusted it contained something of command. Rather than intimidate him, however, it seemed only to make him angry, and for all I could tell he squeezed harder.

I observed that the child had not many seconds of life left in him, and I could not long delay further action. I therefore unsheathed my hanger and held it toward him—pointed precisely at his neck. I meant business, and I would not hold it like a fool making an idle threat.

"I'll not let the boy suffocate while I determine if you take me seriously or no," I said. "In five seconds, if you have not freed the boy, I will run you through. You are mistaken if you think I've done nothing so rash in the past, and I expect I shall do many more such things in the future."

The servant's eyes turned now to slits beneath his protruding forehead. He must have seen the glimmer of truth in my own eyes, for he at once slackened his grip, and the boy fell two feet to the ground, where his comrades came upon him and swept him away. Only a few of them bothered to glance back at me, and one did a sort of officious bow as they all moved backward to the periphery of where we stood—close enough to observe us, far enough that they might escape should the need arise.

The man continued to regard me, now with murderous rage in his eyes. If he could not strangle a boy, perhaps, he thought, he would take his chances with me.

I made it clear I gave no mind to such a thing and sheathed my blade. "Off with you, fellow," I said. "I've no words for a base creature who would delight in cruelty to children."

He turned to the now-distant boys. "You'll stay out of the house!" he cried. "I know not how you gain entry, but you'll stay out or I'll strangle every last one of you." He then condescended to turn his waterfowlish face to me. "Your sympathy is wasted upon them. They are thieves and villains, and your thoughtless actions today will only embolden them to further tricks."

"Yes. Far better to kill a child than embolden him."

The servant's wrath melted into a kind of simmering anger that I believed must be his version of neutrality. "Who are you? I've not seen you before on this street."

I chose not to give my name, for I did not know if my prospective employer wished to advertise his association with me. Instead, I gave the name of the man himself. "I have business with Mr. Jerome Cobb."

Something again shifted in his countenance. "Come with me, then," he said. "I'm Mr. Cobb's man."

The servant made every effort to achieve a more appropriate expression, and so seem to bury his resentment, at least until he could measure my significance to his master. He brought me inside an elegant town house and bade me wait in a sitting room full of chairs and settees of red velvet with gold trim. On the wall hung several portraits with thick golden frames, and between each a lengthy mirror made good use of the light. Silver sconces jutted from the walls, and an intricate and enormous Turkey rug covered the floor. From the house and neighborhood I clearly observed that Mr. Cobb was a man of some means, and the interior showed he was a man of some taste as well.

It is ever the way of rich men to have their lowly servants, such as myself, cool their heels for unreasonable lengths of time. I have never understood why it is that the men who unambiguously hold all of the power in the kingdom have to prove their power continually—I know not if they wish to prove it to me or themselves. Cobb was not like these men—not like them in many ways, I was to discover. He made me wait less than a quarter of an hour before he came into the sitting room, followed close behind by his glowering servant.

"Ah, Benjamin Weaver. A pleasure, sir, a pleasure." He bowed at me and gestured that I should return to the seat from which I had sprung. I bowed at him and sat.

"Edward," he said to his man, "get Mr. Weaver a glass of some of that delightful claret." Then he turned to me. "You do take claret, don't you?"

"Only if it is delightful," I answered.

He smiled at me. Mr. Cobb was indeed a smiling sort of man. He was in his later forties, stout in the way of such men and, I thought, handsome, with a lined face and bright blue eyes full of sparkle. He appeared jolly enough, but I had long since learned to be suspicious of jolly men. Sometimes they were what they appeared, and sometimes they were men who used the affect of good humor as a disguise to mask hidden cruelties.

Once Edward had placed the claret in my hands—it was, indeed, delightful and was contained in an ornate crystal goblet with a ribbed bowl, engraved with what appeared to be dancing fish—Cobb sat across from me in a red and gold chair, sipped at his wine, and closed his eyes with pleasure. "I have heard much approbatory discussion of you, Mr. Weaver. You are said to be the very man for finding lost things. It is also said of you that you know how to disguise yourself well. No small trick for someone about whom the papers have had so much to say."

"A gentleman might know my name without knowing my face," I said. "It is only the keenest of eyes that will recognize a face out of context. The properly chosen wig and coat will see to that. I know of such matters from experience."

"Your expertise in such things has been well reported. Consequently, I have a task I'd like to ask you to perform for me, which will require that you present yourself in disguise. It is an evening's work only and demands little more than that you go to a gaming house, drink and consort with whores, and play at cards with money not your own. I will pay you five pounds. What say you?"

"I say that if every man could make five pounds from behaving thus, there would hardly be a debtor in London."

He laughed and proceeded to tell me about Bailor, a card cheat who had defrauded Cobb in the most outrageous fashion during a game of cacho. "I can abide losing," he said, "and I can even abide being made to look the fool for doing so. However, when I learned that this Bailor is a Gypsy cozener, I could not abide that. I must have my revenge on him." Cobb then told me what he had in mind. Bailor would be at Kingsley's the next night. Cobb had already struck a bargain with the cacho dealer, so no more of me was required but that I draw attention to myself and entice Bailor to engage me in a challenge. Informed as I was of Bailor's dislikes, we easily agreed that I should go dressed as a foppish Scotsman. Cobb was nearly ready to hug himself with pleasure. "The trap shall be so easily sprung, I only wish I could see it for myself. But I fear my presence would alert him, so I shall stand down."

I then raised the issue of funds, and Cobb said he would make things easy on that score. He opened his pocketbook that rested near to his disposal and withdrew an impressive stack of banknotes. "Here are twelve hundred pounds," he said, though he made no indication that he wished to place them into my hands. "You must lose a bit here and there to entice him, but I wish the final blow to be as near to a thousand as you can make it." He continued to clutch the notes.

"You concern yourself, perhaps, with the safety of your money?"

"It is a great deal more than I am paying you."

"I believe, in even the most negative reports of my reputation, you have never heard it suggested that I am a thief or a cheat. I give my word that I shall deal with your money as you request."

"Yes, of course." Cobb rang the little bell on the table next to him.

The servant entered the room once more, this time with a dour man of approximately my age, which is to say, close to but not quite thirty. He had either a low forehead or his wig was pulled down too low, though I suspected it was the former, for he had other deficiencies of countenance—a nose too large and lumpy, sunken cheeks, a receding chin. He was, in short, a most unattractive man, and along with the servant they composed a pair of most unpleasant faces. I do not much hold to physiognomy, but something in their ugliness told me that their characters were stamped on their faces.

"Mr. Weaver, over there you see my nephew, Mr. Tobias Hammond, a dedicated servant of his majesty at the Customs House."

Hammond bowed stiffly. I rose and returned the greeting.

"He is employed at His Majesty's Customs House," Cobb reiterated.

"Yes," I answered.

"I merely wished to point out his affiliation with the Customs House," Cobb said.

"Yes, Uncle," Hammond answered. "I believe he understands that."

Cobb turned back to me. "Though, as you say, I have never heard a believable word uttered to impeach your honesty, I hope you will not mind that I bring in a pair of witnesses to see that I am entrusting twelve hundred pounds to your care. I expect you will return it no later than Thursday morning with whatever winnings you should earn off it. As these winnings will be collected through my own machinations, I trust you will not claim a percentage of them for yourself."

"Of course. I can return the money to you that very night, if you prefer. I should be more comfortable having it in my possession for the briefest period possible."

"Lest you be tempted to steal it, I suppose?" He let out a laugh.

"It is a great deal of money, so of course I shall be tempted, but I have ever been used to mastering my temptations."

"Uncle, are you quite certain this is wise?" asked the nephew, Mr. Hammond of the Customs House.

"Oh, it's the thing," Cobb answered.

Hammond screwed his awkward face into an even more unappealing mask of discontent. He turned to the servant. "That will be all, Edmond."

Edmond, I thought. Cobb had called him *Edward.* Once the servant had left, Mr. Hammond regarded me with hard brown eyes.

"I understand that Mr. Weaver has an acceptable reputation," he said, "but it cannot be a sound practice to trust any man with this sum, more than he could hope to gain honestly in many years."

"It is a substantial sum," I agreed, "but stealing it would mean I must hide myself, abandon my good name, and have no prospects for future income. Furthermore, if after this employment word should spread that I had been entrusted with this sum and that Mr. Cobb's trust was safe, then my future income can only grow. It would be a poor investment indeed for me to act the thief. Nevertheless, this is

Mr. Cobb's plan and not my own. I did not ask to be so entrusted, and I shall not insist upon it."

"I should have him sign a note if it were my money," Hammond observed.

"If it were your money, you could do as you like, as I shall do with mine." Cobb spoke entirely without bitterness. Indeed, there was a certain good nature to his tone, as if he were unfamiliar with pique. "What means papers when we have witnesses? It is all one, and I believe no paper can stand the surety of Mr. Weaver's reputation."

"As you like, sir." Hammond bowed and retreated.

Mr. Cobb spent the next half hour or so telling me more of what he knew of the dealer and of Bailor and what I was to say when I defeated him. I left confident that I could earn my five pounds without fail, but I also felt uneasy, for no man can have upon him twelve hundred pounds in negotiable bills and feel at ease. I wanted only to do what was asked of me and return with all deliberate speed.

As I left the house I saw the servant waiting by the door to watch me leave. He had an air of suspicion in his eye and seemed to want to make certain I did not steal anything on my way out. I hardly knew why I should choose to do so when his master had entrusted me with so much ready money.

Before leaving, I turned to him. "Mr. Cobb called you Edward, but Mr. Hammond called you Edmond. Which is it?"

"Edgar," he told me, closing the door upon my face.

GIVEN EVERYTHING I KNEW of the plot Cobb had set forth, I came to one likely conclusion: The dealer had betrayed the plan to Mr. Bailor. He was, as I understood it, the only person besides Cobb, Hammond, and myself included in the secret; also, as he controlled the cards, no one else could have orchestrated things to so bad a result. He might well have offered some sort of amiable distribution of funds with Bailor. I thought to go find the scoundrel and pummel a confession from him before returning to Cobb's town house, but my good sense held me back. It was certainly true that the dealer might have changed the outcome to favor Bailor, but I could not prove it, and I needed more information in order to proceed. That the dealer's complicity was the most likely explanation did not make it the only explanation. I had seen animosity toward Mr. Cobb from both his servant and his nephew, and it was at least possible that one of them also had a hand in things.

To salvage my honor, I concluded I had no choice but to return to Mr. Cobb, tell him all that had happened, and volunteer not only to recover his funds but also to discover how his plan had gone wrong. There was much I did not know about the man, and I could not vouch for his prudence. It might be, I thought, that he was too foolish to keep quiet about the scheme beforehand. It is possible Bailor might have found out from a friend or some such thing, and it seemed unwise to pursue any course without further information.

I knocked on the door and the servant opened it at once, greeting me with his bill-like lips pressed into a sneer. "Weaver the Jew," he said.

"Edgar the child-strangling bootlick whom no one regards sufficiently to recall his name," I answered, for I was angry and tired and had no wish to play games with the man.

He showed me once more into the sitting room, where this time I did have to wait—perhaps three quarters of an hour—and every tick of the standing clock struck me like a blow. I felt very much like a man waiting for the surgeon to remove his kidney stones: I dreaded the operation but understood its inevitability and wanted it started that it might be over the sooner. At last Edgar returned and invited me into the parlor. Mr. Cobb, dressed in a sedate brown suit, stood in anticipation, smiling with the eagerness of a child who anticipates a sweetmeat. Sitting in an armchair across the room, lumpy nose lost in a newspaper, lurked Mr. Hammond. He raised his eyes toward me but then returned to his reading without comment.

"I trust you have news, sir," Cobb said. His hands clenched and unclenched.

"I do," I told him, when he sat, "but it is not *good* news."

"Not good news." The smile flickered. "You do have the money to return?"

Now my presence captured Hammond's interest. He set down his newspaper and glared at me, his eyes, like the reluctant head of a turtle, just visible from under his bob wig.

"I am afraid I do not," I told him. "Something went quite wrong, sir, and though I do not love to offer excuses for myself, the matter was beyond my ability to alter. It is possible you may have been betrayed by the dealer, for the cards he gave me did not answer, and after the failure, he showed no signs of distress. I have given the events of last night a great deal of thought, and I believe—"

"It's as I predicted," Hammond said evenly. "The Jew has taken your money."

"It's been lost through perfidy," I replied, making the utmost effort to avoid sounding either haughty or wrathful, "but not mine, I assure you."

"Very likely you would tell us otherwise." Hammond harrumphed.

Cobb cooled his ardor with a look, however. "If you had stolen the money, I very much doubt you would be here to tell us of it."

"Bah," said Hammond. "He wants his five pounds in payment on top of what he's stolen. There's a rascal for you."

"Nonsense," Cobb said, more to me than his nephew. " Nevertheless, you do appear to have lost it, which, while a less contemptible offense, is hardly a forgivable one."

"I did lose it, and though I cannot blame myself, I consider myself both wronged and nearly involved. I assure you that I shall not rest until we discover who—"

"You assure *me*?" Cobb asked, something dark slipping into his voice. "I entrusted you with that money, and you assured me you would not betray my trust. Your assurances, I fear, may not answer."

"Anyone might have predicted this outcome," Hammond observed. "Indeed, I believe I did so myself."

"I did not betray your trust," I told Cobb, feeling myself growing hot. I had been as wronged as he and did not like his implications. "I must point out that it was your plan in which the trouble manifested itself. But that is no matter, for I am determined to—"

Cobb broke in once more. "*My plan,* says he. You are turning out to be a saucy fellow, Weaver. I'd not have thought it. Well, you may be as saucy as you like, but, once we have concluded with your efforts to lay this loss at my doorstep, you will accept that you owe me twelve hundred pounds."

Hammond nodded. "Quite right. He must repay at once."

"Repay? I must first learn who took it from you, and I will need your help. If you will take some moments to answer my questions, I believe we can discover who is responsible."

"What effort is this to screen yourself?" Hammond demanded. "You vowed to return the money this morning. Edward and I heard you say as much. Let us not see you attempt any base tricks now. You have either stolen or lost a great deal of money, and you wish to put my uncle to the question. That is great nerve, if you please."

Cobb shook his head. "I'm afraid my nephew has the right of it, Mr. Weaver. I should be undone in my finances if I were to ignore this debt. Sadly, I must demand you return the money now, this morning, as you agreed. If you cannot, I will have no recourse but to swear out an arrest warrant."

"An arrest?" I spoke more loudly than I should have preferred, but my passions were beginning to wriggle loose of their tethers. "You cannot be serious!"

"I am most serious. Can you pay of your own funds or not?"

"I cannot," I said, my voice as hard and resolute as the last words of a highwayman upon the gibbet. "And if I could, I would not." I might expect Cobb to be unhappy with how events had transpired, but I never imagined he would treat me in this fashion. It was his other man who had failed him. Still, I recognized that he had me in a ticklish position, for he possessed witnesses who would swear they heard me promise to return the money, and I could not do so.

Thus, matters being as they were and Cobb making demands such as he did, I began to feel the tingle of suspicion. There was more to this than I understood. Cobb had made certain that the witnesses heard my agreement to return the money, but they had not heard—at least that I could swear to—the details of the evening at Kingsley's.

"Are you suggesting," I asked, "that I must find such money or go to prison? How can that possibly be in your interest when I am not the one who cheated you and, if I am imprisoned, I cannot recover what you've lost?"

"Nevertheless, it is the situation in which you find yourself," Hammond said.

I shook my head. "No, this is not right." I did not speak to the justice of these matters, but rather to their orderliness. Why should Cobb insist that I pay him now, that moment? The only reason I could devise left me nearly breathless with astonishment. I could not but conclude that the dealer had been working with Cobb and so had Bailor. The money was not lost at all. I was.

"You say that you wish me to pay or go to prison," I said. "And yet I suspect you are on the verge of proposing a third option."

Cobb let out a laugh. "It is true that I should hate to see a man of your talents ruined by such a debt, a debt he could surely never pay. I am therefore willing to let you, shall we say, work the debt off, much as transportees work off their debts through their labor in the New World."

"Quite right," Hammond agreed. "If he cannot return the money, and he does not wish to go to prison, he must take the third choice— that of being our indentured servant."

I rose from my seat. "If you think I will countenance such treatment, you are mistaken. You shall see, sir, that I am not about to endure your contrivances."

"I shall tell you what I see, Mr. Weaver," Hammond answered, rising to meet my height. "I see that your preferences in this matter don't signify. Now take your seat and listen."

He returned to his seat. I did not.

"Please," Cobb said, in a cooler voice. "I understand you are angry, but you must know I am not your enemy, and I mean you no harm. I merely wished to secure your services in a more reliable way than the usual."

I would listen to none of it. I hurried past him and into the hall. Edgar stood by the door, grinning at me.

From behind me, Cobb said in an easy and calm voice, "We shall work out the details upon your return. I know what you must do, and I expect you to do it, but when you are done, you will return to me. I'm afraid you have no other choice. You will see that soon enough."

He spoke the truth, for I had no choice. I thought I did. I thought I had a difficult choice, and I went to pursue it, only to discover that my situation was far worse than it already appeared.

CHAPTER THREE

—

*I*T WAS NO LATER THAN MIDMORNING WHEN I LEFT COBB'S HOUSE, but I staggered in the streets as though I had drunkenly removed myself from an alehouse or bagnio in which I had reveled all night. I therefore made all efforts to master myself, for I had no time for beating my breast like Job to lament unjust suffering. I knew not why Cobb should have gone to such considerable trouble to make me his debtor, but I was determined to remain ignorant until I was no longer in his power. Once I had cleared myself of his debt, let us say, and knocked him upon the floor with a blade to his throat, I should be happy to inquire as to his motives. If I asked while he could threaten me with arrest, I should scarce be able to endure the feeling of being his supplicant.

Supplication, nevertheless, would be the order of the day, and though I could not bring myself to live in Cobb's power, there were, I told myself, more benevolent forces in the world. I therefore endured the expense of a hackney—reasoning that a few coppers could hardly alter the shape of my now monstrous debt—and went to that rank and foul part of the metropolis called Wapping, where my uncle Miguel maintained his warehouse.

The streets were too clogged with traffic and peddlers and oyster women for me to dismount directly before the building, so I walked the last few minutes, smelling the ripe brine of the river and the only slightly less ripeness of the mendicants around me. A young boy wearing a tattered white shirt and nothing more, despite the bitter cold, tried to sell me shrimps that had likely turned sour last week, and their perfume sent my eyes to tearing. Still, I could not help but observe with pity his bloody and coal-encrusted feet, filth frozen into his flesh, and out of an eleemosynary impulse I dropped a coin upon his tray, for I thought that anyone desperate enough to try to sell such rubbish must be on the very brink of starvation. Only after he walked away, a little gleam in his eye, did I realize that I had fallen into his very trap. Was there anyone left in the metropolis, I wondered, who was what he appeared?

I expected to be assaulted by the usual chaos of business when I stepped into my uncle's warehouse. He earned his respectable income in the trade of importer and exporter, calling upon his connections with the far-flung communities of Portuguese Jews throughout the world. He would bring in all manner of goods to sell—ambergris, syrup, dried figs and dates, Dutch butters and herrings—but the bulk of his trade was in the acquisition of the wines of Spain and Portugal and the sale of British woolens. Here was a trade I could much admire in so near a relative, for every time I visited his house I could anticipate a gift of a fine bottle of port or Madeira or canary.

I was accustomed, upon entering the warehouse, to being bombarded with countless men in the process of moving boxes and barrels and crates from this place to that, intent upon their work and as confident in their destination as the myriad ants of a swarming colony. I expected the floors to be stacked high with receptacles, the smell of the building to be full of the richness of spilled wine or the sweetness of dried fruit. Today, however, only a few porters milled about, and the air in the building was thick and humid, heavy with the scent of British woolens and with something more pernicious as well. Indeed, the warehouse appeared to be cold and nearly empty, and few of his regular laborers went about their business.

I glanced about, hoping to see my uncle, but I was instead approached by his longtime assistant, Joseph Delgado. Like those of my family, Joseph was a Hebrew of the Portuguese nation, born in Amsterdam and moved here as a child. To the casual observer, he would appear as nothing but an Englishman, however, for he dressed like a man of the trading ranks and wore his face cleanly shaved. He was a good fellow, one I had known since I was a boy, and he had ever had the kind word for me.

"Ah, young master Benjamin," he cried out. I had always taken amusement in his addressing me as though I were still a child, but I understood it well. He did not like to call me by my assumed name, Weaver, for I had taken it when I'd fled my father's house as a boy and it was a marker of my rebelliousness. He could not understand why I refused to return to the family name, Lienzo, so he would call me neither one nor the other. In truth, now that my father was dead and I had grown to live on such familiar terms with my uncle and aunt, the family name no longer sat ill with me. However, the world knew me as Weaver, and I earned my bread based upon my reputation. There was no turning back.

I took his hand in greeting. "It has grown quiet here, I see."

"Oh, aye," he said gravely. "'Tis quiet indeed. Like a graveyard quiet."

I studied his weathered countenance as a dark mood fell over him. The lines and crevices of his face appeared now gulfs and jagged valleys. "Is there some trouble?"

"I reckon that's why your uncle called for you, ain't it?"

"My uncle didn't call for me. I came on my own business." Then, seeing the hidden implication in the words, I thought I had cause to fear the worst. "Is he unwell?"

He shook his head. "No, not that. He is no more distressed than his usual. Things are bad enough. I wish only that he would entrust to me—or someone, I care not who—more of the trade. I fear his responsibilities harm his health."

"I know it," I said. "I have spoken to him before."

"It is that he has no son," Joseph said. "If only you, sir, would agree to shoulder—"

I shook my head. "I want my uncle to recover, not perish from the misery of watching me destroy his business. I know nothing of his trade, and I have no desire to learn it while each mistake could do him harm."

"But you must speak to him. You must implore him to rest. Now, he's in his closet. Go on back, my lad. Go on back."

I strolled to the far end of the building, where I found my uncle in his small office, seated behind his desk, strewn with ledgers and maps and manifests. He drank from a pewter cup full of thick wine—port, I supposed—and stared grimly out his window toward the Thames. He did not hear me enter.

I knocked upon the door as I walked in. "Uncle," I said.

He turned slowly, set the cup down, and rose to greet me, managing the task only by keeping one frail hand pressed hard on an ornate walking stick, an elaborate dragon's head composing the top. Even with the stick, each step was labored and sluggish, as though he waded through water. Nevertheless, he embraced me warmly and gestured for me to take my chair. "'Tis well you've come, Benjamin. Fortuitous, I suppose. I was going to call upon you."

"Joseph said as much."

He filled an identical pewter cup with the rich smelling port and gave it to me with a wavering hand. Even with much of his face covered by his neatly trimmed beard, I observed his skin to be dry and sallow and his eyes sunk deep in their sockets. "There is something you might be able to help with, but I presume you have your own business, so let us hear from you first, and then I will trouble you with my difficulties."

The words came slowly and with a rattling hollow sound as he drew a painful breath. For the past several months, my uncle had been suffering from a pleurisy that would lay him low with labored breathing and great pain in his chest. It would bring him, so we feared, to the very brink of a piteous end, and then, having so terrified him and those who cared for him, it would relent and his breathing would return to what we now thought of as normal—though it was far more constrained and troubled than it had been before the onset of the illness. Though he received frequent visits from a fashionable physician of good reputation, endured regular bleedings, and had each order for the apothecary filled at once, he continued to decline. Little would help, I believed, but a quitting of London, whose air was too filthy in the winter months for any man with diseased lungs. My uncle would not hear of it, however, being unwilling to relinquish his business, arguing that his trade was all he had done for his entire life, and he knew not how to live otherwise. Indeed, he supposed idleness would kill him faster than labor and soiled air. I believed my aunt still occasionally made an effort to work her entreaties upon him, but I had long since quit, believing that the argument did him harm and no expostulations I might offer would put him in a different frame of mind.

I watched him shuffle with old man steps to sit again at his large oaken desk, which sat before a well-tended fire. My uncle was not a tall man, and in recent years he had waxed plump like a good English merchant, but since growing ill this summer, much of that weight had melted like ice under the sun.

"You don't appear well, Uncle," I said.

"That is no kind way to begin a conversation," he said, with a thin smile.

"You must entrust Joseph with more duties and tend to your recovery."

He shook his head. "There may be no recovery."

"I will not listen—"

"Benjamin, there may be no recovery. I have accepted that it is so, and you must too. My duty to my family is to make certain that I leave behind a thriving business, not a vortex of debt."

"Perhaps you might summon José," I proposed, referring to my estranged brother, with whom I had not spoken since we were boys.

My uncle's eyebrows raised ever so slightly, and for a moment he appeared to be the healthy man I recalled from only half a year earlier. "You must be worried indeed to suggest such a thing. But, no, I have no wish to trouble him. He has business and a family of his own in Amsterdam. He cannot abandon his life to put my affairs in order. And I assure you I have will and strength enough to do what I must. Now, what is it that brings you here? I pray for the sake of domestic peace that you come not on your aunt's request, for I endure her pretty speeches enough at home."

"She had no need to instruct me, as you have seen. But I hesitate to add to your troubles, sir."

"Do you think you would not add to them if you refrain from letting me help you when I can? In sickness I see more clearly than ever that little matters beyond family. If I can assist you, it will give me pleasure to do so."

I could not but smile at his generous spirit. Only a man of my uncle's good nature could make it seem as though I aided him when I asked for help. "I find myself in trouble, Uncle, and though I wish not to add to your burdens, I fear you are the only person to whom I can turn."

"Then I'm glad you've come to me."

I, however, was not. On many occasions he had, suspecting my finances were none too mighty of stature, made it clear that he was ready to provide any assistance I might require. For my part, I made it a habit to refuse these offers, even on occasions when I was sneaking about the city to avoid capture by bailiffs with warrants sworn out by some exasperated creditor or other. Yet here was a new matter. This was not a case of my spending more than I earned—who of my station was not guilty of such an indiscretion?—but of my having been trepanned so vilely that I could not resolve my troubles without assistance. It made it easier to ask for money because the need was not my fault, but it was still no easy thing.

"Uncle," I began, "you know I have always loathed the thought of presuming upon your generosity, but I am afraid I find myself in the most awkward of positions. I have been wronged, you must understand—sorely wronged—and I require a loan of some funds to undo the crime that has been perpetrated against me."

He pressed his lips together in an unreadable expression, perhaps sympathy, perhaps physical pain. "Of course," he said, with far less warmth than I had anticipated. Here was a man who ever sought to thrust a purse in my hand. Now that I asked for it, he demonstrated reluctance. "How much will you require?"

"It is a great deal of money, I'm afraid: twelve hundred pounds. You see, a man has contrived to fabricate a claim of debt against me, and I need only pay it to relieve myself of danger. Once so free, I will be able to discover the mischief and, I believe, recover the sum—"

I stopped because I saw my uncle's face had gone pale. A silence fell upon us, broken only by his labored wheezing.

"I see," he said. "I had anticipated something more on the order of thirty or forty pounds, perhaps. I could even manage as much as a hundred, if need be. But twelve hundred I cannot do."

It was a large sum, but his hesitation surprised me. He dealt quite regularly with far larger sums, and he had extensive lines of credit. Could it be that he didn't trust me?

"Under usual circumstances, I should not hesitate to give you what you ask and more," he said, a loud rasp now entering into his voice, a sign, I had come to know in recent months, of his agitation. "You know I ever seek the opportunity to offer you aid, and I rankle at your refusal to let me, but there has been a catastrophe in my affairs, Benjamin. It is for that reason I thought to call you. Until this knot is untangled, I can't produce any sum of that sort."

"What knot is this?" I asked. I felt something uneasy churning within me. Some vague shape began to appear from the fog.

He rose to poke at the fire, working up, I presumed, the strength to tell his tale. After a minute or so of jabbing logs and sending sparks flying, he turned back to me. "I recently brought in a large shipment of wines—a very large shipment indeed. I import Portuguese wines as a matter of course, as you know, and there are one or two shipments each year to stock the warehouses and keep them full. This was one of them. As always, I purchased insurance upon the cargo to protect against this sort of thing, but it has done me no good. You see, the shipment arrived as it was supposed to, was delivered to the Customs House, and was registered there accordingly. Once it was unloaded, the maritime insurance ended, for the goods were considered safely delivered, but now they have disappeared."

"Disappeared," I repeated.

"Yes, the Customs House claims they have no record of my shipment. They claim my records are false, forged. Indeed, they have threatened me with prosecution if I choose to press the case, emphasizing as they do so the little justice members of our nation can expect in this country. I cannot understand it. I've dealt with these people for decades, you understand, and I have always provided the necessary payments to keep the customs men my friends. I've never heard a word of complaint from them, that I did not do my share or any such thing. I received no evidence that they were dissatisfied with my generosity. And now this."

"They toy with you? They hold your cargo hostage?"

He shook his head. "There is no implication of anything of the sort. Indeed, I have spoken to my longtime contacts there, men I consider nearly friends, men who hate to see me harmed because they have grown fond of my payments. They are as perplexed as I am. But the result is, Benjamin, that until this cargo can be discovered I am in rather severe debt. I have letters of credit being called in, and it is taking an inordinate amount of shifting and accounting maneuvers to keep from being discovered and ruined. If it were a few coins you required, it would make no difference, but I cannot discover anywhere a spare twelve hundred pounds. Removing such a brick from my edifice would make the building collapse."

"But the law," I proposed.

"I have begun legal proceedings, of course, but you know how these matters are. It is all delay and blockage and obscuring. It should be years, I think, before there is any answer from the law."

I took a moment to consider what I heard. Was it strange that my uncle should find himself in considerable debt at the same moment I did as well? No, it was not strange at all, it was design; I had no doubt of it. As Cobb had gone to such lengths to make clear, his nephew, Tobias Hammond, worked for the Customs House.

"Do you think, Benjamin, I could prevail upon you to look into this matter? Perhaps you could discover what has happened, and with that knowledge we might force a resolution more quickly."

I slammed my hand hard against his desk. "I am sorry this has happened to you, Uncle. You have been ill used on my account. I see now that someone has undone your business to keep me from receiving relief."

Briefly I told him of my dealings with Cobb, in part because I wished to know if he had any familiarity with these men and could tell me something of them. In truth, though, I wanted to explain to him all that had passed in the hopes that he would not judge me too harshly for whatever role I might have played in creating these troubles for him.

"I've never heard of either of these men. I can make inquiries if you'd like. If this Cobb has so much money to squander on making you his subject, he must be known."

"I would appreciate anything you might tell me."

"In the meantime," he said, "you must discover what it is he wants."

I hesitated for a moment. "I am not eager to do so. I cannot bear that I should be a puppet on his strings."

"You cannot fight him if you don't know who he is or why he would work so diligently to render you toothless. In revealing to you what he has in mind, he may also reveal to you the secret of how to defeat him."

IT WAS GOOD ADVICE and I could not ignore it, at least not for long. Nevertheless, I was not yet prepared to return to Cobb. I wanted more counsel before I did so.

I made arrangements to meet my friend and frequent collaborator, Elias Gordon, at a coffeehouse called the Greyhound off Grub Street, where I expected to find him inside with a newspaper and a dish of chocolate or perhaps a drink of some more considerable strength. Instead, I observed upon my approach that he was outside the coffeehouse, standing on the street, ignoring the snow that fell with increasing strength, and speaking most heatedly with a person I did not know.

The man with whom he engaged in this hot discourse was far shorter than Elias, as most men are, but wider and more manful in build—indeed, as most men are. Though dressed a gentleman in a fine-looking greatcoat and an expensive tie periwig, the stranger's face was red, his chest puffed out, and he spoke with the venom of a cornered street tough.

Elias had many fine qualities, but managing street toughs, or even rude men of breeding, was not among them. Tall, gangling, with long limbs too thin even for his slender form, Elias had always managed to radiate not only poise but a kind of good humor that I had many times observed the ladies found to their liking. So too did men and matrons, for Elias had, despite his humble origins in Scotland, risen to become a surgeon of some note in town. He was oft called upon to drain the blood and tend the wounds and pull the teeth of some of the best-situated families in the metropolis. Nevertheless, as with many men skilled at ingratiating themselves, he would inadvertently make enemies along the way.

I hurried forward to make certain that Elias would come to no harm. A man who has made his living through his fists learns perforce that other men do not love to be treated as children and overprotected, so I would make no overt threats to his enemy. Nevertheless, I hoped my presence would give some pause to any hasty violence.

The streets being mostly clear of all but pedestrians, I had no trouble crossing, and I soon found myself by Elias's side.

"Again, sir," he said, affecting a deep bow that caused his tie periwig to lurch forward, "I had no knowledge of your connection to the lady, and I am most sorry to have given you grief."

"You will be most sorry," said the other. "For first I shall pummel you like the street rubbish you are, and then I shall make certain that no lady or gentleman in the city allows so pernicious a Scots conniver as you into his home again."

I cleared my throat and stepped forward, inserting myself between the gentlemen. "May I inquire the nature of this dispute?"

"Damn your eyes, I know not who you are, but if you are a stranger, be gone. If you are a friend of this knave, keep quiet lest I make my displeasure known to you as well."

"This is a terrible misunderstanding," Elias said to me. "A deuced mishap, is all. I formed an attachment to a most amiable—and chaste, let me say, very chaste—young lady, who it appears is engaged to marry to this gentleman here. May I present Mr. Roger Chance? Mr. Chance, may I present Mr. Benjamin Weaver?"

"Damn you, Gordon, I have no interest in meeting your friends."

"Oh, but you may know Mr. Weaver's name, for he is a celebrated pugilist—most skilled in the arts of violence and now famous as a ruffian for hire." I may have been reluctant to insert myself into the fray, but Elias, it seems, was not reluctant to assert my qualifications. "In any event," he continued, "this young lady I met—well, she and I formed a friendly but purely chaste—I believe I mentioned that—attachment. We merely discussed philosophical principles of interest to inquiring young ladies. You know, she showed a very keen understanding of Mr. Locke. . . ." His voice trailed off as he, perhaps, came to understand the absurdity of his claim.

"And did these philosophical principles involve the removing of her petticoats?" Chance demanded.

"She had a question of anatomy," Elias explained weakly.

"Sir," I ventured, "Mr. Gordon has offered his apologies and pled ignorance. His reputation is known—"

"Reputation as a rascal!" Chance exclaimed.

"His reputation is known as a man of honor, and he would never have imposed upon an understanding between a man and a woman had he known it to exist."

This was perhaps the greatest nonsense I had ever uttered, but if it would preserve my friend, I would deliver it most earnestly.

"This coward refuses to duel," Chance said to me, "so I shall have no choice but to beat him like a dog."

"I never love to duel," Elias said. "Perhaps I can offer you some medical services as restitution."

Though I am Elias's friend, I cringed at this suggestion, and Chance was about to answer it as it deserved when a rumbling sound interrupted our discourse. We all at once attended to the noise; though we as yet saw no cause, we nevertheless witnessed the surprised shouts of pedestrians, whom I saw fleeing from the roadway farther up Grace Church Street. Seconds later, the first of several phaetons came careening toward us.

Icy as the streets were—and thickly populated by pedestrians, vehicles, and occasionally cattle—they made a poor surface for a phaeton race, yet such races had become all the rage that season, possibly because it had been an exceptionally icy winter and conditions were accordingly dangerous, appealing to the reckless pleasures of the rich, young, and idle. Thus far I had heard of as many as ten innocent Londoners killed and one racer severely wounded in these antics, but as these gladiators tended to be offspring of the better families in the kingdom, little had been done to curb the mayhem.

Elias and I instinctively pushed back to the buildings as the first of the phaetons whipped by, and Mr. Chance did the same, though he kept distance from us, lest we believe that we were allies in adversity.

I could not help but curse the foolishness of this sport. Even upon rural roads, where a small carriage driven by a single man and propelled by a single horse might race without risk to others, these vehicles were hardly built for high speeds. The driver stood in the open carriage, and the slightest bump could send a man flying to his doom. As the phaetons tore past us, each driven by a sniveling lordling or haughty young squire, I had cause to lament that none of these men had yet met with so deserving a fate.

After the cluster of phaetons passed, we let out a sigh as a single community, and many of the pedestrians began to go about their business. All, however, was not over, for there was one more adventurer, a young man in a green and black machine who had apparently fallen behind and now raced furiously to catch up with the pack.

"Out of my way, damn you all!" he cried as he came charging through the now-repopulated streets. Again, the pedestrians ran to press against the walls, but one little boy, not five years old, appeared to lose both his way and his mother and stood directly in the phaeton's path.

It is easy to think that a man with whom one has a disagreement must be a villain, but such is often not the case, and now I observed that Elias's enemy, Mr. Chance—whom I must point out, lest ill be thought of me, was the closest of all of us—darted forward, taking not an instant to assess the risk to his own person, and lifted the boy out of danger. He spun with the child in his arms, and set him down out of the phaeton's way. At least it should have been out of the way, but the fool of a driver careened too far toward our side of the road.

"Clear the road, rascal!" he cried to Chance, but the thought of slowing his horse apparently never occurred to him, and so it was that he charged directly into the man who had so recently been the savior of an innocent boy.

Chance spun and was able to avoid the hooves of the horses, but he was nonetheless knocked to the ground, where he slid away from the phaeton. He did not slide enough, and one of its wheels rolled directly over both his legs. The driver of the phaeton turned, saw what he had done, and spurred his horse farther away. The onlookers shouted and reached into the gutters for turds to hurl, but he was far too fast for their missiles to strike home.

Mr. Chance uttered the most pitiable of cries, but then fell silent and lay like a broken geegaw in the street. Elias rushed forward and first examined the man's face, to determine if he lived and then if he was conscious. Seeing that he was alive though dead to the world, he then examined his legs. He ran his hands down each one, and they came up covered with blood. Elias's face grew dark with concern.

"One leg merely has contusions," he said. "The other is quite broken."

I nodded, trying to think nothing of the pain of the thing, for I myself had suffered the breaking of a leg—a wound that ended my career as a pugilist. Elias had tended to me, however, and though many thought I should lose the limb outright, or at the very least never walk again, he had nursed me to near full recovery. I doubted his enemy, even if sensible, could understand his good fortune in his surgeon.

"Help me get him inside!" he shouted to me.

Together we took the man into the tavern and set him down upon a long table. Elias then gave a boy a list of supplies and sent the young fellow to the nearest apothecary. During this dismal period of waiting, the unfortunate Chance became sensible and cried out in the greatest pain. Elias fed him small sips of wine, and after a moment he managed to utter a few words.

"Damn you, Gordon," he said. "If it comes out that you killed me so you would not have to duel, then you shall hang for it."

"I confess it had been my plan," he answered, "but now that you have discovered it, I shall have to formulate another."

The jest appeared to confuse Chance, who swallowed more wine. "Save my leg," he said, "and I shall forgive your crime."

"Sir," Elias said, "I am so awed by your bravery and sacrifice in saving that boy that I promise I shall comply with your challenge upon your recovery, if the prospect of shooting me full of lead will encourage you to heal the sooner."

The man then lost consciousness, mercifully so, I thought. Soon thereafter, the boy arrived with Elias's equipment, and he went to work setting the wound and then delivering the man to his home. I shall not have occasion to speak of Chance in this history again, but I will tell the curious reader that he made a near full recovery, and thereafter sent Elias a note expressing that the debt between them was, in his mind, paid. I do not know if such a thing would have transpired had I not talked Elias out of sending Mr. Chance a bill for the services rendered and expenses laid out. Nevertheless, I believed Elias had the better bargain.

Once all was over, we sat in an alehouse while Elias calmed himself and recovered his spirits. He was mightily tired from his exertions, and in him such fatigue always led to a strong appetite for food and drink. He hunched over his plate, eating quickly of cold meats and buttered bread, talking excitedly between bites. "A rather funny business, don't you think, all this fussing about women? *Oh, you have ruined my wife! Oh, you have ruined my sister! Oh, you have ruined my daughter!* Can they not leave me alone?"

"Perhaps," I proposed, "you might consider being more prudent before bedding any more women. It may be inconsequential to you, but clearly it is not inconsequential to the men with whom they must deal. I suspect your presence is felt long after you've departed."

He grinned. "I like to think so."

"You know that's not what I mean. Surely you cannot imagine that these women can go back to their happy lives once their husbands or brothers or fathers have discovered their dalliances. Have you no concern for that?"

"Really, Weaver, you are being rather a bore about this. It's not as though these women don't understand the nature of their actions. If they choose to have a bit of fun with me, why should I deny them the pleasure?"

It would have been easy to explain why, but every bit as pointless. Elias had no ability to refuse women, even plain and ungainly ones. He had never had any restraint in this matter for as long as I'd known him, and it would be foolish to imagine that any efforts on my part would alter his behavior now.

He looked at me, as though awaiting more lecturing, and when he did not receive it he swallowed a mouthful of chop. "Well, Weaver, you wanted to see me about something before. I own there was a bit of a distraction, but we can discuss the business now. Good a time as any." He gulped down some ale. "I expect you need my assistance in some inquiry or other. I'm happy to provide it, but you ought to keep in mind I laid out all my ready on the surgical equipment for Chance. Pay my reckoning, and you shall have my full attention."

I was hardly a man with an excess of cash, and I resented his proposing this arrangement only after ordering heartily, but I lacked the will for argument, so I acquiesced.

"Can you listen or are you too disordered by the day's events?"

"I cannot say," he answered. "You had better make the tale interesting."

"Oh, I think this one will not fail on its own merits," I said, and began to recount to him all that had happened, from my first meeting with Cobb to my most recent encounter with my uncle. During the course of my tale, Elias ceased to eat. Instead he stared, half at me, half at nothing at all.

"Have you ever heard of this Cobb?" I asked when I was finished.

He shook his head slowly. "Never, which I think you'll agree is remarkable. A man of that sort, with so much money—it seems impossible that I should never have heard of him, for I know everyone who is known."

"You appear to be too stunned to eat," I observed. "I admit that my tale is strange, but you've heard stranger. What, then, startles you so?"

He pushed the plate away, apparently experiencing an unprecedented loss of appetite. "As you well know, Weaver, I'm not a man who likes to live within his means. That is why the Lord invented credit, so we can use it. And I am, in general, quite good at managing my affairs."

Discounting those times that I'd been called to rescue him from sponging houses after an arrest for debt, he was generally correct, and I said as much.

"I've discovered that, in the past few days, someone has been making a point to purchase my debts. Not all that I owe, mind you, but a good amount. As near as I can tell, some three or four hundred pounds' worth of arrears has been consolidated into a single hand. I've been wondering why, and why this person hasn't contacted me, but I believe I now understand."

"Cobb pursues my friends," I mused. "Why? You could not relieve my burden with him, so your debt will not make the difference. Why should he wish you to owe him?"

Elias seemed now to recall his appetite, and he brought his plate closer. "I don't know," he said, giving the meat a stab with his knife, "but I think it might be wise to find out. Sometime before I am arrested, if you please."

CHAPTER FOUR

—

*T*HE MOMENT I TURNED THE CORNER ONTO SWALLOW STREET AND approached Cobb's house, I found myself surrounded at once by a crowd of some four or five urchins, the very ones I had seen during my previous visit. "I know you," one of them said. He was not ten years old; his face and hands were covered with soot, and a pasty brown substance I did not care to ponder streaked his young face, making his bright blue eyes seem all the brighter. "You're that spark what saved Crooked Luke from the fart catcher, ain't you?"

"I never heard his name, but I did help the child," I agreed.

"What's your business with them, then?" he asked, gesturing with his head toward Cobb's house.

I stopped and studied the young fellow. "What's yours?" I held up a pair of coppers to sweeten our discourse.

He laughed and snatched the coins from my hand with such speed and dexterity it gave me cause to wonder if I'd ever held them at all. "Oh, I ain't got much business with that Edgar and his gents. Nah, we just love to give them something to get angry about, on account of Edgar thinking he's so much above us. He loves to chase us off, he does, and it drives him devilish angry when we break open their place, which is half the reason we do it."

"And what is the other half?"

He grinned at me, showing a mouth full of the black teeth of an old man. "The other half is for the rhino. They got plenty what's easy to sell for it."

"What do you know about Cobb?"

He shrugged. "Not much as I can say. He don't come out a lot, and when he do, he gets pushed into his coach right quick. We've jeered at him like we done with Edgar, but he don't pay us mind."

"Do they receive visitors often?"

"Not what I seen."

"Have you seen anything unusual about them?"

He gave this question some thought. "Only that there's hardly anyone in there. Big house like that, with two gentlemen and just the one servant, if you can credit it. Other than that, I can't say much about them. They stay all quiet-like."

"That will have to do for the moment, then." I handed him my card. "If you observe anything of note, come find me."

He looked at the card with the blank curiosity of the most ignorant savage. "What is it?"

"It's a card," I said. "It has my name and directions upon it. If you need to find me, ask someone to read it for you."

He nodded, as though I had explained some ecclesiastical mystery.

With the urchins continuing to watch me from the street, I knocked upon the door, and in a moment Edgar came and looked me over with a critical eye. "I'm surprised it took so long for you to return."

"Are you, now?" I punctuated my question with my fists. I struck him squarely in the nose, more with finesse than strength, and that organ erupted at once in a fount of blood. The servant fell back against the door, and I stepped forward, launching another blow to his face before he could sink to the ground. This one struck his jaw, and I felt confident I dislodged a tooth or two.

The gathered urchins let out a cheer, so I dragged the footman to the stoop and closed the door behind him. I would let the children make of him what they would. My only concern was that I deal with Cobb while he was free of anyone who might interfere.

I marched into the sitting room and found Cobb, as though prepared for me. I thought it fortunate that Hammond was not present, as he took a much harder position than did his uncle. Indeed, the older man sat placidly, sipping at a glass of wine and wearing his amiable smile. I would have none of it. I drew my blade and put it to his throat. "What do you want?"

He looked at the blade but did not flinch. "You're the one who's come bursting into my home," he pointed out. "Perhaps that is my question for you."

"Don't play games with me, sir, or you shall find yourself answering my questions while you stare at the tip of your nose on the floor."

"I don't think you want to antagonize me, Mr. Weaver. Not while I'm in a position to hurt you and your friends. As you have surely discovered by now, not only you but some of your associates have become my debtors. I should hate that any or all of you should rot away your lives in debtor's prison, though I suspect your uncle could resolve his problems should he sell his business and beggar himself, but I am certain he is loath to do that. Yet the fortunate news is that he need not do any such thing. That more salutary outcome is, as you have surely surmised, in your hands."

"What is it you want of me?"

"Put away the blade, sir," he said. "It shan't do you any good. You won't hurt me while I have so much power of you, and there is no reason why we cannot be friends. I think, when you hear what I have to say, you will find I am not an unreasonable man. I have no doubt that my methods will remain distasteful to you, but things will be far easier than you perhaps imagine."

He was certainly right that I could not stand all day with a sword to his throat, and I would be loath to harm him when he could do so much damage to my friends. I sheathed the blade, helped myself to a glass of wine, and sat across from Cobb, staring at him contemptuously. "Tell me, then."

"It is a simple matter, Mr. Weaver. I have a great deal of admiration for you and your abilities, and I wish you to work for me. I went to considerable trouble to ensure that you will do so. I hope you will forgive the masquerade I constructed, but I believed it the best way to secure your services and for you to understand that you dealt with no ordinary man."

"The trouble of making me your debtor, destroying my uncle's business, and buying Mr. Gordon's debts was surely more costly and laborious than simply hiring me. Why did you not offer to pay me for my services?"

"I did, but to my regret you declined." He must have seen my unknowing gaze, for he let out a breathy sort of laugh, took a drink, and began to answer my unstated question. "Not me, personally, you understand, but an associate. Not two weeks ago, a Mr. Westerly called upon you—perhaps you recall—offering quite a bit of money to perform a service, but you would have none of it. When it became evident you could not be hired for our needs, more extreme measures had to be devised."

I recalled this Mr. Westerly, a short, obscenely fat man who could walk only by swinging his arms with considerable strength to gain the momentum he required. He had been polite enough, deferential, full of encomiums upon my talents. None of that signified, however, for what he asked me to do had not only been impossible but foolish to the extreme, and I had turned him away with apologies. "Westerly works for you?"

"The precise hierarchy is not, in my opinion, important. Suffice to say, I have already taken your advice and attempted to hire you, and you have said no. As I could not do without you, and you would not sell your time by choice, I was forced to compel you to serve."

"And if I refuse to do what you ask, you will then ruin my friends and myself?"

"I should hate to do that, but yes."

"And if I do comply?"

Cobb smiled winsomely. "If you do all I ask, I shall make your debt disappear, and your friends' difficulties shall likewise vanish."

"I mislike having my hand forced," I told him.

"I should be very surprised if you did like it, but I promise all will be made easy. I shall happily pay you thirty pounds for this particular service, which I think you will agree is a very generous fee. And when you have done all that is required, you and your friends shall be under no further obligation to us. All very reasonable, I think you'll agree."

I felt anger surge through me. I hated, hated to my core, to allow this man to treat me as his plaything, to serve him whether I would or no—his thirty pounds be damned—but what choice did I have? He had been careful to learn what he could of me, and while I would have allowed myself to be dragged off to debtor's prison rather than do his bidding, I could not let my friends, who had come to my aid so often in the past, suffer now for my pride.

"I cannot like this," I told him, "and you must know that when I have fulfilled all obligations, you will have to be careful to avoid crossing my path, for I cannot let this treatment be forgotten."

"It is perhaps a poor negotiating strategy to discourage me from releasing you and your friends from my bonds."

"Perhaps it is," I agreed. "But you must understand the devil's bargain you make."

"Nevertheless, I feel confident that once we part ways you will come to feel differently about me. You will come to understand that though I have forced your hand, I have treated you with generosity, and you will have nothing ill to speak of me. That is the reason why I shall not let your threats deter me from my generous offer."

It seemed I had no choice but to act as his pawn for the moment, and the means and method of demonstrating my resentment would have to take shape at a later time. "Perhaps now it would be wise for you to remind me of what it is you wish."

"Very well," he said. He suppressed a smile, but I could see he was mightily pleased with himself. I had capitulated. Perhaps he knew I would, but perhaps he had not expected it to be so easy.

I felt a pang of regret. I should have been more intractable, I thought. I should have made him pay for this victory with blood. And then I thought of the brutalized Edgar and comforted myself that his had not been an entirely peaceable victory.

Cobb began at length to explain what it was he wished me to do. He gave no information on why, nor certainly on how, to achieve his goal. There was no mistake, however, that he wished it done, and quickly too. "Had you allowed Mr. Westerly to secure your services, we would have more time to plan, but we haven't that luxury now. Within the next two or three days, I believe, there is an opportunity that must be seized."

It was very short time, short time indeed, for me to don the role of housebreaker and force my way into the most heavily guarded estate in the kingdom—a property inhabited by some of the most powerful private men in the world. A scheme of this sort is well planned over the course of months, not days.

"You are mad," I told him. "How can I hope to break open such a house? They have watchmen and dogs and who knows what matter of protection."

"It is your task to discover the way," Cobb said. "Your friends are counting on your ingenuity, are they not?"

"And if you care nothing for your kinsman and associates, the thirty pounds ought to be enough incentive." It was Hammond. I had not seen him enter, but he now stood at the doorway, sneering at me in his low, pinched way.

I ignored Hammond and turned to Cobb. "Kinsman and *associates*?" I asked. "Have you pursued men other than my uncle and Mr. Gordon?"

"Ha!" Hammond barked. "The great thieftaker has not yet discovered all. Perhaps, Mr. Cobb, you have overstated his worth."

"There is another," Cobb said quietly. "You must understand that our goal is of the greatest importance, and we cannot risk even the possibility of failure, so in addition to the two men you have smoked, we have also meddled with the affairs of—"

"Wait, sir." Hammond clapped his hands together with a childish glee that upon his ugly face engendered a countenance too grotesque to be imagined. "Perhaps the pull of responsibility might be stronger if you withheld that information. Let him worry whose foot might next step into the trap. That's the very thing. Have you read Longinus on the sublime? He observes that darkness holds far greater terrors than any monstrosity, no matter how terrible, revealed in the light."

"I hardly think we needs must leave the gentleman on the rack in that regard," Cobb said easily. "Nor must we apply poetical theory to human affairs. I beg you, nephew, not to mistake cruelty for strategy. Though we force his hand at the first, we want Mr. Weaver as our friend when all is settled." He turned to me. "The third man we have so set upon is a Mr. Moses Franco, a neighbor of yours, I am told, and a particular friend."

I felt my color rising. The outrage of having my closest relation and dearest friend put under this burden was terrible enough, but to bear the responsibility for a man to whom I had so slight a connection was even worse. My uncle and Elias knew and trusted me and would have faith that I would do all I could in their service, but to see a man, hardly more than an acquaintance, dangle by the thread of my compliance drove me to distraction.

"Franco?" I spat. "The man is nothing to me. Why draw him into this madness?"

Hammond let out a chortle. "Nothing to you? Rot."

Cobb rubbed his hands together gently, mournfully, like a physician looking for the words to deliver an unpleasant prognosis. "I was led to believe, sir, that there is a connection between you and the Jewess, Miss Gabriella Franco. Do I not have the right of it?"

"You do not," I told him.

It had been for some three years or more my greatest wish to marry my cousin's widow, Miriam, but that affair ended badly and with no hope of felicitous resolution. Though my uncle Miguel had sought that union, he too understood that the fortress lay in ruins, and he had accordingly made some efforts to secure matches for me that would be, in his mind, advantageous to my domestic economy and happiness. Though it was my habit to resist these advances, I would, on occasion, call upon a lady of his choosing if I thought her of sufficient interest. Miss Franco was indeed a very fine woman with a sprightly character and a distractingly pleasing shape. Should a man marry for shape alone, I declare I should have already surrendered myself to Hymen's estate. Yet there must be other considerations, not the least of which is match in temperament. While I found her agreeable in many ways, for Miss Franco seemed all but designed to appeal to a prodigious quantity of my tastes in the more delicate sex, the lady was of a sort more to appeal to my casual rather than matrimonial impulses. Were she not the daughter of a friend of my uncle's, and a man I had come to esteem upon my own account, I might have pursued a connection of a less permanent nature, but I refrained out of respect for my uncle and the lady's father. Ultimately it was of little moment, for after I had made three or four visits to the Franco house, where I developed, I daresay, as much of a liking for the father as the daughter, the young lady's grandmother had fallen gravely ill in Salonica, and the lovely angel immediately departed to care for her relation.

Though I had meant to continue a friendship with the very agreeable father, I had not yet had the opportunity to pursue the matter. I feared there would be no strong bonds of friendship forming now that I was certainly the source of the most imposing and unjust distress.

"I have no obligation to the Franco family nor that family to me," I announced. "Their affairs are of little more interest to me than of any other casual acquaintance of my neighborhood. I ask that you not involve them in our concerns."

"'Pon my honor," Hammond called out, "it would seem the plight of the stranger causes him more distress than the plight of a friend. I think we'll leave Mr. Franco's debts safely—which is to say, precariously—in our charge."

Cobb shook his head. "I am sorry, but my nephew has the right of it. Perhaps if you prove yourself a willing partner, we can release him soon. In the meantime, as it appears to offer some guarantee of your cooperation, we shall hold on to Mr. Franco's credit."

"You are mistaken," I said in a low voice, "if you think I care for him above my uncle. Indeed, my uncle is unwell, and these debts of yours can only strain his already taxed constitution. If you will but release him from your bonds, I will serve you as you ask. You will have the additional surety of Franco and Gordon."

"I must admit I know he suffers from a pleurisy, and I have no love of making him suffer—" Cobb began.

"Oh, bother!" Hammond announced. "You do not dictate conditions, Weaver, we do. If you treat fairly with us, your uncle has no need to concern himself, no need to tax his health. You are in no position to negotiate, since you have nothing to offer us but what we have already asked. The sooner you comply, the sooner your friends will be relieved."

There was no other way, I saw. The peace of three men—and in the case of Franco and my uncle, their families—would rest upon my willingness to obey Cobb's orders. That the nature of those orders would put my life and safety at risk appeared of no account to such men as these. They acted as though they wanted nothing more of me than to run a simple errand, when what they wished was that I break open a house very like a fortress, filled with men of such power and greed that the very thought of this task filled me with cold terror.

—

CHAPTER FIVE

*T*HE BRITISH EAST INDIA COMPANY CONDUCTED ITS LONDON BUSI-
ness at Craven House, located at the intersection of Leadenhall and
Lyme streets. Here was not only the mansion with the Company's directors but the whole of the India House yard—an increasingly large
portion of the space bordered by the two streets mentioned—as well as
Grace Church Street to the west and Fenchurch Street to the south. As
the East India Company grew in wealth, so too grew the space required
to house spices, teas, precious metals, and, of course, the linens and
muslins and calicoes the Company imported and for which the British
public demonstrated an insatiable appetite. At the time I write these
memoirs, so many years after the events, the Company has become
synonymous with teas, and in the time of my infancy it was one and the
same with spices. In the days I write of, however, the world knew the
Company for its Indian textiles.

During all daylight hours of the warmer months, each day but the
Christian Sabbath, a steady stream of porters and wagoners, burdened
with their precious cargoes, could be seen making the trek between the
India House yard and the Billingsgate dock, where the ships were
loaded and unloaded. Even in cold months, when ship traffic was all
but eliminated, a steady procession moved in and out, for the adora-
tion of that most esteemed idol, profit, knows no season.

I understood relatively little of the particulars of the East India
Company, but I did know as much as this: Craven House was guarded
by a near army of men whose task it was not only to protect the con-

tents of the warehouses but the interior of Craven House itself. Unlike the other trading companies—the Africa, the Levant, and, of course, the South Sea Company, now notorious throughout the nation and the world—the East India Company no longer held a monopoly on its trade. It was fully established, and had been so for these hundred years or more, and serious rivals were few and weak, but the Company directors had good reason to guard their secrets. It is a foolish man, a very foolish man, who dares to challenge one of the trading companies. I might be swift and clever in the ways of housebreaking, but when a man crosses a power that can spend millions of pounds with the ease I spend pennies, he is sure to come out the loser.

It was for that reason I had declined Mr. Westerly's offer when he'd come to me weeks ago, offering me forty pounds (clearly the remuneration had decreased as expenses had increased) to perform an act I considered unthinkably foolish: break into Craven House, make my way to the office of one of the directors, and steal documents vital to a forthcoming meeting of the Court of Proprietors, the large ruling council of the organization. The risk of capture, I explained to Mr. Westerly, was far too great, and the consequences too dire.

I recalled a celebrated incident of some years back: A rogue by the name of Thomas Abraham had managed to steal some sixteen thousand pounds from Craven House. He had done it by secreting himself inside, acquiring his goods, and waiting for the grounds to be vacated for the night. Unfortunately, he had too well fortified his courage with drink beforehand and was consequently forced to abandon the security of his hiding place in order to empty his water, and during this unfortunate if necessary excursion he was apprehended. Mr. Abraham was sentenced to death for his infraction, but in a rare moment of generosity, the Company commuted his sentence to perpetual servitude in one of its East Indian outposts. I did not consider the life of a slave in a tropical habitation of heat, disease, famine, and war much of a mercy and wished very keenly to avoid a similar fate.

On the other hand, I discovered that Mr. Cobb was sympathetic to the difficulties I faced, and desirous as he was that I should succeed in my mission, he agreed that he would be willing to expend such funds as were necessary in order to ease my way inside, provided I could demonstrate the value of each expenditure. Therefore it was with the promise of such funds that I left Cobb's house and proceeded on a journey that I feared could only end in disaster.

Upon leaving my meeting with Cobb, I stepped outside, extending my legs over the body of Edgar the servant, who, though alive—for I could see the rise and fall of his chest—had been used roughly by the urchins. He was, for one thing, entirely naked, having been stripped of his clothes, no kind treatment during a time when the air was so cold, the ground so icy. For another, he had cuts and bruises about his eyes that I had not delivered, and I felt certain the boys had been quite harsh with him. I would have to be very certain not to expose any weakness to Edgar, who would be sure to make me suffer for it.

I took a hackney to Spitalfields and to an alehouse called the Crown and Shuttle, for it was the haunting ground of a man with whom I dearly needed to speak. It was early yet, I knew, but I had no other business that could possibly intrude upon my affairs, so I ordered an ale and sat thinking of the troubles ahead. I was nearly apoplectic with resentment, and the thought of being used as I was filled me with a simmering anger that, even when I turned my thoughts to other subjects, never quite left me. However, I admit I was intrigued. Mr. Cobb had presented me with a problem—a very troubling problem—and it was now my task to uncover the solution. Though I had told Mr. Westerly that the task was impossible, I now came to understand that I had overstated the difficulty. No, not impossible—only improbable. But with the appropriate amount of planning, I could do what was required of me, and do it perhaps even easily.

It was these things I contemplated over the course of two or three hours and five or six pots of ale. I confess I was not at my most finely sharp when the door to the tavern burst open and a set of six burly young men came in, all clustered around a central figure. This figure was none other than Devout Hale himself, the man of whom I had come in pursuit. He made no attempt to hide his misery; his head slumped and his shoulders slouched, while his comrades, dressed in undyed rough cloth one and all, gathered about him to offer their support.

"You'll get him next time," announced one.

"He almost saw you. He was turning your way when that sodden whore with her baby cut you out," said another.

"It was the rottenest luck, but you'll get him yet," asserted a third.

From the midst of the throng of well-wishers emerged the gloomy principal, a rough man in his middle forties with an unruly flourish of luminous red hair and a fair skin full of untended beard and unfortunate blemishes—both the kind associated with his coloring and those of a more dire nature. He had, however, sparkling eyes of green, and though his face bore freckles and lesions and a hundred scars from the battles he'd fought, he still appeared a robust man, no less defeated in his sadness than Achilles in his brooding.

"You're good friends, lads," he announced to his companions. "Good friends and companions all, and with your help I shall be victorious in the end."

He moved forward now, pressing upon the tabletop for support. I could not mistake that his condition had grown worse since I'd last laid eyes upon him, and inevitably in his infirmity he brought my uncle to mind, and a new wave of sadness crashed over me, for I felt as though everyone I knew had fallen into a state of decay.

Though thick in the shoulders and chest, this man had grown more slight with his disease. The swelling on his neck, though he made an effort to hide it with a gravy-colored cravat that had once been white, was more pronounced, and the lesions on his face and hands hinted to the ravage that lay under his clothes.

With great effort, he brought himself to a table where he would no doubt drown his sorrows in drink, but as he moved he scanned the room with the cautious eye of a predator who fears something worse than itself. Thus it was he saw me.

His face, I was heartened to observe, brightened some little bit. "Weaver, Weaver, welcome, friend, but you've come at a terrible time, I'm afraid. A terrible time. Come join me here, all the same. Danny, fetch us our pots, would you, lad? That's a good fellow. Sit here with me, Weaver, and make me no sadder, I pray."

I did as he bid and, though in no need of more ale, I did not instruct his fellow to forbear. Indeed, I had hardly lowered myself before the pots appeared before us. I sipped at my drink, but Devout Hale drank half of his down in a greedy gulp.

"I don't mean to evade you. Hardly that at all, but these times are hard, my friend, right hard, and once the family's been fed and the landlord's greed answered, once the candles are bought and the room heated, there's scarce a farthing to spare. But when there is, by the devil's tits, I swear I'll give you what you're owed."

I would not go so far to say that I had forgotten that I was Devout Hale's creditor, but that little obligation he bore me inhabited no significant status in my mind. I have worked for many poor men, and I ever permitted them to pay me when they could. Most paid in the end, whether out of gratitude for my service or fear of the consequences I cannot say—though with Mr. Hale I was dependent upon the former rather than the latter. He and his followers could hardly fear a single man—not when they had taken on and vanquished such enemies as they made.

However, I had done him a good turn, and it was this fact upon which I depended. That he still owed me four shillings in payment only meant he might be more inclined to listen to my proposal. Some three months ago one of his men had gone missing, and Hale had asked me to find his whereabouts. This man was a special favorite of his, a cousin's son, and the family had been exceptionally uneasy. As it turned out, there was no cause for alarm—he had run away with a serving girl of poor reputation, and the two of them had been living in Covent Garden, joyously consummating their union while earning their keep through the ancient art of picking pockets. Though Mr. Hale had been disappointed and angered at his kinsman's behavior, he had been relieved to find the boy alive.

"It's come harder than I can scarce remember," Hale was saying, "to keep a man's family in bread. What with the competition from the cheap cloths from foreign lands where they don't pay their workers nothing and the local boys what set up outside the confines of the metropolis so they aren't beholden to the rules of the London Company. Those fellows will take half the wages we need just to keep from starving, and if the workmanship ain't so good, there's plenty of folks that won't care. They'll buy the cheaper and sell it as though it were the dearer. There's ten thousand of us in London, ten thousand of us in the silk-weaving trade, and if things don't change soon, if we don't make matters better, we're as like to become ten thousand beggars as not. My father and his father and grandfather worked this trade, but no one cares now if there's another generation to weave their cloths so long as they have the cheap of it."

It was my task, I knew, to set him at ease. "I haven't come to demand payment. In fact, I've come to offer you money."

Hale looked up from his drink. "I hadn't expected that."

"I should very much like to give you five pounds in exchange for something."

"I tremble to hear what you ask that is worthy of so great a fortune." He stared at me skeptically.

"I want you to riot against the East India Company."

Devout Hale let out a boisterous laugh. He slapped his hands together. "Weaver, the next time I feel the melancholy upon me, I shall summon you at once, for you have restored my good humor. It's a marvelous game when a man offers you five pounds to do what you'd like as not do for free."

Devout Hale had spent his entire life as a silk weaver—indeed, he was now a master silk weaver—and, through his industriousness and his inclination to hurl stones at his enemies, he had become something of a leader of these laborers, though his status was as unofficial as it was unshakable. He and his fellows had been involved in a war for the better part of a century now against the East India Company, for the goods the Company brought in to the island—their fine India cloths—cut deep into the fustians and silks these men labored so hard to produce. Their main means of protest—the riot—had served them well in the past, and Parliament had on more than one occasion capitulated to the silk weavers' demands. Of course, it would be foolish to suggest that these men could get their way simply through a bit of rioting, but there were men of power in the kingdom, and in the city in particular, who feared that the East India Company's imports would permanently harm the trade in native British cloths and enrich a single company at the expense of a national industry. Thus the violence of the silk workers and the machinations in Parliament of the wool interest had proved, when combined, a reasonable counter to the might of the greedy schemers of Craven House.

Hale's smile began to fade and he shook his head slightly. "At least, we have been inclined to riot in the past, but we've got no cause now. Parliament's thrown us some scraps, and we're content for the time being. The Company ain't given us a reason to knock 'pon their gates. And as we've won the last battle of our little war, it would be unseemly for us to launch a new campaign."

"I believe I mentioned an incentive to wink at the unseemliness," I said. "Five pounds. And, I hardly need mention, a cancellation of your debt to me."

"Oh, you might mention it. It's worth mentioning, all right. Make no mistake. But I don't know that's the offer I'll take."

"May I ask why?"

"Do you know where I was tonight, with my companions there, who have been so kind to me? I went to the Drury Lane Theater, where I learned from some contacts I've made over the years—I shan't tell you who—that the king himself was to make a surprise attendance. And do you know why I should wish to be in the path of his Germanic majesty?"

I thought at first that there must be some political reason, but I quickly dismissed the idea. The answer was all too obvious. The lesions on Devout Hale's skin and the swelling about his neck arose from scrofula, which poor men called *the king's evil*. He must give credit to the stories told, that only a touch from the king could cure his affliction.

"Surely," I said, "you don't believe such nonsense."

"Indeed I do. It has been known for many centuries that the king's touch cures the king's evil. I know many people who say their kinsmen know those who have been cured by the king's touch. I mean to put myself in his way, that I might be cured."

"Really, Devout, I am surprised to hear you say this. You have never been a superstitious man."

"It's not superstition but fact."

"But come, only think of it. Before Queen Anne died, our King George was merely George, Elector of Hanover. Could he cure scrofula then?"

"I very much doubt it."

"And what of the Pretender. Can he cure scrofula?"

"Don't stand to reason. He wants to be king, but he ain't."

"But the Parliament could make him king. If it did, could he cure you then?"

"If he were king, he could cure me."

"Then why not petition the Parliament to cure you?"

"I've no mind to play at sophistry with you, Weaver. You can believe what you like, and my believing what I like don't give you no hurt, so there's no need to be unkind. You do not suffer from this disease. I do.

And I tell you a man with the king's evil will do anything—anything, I say—to be rid of it."

I bowed my head. "You are quite right," I said, feeling foolish for having tried to dash an afflicted man's hopes.

"The king's touch can cure me, that's the long and short of it. A man's got to put himself in the king's way to get his touch, and that ain't always as easy as one would like, now, is it? 'Tis said," he announced, in a tone that suggested a shift in conversation, "that when you was a fighting man, amassing your victories in the ring, the king himself was something of an admirer."

"I've heard that bit of flattery myself but never seen any evidence to prove it."

"Have you sought evidence?"

"I can't say I have."

"I suggest you do."

"Why should I care one way or the other?" I asked.

"Because of the king's touch, Weaver. That's my price. If you want my men to riot at Craven House, you must swear to do all in your power to get me the king's touch." He took another deep drink of his ale. "That and the five pounds four shillings you mentioned."

IN THIS CONVERSATION, we circled each other many times. "You are sadly mistaken," I explained, "if you believe I have any connection of the sort you require. You seem to forget the troubles I earned for myself in the late election. I made no shortage of political enemies."

"We have but two political parties in our land, so any man who makes enemies must, in the same stroke, make friends. I would present that to you as a law of nature, or something very like."

I cannot say how our conversation would have resolved had it not been interrupted by a sharp explosion of noises—a burst of angry voices, the overturning of chairs, the hollow *clang* of pewter knocking pewter. Hale and I both turned and saw two fellows standing in close proximity, faces red with anger. I recognized one of them, a short stocky man with comically bushy eyebrows, as a member of Devout's company of silk weavers. The other fellow, taller and equally well built, was a stranger to me. It took but one glance at Devout to see he was a stranger to him as well.

Though large and ungainly, Devout Hale was upon his feet and lumbering toward them as best as his frail and ungainly body would allow. "Hold there, what is this?" he demanded. "What's the ill, Feathers?"

Feathers, the shorter man, addressed Hale without once taking his eye off his adversary. "Why, this rascal has insulted those of us whose parents come over from France," he said. "Said we're naught but Papists."

"I never said anything of the sort," the taller man said. "I believe this fellow is drunk."

"I'm sure it ain't but a misunderstanding," Devout Hale said. "And we can't have any unpleasantness here, so what say I buy you both a drink and we make ourselves friends?"

The one Hale called Feathers sucked in a breath, as though steeling himself for peace. He would have been wiser to steel himself for something else, however, for his adversary most unexpectedly threw a punch directly into Feathers's mouth. There was a spray of blood before the man sank, and I thought for certain the author of this violence should find himself destroyed by the injured man's companions, but all at once there was the sound of a constable's whistle, and we turned to find two men, dressed in the livery of their office, standing alongside the mayhem. I scarcely had time to wonder how they could have arrived so quickly before they began to collect the fallen Feathers.

"This one was looking for trouble," one of the constables observed.

"No doubt, no doubt," the other agreed.

"Hold on, there!" Hale cried. "What of the other?"

The other was not in sight.

IT WAS ONLY WITH GREAT EFFORT that Mr. Hale was able to convince his brother silk weavers to stay in the tavern while he accompanied the victim of injustice to the magistrate's office. His proposal produced much discussion, and I was led to understand that my friend was not upon good terms with the unfortunate Mr. Feathers, but he nevertheless convinced the others that he should make the best possible representative for their injured brother, and that arriving in the chamber in great numbers might only give the magistrate cause to claim intimidation. He asked, however, that I accompany him on his mission, as I knew something, as he put it, of the workings of the law.

I did know a thing or two about the law, and I knew I did not like what I had seen of the business thus far. Those constables had been too quick to appear, the assailant too quick to disappear. There was some mischief afoot.

The office of Richard Umbread, magistrate in Spitalfields, was spare and quiet at night, with only a few constables and a clerk milling about in the poorly lighted space. A fire burned in the fireplace, but it was small, and there were far too few candles lit, giving the room the air of a dungeon. Mr. Feathers, who dabbed at his bleeding nose with an already crimson-soaked handkerchief, looked up in a daze.

"Now then," the judge said to Feathers. "My constables tell me you instigated a drunken attack upon your fellow. Is this true?"

"No, sir, it ain't. He insulted my parents, sir, and when I objected, he hit me without cause."

"Hmm. But as he is not here and you are, it is a rather easy thing to set all the blame upon him."

"There are witnesses to that effect, sir," Devout Hale called out, but the judge offered him no mind.

"And I am made to understand," the judge continued, "that you have no gainful employment, is that correct?"

"That ain't right either," Feathers corrected. "I am a silk weaver, sir, and I work along with a company of silk weavers hard by Spinner's Yard. That man standing over there, Mr. Devout Hale, works alongside me, sir. He knew me as an apprentice, though I was not 'prenticed to him."

"It is a very easy thing," said the judge, "for a man to get his companions to say this or that on his behalf, but it does not alter the fact that you are a man without employment and so inclined to violence."

"That's not the case at all," Feathers shot back. His eyes were now wide with disbelief.

"You can offer me no evidence to the contrary."

"Excuse me, your honor," I ventured, "but I believe he has offered you ample evidence to the contrary. Mr. Hale and I witnessed the conflict, and we will swear that Mr. Feathers was the victim rather than the cause. As to his employment, Mr. Hale will swear to it, and I'm sure it would be no hardship to find a dozen or so men who will swear similarly."

"Swearing don't signify when it is all falsehood," the judge said. "I have not sat these many years on the bench without learning to see what stands before me. Mr. Giles Feathers, it is my experience that men of violence and no account want a useful skill to teach them to better their ways. I therefore sentence you to the workhouse at Chriswell Street, where you may learn the trade of silk weaving over the three months of your detainment. It is my hope that such a skill will help you to find employment upon your release, and so I will not need to see you here again on similar charges."

"Learn the skill of weaving?" Feathers cried. "But I *know* the skill of weaving and am a journeyman in that trade. It's how I earn my bread."

"Get him out of here," the judge told his constables, "and clear the room of these loiterers."

Had Mr. Hale been a stronger man, I would have expected him to show his outrage in ways that would have landed him in prison as well, but he could not resist the pull of the constable, and it was not my battle to fight, so I followed him out.

"I'd heard of these tricks," Hale breathed, "but I never thought to see it practiced against my own men."

I nodded, for I now understood all too well. "A kind of silk-weaving impressment."

"Aye. Chriswell Street workhouse is a privately run affair, and the men what owns it pays the judge, who pays the constables, who get men with skills arrested on no account of their own. Then they're sent to the workhouse to *learn* a trade—the very irony of it. It ain't nothing but slavery. They get three months' worth of unpaid labor out of Feathers, and if he makes a fuss, they'll jut punish him with more time."

"There's nothing to do?" I asked.

"No, there's what to do. I must go now, Weaver. There's legal men to be hired and testimony to be sworn. They're depending on us being foolish and ignorant of our rights, and in most cases the men they snatch will be. But we'll sting 'em, don't you doubt it. They'll think twice before they go after one of my fellows again."

"I'm glad to hear it. Now, I hate, when you have such other concerns, to raise the issue once more—"

"Your riot, is it? Well, you need not fear about that. I've got the anger in me now, and a good riot shall make me feel right and proper. You just get me the king, sir. Swear you'll do all in your power. That will have to be enough."

—

CHAPTER SIX

I DID SWEAR. TO MY MIND, THIS WAS LIKE PROMISING A MAN HIS lottery ticket would answer with a fortune. Worse than that, for a lottery, as a game of chance, can be manipulated—as I knew well—but there could be no counterfeiting a meeting with the king. Still, the promise did the business, and two nights later, I found myself in the green market to the west of the East India complex, where I contrived to busy myself in the examination of discounted cabbages—for these were the goods that had not sold that day, and the clever and unhygienic consumer could find a bargain if he didn't mind a bit of maggot with his leaves. The air had grown quite cold over the course of the afternoon, and I ran my gloved hands over a variety of vegetables and squinted in a show of disappointment. My coat was of a better quality than any of the scavengers, and I attracted more notice than I should have liked, so I was most relieved when the operation commenced.

At only a few minutes before the striking of the eight o'clock hour, I heard a woman cry out in fear, and I knew Mr. Hale and his men had upheld their part of the bargain. Along with the other late patrons—many of whom used the distraction as an excuse to depart the premises without paying for their moldy greens—I ran out to Leadenhall Street and observed a group of some thirty or forty silk weavers standing by the premises, braving the cold in their inadequate coats. A half dozen or so held torches. Another half dozen tossed chunks of old brick or rotten apples or dead rats at the walls surrounding the structure. They shouted a wide array of criticism at this barrier, claiming the Company practiced unfairly against common laborers, contrived to lower their wages, diffused their markets, and corrupted the common taste with Eastern luxuries. There were some epithets against France thrown in as well, because the Englishman has not been born who knows how to riot without mentioning that nation.

Though many have had cause to complain about the sluggish motion of British justice and the enforcement of laws, here was a case in which a certain slowness served me in good stead. In order to make the silk weavers disperse, a constable would have to rouse a justice of the peace brave enough to stand before them and read aloud the substance of the Riot Act. At such a point, the mutineers had one hour in which to disperse before the army might be deployed to end the violence—ironically, through the use of violence. Here was an old system, but one borne out by time, and many experiments had proved that the firing of muskets into one or two of the troublemakers would send the remaining rebels a-scatter.

Devout Hale had assured me that he and his men would prosecute my cause for as long as possible before the risk of harm overtook them. They would not, in short, endure musket fire on my behalf, but they would continue to fling dead rodents for as long as they might do so in safety.

Such was the most I could request of them. If I were to attempt to be truly safe, I would need to enter the premises, get what Cobb desired, and exit before the soldiers scared away the mischief makers. I therefore made my way past the riot, feeling the heat of the burning torches and smelling the rank perspiration of the laborers, and hurried around the corner to Lyme Street. Darkness was now fully upon me, and as any perambulators would have been drawn to the spectacle of riot, and the guards within the complex would be preparing for a siege of silk workers, I felt I might scale the wall with some reasonable hope of success. Should I be discovered, I decided, I would merely explain that I was being chased by a crazed rioter who believed me affiliated with the Company, and as that organization was the source of my woes, I hoped they would be willing to be the source of my succor as well.

Because I needed to explain myself if apprehended, I could not bring with me grappling equipment, for it is the rare innocent spectator indeed who inexplicably has such engines about him. Instead, I climbed the wall in the more primitive method practiced by boys and housebreakers without expensive tools and found the climb rather easy—more particularly so as the street was deserted, any perambulators having gone to observe the mayhem on Leadenhall. During a daylight surveying of the area, I had observed numerous cracks and crevices, and these proved more than equal to the task of providing footing up the ten feet to the top. The greatest difficulty lay in climbing while holding on to the rather heavy sack I carried, containing as it did its measure of living creatures, who writhed unhappily within.

Nevertheless, I managed, occasionally shifting the weight of the sack from my hand to my teeth, and in that manner I scaled the outer wall. I then lay prone for a moment to survey the grounds. The bulk of the watchmen, as I had anticipated, had abandoned their stations and now engaged themselves in the manly art of hurling insults at the rioters while the rioters hurled carrion at them. In addition to shouting, I heard incessant metal clanging and knew the rioters had improvised drums of some sort. These were good fellows, for they knew the more distraction and irritation they could devise, the greater the chance that I might enter and exit with impunity.

Getting down the wall would prove more complicated that getting up, but some twenty feet to the south, closer to the warehouses, a hillock rose by the wall, and there the drop would be no more than half my body length, so, snakelike I slithered to that spot and prepared to enter the grounds.

At that moment the dogs observed me; some five dragon-headed mastiffs sprang forward, thunderous barks booming from their terrible jaws. As they approached, I reached for my cumbersome sack and took out the first of the rabbits I had purchased at market that afternoon. I dropped it to the ground, where, after an instant of regaining its bearings, it saw the dogs descending upon it and sped away. The advantage went to the rabbit, for the sack had kept it warm, and the dogs were visibly chilled by the coldness of the night. Three of the dogs ran off in frigid pursuit, so I dropped the second of my rabbits, and this one carried the other two beasts off with it. I retained the third, having, I suspected, further use for the creature when I made my exit.

Next, I slipped onto the soft ground, landing in a practiced crouch. I continued to move in such a fashion until I slipped between the warehouses and Craven House itself. My task would prove far more complicated now, for the grounds were lit, and though I was dressed in a sufficiently gentlemanly fashion that my appearance would not send anyone fleeing for help, I presumed that the clerks and workers inside the house would notice an unfamiliar face. I could only hope that most of these men had already left for the day—though I was made to believe that many men worked long hours for the Company—and those who remained would be watching the riot with equal quantities of amusement and concern.

I slipped through the garden, sticking close to such shadows as I could find, and opened the rear door, thinking to find myself in a kitchen of some kind. Instead, two surprises lay in wait for me. The first was that the room I entered was no kitchen but a great meeting hall, a space equal to housing some sixty or seventy men, provided they all stood quite straight and not too many were exceedingly fat. Here was where, I surmised, the Company would hold sales of shares, share exchanges, and auctions of large quantities of East India goods to fairly small numbers of wealthy men. At this time of night, the room had no reason to be occupied, so it made a most agreeable point of entry.

On the less pleasing side, the door had attached to it a bell, which alerted anyone who cared to hear that someone had entered.

I dashed immediately to a far corner and into a slim space between two bookshelves, hoping that, should anyone come into the room, even with a candle, the shadows would conceal me. No one inquired into the bell, however, and I concluded after a few minutes that the coming and going of people was not a matter to send servants running in with torches. I would like to have concluded that it meant that no one was in the house to hear the bell, but that notion was disabused by the creak of footsteps on the floor above me.

I removed my outer coat and placed down my rabbit sack, making certain it was fully closed, prepared now to make my way into the heart of the building. Mr. Cobb had been so kind as to explain to me that the office I wanted was located in the southeast corner of the second floor. He knew no more than that, however, and it was up to me to locate the stairs of this mansion. I slinked across the floor and came to a closed door, one that offered no light spilling between the cracks—a good sign indeed. Trying the handle and finding it unlocked, I opened it swiftly. I was prepared, if necessary, to impersonate a man who had every business in Craven House rather than act like the sneak thief I was.

On the far side of the room, I found another door both unlocked and showing no light. Once more I made bold to open it and now found myself in a hallway. Here, at least, was some improvement. Though my sense of direction had been altered somewhat, I believed I knew which way to find the front of the house, and there, I concluded, I would find the stairs. I had made my way about halfway down the hall when a light entered my path. The glare momentarily blinded me, but after a few blinks I saw a young woman walking in my direction with a candle. Even in the darkness I could see she was a pretty thing, with dark hair only partially hidden by her bonnet and large expressionless eyes of some dark color, though I could hardly say what. And though I ought to have had more urgent things upon my mind, I could not help but admire her womanly shape, which her plain gown might have concealed but was unable to disguise.

"Ah, there you are," she said to me. "With those wretched rioters out there, I thought you should not be able to find your way in, but I suspect you are cleverer than I'd been led to believe."

I almost thought to ask if Cobb had sent her, but I held my tongue. If Cobb could have inserted a woman inside Craven House to do as she pleased, he would not have needed me. No, this was something else. I said to her, "I should hate to think who has been leading you to believe me unclever."

In the darkness, I saw her eyes widen. "I do beg your pardon, sir. I thought you were someone else." I could not be certain, but I believed her skin reddened as well. This mistake deeply embarrassed her, that much was clear.

Ready to make another glib response though I was, I thought it better to hold my tongue for a moment. I needed her to believe I was an East India Company clerk, and I must act that part, not the part of a man who sees a lovely young woman. "Your mistakes are your own and no concern of mine," I told her, hurrying past her in the gruff manner I hoped would be typical of Craven House men.

"Sir," she called out. "Sir, a moment."

I had no choice but to stop as well, for were I to run off she would surely guess I did not belong. Were this a man, I decided, I would take no chances and lash out with a blow that would render the trouble-maker unfit for further interference, but I am too delicate a soul to pummel so pretty a thing, so I merely turned and glared at her with the impatience of an overworked clerk who needed to be doing three different things at that moment.

"What is it?"

She held forth her candle. I felt certain that she did so to study my features, but then I was thinking like a man with something to hide when she would in all likelihood be thinking like a servant. "I see you have no light, and as there aren't many people about, I thought you should like my taper. I should not bother you, sir, but with the rioters outside I feared for your safety."

She put the candle too close to my face, and for a moment I was half blinded by the flame and half blinded by her charm. Some clever remark bubbled up inside me, perhaps about how no mere tallow and wick could outshine her beauties, but I choked it down, thinking it inappropriate for the identity I assumed, and snatched away her offering. "Kind of you," I muttered and took the light, wondering what sort of man takes a light from a lady because there is danger about. The answer came easily enough: an East India man. I headed in the direction to which I'd set out.

I hardly wanted the candle, and I extinguished it the moment she was out of sight, but she had provided me with some useful intelligence, mainly that the house was mostly deserted. This knowledge gave me the courage to act with an eagerness that bordered on recklessness. I strolled forth confidently and, finding the stairs, climbed them like a man who visited Craven House both regularly and licitly.

At the top of the stairs I quickly checked for unwanted observers, but the space was as dark and abandoned as the rooms below. Getting a sense of direction, I quickly found which office I needed, or believed I needed, for I could in no way be certain if I had discovered the right place. With no choice but to hope I had struck home, I strode in, finding the room empty and made ready to plunder.

I was operating under a number of disabilities that made my task more complicated. It was dark; I had no familiarity with the documents I sought or the man who possessed them; I had a limited amount of time to find what Cobb wanted; and the consequences of being caught or failing were both dire.

My eyes were fairly well adjusted to the dark. Indeed, the lights of the mayhem outside helped illuminate the room; there were even muted cries of defiance from the silk weavers. I ignored the sound and took in as much as I could. The light was sufficient for me to make out the furnishings—a desk, a few chairs, bookshelves, side tables, and so forth—but insufficient for me to read the titles of the books without getting very close or to make out what images were within the frames upon the wall. There were a number of piles of documents upon the desk, and it was with these that I thought to start.

Cobb had told me as much as he thought I needed, and he had clearly thought it best to tell me no more. I was to look through the papers of a Mr. Ambrose Ellershaw, a man conveniently gone to his country estate for the next two days, who was one of the members of the Court of Committees. This group was currently preparing for a quarterly meeting of the much larger Court of Proprietors, the two hundred or so men who controlled the fate of the Company. Each member of the smaller Court was charged with preparing data for the larger meeting, and it was Ellershaw's responsibility to report on the data involving the import of India cloth to the British Isles and the sales of forbidden cloths to European and colonial markets. In order to prepare these figures, Mr. Ellershaw would need to comb through countless records of accounting data to obtain the information he required.

My task was to find the only existing copy of his report and take it with me. How Cobb could know there were no duplicates I could not say, nor was it in my best interest to ask. I had no desire to find ways to make my task more difficult. Cobb said he could not know with any certainty how Ellershaw would store his report, only that it would be in his office and would be clearly marked.

I began to make my way through the documents on his desk, but I found nothing but correspondence. The light was insufficient for me to read the texts easily, but as I had no interest or reason to know more of his letters, I had little concern for this difficulty. Time was lost to me in my frantic review of the papers, and I know not how long it took to make my way through the documents on the desk. I only knew I was finishing up the last two or three pieces of paper when I heard the clock strike nine. The silk weavers might depend on rioting another half hour, three quarters at most, before their safety was at risk. I had to find what I wanted, and soon.

I was moving to open one of the desk drawers when something terrible transpired. There was a metallic groan I recognized in an instant—it was the sound of someone turning the door handle.

I dropped at once to the floor and hid myself behind the desk as best I could. It was not the hiding place I would have chosen—in the corner would have been preferable, since the person might have business with the desk and ignore a corner—but I had no time to discriminate. I listened and heard the door open, and the room was suddenly awash with light.

I overstate the case, for even hidden from view I could tell it was but the single flame of a candle or oil lamp, but it penetrated my precious protective darkness and left me feeling naked and exposed.

I could only hope that the intruder wanted a book or a document from the top of the desk, but such was not the case. I heard the muffled tap of something—I presumed the candle—being set on the top of the desk.

"Oh," a female voice said.

I looked up and saw the young woman who'd given me her candle looking down at me with an entirely understandable curiosity.

I HAVE BEEN, I admit, in difficult situations before and one does not survive them without an ability to improvise upon the moment. Rather than suggest she call the estate guardians to take me to the nearest constable, instead I begged her to bring her light down to the floor. While she did so, I slipped a pen knife from my pocket and slid it under the desk. While she held the light for me, I went through the motions of finding it and then rose to a more dignified position.

"Thank you, my dear," I said. "That knife, while it may look like a trivial thing, belonged to my father, and I should have hated to lose it."

"Perhaps if you had not extinguished your own candle," she suggested.

"Ah, well, it was a bit of a disaster. My candle went out, I dropped my knife—you know how such things go. One little accident leads to another."

"Who are you, sir?" she asked, peering more closely at me now. "I don't believe I've seen you before."

"Yes, I am rather new here. I'm Mr. Ward," I said, hardly knowing why the name of that scandalous poet rose to my mind before all oth-

THE DEVIL'S COMPANY | 67

ers. "I am a new clerk in the service of Mr. Ambrose Ellershaw. I've not seen you before either."

"I am here most regularly, I assure you." She set down the candle but continued to stare.

"Please sit, miss . . ." I let my voice trail off.

"Miss Glade," she said. "Celia Glade."

I bowed at her and then we stood together, somewhat awkwardly. "I am pleased to meet you, Miss Glade." Who, I wondered, could this woman be? Her mode of speech was most proper, and she sounded nothing at all like a servant. Could she be some sort of a female clerk? Was it possible that the East India Company held to such modern notions?

My confusion was not a little increased by the impropriety of being in so dark and private a space with a remarkably attractive woman of apparent breeding.

"Mr. Ward, what brings you to Mr. Ellershaw's office this night? Would you not rather be outside watching the silk weavers toss manure at the guards?"

"It is a temptation, I am sure, but I must sacrifice my pleasure for my work. Mr. Ellershaw, whom you know to be out of town for another two days, has asked me to review his report to the Court of Proprietors. I left for the day and was prepared to go home when I recollected the report and thought to come back, take it, and review it this night in my rooms. And then I dropped my knife and so forth. But I'm glad to have you here to help me relight my candle."

I lifted my taper and allowed my wick to touch hers, and the gesture felt to me so ripe with amorous suggestion that I feared that more than wick and wax might burst into flame. I set the candle down. "Now, if only I could recollect where Mr. Ellershaw said he put the devilish thing. Pardon the coarseness of my language, Miss Glade."

She let out a musical laugh. "Think nothing of it. I work among men and hear that sort of talk all the day. Now, as for that document." She rose and approached the desk, moving into such close quarters with me that I could smell the womanly scent of her. She slid open one of the desk drawers and withdrew from it a leather packet thick with papers. "I believe this is Mr. Ellershaw's report to the Court of Proprietors. It is a rather lengthy document. You'll be up rather late if you review it tonight. You might be wise to leave it here and read it in the morning."

I took it from her hand. How could she know of its location? Presumably, my lady clerk theory had proved well founded. "In the morning I shall have other work that requires my attention. I thank you for your concern, however." I rose, and she backed off accordingly.

With the packet tucked under my arm and one of the candles in my hand, I approached the door.

"Mr. Ward," she called out, "when did Mr. Ellershaw take you into his employ?"

I stopped at the door. "Just this past week."

"It is very unusual, is it not, for there to be a new position prior to the meeting of the Court of Proprietors? From where did he obtain the funding?"

I thought to say I had no idea how he should obtain the funding, but surely Mr. Ellershaw's clerk would be aware of such issues, wouldn't he? Of course, I had no real idea of what a clerk did, let alone Ellershaw's clerk, but I felt certain I ought to say something.

"Mr. Ellershaw has not yet received funding from the Court, and until he does he is paying me from his own funds. As he prepares for the meeting, however, he wished to avail himself of additional hands."

"You must provide him with vital services."

"It is my most earnest desire to do so," I assured her, and excused myself from the room.

I wasted no time in extinguishing the candle, making my way down the stairs, and toward the back door. Ring be damned, I thought. I would be far away before anyone thought it odd that I should leave through the rear. And, in truth, there was nothing odd, for why should I vacate by way of the front while riot raged?

I reclaimed my coat and my sack, and was fortunate enough to find the grounds still free of guards, who continued to trade words with the rioters. I observed none of the dogs, but I clutched my remaining rabbit most tightly. From the front of the building I heard curses, now mixed with threats that the soldiers would soon be upon them and they would have a hard time tossing filth with a musket hole through their chests.

Returning to the hillock, I once more scaled the wall. Now I would have a much harder time approaching the other side, for I did not wish to drop all ten feet, and there was no higher ground on which to land. Instead, I clambered down as best I could to close the gap between me and the ground, and then, when the distance looked manageable, I let go and fell to the earth. It was an uncomfortable landing, but not a terribly dangerous one, and I emerged from my efforts unharmed and remarkably unmussed. I then opened the bag and freed the rabbit, allowing that it might run at its liberty and do the best it could. Certainly it was better that one of us might do so.

I HURRIED BACK to Leadenhall Street, where the silk weavers shouted and tossed filth and pranced about in the shadow of a company of red-clad soldiers whose expressions bespoke a frightening combination of tedium and cruelty. In the space it took me to approach, I saw the officer in charge glance twice at the tower clock of St. Michael's. He would, I knew, discharge his ammunition the very moment so permitted by law. Therefore it was with great relief that I found Devout Hale and informed him that I had done my duty and he and his men might disperse freely. He made the call, and the silk weavers desisted at once and marched off peaceably while the soldiers taunted them, accusing them of not being men enough to take their musket fire.

I could not be more delighted that my time of servitude was at an end, so rather than wait until morning I took a hackney to the vicinity of Swallow Street and knocked upon Mr. Cobb's door. When Edgar answered I immediately had cause to regret the roughness with which I treated him. Not that marks of a severe thrashing upon his face gave me pain. I should have been only too happy to serve him with the same sauce again should he deserve it. Nevertheless, I knew I had made an enemy, and one who would be unwilling to forgive me even when his master had cause to forget.

"Weaver," he groused, his voice slurred from the bruises and loss of teeth. The swelling of his muzzle only increased the duckishness of his appearance. "You are damnably fortunate that Mr. Cobb has told me not to harm you."

"I feel fortunate," I assured him. "And whatever the source of your divine mercy, I shall always be grateful for it."

He only squinted with his unmaimed eye, seeming to think my words none the most honest, and led me to the sitting room. I delivered unto him my coat and gloves, and he took them with all the disdain he could summon.

After my ordeal in Craven House, it seemed to me the height of luxury to sit in so warmed and well-illuminated a space. Each sconce on the wall held a lit candle, and there were lit lamps about the room as well, and a well-tended fire took the chill from me. A rather expensive indulgence, I thought, unless Cobb knew he was expecting a visitor. I could only conclude then that either someone else was due to visit that night or he had had an agent watching my progress at the mansion, one who informed him I was on my way.

After what felt like an interminable time, Cobb entered the room and took my hand. I should like to have ignored this gesture, but I returned his grip out of habit.

"Have you got it?" he asked.

"I believe so," I said. It occurred to me for the first time that I had not reviewed the contents of the package. What if Miss Glade had been deceiving me? I could not imagine why she should do so, but then I could not imagine why any of these things transpired.

Cobb opened up the leather folder and removed the pages, which he examined quickly. "Ah, yes. Just so. The very thing." He put them back and slid the folder onto the table. "Well done, Weaver. Your reputation is well deserved. There's hardly a more secure ground in London, and yet you've somehow got yourself in, took what you desired, and removed yourself. I am awed by your talents, sir."

Without waiting to be asked, I sat by the fire and stretched out my hands before it. "Your pleasure signifies little. I've done what you asked, so now it is time to release me and my friends from your obligation."

"Release you?" Cobb frowned at me. "Why should I do such an absurd thing?"

I jumped to my feet. "Do not toy with me. You told me if I did what you asked, you would undo the harm you've done. And I've now done what you asked."

"As I recall, I said you must do *all* I asked. You've done the first thing, to be sure." He little moved, seemed not to recognize that I was on my feet, my fists balled. "There is more, much more, that I require of you. Oh, no, Mr. Weaver. Our work is just beginning here."

Perhaps I ought to have anticipated this turn, but I hadn't. Cobb, I had believed, wanted these documents, and once they were in hand he would have no more use for me. "How long do you think to abuse me thus?"

"It's not a matter of time, really. It's a matter of goals we must achieve. I need certain things. Only you can provide them. You would not agree to do so. We will work together until my goals are met. It is that simple."

"I shan't keep breaking houses open for you."

"Of course you shan't. Nothing of the sort. I have a much more delicate business in mind."

"What business is that?"

"I cannot tell you, not in such detail as you would desire. 'Tis too soon, but you will find I'm very generous. Sit, sit. Please sit."

I don't know why, but I sat. Perhaps it was something in his voice, and perhaps it was my recognition of the futile position I inhabited. I could not harm him, not without bringing horrific ruin upon my head and the others'. Cobb had managed his affairs masterfully, and I needed more time if I were to discover a means of besting him. I could not use my fists and end this tonight.

"Now," he continued, "you will, for the time being, allow yourself to be hired no more. I will be your only patron. In addition to the thirty pounds I have promised you for this task, I will pay you another forty pounds per quarter, which is a very generous sum—I suspect quite as much as you would earn in a typical span of time, and perhaps rather more. In addition, you will not have the distress of wondering whence your income will arise."

"I will have the distress of being slave to another man's whims and having the lives of others hanging upon my actions."

"I think of that as less a distress than an incentive. Come, only consider upon it, sir. If you are loyal to me and give me no cause to prod you, none of your friends will find themselves in any harm."

"And for how many quarters will you require my services?" I asked, forcing my teeth to ungrit.

"That I am unable to say. It may be a few months. It may be a year or even more."

"More than a year!" I barked. "You cannot leave my uncle in his current condition for a year. Return his shipment to him, and I will consent to move forward."

"I'm afraid that won't do. I cannot believe you would feel obligated to keep your word to a man who has used you as ill as I have. In a few months' time, perhaps, when you have further committed yourself, when you have too much to lose from ending this yourself, we can discuss your uncle. In the meantime, he will help make certain you do not stray too far from our goals."

"And what are those goals?"

"Come see me in three days, Weaver. We'll discuss it then. Until that time, you may away with your earnings and indulge your liberty. Edmund will pay you for tonight's adventure and your first quarter's wages on your way out."

"I'm sure he will delight in paying me."

"His delights are no matter to me, and if you think you incur my anger by thrashing him, you are mistaken, so you may cease doing so."

"You might give me a better motivation."

"If beating upon my servant calms your humors and makes you more agreeable, then beat him as you like, and I'll consider his wages well earned. There is one other thing, however. I cannot help but presume that you are curious as to why I go to such extremes to pursue this end. You will want to know about these documents and Mr. Ellershaw and so forth. It is my advice that you dampen your curiosity, snuff it out entire. It is a spark that could lead to a great conflagration that would destroy you and your friends. I do not want you looking into me or my goals. If I find you have not heeded my words, one of your friends will suffer to prove my earnestness. You must content yourself with a state of ignorance."

I'd been dismissed. I rose and stepped out into the hall, but Cobb called me back.

"Oh, Weaver. You mustn't forget this." He held out the documents.

I stared at the papers in his hand. "You do not want them?"

"They are worthless to me. Take them, but keep them safe. You will have need of them in a few days."

By the door, Edgar returned my things to me and placed a purse in my hand without a word. It was well for me that the thieves who haunted the streets like hungry ghosts did not smell my silver, for they would have had an easy target that night. I was too dazed to fight back, or perhaps even to understand danger when I saw it.

chapter seven
—

THE NEXT EVENING I ARRANGED FOR A MEETING AT MY UNCLE'S HOUSE that Elias also attended, for the three of us were the men most nearly connected with this trouble—with the exception of Mr. Franco, but I shall speak more of him later. We sat in my uncle's study sipping his wine, though, in Elias's case, gulping might be a more accurate description, for he had a hard time balancing the needs of clarity of thought with the quantity of claret in a wine merchant's home.

"I have been unable to learn anything of the man, this Mr. Jerome Cobb," my uncle said. He leaned back in an armchair, looking small and frail in its clutches. Despite the fire, he sat under a pile of heavy quits and had a scarf wrapped around his neck. His voice emerged with a rattling wheeze that made me most anxious for his health. "I've asked around, quite discreetly you understand, but his name produces nothing but blank stares."

"Could those of whom you inquire be dissembling?" I asked. "Perhaps they are so afraid of Cobb they fear to cross him."

My uncle shook his head. "I don't believe so. I have not been a merchant for all these years without learning to sniff out deception—or, at the very least, uneasiness. No, Cobb meant nothing to those I asked."

"What of the nephew, the customs man?" I asked.

My uncle shook his head. "He is known to work there, but he is well situated and aloof. Many men I spoke with had some passing knowledge of him and could report having seen him, but they could say no more."

Elias, who was wiping his mouth with the back of his wrist, nodded vigorously. "I can report little more. I've learned that his servant arranged for a lease upon his house at auction, offering a generous amount and paying three years in advance. He did so some six months past. Beyond that, I have heard nothing. No one of means lives in London without attracting the notice of society. Since it became clear he had designs upon you, I've let the blood out of some of the most fashionable arms in London, pulled some well-placed teeth, and removed a rather lofty kidney stone. I even had the delight of applying cream to a rash upon a pair of the most exceedingly fashionable breasts in London, and no one of import has heard the name. And you know how these affairs go in the world of fashion, Weaver. A man of this sort, with wealth not merely claimed by him but put into undeniable action, cannot enter the metropolis without generating attention. Yet he has managed to avoid all notice."

"He appears to have no servant but his unpleasant man, so it would seem he has no cook," I noted. "He must therefore eat out. Surely someone has observed him about town."

"An astute question," Elias said. "I believe I may be able to learn a thing or two on that score. I will redouble my efforts. There is a very fashionable son of a duke—a third or fourth son, so of no real consequence, you understand—who lives not far from Cobb. He suffers from some rather painful boils upon his arse. Upon the next lancing, I will inquire if he has made any observations on his neighbor."

"You'll provide us, I hope, with only his answer and no other details," I said.

"Is it then only my love of human health that makes me so enjoy the sight of a lanced boil?"

"Yes," I assured him.

"Well, look, Weaver, I hate to even mention this, but I think it worth saying. This Cobb fellow is quite obviously a man of some power and cunning. Would it not benefit you to seek an alliance with another man of power and cunning?"

"You mean that scoundrel Jonathan Wild," my uncle said with evident distaste. It required some considerable effort, but he pushed himself forward in his chair. "I shan't hear of it."

Wild was the most famous thieftaker in the city, but he was also the most cunning thief in the nation, probably in the world, and very possibly in the history of the world. No one, as far as I knew, had ever established a criminal empire of the scope Wild had constructed, and he did it all while passing himself off as a great servant of the public. The men of power in the city either knew nothing of his true nature or pretended to know nothing because ignorance served their purposes.

Wild and I were adversaries, there could be no doubt of that, but we had also formed uneasy alliances in the past, and I had a cautious respect for Wild's nearest lieutenant, one Abraham Mendes, a Jew of my own neighborhood.

"To speak the truth," I explained, "I had already considered that option. Unfortunately, Wild and Mendes are pursuing their operations in Flanders and are not expected back these two or three months."

"That's rather bad timing," Elias said.

"Not in my opinion." My uncle settled back in his chair. "The less business you have with that man, the better."

"I'm inclined to agree," I said. "Were he here, I would have no choice but to seek his advice at the very least, possibly even his aid. That would be a dangerous precedent. I have worked with him before when we had overlapping goals, but I should hate baldly to ask him for a favor. To do so would be to grant him too much power."

"Quite so," my uncle intoned. "Nevertheless, Mr. Gordon, your suggestion is appreciated. I value your help."

"I am hardly helping you," Elias pointed out, "for my own finances and futurity are as bound up in this as yours."

"Nevertheless," my uncle continued, "I am in your debt, sir."

Elias rose to bow.

"Now, I hope you will excuse us but I have a need to speak to my nephew alone."

"Oh," Elias said, understanding my uncle's praise as an awkward transition. He looked somewhat dejectedly at his half-full glass of claret, wondering—I could see from the mournful look in his eye—if to finish it off now in a quick gulp would be an unforgivable rudeness. "Of course."

"On the way out, tell my man I'm instructing him to present you with a bottle. He'll know where to find it."

This pronouncement brought all the joy back to my friend's countenance. "You are too good, sir." He bowed once more and took his leave.

When he was gone, we sat together in silence for some minutes. Finally, it was I who spoke. "You must know how sorry I am to have brought this upon you."

He shook his head. "You've done nothing. You are being harmed and have done no harming. I only wish I could offer you some assistance."

"And what of you? How will you endure these trials?"

He raised to his lips a glass of a steaming wine posset, so thick with honey I could smell its sweetness across the room. "Think nothing of it. This is not the first time in my career that money has been hard to find. It shan't be the last. A skillful merchant knows how to survive. See that you do the same."

"And what of Mr. Franco? Have you heard anything from that quarter?"

"No," my uncle said. "It may well be that he has not yet discovered his embarrassments."

"Perhaps he need never discover them."

"No, I don't think that's right. He may never learn that his fate is bound up with yours, but if he should be carted off to prison on your account, I think he should have heard something of the matter first."

My uncle had the right of it, and I could not deny his wisdom. "How well do you know Mr. Franco?"

"Not so well as I would like. He has not lived here long, you know. He is a widower, and he and his lovely daughter removed themselves from Salonica to enjoy the liberties of life in Britain. Now the daughter has gone back. I still don't understand why you did not pursue her more forcefully," he added.

"Uncle, she and I would not have been a good match."

"Come, Benjamin. I know you hold out hope for Miriam—"

"I do not," I said, with all the force of conviction I could muster, much of it sincere. "Things with her are irrevocably broken."

"They seem to be broken between the lady and myself, as well. I hear very little *of* her and nothing *from* her," he told me. "Upon her conversion to the English church, she severed her connections with this family entire."

"She has severed ties with me as well."

He looked at me with some skepticism, for he did not believe it was her conversion and marriage that ended our friendship so permanently. Nor should he have believed it. "I suppose there's nothing to be done, then."

"No," I said. "Now let us return to the subject of Mr. Franco."

My uncle nodded. "He was a trader in his youth and did moderately well, but he is not a great man by any means. His desires are fairly modest. I understand he has no active life in the markets now and interests himself in reading and enjoying company."

"And," I noted with great unhappiness, "if he has collected only enough upon which to retire in relative comfort, a major burden of debt could quite destroy his comfort."

"Just so."

"Then I suppose I had better speak to him."

MR. FRANCO KEPT his handsome and tastefully appointed house on Vine Street, an easy walk from my own residence and my uncle's. Given the hour, it was possible, perhaps likely, that he should be entertaining or out, but I found the man at home, and eager to receive company. He saw me in his parlor, where he offered me a fine chair and a cup of cleverly mulled wine.

"I'm delighted to see you, sir," he told me. "After Gabriella's return to Salonica, I feared there would be no further connection between us. I expect her back soon and am glad of it, for a man should be with his family. It is a great blessing in one's later years."

Mr. Franco smiled kindly at me, and I felt hatred toward myself and rage toward Cobb for what it was I must tell him. He was a kind-looking man with a round face that suggested a plumpness of body he did not possess. Like my uncle, he eschewed London fashion and wore a closely cut beard that drew an interlocutor's attention to his warm, intelligent eyes.

He was, in many ways, an unusual man. Part of the reason my uncle had been so eager for me to pursue the match was that, unlike many respectable Jews of London, Mr. Franco would not have regarded an alliance with a thieftaker as an insult to his family. Indeed, he rather took pleasure that I had achieved some recognition among the Gentiles of the city and regarded my successes as a sign—an overly optimistic one, in my estimate—of a greater tolerance to come.

"I had feared that when there failed to be a connection between my daughter and yourself—no, no, don't protest. I see you would correct me, but it is not necessary. I know my daughter is charming and beautiful, so I need not hear it from you. I also know that not every charming and beautiful woman can appeal, in a matrimonial way, to every man, or the world would be a strange and awkward place. I take no insult. You will both find fine matches, and I wish it upon you sooner rather than later, for a man should know the blessings of matrimony."

"You are very kind." I bowed from my seat.

"I am led to understand that you had some connection to your uncle's daughter-in-law," he said probingly. "Perhaps this woman is an obstacle between you and my daughter?"

I sighed, for I felt I could not avoid this troublesome topic. "At one time I did indeed wish most earnestly to marry the lady," I admitted, "but she sought happiness elsewhere. She is no obstacle to anything in my life."

"She converted to the Church of England, they say."

I nodded.

"But it is my understanding that she has since been widowed a second time."

"You understand correctly," I informed him.

He laughed softly. "And I perceive that you do not wish me to pursue this topic further."

"I hope you will feel free to discuss any matter you like with me, Mr. Franco. I cannot take offense when a man of your good nature speaks with a free and open heart."

"Oh, you may stop being so formal with me. When you and Gabriella failed to pursue a more solemn connection, I feared that we must cease being friends. I do hope that is not the case."

"I, too, had flattered myself that we might continue our friendship," I said, "although when you have heard what I have to say, you may find yourself wishing you had never invited me into your home. I am afraid that I must be circumspect and keep more details from you than I would like, but the truth is, sir, that someone means to do you harm as a means of doing me harm."

He leaned forward, and the creak of his chair startled me. "Do us both harm? What do you mean?"

I explained, as clearly as I could despite my discomfort, that my enemies had selected a few of my nearest contacts whose finances they disrupted. "It appears that because of my frequent visits, they mistook you for a very near connection."

"But there is nothing wrong with my finances."

"Have you any debts, Mr. Franco?"

"All men have debts," he said, his voice now strained.

"Of course. But what these men have almost certainly done is to buy up such debts as they can find. If all of your outstanding debts were to be called in at one time, would you find yourself in great difficulty?"

He said nothing for a few moments, but his face had gone pale around his beard, and his fingers, locked around his cup, also turned toward an ivory color.

"I am very sorry to have visited this upon you," I offered, wincing at the weakness of it.

He shook his head. "From what you tell me, you have done nothing. These men must be base enough to prey upon your good nature, knowing that you could endure suffering for yourself but not for others. I am indeed angry, Mr. Weaver, but not at you, who have done no harm."

"I do not deserve such understanding, though I am grateful to receive it."

"No, but you must tell me more. Who are these enemies of yours? What do they want from you?"

"I think it best I not say too much. But they wish me to perform services I would not perform otherwise."

"What sort of services? You must not, even to preserve me from prison, do anything that conflicts either with your own sense of moral duty or the laws of this kingdom."

I thought it best to ignore this point. "As to the nature of the services, perhaps the less said the better."

"You may have done no wrong to put me in this predicament, Mr. Weaver, but I am in it, and it would be unkind to leave me ignorant."

He was undeniably correct, and so after impressing upon him the need for secrecy, for his own good as well as that of others, I told him as much as I thought safe. I explained that a very wealthy man of great influence wished to deploy my services against one of the East India Company directors.

"Ha," he said, with a kind of triumph. "I've had dealings with the East India Company and their competitors too. I promise you I am no novice in this game, and we shall outmaneuver them."

"That may not be done so easily," I said.

He smiled a knowing smile at me. "You think because these men are rich and great they cannot be dealt with? That is the beauty of 'Change Alley. Fortune is a fickle goddess and can strike blows where no one expects and elevate the mendicant to great heights. The East India men have no cause to love me, but their enmity has never done me harm. There are rules in this game we play, you know."

"Given that you, I, my uncle, and my dear friend are now dangling with our feet over the flames of ruin, I would say the rules of the game have changed."

"It does sound rather like. Tell me then, who is the man who wishes the Company harm? What is his name? What are his connections?"

"No one has heard of him, and I dare not speak his name more often than I must. I believe the slightest slip could have disastrous results for you or one of my other friends. Indeed, I have been warned not to have conversations precisely like this one, and I risk it only because I believe you deserve to know that there are invisible agents who act upon you. Yet, though this knowledge is your right, I must urge you to resist all temptation to act upon it. Until I see a better opportunity, there is little for any of us to do but appear as placid as sheep while we wait for the main chance to present itself."

"You do not know me very well, Mr. Weaver, but I think you know I am not a man who would break his oath. I can assure you I am even less inclined to do so when breaking my oath will land me in the Marshalsea or some other equally terrible place. In addition, I have traded—indirectly, mind you—with the eastern-looking companies of this nation as well as of the Dutch and the fledgling project of the French. If this man is an actor upon the East Indian stage, I will know him, and you will then have an advantage you did not previously possess."

I could not deny the request, so with an unexpected amount of difficulty I spoke his name. "Jerome Cobb."

Mr. Franco said nothing for a long while. "I've not heard of him."

"No one has. Neither my uncle nor the other victim, my friend Elias Gordon, a well-connected surgeon, can discover anything of him. He is a man with a great deal of money, and yet no one in London knows him."

"Perhaps it is not his real name."

"I have already considered that."

"No doubt. In truth, Mr. Weaver, this certainly presents some difficulties. I beg you will keep me informed of your progress. If I am to find myself in debtor's prison, I can only ask for some advance warning. And as I know the trade, I may be able to provide some advice."

I assured him I would do as he asked, and indeed I felt that Mr. Franco might prove an unexpected ally in these matters, but to use his services I would have to jeopardize his freedom, and I did not know how much of a risk I dared to take.

—

CHAPTER EIGHT

*M*Y UNCLE AND MR. FRANCO BOTH MADE THEIR HOMES IN THE parish of St. James's, Duke's Place. I had for some years been living in the same parish, but upon the far less fashionable street of Greyhound Alley. Here the houses were full of Jews, both my family's sort—the speakers of Portuguese, though coming from many nations—and those whom we called the Tudescos. They had their own name for themselves, but I could not say I knew what it was. These were the people of the Eastern European nations—Poland and Muscovy and the like—and they had been coming to this kingdom in increasing numbers. This fact caused some consternation among the Portuguese Hebrews, for while we had our share of the poor among us, these Jews were poor almost to a man and, with their old clothes trade and peddling, created a poor reputation for us among the Gentiles.

Most of those who lived in my house were Portuguese Jews, and I flattered myself that I possessed the finest rooms in the establishment. Here lodgings were inexpensive, and I had little trouble taking for myself three spacious rooms, airy in summer courtesy of several working windows and warm in winter from an adequate fireplace. Indeed, I suspected my landlord went to special trouble to make certain I remained comfortable, perceiving that having a man of my reputation about kept his house safe from intrusion and crime.

I would have liked to believe the same thing, but as I entered my rooms that night, one hand clutching an oil lamp to illuminate my way, I started to see a figure sitting in one of my chairs, hands folded in his lap, waiting patiently. I thought to drop my light and reach for a weapon, but in the flash of an instant I saw he made no hostile move. Whatever he wanted, he had not come to surprise me with violence. I therefore took my time and lit a few more lights. I never took my eye off of him, but I wished to create the impression that I was indifferent to his presence.

Once the room was sufficiently bright, I turned around and saw a rather large man staring at me with a familiar smile. Here was Mr. Westerly, who had come to me some weeks ago asking if I would attempt a break-in of the East India Company house. Now he sat, plump hands resting in his lap, as though no place in the world suited him so much as my rooms and my chair. His cheeks were pink with contentment, and his overly frizzed wig had sunk low to just above his eyes, creating the impression that he had fallen asleep.

"You don't mind that I used your pot, I hope," he said. "Came nowhere near to filling it, but there's some that don't like it when another man mixes his piss with their own."

"Of the grievances I bear against you, a man who has entered my rooms without permission," I said, "that may be the least. What do you want?"

"You would have been better to have concluded our business differently, I think. Now look at you, Weaver. You have made a bit of a mess for yourself, haven't you?"

"Mr. Cobb strikes me as a tolerably stalwart figure," I told him, applying my most unnerving stare. "You, however, do not. Perhaps I could learn a great deal about Mr. Cobb by applying my attentions to you."

"That is a distinct possibility," he agreed, "one you might be foolish to ignore. I am not a brave man, and I should collapse under torture quite easily, I think. I hate the thought of pain. Hate it tremendous. However, the same shackles that bind you in your actions against my colleague bind you against me. Harm me, sir, and your friends suffer."

"Perhaps you will never be found. Cobb would have no way of knowing that I was the one who encouraged you to disappear."

"My associates know where I am at this moment, have no fear. Claim what you like, sir, but no one would believe you. Indeed, for the sake of your uncle, you must hope I stumble upon no unhappy accidents on my way home."

"For your sake," I returned, "you had better hope I forget not prudence and cause you to stumble upon an unhappy accident within these walls."

He nodded. "You are correct. It is ungentlemanly of me to torment you in this fashion. I have come to deliver a message, and knowing that yours is an uneasy position, I wish to do no more. You must not think we are your enemy, Mr. Weaver. It pains us, you must know, to treat you in this style. But we need you and you would not have us, and here is the result."

"I have no interest in your protests. Deliver your message, and next time recall that I know well how to read. Further communications would be better sent by note than by mouth."

"This one could not wait. I am come to repeat Mr. Cobb's warning not to inquire into his business. It has come to his attention that your uncle and your associate have both been heard to ask inappropriate questions. As you and Mr. Gordon have met with your uncle this evening, and as you have then met with Mr. Franco, I cannot but think that you continue to pursue matters that you've been advised to leave alone."

I said nothing. How could it be that they had known? The answer was most obvious. I was being followed, and not by Westerly, for so large a man could not hope to travel unseen in the streets. There were more who had followed me. Who was Jerome Cobb that so many men served him?

"I met with my uncle and my friend. What of it? We were as like to meet prior to these events as after."

"Perhaps, but you discussed the matters at hand, did you not?"

"No," I said.

Westerly shook his head. "I cannot believe that. And you would be wise, given the fragility of your situation, not only to avoid any wrongdoing but to avoid the appearance thereof."

"I shan't shun my friends," I answered.

"No, pray don't. But you must ask them to make no more inquiries." Westerly pushed his bulk from my chair and steadied himself with his walking stick. "We know your nature, and know these efforts were inevitable, so you shan't be punished this time. Now, however, you see that you cannot escape our gaze. Cease looking to wiggle free of the net. Accept your generous employment and do our bidding. The sooner our goals have been met, the sooner you will be free of our demands."

Mr. Westerly bade me good night and departed my rooms.

TWO DAYS LATER I received a visit from Edgar, who wordlessly handed me a letter and then withdrew. His contusions had healed somewhat, but he nevertheless appeared badly used and was in no disposition to make friendly conversation with me.

In the privacy of my rooms, I opened the note and discovered the instructions Cobb had promised would be forthcoming. I was now to contact Mr. Ambrose Ellershaw of the East India Company, the man whose document I had stolen, and explain that, in the course of some unrelated thieftaking activity, I had happened upon the enclosed report. Recognizing the papers to be of likely importance to their rightful owner, I now wished to return them.

I took no pleasure in jumping to do Cobb's bidding, but I did believe that moving forward in this matter was superior to not moving at all. Perhaps I would soon have a clearer sense of what I was to do and why Cobb was so anxious that I should be the one to do it.

I situated myself in a coffeehouse where I was known and sent the note as Cobb desired, instructing Ellershaw to send any answer to that location. I would pass the afternoon, I decided, reading the newspaper and sorting through my thoughts, but I had hardly an hour to myself. The same boy I sent out returned with an answer.

Mr. Weaver,

I am delighted beyond words to hear you have the documents you mentioned. Please come see me at your earliest convenience, which I hope will be this day, at Craven House. I assure you that your delivery and your urgency will be rewarded as they deserve, being the way friends are treated by

Amb. Ellershaw

I finished my dish of coffee, headed immediately to Leadenhall Street, and once more made my way to Craven House and the East India yards, though this time my approach was more direct and less dangerous. A guardian at the door—a handsome young fellow who, by his accent, had recently arrived from the country and could count his good fortune at finding such easy employment—allowed me to enter without molestation.

In the light of day the East India house appeared to be nothing so much as an old and unlovely building. It was, as we now know, outgrowing these old quarters, and the structure would be rebuilt in not many years' time. For the nonce, however, it was spacious and indicated little of its purpose other than the paintings upon its edifice—a great ship bordered by two smaller ones—and the outer gate, which suggested that none but those with purpose might enter.

Inside, I found the house to be full of activity. Clerks rushed from here to there with bundles of papers pressed to their chests. Runners moved from the house to the warehouses, checking on quantities or delivering information. Servants scurried this way and that, delivering food to the hungry directors who labored tirelessly in the offices above.

Though I knew well where to find Ellershaw's office, I inquired for the sake of appearances and then climbed the stairs. I found the door closed, so I knocked, and my actions were met with a gruff call to enter.

Here was the same room I had explored under cover of darkness. Now, in bright daylight, I saw that Ellershaw's desk and bookshelves were of the most ornately carved oak. His window offered him an expansive view not only of the warehouses below but of the river in the distance and the ships upon it that brought him riches from so far away. And while in the darkness I had seen only that his walls were covered with framed pictures, now, in the afternoon glare, I could see the images.

At last I began to gather some understanding of why Cobb had so desired that I, and I alone, should deliver to Ellershaw his missing documents. I still had no idea what Cobb wanted of me and where his manipulations might lead me, but at least I understood why he required that it should be I, and no other, who engaged with Ellershaw.

Not all his pictures, mind you—for many depicted scenes of the East Indies—but many of them had a single focus. There were some dozen woodcuts and prints upon one wall that celebrated the life and exploits of Benjamin Weaver.

They spanned the course of my career. Ellershaw had a print of my early days as a pugilist, when I first made a name for myself. He had a print of my final match against the Italian, Gabrianelli. He even had a rather absurd rendering of me escaping without benefit of clothing from Newgate Prison, a consequence of my unfortunate involvement with parliamentary elections from earlier that year.

Mr. Ellershaw was, in short, an aficionado of the life of Benjamin Weaver. I had met men in the course of my work who recalled me from my days in the ring, and I flatter myself by observing that more than one of these recalled my fights with reverence and regarded me with special notice. I had never before met a man who seemed to collect images of me the way some odd fellows will collect bones or mummies or other curiosities from afar.

Ellershaw looked up from his work and an expression of pleased surprise came over his face. "Ah, you're Benjamin Weaver. Ambrose Ellershaw at your service. Do sit down." He spoke with a curious amalgam of gruffness and amicable cheer. Observing that my eyes went to his prints, he colored not a little. "You can see I'm no stranger to your doings, your comings and goings. I know full well about Benjamin Weaver."

I sat across from him and offered a weak smile. I felt both awkward to be engaged in this charade of returning what I had stolen and embarrassed by his enthusiasm as well. "I am gratified and surprised by your attentions."

"Oh, I have seen you fight many times," he told me. "I even witnessed your final match against Gabrianelli—that was the night you broke your leg, you may recollect."

"Yes," I said stupidly, for I wondered how he thought I might somehow forget breaking my leg in the boxing ring.

"Yes, quite a sight, the breaking of your leg. I am glad you are here. May I see it?"

I own I showed the greatest surprise. "My leg?"

"No, you blockhead," he barked, "the report. Give it me!"

I hid my surprise at the insult and handed the documents to him.

He opened the packet and examined the contents with evident approbation, leafing through the pages as though to make sure all was in order and nothing missing. He then took from a ceramic bowl, painted in red and black in the oriental design, a hard brownish thing that he placed in his mouth and began to chew methodically, working at it as though it tasted both horrible and unspeakably delicious. "Very good," he mumbled, through his chewing. "Not a thing out of order, which is rather fortunate. Should have been a bit of work to replace. When I discovered it missing, I thought, Here is an opportunity to see Weaver at work in his newer capacity, but I was not entirely certain I had not left these at my country house. I had a servant searching, and I was awaiting his report every moment when I received your note instead. How very fortunate. Where did you find this?"

I had a lie prepared, so I answered with easy confidence. "I was in the process of apprehending a notorious dealer in stolen goods when I came across a number of personal items. When I saw these documents, I perceived them to be of significance, and I felt their owner would be happy to see them again."

"Indeed I am," he said, continuing to work his brown nugget with his back teeth. "Very good of you to make so free as to bring them to me. That is the great gift of this island to the rest of the world, you know: our freedom. No arsenal and no weapon in the arsenals of the world is so formidable as the will and moral courage of free men."

"I had not thought of that," I told him.

"Now, what can I offer you in compensation for your efforts?"

I mimicked giving this matter great thought. "The papers have no intrinsic value of their own, and I am used to receiving a guinea for the return of such an item, but as you did not employ me to search for your papers, and as finding them took no more effort than the actions for which I was already employed, I cannot in good conscience demand payment. I ask only that if the East India Company, in future times, requires the services of a man of my skills, you will not hesitate to call upon me."

Ellershaw appeared to chew over the matter along with the strange wad of brownness, which by now had coated his teeth with a sepia film. He twisted his face into an unhappy frown. "Oh, no, that won't do at all. Not at all. We cannot leave things hanging this way."

I thought he should say more, but the conversation came to an abrupt end as he suddenly stopped speaking and winced, as though in the most sudden and excruciating pain. He gripped the side of his desk, clenched his eyes, and bit his lower lip. In a few seconds, the worst of it appeared to have passed.

"The damnable trouble. I must take my emulsion." He pulled at a tasseled rope that dangled beside him, and in the distance I heard a bell ring. "What sort of employment do you seek?" he asked me.

I laughed dismissively. "I am fortunate enough to have no shortage of men in need of my talents, sir. I did not come here to beg employment of you at this moment, only to request that if, in the future, a need should arise, you might consider me your man."

"That won't do at all. I am too delighted to have met you at last to let you walk away on such uncertain terms. I know you are a man of some pride, a fighting man and all that. You won't admit your needs, but it must be of some trouble to have to live from one found employment to the next."

"It has never been a trouble before."

"Of course it has," Ellershaw explained, with an indulgent smile. "And look at you, sir. You put a good face on it with your clean suit and such, but any man can see you a Jew without too much squinting. It must be a terrible burden for you."

"It has been a tolerable burden thus far."

"And though it be a terrible burden, you still enjoy the freedom of an Englishman, almost as though you were one yourself. Is it not a glorious thing? Freedom is, as you must know, the right to question and change the established way of doing things. It is the continuous revolution of the marketplace, whether it be the market for Indian textiles or stolen watches, I suppose."

"I honor your opinion on that subject." I glanced longingly at the door.

"But as for being a Jew, I suppose that is another matter. Burdens are not part of freedom, of course. We must be free despite our burdens. Yet this whole Jew business—I am sure it prevents you from having serious congress with gentlemen, but I promise you that I am not of that sort. I don't care about it, I tell you. I don't care whether you look a Jew or have come here as little more than a beggar returning my stolen papers. It signifies nothing to me, and shall I tell you why?"

I begged that he would do so.

"Because I have seen you fight in the ring, sir. I know what sort of man you are, even if the rest of the world only spits upon you."

"Begging your pardon," I began.

He would not yield his pardon. "To the world, sir, you are but a lowly sneak thief, not suited to sweep their chimneys, but I see in you something far better. Indeed, I have something of an idea of what to do with you. Would you like to hear it?"

I would have to wait to hear of that idea, however, for there was a light knock, and before Ellershaw could answer the door swung open and a serving girl entered with a tray in her hands. Upon the tray rested a pot of some steaming liquid that smelled of mushrooms and lemons. I should hate tremendously to have had to drink it myself, but it was not the strange tea that held my interest. The girl caught my notice, for this creature, hunched over and meek as any female drudge in a house full of brusque East India men, was no other than Miss Celia Glade, the bold woman who had handed me the documents in that very room.

Miss Glade set the bowl on Mr. Ellershaw's desk and curtsied at him. She gave me not a glance, but I knew full well she recognized me.

In the light of day, I observed I had underestimated her beauty. She was tall and remarkably well made, and her face was full both of round softness and sharp cheekbone. Her forehead was high, her lips red, her eyes as black as emptiness itself: a blackness to match the dark of her hair, which set off the delicate paleness of her skin. Only with great difficulty did I prevent myself from staring, either out of confusion or delight.

"Perhaps you would like to have Celia bring you something to drink," Ellershaw said. He spat the remains of his nugget into a bucket upon the floor. "Do you take tea, sir? We have tea, you may depend upon it. We have teas you have never tried, never heard of, teas hardly a white man outside the Company has ever heard of. We have teas we import for our own use here, far too good for selling or wasting upon the general public. You would like such a tea, would you not?"

"I am quite well," I assured him, wanting only for the girl to leave the room and give me a moment to think. I had imagined her before some kind of feminine clerk. Now she showed herself to be a mere servant. How, then, did she so handily know the location of Ellershaw's documents, and why had she been so quick to surrender them to me?

Ellershaw, however, would not be stopped. "Of course you want tea. Celia, bring the man a pot of the green tea from the Japans. He will like it very much, I'll wager. Mr. Weaver is famous as a great pugilist, you know. He is now a great thieftaker."

Miss Glade's black eyes widened and her face colored. "A thief! That's something terrible is what that is." She no longer spoke with the clarity and diction of a woman of education, as she had when we first met. I considered the possibility I might have mistaken the breeding in her voice during our encounter, but I dismissed the notion in a trice.

The girl was something other than what she pretended, and she knew I was as well.

"No, you silly girl. Not a thief, a thieftaker. Mr. Weaver tracks down thieves and brings them to justice. Is that not right, sir?"

I nodded, and now, feeling a bit bolder, I turned to the young lady. "Indeed, that is only part of my work. I am practiced in revealing all manner of deceptions."

Miss Glade looked at me blankly, which I supposed was the appropriate response for her. "I'm sure that's very good, Mr. Ward," she said, with utter obsequiousness, but not missing the opportunity to deploy the false name I'd given her during my nocturnal thieving.

"*Weaver,* you ninny," Ellershaw said to her. "Now go bring him his green tea."

She curtsied and left the room.

My heart beat heavily as I felt the thrill and panic of having escaped— but escaped what, I hardly knew. I could not concern myself with the matter for now, however. I had first to discover what it was that Ellershaw would do with me, though I operated under the severe disability of not knowing what Cobb would have Ellershaw do with me. What if I should do the wrong thing? I could not worry myself with that, for if Cobb had not told me he could not hold me responsible.

Ellershaw took a sip from the steaming bowl the girl had brought him. "This is monstrous stuff, sir. Absolutely monstrous. But I must take it for my condition, so you shan't hear me complain, I promise you, though it tastes as though brewed by the very devil." He held out the bowl. "Try it, if you dare."

I shook my head. "I dare not."

"Try it, damn you." The tone of his voice did not quite match the harshness of the words, but I misliked it all the same, and I should never have endured this treatment were I in possession of the freedom Ellershaw so extolled.

"Sir, I have no wish to try it."

"Oh, ho. The great Weaver afraid of a bowl of medicinal herbs. How the great have fallen. This bowl is the David to your Goliath, I see. It has quite unmanned you. Where is the girl with that tea?"

"It has only been a moment," I observed.

"Already taking the sides of the ladies, are you? You're a wicked man, Mr. Weaver. A very wicked man, in the way I have heard that Jews are wicked. Removing the foreskin, they say, is like removing the cage from the tiger. But I like a man who likes the ladies, and that Celia is a rather tasty morsel, I think. Do you not agree? But let us stop this foolishness, for you won't advance in Craven House if you can think of nothing but getting under the skirts of serving girls. Do we understand each other?"

"Absolutely," I assured him.

"Let us turn our attention to the matter at hand. I have not had much time to consider it, but tell me, Mr. Weaver, have you ever thought of working for a trading company rather than being an independent such as you are, struggling from day to day, wondering where the next bite of bread might be found?"

"I had not thought of it."

"It has just come to my mind, but I wonder how it is that these papers could have gone missing. You know, there was a riot of rotten silk fellows the other night, and my guards were all occupied in jeering at the ruffians. It might be that, in the excitement, one of those rogues could have slipped in and taken this."

Ellershaw cut too close to the truth for my comfort. "But why should they take these papers? Was anything else taken?" I asked.

He shook his head. "I know, it hardly sounds plausible, but I can think of no other explanation. Even if I am wrong, it little alters the fact that we have dozens of low types guarding the premises, but no one who truly supervises them. The ruffian who inspects a departing laborer to make certain he has stolen nothing is himself the next day inspected by the very fellow he previously examined. The Company, in a word, is vulnerable to the treacheries and inadequacies of the very men charged with protecting it. Thus, I have the idea, at this very moment, that you might be the fellow to be head of the guard, if you will, to keep your eye upon them and make sure they are up to no mischief."

I could hardly think of anything I should like to do less, but I understood my place was to seem agreeable to Mr. Ellershaw. "Surely," I proposed, "a former officer in the army might be a better man. It is true I have some experience with thieves, but I have no experience in commanding underlings."

"It hardly signifies," he said. "What do you say to forty pounds a year in exchange for your services? What say you to that, sir? It is nearly as much as we pay our clerks, I promise you. It is a fair rate for such an office. Maybe too fair a rate, but I know better than to haggle over price with a Jew. I shall pay your people that compliment with all my heart."

"It is a very tempting offer, for the stability of the work and the steadiness of the income should be quite a boon to me," I told him, having no wish to make any decision without first consulting Cobb. "But I must think on it."

"You must please yourself in that regard, I suppose. I hope you will inform me of your conclusions. It's what I hope. But you've kept me long enough, I believe. I have much to do."

"The girl is coming with the tea," I reminded him.

"What? Is this a public house that you can order this and that at your leisure? Sir, if you are to work here, you must first understand that it is a place of business."

I apologized for my error, while Ellershaw glared at me with the utmost hostility, and I made my way out of Craven House. I maneuvered around rushing clerks, servants with trays of food and drink, self-important and generally—though not always—plump men in close conversation, and even a few porters, all of whom moved about with such determination as to give the building the feel of a center of government rather than a company office. I both lamented and celebrated that I managed to see nothing more of Miss Glade, for I knew not what to make of that lady. I knew, however, that were I to return on a regular basis, that matter must come to some sort of head.

Once I was clear of Craven House, I had no choice, then, but to visit Mr. Cobb and report at once on everything I had seen. This necessity pained me, for I hated more than anything the feeling of fleeing to my master to tell him how I had served him and to inquire how I might best serve him next. However, I once more reminded myself that the sooner I discovered what it was that Cobb wanted, the sooner I would be free of him.

I had no desire, however, to deal with his injured and malevolent serving man, so I took myself to an alehouse and sent a boy to Cobb, asking that he should meet me there. I thought it a small imposition for him to come to me when he was so eager to treat me as his puppet. And, in truth, ordering him this way or that felt to me a pitiful sort of lubricant but a lubricant nevertheless, to help me swallow the bitter medicine of my servitude.

As I drank my third pot of ale, the door to the tavern opened, and in came, of all people, Edgar the servant, his bruised face hard with rage. He strolled toward me like an angry bull whose baiting had not yet started and stood over me with an air of menace. He said nothing for a moment and then raised his hand and opened it over my table. I was rained on at once by two dozen tiny pieces of shredded paper. It took no close examination to determine that this was the note I had sent.

"Are you such an idiot as to send notes to us?" he asked.

I took one of the pieces of paper and acted as though examining it. "Apparently."

"Never do so again. If you have something to say, you come to us. Do not send a boy from an inn. Do I make myself understood?"

"I'm afraid I don't understand you," I answered.

"Play games to amuse yourself in private," he sneered. "Not upon Mr. Cobb's time nor within his sphere."

"What does it matter if I send a boy?"

"It matters because you are not permitted. Now get up and follow me."

"I am finishing my pot," I told him.

"You are done with your pot." He struck out at once, knocking my pot from the table so it hit the wall, spraying a few patrons who had been hunched over their own drinks. They stared at me and the good manservant. Indeed, everyone stared at us: the patrons, the barman, the whore.

I fairly leaped from my chair and grabbed Edgar by his shirt and thrust his back down on my table. I raised one fist over him that he might know my intent.

"Ha," he said. "You'll strike me no more, for I believe Cobb shan't permit it. Your days of terrorizing me have passed, and you'll come meekly or your friends will suffer. Now let me up, you filthy heathen, or you'll know more of my wrath."

I thought to tell him that Cobb had assured me I might beat Edgar as I like, a term of employment that the good patron had clearly been re-miss in articulating. Nevertheless, I held my tongue, for I did not wish to sound like a child quoting paternal sanction. What shred of power I could reserve for myself, I would have. I therefore justified myself upon my own terms.

"We face a difficulty," I told him. I spoke quietly and with a calm I did not possess. "These people here know me, and they know I would never allow a bootlick such as you to treat me thus. Therefore, that I might better protect Mr. Cobb's secret designs, I have no choice but to thrash you. Do you not agree?"

"One moment," he began.

"Do you not agree that it must appear to the world that I am the same man I have been?"

"Yes," he said.

"Then what must I do?"

Edgar swallowed hard. "Strike me," he said.

I held myself still, for it occurred to me that to strike him when he showed himself in a position of surrender might not prove satisfying. Then I struck him—to find out for certain. I hit the good footman two or three times about the head until he was too disordered to stand. Tossing a bit of silver to the barman for his trouble, I took my leave.

If Cobb thought it strange that I had arrived without the footman in tow, he did not say so. Indeed, he said nothing of the note and the boy, and I wondered if that had been Edgar's fabrication, an effort to try to lord some power over me. More likely, Cobb wished to avoid a confrontation. That appeared to be, at all times, his inclination.

His nephew, however, seemed to me a man who delighted in nothing so much as discord. He too sat in the parlor, and he stared at me with malice, as though I had dragged mud through his house. He remained quiet, however, and made no comment or gesture as I entered the room. Instead, he watched my interaction with Cobb, watched with reptilian dispassion.

I returned Hammond's cool gaze, then faced Cobb and spoke of everything that had happened with Ellershaw. He could not have been more pleased. "This goes precisely as I'd hoped. Precisely. Weaver, you are doing a remarkable service, and I promise you that you will be rewarded."

I did not respond. "Shall I presume, then, that you wish me to take this position at Craven House?"

"Oh, yes. We cannot miss the opportunity. You must do everything he requests of you. Take his position, of course, but you were wise, oh, so wise, to claim to need to think on it. Gives it a bit of verisimilitude, you know. But you must go to him in a day or two and take what he has to offer."

"To what end?"

"That doesn't matter just now," Hammond said. "You will learn when we wish you to learn. For the moment, your only task is to get Ellershaw to like you and trust you."

"Perhaps we should be more particular now," Cobb said. "I should hate for Mr. Weaver to lose an opportunity because we have not told him the reason for his presence."

"And I should hate for our plans to crumble to dust because we have spoken too soon," Hammond replied.

Cobb shook his head. "It is more dangerous to leave so important an agent directionless."

Hammond shrugged at this point, more a condescension than a concession. "Tell him, then."

Cobb turned to me. "You will have many tasks to accomplish while at Craven House, but perhaps the most significant is to discover the truth behind the death of a man named Absalom Pepper."

It would seem that they had hired me to conduct an inquiry. For some reason, this revelation cheered me. At least now I was upon familiar ground.

"Very well," I said. "What can you tell me about him?"

"Nothing," Hammond snapped. "That is the difficulty of it. We know virtually nothing of him, only that the East India Company arranged for his death. Your task is to find out what you can of him, why the Company viewed him as a threat, and, if possible, the names of the particular people who committed the crime."

"If you know not who he is, why should you care—"

"That," Hammond said, "is not your concern. It is ours. Your concern is to do what you are told and keep your friends from languishing in prison. Now that you know what you must do, listen well to how you must do it. You may not ask questions of this matter, not in Craven House or anywhere. You may not speak the name of Absalom Pepper unless someone raises the name unbidden. If you violate these rules, I will hear of it, and you may depend that I will not let the crime go unpunished. Do you understand me?"

"How am I to discover anything of this man if I may not conduct an inquiry?"

"That is for you to sort out, and if you wish to redeem your friends I suggest you work hard at making that discovery."

"Can you tell me nothing more of him?"

Hammond let out a sigh, as though I tried his patience. "We are led to believe that the East India Company arranged to have him attacked late at night, and accordingly he was beaten most likely to death. If not so, then it was the drowning that killed him, for he was tossed into the Thames and there abandoned to his fate. As is often the case with such unfortunates, he was undiscovered for many days, and by the time he was retrieved, the water creatures had nearly devoured his extremities, though his face remained sufficiently intact and he was accordingly identified."

"By whom?"

"Damn you, Weaver, how am I to know? What little information I have is based upon intercepted correspondence. It is all I know."

"Where was he found?" I asked. "I should like to speak to the coroner."

"Are you deaf? I told you we know nothing more. I cannot say where he was found, where he was buried, or any other such detail. Just that the Company had him killed and we must know why."

"I shall do what I can."

"See that you do," Hammond said. "And do not fail to recall your restrictions. If we learn you have spoken this man's name aloud, we shall declare our business with you finished, and you and your friends may all live happily together in your imprisoned state. Do not forget this warning. Now, go off and do as you are told."

I hardly knew how I could do as I was told, but I had no choice, so I took my leave and returned to my rooms for the afternoon. The confinement did little to soothe my anxiety, but I had nowhere to go and nothing to do, and the entire metropolis had begun to feel alien and dangerous to me.

As it grew dark, I went outside to St. Mary Axe, where there was an inn that catered to the dietary requirements and preferences of Portuguese Jews, and there I ordered my dinner, for though I was not hungry I was determined to eat in order to maintain my strength and wits. Several of my fellows called to me that I might join them, but I dismissed their offers with requisite politeness, declaring that I wished to dine alone. These men knew my character well enough and understood that though I could be a merry and sociable fellow, I might also be of a brooding disposition, and no one deployed excessive effort to force me to be good company. For this consideration, I was most grateful.

I had not been sitting five minutes when a gentleman entered who caught the attention of the whole room. He was an Englishman, dressed in a plain suit and prim little wig, and he kept clutched to his side a leather envelope. He appeared quite out of his element and, indeed, frightened to be surrounded by so many Jews. He spoke a word to the proprietor, and that good man, with evident hesitation regarding my desire for solitude, pointed toward me.

The Englishman hurried over. "You are Mr. Weaver, yes?"

I nodded.

"Your landlord, sir, said I might find you here."

I nodded again. I concluded at once that this fellow had come to hire me for my thieftaking services, and by Cobb's decree I would have no choice but to send the fellow off.

It was soon revealed, however, that I need perform no such task. "My name is Henry Bernis, sir. May I impose upon you for a moment?"

I again nodded, keeping my face sullen and hard, for I had no desire that he think me in too convivial a humor.

Bernis studied me for a minute. He stretched out his neck to look at one side of my head and then the other. "Might I beg you to stand for me."

"What is it you want, sir?"

"Come, now. On your feet. Let's have a look at you."

I don't know why I complied, but I felt a strange curiosity, so I stood. He asked me to turn around, but I refused. "I shan't dance for you," I told him.

"Oh, heavens. No dancing. None of that. No cutting capers or prancing about. I just wish to make certain you are healthy. To protect the investment. May I view your teeth?"

"You haven't hired me yet," I pointed out. "You have not yet told me what you want, and a thieftaker is not a horse, sir. I shan't be used as such, not even if the king himself wishes to hire my services."

"Hire you? Heavens, no. I haven't any desire to hire you. What should I want with a thieftaker?"

I sat down. "I haven't any idea, but you are starting to irritate me, Mr. Bernis, and if you don't make yourself better understood, you are going to be in need of a surgeon to set your bones."

"Please, no threats," he said. "I hate them. And no violence whatsoever, if you please. Any time you engage in violence, you risk your own safety, and we cannot have that. You must protect yourself from harm, good sir, I beg of you."

"By the devil, what do you want?"

"You shan't offend me by swearing, sir. It offers no harm to you or to me, and if a man be damned for swearing, what of it? The next life is no business of mine. I care only for your well-being in this one. Now, you have not been sick of late, I trust?"

"No, but—"

"Any injuries of a permanent sort? I am aware of the broken leg that took you from the ring, but that was some years ago. Anything of a similar nature since?"

"No, and I don't think—"

"You are not planning any trips abroad, are you?"

"No, and that's the last question I'll answer until you tell me what you want."

"I merely wish to ascertain your health."

"Whatever for?"

"I am sorry. Did I not say? I work with Seahawk Insurance Office. I am merely making certain we haven't made a mistake."

"Insurance? What do you tell me?"

"No one quite knew it was happening—a matter of too many clerks not speaking to one another—but it seems we have sold three insurance policies with your name attached in the past few days. We merely wished to make certain that there was nothing deceptive planned against us. But I must say that you seem in remarkable health."

"What sort of policies?" I demanded.

Mr. Bernis wrinkled up his face. "Why, life insurance, of course."

I knew well the business of insurance, for my uncle used it to protect his shipments. I knew less of life insurance, but I had heard something of it. I knew it to be a form of gambling in which people might bet on the longevity of a famous person, such as a pope or a general or a king. I also knew that policies were bought to protect an investment, so that if you were a merchant who sent an agent abroad, and this agent had particular skills, you might insure his life, so that if he were killed or stolen by Turk pirates, the merchant could be compensated for his loss. I hardly knew why anyone would buy a policy against my death.

"Who bought this?" I demanded.

"I cannot tell you that, sir. I don't know myself, to be honest, though if I did, I could not reveal that information. I merely wished to ascertain your health, which looks to me quite good. I thank you for your time."

"Wait a moment. Do you mean to tell me that there are men, multiple men, who have laid out money to the effect that they will benefit if I die?"

"Oh, no, heavens, no. Nothing like that. No one should have invested in your death. That would be monstrous, sir, most monstrous. No, these men have laid out money so that they will not suffer losses if you die. That money is not a wager, sir, but a protection of their investment in you."

I could ascertain from his simper that this was mere fluffery. I had hit it right the first time.

"Who holds these policies?"

"As I mentioned, I do not know. In any event, I am made to understand that the policyholders wish to keep their business a secret. I respect that, and I think you should too."

"I think I shall be paying your offices a visit," I said.

"I don't think you ought to waste your time. It is all quite legal, and you'll find it is our policy not to reveal such things."

"So one man may take out such a policy on another man and not have to answer for it? That is diabolical."

"How can it be diabolical when it is the law?" he asked.

And, indeed, his question contained such oceans of absurdity that I had no answer for him.

CHAPTER NINE

—

THE NEXT MORNING, AFTER A BRIEF EXCHANGE OF NOTES, I RETURNED
to Craven House, where despite my appointment I found Mr. Ellershaw
already engaged in his office. He motioned me inside, where he entertained a trio of gentlemen, dressed most exquisitely in widely flaring
coats, widely cuffed sleeves, and ornate embroidering—one with gold,
the other silver, the third both and a black thread as well. Each of them
handled samples of fine Indian calicoes, which they passed along back
and forth, commenting most minutely.

Ellershaw introduced me to the men, whom I recognized as fashionable figures of the metropolis, one the heir to a large earldom, another the son of a wealthy Sussex landowner, the third a young duke
himself. They took no notice of me at all, even when Ellershaw pointed
to the prints upon my wall, remarking how fantastical it was that I
should be in his prints and in his office simultaneously. These men,
however, would not be distracted and studied the cloths with all the interest of a milliner.

"These are very fine," the young duke said, "and I thank you very
much for your gift, Mr. Ellershaw, but what does it signify for you? Our
wearing this shall not change how matters stand."

"I want a run, sir. I want that you should appear in public in these
new cloths and make it known that you will wear what you can when
you can. I wish more than anything that the three of you, so dressed,
will create a mania to drain out the contents of our warehouse before
Christmas."

"That is a good joke," the duke said. "To make the beau monde shell out a pretty penny upon what they can wear only for another month? Yes, I like your joke tremendously."

The earl's heir laughed. "I'll set my tailor to work at once, and I shall be in these new things by the end of the week."

The men thanked one another and there were many words of approbation before the trio departed.

Ellershaw walked over to his writing desk, where he removed one of his brown nuggets from the bowl and cracked it between his teeth. "That, Weaver, is what I call the Holy Trinity." He laughed at his joke. "Those buffoons could appear in public wearing only the bearskins of an American savage, and within three days there would not be a gentleman in London out of bearskins. I have a group of ladies who serve a similar purpose. So I must congratulate you. You have been in my employ not ten minutes, and you have already discovered the great secret of the India cloth trade at home: give your goods away to a few fashionable people who have the power to set trends, and the trend is set. The new style is written of in the papers and the monthlies, and soon the provinces hear of them, and they clamor for our cloths. They beg us—beg us, I tell you—to sell them our goods for whatever price we care to name."

"It sounds most agreeable," I told him.

"It is the business of the modern world. You are still close enough to being a young man, I daresay. When you were born, men brewed their own beer, women made their own bread, sewed their own clothes. Need drove commerce. Now all of those things are bought, and only the most backward of bumptious fools would think to do their own baking or brewing. In my lifetime, thanks to my own work in the Indies, it is not need but desire that drives commerce. When I was a boy, a man might kill for silver enough to buy a morsel to feed his family. I cannot recall the last time I heard of such a thing, but the week does not pass where we do not hear of some heinous crime because a man wanted silver to buy a new suit or a jewel or a fashionable hat or bonnet for his lady."

I applauded his role in giving rise to such progress.

"It is the growth of industry and wealth, and that is the greatest progress the world has seen. And this growth can have no limit, for there are no limits to the Englishman's capacity. Or yours, I suppose."

We took our seats amiably. Not wishing to appear overly susceptible to self-love, I attempted to avoid casting my gaze too often over the prints on the wall depicting the exploits of my own life. It is, nevertheless, a curious thing to find oneself memorialized in such a fashion, and while it was in a particular sense gratifying, I also found it excessively disturbing.

"So you've chosen to be one of our brotherhood here at Craven House, to serve the Honorable Company, as we style it," Ellershaw said, while he chewed his mysterious kernel. "That's just the very thing for you. A rare opportunity, Weaver, one not to be missed. For both of us, I believe. You see, I sit on the subcommittee that oversees the warehouses, and I believe I shall earn the approbation of the Court of Proprietors when I inform them I've brought you along. Now, let's go have a look about, shall we?"

He led me down the hall and into a small and windowless closet, where a young man sat at a desk poring over a stack of papers and making notations in a complicated ledger. He was only in his early twenties, but he looked studious and dedicated, and his brow wrinkled with bookish labors. He was also, I noticed, rather slight in build, with drooping shoulders and remarkably thin wrists. His eyes were filigreed with red and the bags underneath were of a bluish black complexion.

"The very first thing I must do is introduce you to Mr. Blackburn," Ellershaw said, "lest he hear of you on his own and come demanding explanations. I want you to have no surprises, Mr. Blackburn."

The young man studied me. He had a more severe face than I had at first realized, possessed of something of a predatory nature, an impression augmented by a large beakish nose that hooked sharply. I wondered at what personal cost he labored, for he possessed a beleaguered expression one is more like to see in a man twice his age. "Surprises lead to three things," he said, holding up three fingers. "First, inefficiency. Second, disorder. Finally, diminished returns." With each of these, he clutched the finger of his right hand between the thumb and forefinger of his left. "I do not love surprises."

"I know it, and so I have done what I could to keep you informed. This is Mr. Weaver. He will be working for me, overseeing the watchmen on the premises."

Blackburn reddened a little. At first I thought this was some inexplicable embarrassment, but I soon realized it was anger. "Working for you?" he demanded. "Now? How can you have someone new come to work for you now? The Court of Proprietors has not approved any such post, and no posts can be funded without their approval. I don't understand this, sir. 'Tis most irregular, and I cannot think how I am to account for it in the employment ledger."

"Irregular, to be sure," Ellershaw agreed, his voice all soothing tones, "and because the Proprietors have not discussed it, Mr. Weaver will, until further notice, receive his pay directly from me."

"Payment from *you*?" Blackburn demanded. "There are no East India employees who are paid directly by other employees. I have never heard of this. How shall I make note of it? Is this to be a new entry in the books? A new sort of book? A special book just for this, sir? Are we to have new books every time a member of the Court takes a whim into his mind?"

"I had thought," Ellershaw said, "to leave Mr. Weaver unmentioned in the books altogether." It struck me that Ellershaw kept his voice remarkably even. To my surprise, though Blackburn was evidently the subordinate, he was the one demanding explanations.

Blackburn shook his head and held up two fingers. "Two things, sir. First, no one is unmentioned in the books." He tapped one of the folio-size volumes, bound in a very grave sort of black leather. "Everyone is in the books. Second, if we begin to make exceptions, write rules as the notion takes us, then these books are for nothing, and my work is for nothing."

"Mr. Blackburn, you may either take the time to integrate Mr. Weaver's unique position, really as a servant to me, into your existing scheme, or you can accept that he is outside of your purview, not your responsibility at all. That being the case, you can safely ignore him altogether, as you would my footman or my pastry cook. Which would you like?"

This pointed argument appeared to gain some sway with the clerk. "Your servant, you say? Like a pastry cook?"

"Precisely. He helps me do my work more efficiently, and so it is my choice to take him on, and it is my wish to pay him out of my own monies. You need not account for him at all."

Blackburn gave Ellershaw a curt nod. "I accept your proposal," he said, though, as far as I knew, nothing had been offered.

"A fine plan, Blackburn. Very fine. But one more thing. I would rather you not discuss this matter with anyone. If anyone asks you, say only that everything is in order. I don't believe most men would pry more, lest they hear about facts and figures and tables in which they have no interest. Can you keep this to yourself?"

"Of course," Blackburn said. "I have no desire to advertise this irregularity. You see, Mr. Weaver, you are something disorderly, and I hate disorder. I like things to be regular and predictable and easily accounted. I certainly hope you won't bring disorder with you."

"I had thought to," I said, "but upon your request, I shall refrain."

When we left Mr. Blackburn's office, we nearly collided with a tall gentleman of fine form who appeared to hover in the hall awaiting our arrival.

"Ah, Forester, well met," Ellershaw said. He put a hand upon the man's arm. "I want you to meet Weaver. He'll be aiding my work on the warehouse subcommittee."

Forester's dull blue eyes grazed Ellershaw's hand on his arm before settling upon me. It could not have been plainer that he cared little for Ellershaw, but my new patron's monkey grin told me he observed none of this animosity.

Forester nodded. "Good. Things in the warehouses would benefit from more attention."

"Yes, yes. If you see Weaver around, think nothing of it. He is my fellow, you know. All is just as it should be."

For some reason, this prompted Forester to study me more closely. "Your fellow?"

"Yes, yes. You needn't worry." Then to me, he said, "Mr. Forester is serving his first term upon the Court of Committees. Very new to everything, you see. But his father—ah, Hugh Forester. Now, there was a great servant to the Honorable Company. A great man both in the Indies and in London. The younger Forester has much to live up to, I think." And here he offered me a wink.

Forester walked off and Ellershaw remained still, his face frozen in a foolish smile, like a young man who has exchanged charming pleasantries with the lady of his fancy. "I like that young man," Ellershaw told me. "I like him enormous. I believe he shall go far with my help."

I found this approbation astonishing. Forester's disposition, which might flatteringly be called indifferent, had been unmistakable. How could Ellershaw not see the contempt with which this admirable young man regarded him?

For want of anything more decisive to say, I merely remarked that he must know best the character of the men with whom he worked.

"Indeed, I do. I love to spend my time with the Company men, inside Craven House and without. As it happens, I am to have some guests at my home four nights hence. I wonder if you would be so good as to join us."

I could not have been more astonished. I was Ellershaw's underling, his plaything even, little more than a toy. The vast difference in our stations made this invitation both strange and unexpected, and I could not but doubt that I was invited to attend in the role of a curiosity, something at which his guests might marvel. Still, in light of my directions from Mr. Cobb, I could hardly justify excusing myself. There was more, however, to it. I was beginning to find Ellershaw more than an interesting specimen of unlikable man, I was beginning to find him fascinating in his obliviousness, and much as he surely planned to hold me up as an object of fascination, I wished to do the same with him.

"You do me too much honor," I told him.

"Nonsense. You'll come?"

I bowed and said I should be delighted, and in doing so I set into motion one of the most important phases of this history.

ELLERSHAW NEXT LED ME down the stairs and out the back door, which I had previously entered on my covert first foray into Craven House. The grounds, in the light of day, seemed almost a small city, or perhaps even like one of the Company's encampments in the Indies. Three or four large houses—converted homes, as I understood it—hulked about the grounds, but while the outer structures had surely not changed since the Company acquired them, they had lost all air of anything domestic. On the lower floors, windows had been boarded up, no doubt as much to save on the window tax as to provide security, and the bricks all had a dull gray cast to them.

Except they teemed with life. Scores of men and wagons, like monstrous insects of the Indies themselves, filed in and out of the compound, bringing goods to and from the East India docks at the river. The air was full of grunts and cries and orders shouted, the squeak of wheels, the creaking of wagon wood. Smoke puffed out of the warehouses' chimneys, and from not too far away I heard the clang of a blacksmith, at work, no doubt, on some poorly abused wagon component.

And then, of course, there were the guards. I distinguished them from the laborers because they carried nothing, they hurried nowhere. They merely strolled around the grounds, looking at once suspicious and bored. Occasionally one would stop a wagon and examine the contents. I observed one fellow demand to see a manifest of some sort, but from the way he held it, I divined at once that he could not read.

Ellershaw led me to one of the largest of the structures, situated in the middle of the yard and facing the open gate. The wagons of goods went around toward the back of the house, where I presumed I would find some sort of dry dock for the loading and off-loading of cargo. The front maintained the illusion of a house. When I walked in, however, the illusion shattered at once. The interior of the house had been gutted but for the supporting walls required to keep the second story from crashing down on the first. Here I found a vast expanse of crates and barrels and boxes, not unlike my uncle's warehouse of woolens and wines. And here, as in the days before Mr. Cobb wielded his malicious influence, the space was bustling with activity and energy.

"Move your arses, then," a man shouted behind us, and divided Mr. Ellershaw and myself as he walked between us carrying a pile of boxes that rose three or four head lengths above the top of his hat. If he noticed to whom he spoke and felt regret, he offered no indication.

"You there," Ellershaw shouted at a portly fellow with heavily hooded eyes leaning against the wall, watching the proceedings lazily. "What's your name, you slothful miscreant?"

The man looked up as though the effort of doing so pained him. He was not yet old, but he was close, and he had the look of a fellow who'd spent his life in the service of something about which he cared nothing. "Carmichael, sir."

"Very well, Carmichael. Are you 'pon the watch?"

"That I am, sir, and at your service." He offered a hesitant bow, clearly understanding that he spoke to someone important. "I am at your service, sir, and one of the watchmen too, as your worship observed himself."

"Yes, yes, that's fine. Now gather your fellows here, I wish to address them."

"My fellows?" he asked. "Begging your worship's pardon, your worship, but I'm not aware in any wise of your meaning."

"My meaning," Ellershaw said, "is that you will gather your fellows—the other watchmen. Go and gather them. I wish them gathered."

"As regards your worship's meaning," the guard answered, "I understood as much as that. But as regards to the *how* of your worship's meaning, I am less certain. How is it that I am to gather my fellows?"

"How the devil am I to know? How do you usually do it?"

"Begging your worship's pardon, but I don't, nor does no one. There ain't no method to do so of which I'm aware."

"Mr. Carmichael, do you mean to say," I inquired, "that you have no means of gathering about you the various guardians of the grounds?"

"It is as your other worship says," he informed me.

"How are new orders conveyed and how is new information disseminated?" I said, pursuing the matter.

"One fellow tells another, is how it's always been done."

"This is done very poorly," I said to Mr. Ellershaw, with an air of gravity, taking upon me the full role demanded by Cobb. "Very poorly indeed, for this lack of organization is most disastrous. You must go about the grounds and shout," I told Carmichael, "ordering such guards as you can find to gather here. Tell them, if they ask, that Mr. Ellershaw of the Court of Committees demands it."

Carmichael bowed his ungainly form nearly to the ground and scurried out. While we waited, Mr. Ellershaw praised me for my masterful handling of the low fellow and then begged me to amuse him with some stories from my time in the ring. I did so, and after perhaps a quarter hour, there were a sufficient number of men gathered about us for Mr. Ellershaw to proceed.

I counted some two dozen guards. "How many are there employed at this time? How many are missing?" I asked him.

"I have no idea."

I then put the question to the gathered group, but they were as confused as Mr. Ellershaw.

Ellershaw turned to the men. "Fellows," he shouted, "you have acquitted yourselves poorly, for something of mine has gone missing, and I shan't tolerate it. I have therefore decided to put in charge of you one man, who shall organize your comings and goings and duties. You shan't laze about further on Company time, I promise you, for I have employed as your overseer the famous pugilist Benjamin Weaver, who shall tolerate none of your knavery. I give him to you now."

A murmur arose among the men, and I observed that they spoke confusedly to one another. My initial impression was that they had no notion of the idea of an overseer. I soon saw, however, that I was mistaken.

"Begging your worships' pardons," Carmichael said, stepping forward hesitantly, "but perhaps you don't know that we already have one of them."

Ellershaw stared blankly at the gathered company, and then, as if in answer to a question he dare not ask, a figure pushed its way forward. And what a figure he was. Here was a man of well over six feet in height, of enormous stature and commanding presence. He was dark, almost as dark as an African, but dressed as a working Englishman would dress in such weather, in rough woolens, a heavy coat, and a cravat about his neck. His face was of the cruelest sort, with a large flat nose and small eyes and a long, sneering mouth, but what made it most distressing were the scars that crossed his flesh as though he had been whipped in the face. His cheeks, across his eyes, even his upper lip, bore the deep craters and crevices of some unknown conflict. Upon the street, I might have wondered at the land of his origin, but here, in this place, there could be no mistaking it. He was an East Indian.

"What this?" he demanded, as he pushed himself forward. "Warehouse overseer? I warehouse overseer."

"And who the devil are you?" Ellershaw asked. "Why, you look like the devil for all that."

"I Aadil. I warehouse overseer." He grunted.

"That's Aadil," Carmichael chimed in. "He's the warehouse overseer that we already got. What do we need another one for?"

"A warehouse overseer?" Ellershaw bellowed. "No such thing."

"I warehouse overseer," Aadil responded, now smacking a massive hand against a massive chest. "It me. All men here agree me overseer."

"How come I never heard of this?" Ellershaw demanded. A good question, particularly since he governed the subcommittee on the warehouses.

No one had an answer for his unanswerable inquiry, which Ellershaw took as some sort of victory. "There it is, then," he said. "You." He jabbed a finger at the East Indian. "You've done a poor job, so I'm demoting you. You are now one of the guards. Weaver here is the new overseer."

Aadil glared at the two of us but said nothing, accepting loss of status with what I regarded as Oriental stoicism. At least I hoped it was that, for the fellow looked angry—enraged, even—and I should hate to have to manage affairs with a wrathful barbarian under my command.

"Now that we've resolved this business," Ellershaw said to me, "perhaps it would be best for you to speak a few words to your men."

I turned to the gathered crowd, possessing no notion of what to say. I had not known to prepare any oratory, but the situation provided me with little choice but to make the best of it. "Men," I said, "there have been mistakes in the past, that much is true. But you have been given a difficult duty and you have been hampered by a lack of organization, and that shall plague you no longer. I am here not to torment you but to make your duties easier and more clearly understood. I hope to have more information for you shortly, and until that time I trust you will acquit yourselves as best you can." Having nothing more to say, I took a step backward.

Mr. Ellershaw, it would seem, had no better idea than I of what to do, and we stood in awkward silence for a long moment. Then one of the men leaned to his left and whispered something in Carmichael's ear, and that worthy let out a too loud and too shrill titter.

Ellershaw turned red at once and pointed his walking stick at the laughing man. "You there," he boomed. "Step forward."

He did. "I am sorry, your worship," Carmichael said, with a nervous stammer that seemed to suggest he knew he had crossed a line. "I meant no harm or nothing like it."

"Your meaning is your own, I can't speak to it," Ellershaw said. "Your behavior, however, is another matter. To demonstrate that our affairs shall be far more orderly under Mr. Weaver's guidance than under that black fellow's, I believe it is best that this fellow receive a stout beating. It is just, and it shall provide Mr. Weaver with a fine opportunity to use his pugilistic skills once more."

I examined his face, hoping to find the unmistakable mask of humor. Instead, I saw only a hard determination. My agitation now ran high. How could I acquit myself to the satisfaction of Ellershaw—and so consequently my true master, Cobb—if I were to shirk from this cruel task? "That is, perhaps, excessive," I ventured.

THE DEVIL'S COMPANY | 111

"Nonsense," Ellershaw told me. "I have had men under my command, and in India too. I know something of maintaining order." He called forth two men from the crowd to hold tight Mr. Carmichael, whose eyes were now big and moist with fear. Ellershaw ordered one of the men to hand me a thick pole of wood, some three feet long and four inches wide. "Strike this fellow about his buttocks," he commanded me. "And feel no need to restrain. It is a sturdy piece of wood, and no mere human flesh will harm it."

I took the plank but made no motion with it. I merely stared dumbly.

If Ellershaw saw my hesitation, he made no sign of it. Instead, he turned to the immobilized man. "You are a lucky fellow. You are about to be flogged by one of the great fighters of this kingdom. You may tell your grandchildren of this." And then to me, "Go on, then."

"I think it overly cruel," I said. "I have no wish to flog the fellow."

"But I wish you to," Ellershaw returned. "If you wish to keep your post, I suggest you listen."

When a man is in disguise and acting as something he is not, he must inevitably face such moments as this, though not only with such dire consequences to another human being. If I were to act as myself and do what I thought right, I must refuse my charge and so jeopardize my standing with Mr. Cobb. To refrain from flogging the innocent would be to risk my uncle and my friend. On the other hand, I could not in good conscience beat a fellow with a heavy stick just to placate Ellershaw's thirst for thrashed buttocks.

I struggled in my mind to come to a solution, but came up instead only with a justification. I was disguised, it is true, but as myself, and I like to believe that those who knew me would think me unwilling to beat someone who had done me no harm. Mr. Ellershaw had hired Benjamin Weaver, and he could not fault me for acting as myself. If I were to lose my place, I could explain to Cobb that I wished only to act as myself, thinking the order something of a test. I hoped that would be enough to preserve my friends from harm.

I handed Ellershaw the stick. "I think a beating unnecessary," I said. "I won't do it."

"You risk your situation with us," he informed me.

I shook my head. "It is a risk I am prepared to take."

Ellershaw glowered at me. I thought for a moment that he would beat the fellow himself, but instead he tossed the wooden plank to the ground and made a wild gesture with his hand. "Let the wretch go," he told the watchmen holding Carmichael.

A cheer of joy rose from the men, and I heard my name called out approvingly as well. Ellershaw frowned at me and at them. "I beg you await me outside, by the front of this house," he said, "where I trust you will offer an explanation for this mutiny."

I bowed and took my leave among the men's huzzahs, for they appeared to have come to love me for my act of defiance. Only the East Indian, Aadil, hung back, glowering at me with foreign menace. I dreaded finding Ellershaw once more, for I felt certain he would dismiss me, and I would be forced to explain these events to Cobb. I was quite mistaken, however, for the Company man met me with a large grin and clapped me on the shoulder.

"Finely done," he said. "The men now love you, and they shall follow you as you wish."

I remained speechless for a moment. "I don't understand. Do you mean to say you desired that I refuse to flog the fellow? I wish you had made your pleasure better known, for I believed I had openly defied you."

"Oh, as to that, you did defy me. I had no desire that you refuse, but the end result is excellent, and I shan't make a fuss of it. Come then, back to my office. There is something of great importance to discuss."

"And what might that be?"

He observed from my voice how ill at ease I felt and let out a little laugh. "Why, you mustn't take this warehouse business too seriously, Weaver. What I wish to discuss with you is the true reason I've taken you into my employ."

chapter ten

—

*W*E CLIMBED THE STAIRS ONCE MORE. ELLERSHAW, AS THOUGH made giddy by our episode in the warehouse, had to cling to the polished banister, and once he almost fell backward upon me. When we reached the top he looked back and grinned at me, exposing a mouth full of mashed brown pulp.

Once he opened the door to his office, however, he was surprised by a fellow of some forty years, plump in body, with a round face offering a nervous grin meant to appear like a smile of familiar pleasure.

"Ah, Mr. Ellershaw. I hope you don't mind my taking the liberty of awaiting you."

"You!" Ellershaw cried. "You! How dare you show your face here? Did I not banish you on pain of death?"

The strange man half crouched and half bowed. "Mr. Ellershaw, I told you from the beginning that yours was a delicate concern, sir, and that you would need to follow my orders to the letter, and you would need to be of a patient disposition. I have observed that you have not followed my advice on either account, but if we begin again, I believe we may—"

"Get out!" Ellershaw cried.

"But, sir. You must believe me when I say—"

"Get out, get out, get out!" Ellershaw screamed, and then surprised us both by embracing me as though he were a child and I his mother. He smelled of chop grease and a strange, bitter perfume and felt unnaturally heavy against me. Most shocking of all, I could feel the warm trickle of tears against my neck. "Make him get out," he sobbed.

Against my own desires, I found myself patting his back in a cold approximation of comfort. With the other hand, I flicked away the intruder, who crept backward out of the room, closing the door behind him.

Through his tears, Ellershaw began to say something I could not quite make out. At first I thought to ignore it, but when he repeated the same murmurings I told him gently that I could not understand him. He murmured in the same high-pitched, baby-bird tones once more.

"I'm afraid I still don't understand you, sir."

Ellershaw startled me by pushing me away violently. He glared at me from three or four paces away. "Damn you, man, do you not understand English? I asked you if you knew of a reputable surgeon to recommend?"

I own it took all the self-control I could muster to suppress a grin. "As a matter of fact, Mr. Ellershaw, I know just the man."

ONCE THE INTRUDER, whom I deduced to be Mr. Ellershaw's now-erstwhile surgeon, had taken his leave and I had provided my employer with Elias Gordon's name, matters calmed considerably. There were no signs of the previous intimacy other than Ellershaw's overly mannered correcting of his clothes—pulling at his sleeves, dusting off his coat, and the like. After a moment of harrumphing and ahemming, Ellershaw rang his bell and summoned a girl, fortunately not Celia Glade, to bring us some tea.

While we waited, Ellershaw refused to say much of substance, and spoke instead only of a play he had seen and the scandalous French dancers who had performed afterward. Finally, the tea arrived—the green mixture of which he had previously spoken—and I drank it with some pleasure, for it had a delicate grassy quality I had not previously known.

"Now, sir," he began, "you have no doubt begun to wonder as to why I should hire you to oversee the watchmen when we already have such a man."

He spoke, of course, of the East Indian, Aadil, but I had been under the impression he'd been ignorant of the man's existence. Now I knew not how to judge if his previous actions had all been a masquerade or if he played at some much deeper game.

"I presumed," I began cautiously, "that there had been a misunder-standing, which you chose generously to settle to my benefit."

He slammed the desk with his open palm, rattling the china. "You think me such a fool, then, do you? You shall soon see, sir, that I am no fool. I see it all; I see everything. And I see something else as well. When the Court of Proprietors meets in just over two weeks, there is a faction that will exert its utmost power to have me thrust from my position—thrown onto the streets, sir, after all I've done for this Company."

"I am distressed to hear it."

"Distressed? Is that all? Where is your rage, sir? Where is your sense of justice? Have I not toiled for this Company from the time I was old enough to walk? Did I not squander my youth in the inhospitable climes of India overseeing the factory in that fetid hell called Bom-bay? Have I not, with these very hands, been made to strike dead wild natives—and not just men, mind, you, but women and children—for failure to heed my directives? I've done all that, sir, and more, in the name of the Company's profits. And then I return to this island and take my rightful place in Craven House, where I lead the Company to greater success than it has ever known. After a life of service, now there are those who want me gone, who say my time is finished. I won't have it, and with your help I shall destroy them."

"But who are these men?" I asked, sensing I was upon something of import.

His color subsided somewhat. "That I cannot determine. They use strange and clever engines of deception to hide themselves and their motives. I know not who they are or even why they wish me gone, other than that they wish their man in my place. You see, I don't believe I am their enemy, sir. Rather, I believe they see my place as vulnerable, and so they have set their sights on it. The destruction they have planned for me is but a circumstance of their ambition, not the cause of it."

"How do you know all this?"

"Rumblings, sir, rumblings. You do not get to my lofty place without learning to hear them, to feel them. I know the weather before it breaks, I promise you. I've built my life on it. A look here, a glance there. Craven House is a place of secrets, Mr. Weaver. It always has been. We on the Court of Committees each have our separate responsibilities, but it has often been our way to establish secret committees—committees whose tasks are known only to the members. We love our secrets, and for some time I have felt that there is a committee that works against me. Those papers you found, you know. I believe they were stolen by an agent of that secret committee."

"But surely a man who has served the Company his whole life cannot be tossed aside for losing some accounting records. It seems petty."

"You have the right of it. But they mean only to show a pattern, for there is a great edifice upon which they mean to build their attack: the legislation of 1721."

I gave him a quizzical look. I have never been a political creature, and though I'd received a rude education in the late election, I knew not of what he spoke.

"You are utterly ignorant," he said, with evident disgust. "I see that now. Very well. Listen carefully, Weaver, but do not expect this to be a happy story, for it is a story of government men, and that can never be good. These government men, Weaver, they scheme of how to hurt the man of business, how to take away his money. And they have little minds, for were it otherwise, the world of business would hire them away. Shall I tell you of their calumny?"

"Please do."

"Cures have been developed when there is no disease, I tell you. And so, as of this Christmas the wearing of imported calicoes will be made illegal. With the exception of a few items, like neckcloths or blue fabrics that are so deeply entrenched in our society Parliament would not dare act against them, those scoundrels in the Commons have stood up for the wool interest and those villainous silk weavers and acted against the Company."

I knew from my associations with Mr. Hale that the wealth and influence of Britain's indigenous wool interest had wedded very nicely with the blistering violence of the silk weavers. Hale and his men had rioted, demonstrated, and lashed out. They had struck down men and women in the streets for wearing India prints. They broke the windows of shops that sold imported calicoes. The nation had been moving steadily away from fabrics made or woven at home, but the silk weavers did a fine job of making any man who stepped in the street with foreign-woven threads on his back feel as if he had an archer's target upon him. Now I understood that Parliament had bowed to the pressure of the wool interest, who, Ellershaw explained, had succeeded by threatening to withhold support for candidates in the late election. Thus, as of December 25, I, and every other citizen in the nation, would be empowered to bring before a magistrate any person wearing imported fabrics, and if the victim should be found guilty I should receive five pounds.

Ellershaw recounted all this for me, though his descriptions were peppered with condemnations of the silk workers and the wool interest and praise of the effects of imports upon the British economy.

"The men who were in my office earlier," he said, "the Holy Trinity, as I style them—they understood the absurdity of contriving to convince the populace to purchase goods they will soon be fined for wearing, but we shall do our best. We must surely sell what we can when we can by what means we can contrive."

I nodded, wishing to give no more sign of my feelings.

"So, there you have the long and short of it, Mr. Weaver. I chaired the Company's Parliamentary Committee meant to prevent such legislation, and now that the fruits of that year are coming to ripen, this legislation will be wielded against me as a weapon by my enemies, men who tell themselves they work for the best interest of the Company. Perhaps they even believe it."

"Surely," I proposed, "such men always work in their own best interest, and the interest of the Company be damned."

He nodded most approvingly. "I believe you have the right of it, sir. They will sacrifice me on the altar of their ambition, for this disaster is no fault of mine. You must understand that I had my men in Parliament, I had my men in the Lords, I worked quite hard to counter this business. But with the general election looming, the Parliament took the coward's way out."

"What will the Company do?"

He waved his hand. "Without the home market, you mean? Well, I shall tell you what the other members of the Court believe we will do. We will keep selling to the European and colonial markets. They look upon past colonial and continental purchases and believe these shall predict future purchases, but they know nothing. Those fabrics we have sold abroad before sold only because they were fashionable in the home market. Without British fashion to lead the charge, I cannot say how the other markets will respond."

"How could you predict that the clothes you sold would remain fashionable at home?" I inquired.

"Oh, that was the very beauty of it. When we sold to the home market, we could contain the trends, you know. Say the little black buggers in India were producing more white fabric with red design than we would wish for. It was nothing to give these fabrics to my Holy Trinity of men or my collection of ladies. We could make the fashions bow to the warehouses rather than take the trouble of stocking warehouses that bowed to fashions. With the markets moved overseas, that will be much harder to do. The truth is, sir, we have to undo the legislation of 1721. We have to take the power back from the Parliament and put it where it belongs."

"With the East India Company?" I proposed.

"That is exactly right: with the East India Company, and the chartered companies, and those men of wealth and ingenuity who wield the power in our economy. To them must go the spoils of the earth, not members of Parliament. Government growing beyond our consent has become a lumbering giant, sir, slamming shut the gates of opportunity, threatening to crush the very roots of our freedom. What will bring us back? The Englishman of means will bring us back—with quiet courage and common sense; with undying faith that in this nation the future will be ours, for the future belongs to the free."

Having spent so much of my life in close contact with the poor, laborers who struggled to earn enough silver each week to fend off starvation, who lived in terror of an illness or a disruption in their work that would drive them and their families to ruin or death, this notion seemed almost comical. While I could not easily believe that the men of Parliament had acted in an entirely altruistic way, the legislation Mr. Ellershaw railed against seemed to me a perfectly reasonable corrective to balance the unrestrained power of the Company, for it protected the laborers at home from those abroad and favored the native woolen industry over foreign trade. It looked after Englishmen before foreigners and companies. Yet as he spoke one would think it were a crime against nature to prevent these companies, though they were possessed of massive wealth, from doing anything they liked to amass more wealth at the cost of anyone they chose.

On this point, however, I knew to hold my tongue.

"Mr. Ellershaw," I began, "you speak of the doings of people and institutions far beyond my power. I hardly see what I can offer to help shape the course of the East India Company or of Parliament."

"Nevertheless, I see it, Mr. Weaver. I see it with remarkable clarity. You will be my club to wield, sir, and wield you I shall. By the devil, we will fight back against those rascals, and when the Court of Proprietors meets, no one shall dare speak a word against me. And that, sir, is why you must be at dinner at my house. Do you imagine I don't know how scandalous it is to have a Jew sitting at my table? Not even a Jew of wealth, which might be excusable, if someone there needed something of him. But you, a man who now, by my charity, earns forty pounds a year? I know it, sir, but you may leave it to me. You may leave it all to me."

chapter eleven

—

*I*TOOK MYSELF TO MR. COBB'S HOUSE, THINKING I HAD BETTER INFORM him of what I'd done with Elias's name. As he did not want me plotting with my friend, I suspected he might be angered that I had recruited my near associate and fellow victim. On the contrary, Cobb regarded my decision with approbation.

"I trust you can control your friend," he told me. "He must get a sense as quickly as possible of what it is Ellershaw wants to hear, and he will tell him that. Placate the man in any way you can. Earn his love through your surgeon. Do not think of discussing other matters with him, however. No matter how private you believe yourself to be, I can assure you I will know of your conversation."

I said nothing, for there was nothing to say.

OVER THE NEXT TWO DAYS, I began to make something of a routine of my work at the East India House. After the first day, when I wandered in at ten in the morning, Ellershaw informed me that I was expected to keep company hours, from eight to six, like everyone else, but otherwise my work was unsupervised. I began by obtaining from the fastidious Mr. Blackburn a list of every watchman hired by the Company. Once I explained that I wished to establish an organized schedule of work and routine, he warmed to me considerably and praised my sense of order.

"What do you know of that East Indian fellow, Aadil?" I asked him.

Blackburn spent a few moments looking through some papers before announcing that he earned twenty-five pounds per annum.

I realized I had to clarify the question. "I meant to say, what sort of man is he?"

Blackburn looked at me, the vaguest hint of puzzlement on his face. "He earns twenty-five pounds per annum," he repeated.

I saw that I should not get very far with this matter, so I attempted to shift to another area of inquiry. I had not forgotten my curious encounter with the gentleman from the Seahawk Insurance Office, and I thought perhaps Mr. Blackburn might be able to help me in that matter. Accordingly, I asked what he knew of them.

"Oh, yes. They have their offices at Throgmorton Street, near the bank. Mr. Slade, the director, lives above the office. They run a good business, indeed."

"And how do you know that?"

He colored slightly. "I own that my services are in demand, sir, and not only by the gentlemen of Craven House. On occasion I am contracted by various concerns to set their records in order, and my reputation is well known in both the mercantile and insurance worlds. Last year, in fact, I spent several consecutive Sundays restoring order to the books at the Seahawk."

Here was good news indeed, but I could not appear overly eager and thereby raise his suspicions. "Can you tell me how you went about such a thing? I am marvelous ignorant of how a man might reorder a set of records."

No question could have made the gentleman happier, and while it meant that I listened to an astonishingly dull tale that stretched out over the most expansive hour I have ever endured, I learned a number of highly valuable details—namely, that the records of the company's interactions were kept on the main floor, in the offices of a Mr. Samuel Ingram, one of the principal figures in the office, generally charged with making assessments of the riskiest propositions.

Having obtained that information, the moment I could politely extricate myself, I did not fail to do so. I could see, however, that my inquiries, rather than incurring the suspicions of Mr. Blackburn, had instead endeared me to him.

—

THE ROUTINES OF MY NEW life took only a day or two to puzzle out, and I began then to post a schedule at the main warehouse. It indicated who worked when and for how long, what patrol each man was to take, and so forth. Those men who could read were obligated to inform those who could not of their requirements. While the newness of the system produced some consternation in its offing, the men soon discovered that they would work fewer hours if they all attended to their duties. Only Aadil and a small band of some three or four sour-looking fellows, who appeared to be his inner circle, indicated any displeasure with the new arrangement.

Despite the hardly insignificant fact that he continued to earn five pounds per annum more than his underlings, I could hardly be surprised that Aadil resented my intrusion in his little kingdom. Nor could I be surprised that he had gathered a following to himself, for men of force are wont to do so. What did surprise me, however, was that his circle appeared to extend beyond the limit of the rough laborers. On my second day at the warehouses, I wandered down a bit early to find two figures standing directly in front of the main warehouse, huddled together, ignoring the cold and the light precipitation of frozen rain. It was the East Indian himself, in close conversation with none other than Mr. Forester, the young member of the Court of Committees who appeared to hold Mr. Ellershaw in such contempt. The two men stood talking quietly. Aadil, who was tall as well as large, stooped like a giant speaking to a mortal.

I had no desire to intrude upon them, and while I could not imagine what these two worthies might have to say to each other, I hardly thought it my place to impose upon them. I therefore turned away, as though I had business in one of the smaller warehouses. They observed me, however, and while Aadil took only a moment to glare at me with evident displeasure upon his scarred face, I could see that Forester was rather alarmed, either by my presence or my having discovered him with the ruffian. He blanched and turned away hurriedly, dusting from his greatcoat the tiny chunks of ice that had landed upon him and melted.

Aadil marched over toward me, looking less like a man than a bull at a baiting. "You say nothing of him," he told me. "It not your business."

"I should hardly have given it any thought," I observed, "had you not told me to ignore it. If you wish for people not to remark about your doings, you must treat them as though they are unremarkable."

"You say anything, you be sorry," he responded, and then marched off, his heavy boots crunching into the thick crust of ice on the soil.

Later in the day, I found an opportunity to take aside the plump and good-natured Mr. Carmichael, who—after my refusing to beat him—had become my closest confederate in the world of the guards. I could have had a worse, since he appeared to have a fair amount of influence with his fellow warehouse workers. When I knew Aadil was occupied with some task on the far end of the yard, I asked Carmichael about what I had seen with the East Indian and Forester.

"As to that," he said, "you'd be advised to take no notice of it."

"That's what Aadil said."

"He's the reason you should take no notice of it. He and that Mr. Forester are about something."

"What sort of something?"

He looked around to make certain we were unobserved. "I oughtn't to tell you as much as this, but if it will keep you from inquiring further, maybe it is for the best. I don't know exact what they're on to, but it's got to do with the third floor of the south warehouse, the one they call Greene House, on account of it being bought once, long ago, from a spark called Greene."

"What do they do on the third floor of the Greene House?"

"I can't say, as ain't no one allowed there. Any deliveries or removals have to be done by Aadil's men and no one else, and every time he brings something in or takes something out, Mr. Forester ain't too far behind."

"Have you asked him about it?"

"No, I haven't done that any more than I would stick my head in the mouth of a wolf. You only have to look at the cove to see he don't want you asking, and as you value your place here, you'll stay away from the business."

"Is not anything that happens in the warehouses now part of my business?" I asked, with deliberate obtuseness.

He laughed. "I've worked here now the better part of these twenty years, Mr. Weaver, and I can tell you as much as this: Craven House is a place of secrets and hidden alliances and graspings for power that would do any stage play proud. That's how it's always been. The men what want to get ahead have to plot and sneak to destroy their betters. That's all. You ain't got anything to gain by discovering what those two are up to, but on the other hand you got nothing to lose by *not* discovering it. To my mind that means it's best left alone whilst you attend to your own duties."

As for those duties, I was unsure of what I was to be doing with myself for ten hours a day. Once I had worked out the details of the schedule, I saw it would only be a matter of a few hours' work each week to maintain it. Other than wandering about the warehouses and making certain the men appeared to remain vigilant and keep to their posts, I was at a loss. I mentioned as much to Mr. Ellershaw, but he told me only that I should continue my fine work.

Elias informed me that he had, as of yet, received no word from Ellershaw, and I thought it imprudent to pursue that matter as well, so I wandered about the grounds, chatted amiably with the watchmen, and listened to their gossip, hoping to stumble upon some reference to Cobb's mysterious Absalom Pepper. No one spoke the name, and I dared not raise it myself.

On my second day, the same in which I observed the strange interactions between Aadil and Forester, I stayed late at night, on the pretense of observing the men as they went about their later rounds, and I attempted once more to search through Ellershaw's papers. But to find a reference to a single man among so many documents would have required an astonishing amount of luck, and luck did not serve me in this cause. I remained awake nearly the entire night and discovered nothing, obtaining for my efforts only a headache from straining my eyes against a single candle.

ON THE THIRD DAY, however, I had an encounter of particular importance to these events. Late in the morning, I abandoned the warehouses for the kitchens of Craven House, where I hoped to take a glass or two of strong wine to fortify my fatigue against the further obligations of the day. When I entered that room I found it devoid of all servants save one, the lovely Miss Celia Glade, whom I had seen only at a distance or in crowded spaces since our encounter in Ellershaw's office. She was in the process of setting up a tray of coffee dishes, no doubt destined for some director or other. I smiled at her when I entered the room, but I felt my stomach drop, as though I had been tossed from a great height. Here was a woman who knew my dark secret, or at least knew I had one. I was protected from her only because I knew she had one as well.

"Good morning, Miss Glade," I offered.

She turned to me, and in an instant I felt a terrible fear wash over me—a fear that I was not in entire command of my own sensibilities. She was naught but a woman, a remarkable pretty one, yes, and no doubt a remarkable clever one too. But what of it? Was not London full of these? Had I not enjoyed my share of them? Nevertheless, as I stood in her presence I felt that there was something else about her, far beyond beauty and perception. She played a game, as I did, and she played it well. I believed I was in the presence of someone quite capable of undermining my efforts.

She curtsied at me and lowered her face deferentially, but she nevertheless kept her dark eyes fixed upon mine. "Oh, it ain't right to address me in such lofty terms," she said, deploying the accent of daylight hours, not the ladylike voice she'd used during our late-night encounter. "All the folks here calls me Celia—or Celie, those what are my friends."

"And am I your friend, Celie?" I asked.

"Oh, la! I hope so, Mr. Weaver. I don't want to make no enemies."

She frittered about so busily, her brow furrowed in concentration, that for the most fleeting of instants I had to question whether my late-night encounter could have been with this same woman. I could see nothing about her that revealed she was not what she wished the world to believe.

I pressed on. "As I recall, when we first spoke, your voice had a slightly different quality."

"When I brung Mr. Ellershaw his medicine drink? I must surely have been taken with my work, or some very like thing."

"As you say, Celie."

"I must be about my duties, Mr. Weaver," she told me. But as she brushed by, she nearly stumbled with her tray, and I had to reach out to help her right herself. In the confusion, she very deftly whispered two sentences in my ear. She said, "They're always listening," so softly I could scarcely hear it over the rattling china on her tray. And then she said, "The Duck and Wagon in St. Giles—tonight."

"I cannot tonight," I whispered back.

She nodded. "Of course. The dinner with Mr. Ellershaw. Two nights from now?"

"Two nights from now," I assured her.

For a fleeting instant, she took my hand in her own. "Good."

My heart thudded with buoyant pleasure as I watched her leave the room. I had forgotten, it would seem, that I had not been invited to an assignation. I felt a twinge of surprise that she knew I was to eat with Mr. Ellershaw. I had no idea of what it could mean, nor did I know if meeting Miss Glade at the place of her choosing was a sound idea. At best, I would receive some sort of explanation for her duplicitous nature. At worst, I would enter some manner of trap.

CHAPTER TWELVE

———

*P*RIOR TO DRESSING FOR MY EVENING OUT, I WALKED FROM MY rooms to my uncle's house on Broad Court. I had been remiss in my duties as a nephew since my involvement with events at Craven House—partly because I in no way wished to incur the ire of Cobb, and partly because I had been too busy to play the dutiful relative. Those were the reasons I told to myself, but if I am to be honest, I must admit to a further. I avoided my uncle because he seemed to me a living testament to my poor management of affairs. That his health declined could be laid upon no earthly doorstep, but that his finances declined I counted among my failings. To say I felt guilt would be to press the point, for I knew I had done nothing to lead to this end, but I nonetheless understood that I bore the responsibility—if not for his difficulties then at least for their resolution. If I had not yet devised a means of helping my uncle, that in no way diluted my desire to continue the pursuit.

When I arrived, I found that matters were far worse than I might have predicted. In the gloom of evening, a small gang of rough-looking fellows carried from out my uncle's house a chest of drawers. Parked upon the street was a dray wagon attached to a pair of ragged horses that appeared themselves to be half dead from starvation and abuse. In the dray already were several chairs and a pair of end tables. A crowd had gathered to watch the pathetic procession, and the rough men were being followed by Mr. Franco, who barked at them to be careful and to avoid knocking the doorway in between bouts of cursing or naming the men rascals.

"What is this?" I hurried up the drive and placed a hand on Franco's shoulder.

He must not have heard me for he spun around violently, and I believe, had the light been any poorer, he should have struck me and only later troubled himself to learn who had received the blow.

However, he did check his arm. Indeed, at the sight of me, his whole body appeared to grow limp. He shook his head and cast his eyes downward. "Creditors, Mr. Weaver. They've scented blood. I fear it may not be long before they descend upon your uncle like ravens. And they could not have come at a worse time, for your uncle—well, he does poorly."

I turned at once to enter the house, paying no mind to a fellow attempting to balance a chair truly too large for a single man. I knocked him quite soundly but took no pleasure in his broad efforts to keep from tumbling.

Inside, the front rooms were well lit, no doubt to aid the creditor's men. I rushed to the main stairs and up to the second floor, where my uncle kept his room. The door was only slightly opened, so I knocked and heard my aunt Sophia call for me to enter.

My uncle did indeed lie abed, but had this not been his house I should hardly have known him. He appeared to have aged a decade or more since I saw him last. His beard had taken on a new and deeper gray, and the hair on his uncovered head had grown far thinner and more dry. His eyes, open, were deep and reddened and heavily bagged, and I observed that each breath was a struggle for him.

"Have you sent for the physician?" I asked.

My aunt, who sat on the bed holding his hand, nodded. "He has come," she said, in her heavily accented English.

She said no more, so I knew there was nothing more to say. Perhaps he despaired for my uncle; perhaps he did not know. When she showed no optimism for recovery, I could only presume there was none.

I came to the bed and sat upon the other side. "How fare you, sir?"

My uncle attempted a weak smile. "I do not do well," he said. A rattling sound emerged from his chest, and his voice was heavy and labored. "However, I have walked this path before and, though dark and circuitous, I have ever found my way back."

I looked to my aunt, who offered me a half nod, as if to say that he had suffered these attacks previously, but perhaps not so bad as this.

"I am full of remorse that this has happened," I said, keeping my words vague. I hardly knew if he was aware of the outrage that transpired below.

"As to that," my uncle managed, "it is of no moment. Minor setbacks. Soon all will be well once more."

"I know it will," I told my uncle.

I looked to the door and saw Mr. Franco hovering, as though he had something of urgency to discuss. I excused myself and stepped outside.

"The men are done," he told me. "They've taken several pieces, but I fear that is the least of it. If word spreads, the creditors will show no mercy. Your uncle, sir, will lose his house. He will be forced to sell his importing concern, and in its current diminished state, he must sell it very cheap indeed."

I felt my face grow hot. "Damn them."

"I am certain you do what you can," he said. "Your uncle and aunt know it too."

"I am meant to attend this cursed dinner tonight, but how can I go with my uncle so unwell?"

"If you must go, then you must," Franco said. "With whom do you dine?"

"Ellershaw and some other men of the Company. I hardly know any more than that. I must send a note excusing myself. Cobb cannot expect me to be his plaything while my uncle lies so gravely ill."

"Do not excuse yourself," Franco said. "If by attending this dinner you bring yourself any closer to your goal, I am certain your uncle would far prefer you do that than spend the evening looking sad by his side. No, you must find the strength to attend to your duties. Your aunt and I will make certain your uncle has all he needs."

"What did his physician say?"

"Only that he may recover, as he has in the past, or he may decline. This attack, he fears, may be worse than what we have seen before, but he cannot say what that means."

We whispered together for a few more minutes, while I attempted to inform him of some of what had transpired in recent days at Craven House. I kept the discussion brief, in part because I wanted to return to my uncle, but also because I had not entirely recovered from the revelation that my most private conversations appeared to be available to Cobb. I only said that I had, at Cobb's request, become employed by the East India Company, where I looked into any of a variety of internal turmoils. But, I said, as Mr. Cobb's agenda remained opaque, I could hardly say if I grew closer to my end or not.

During this conversation, my aunt emerged from the bedroom with a look of some relief upon her face. "He is better," she told me.

I entered and saw that, in the space of half an hour, he did appear remarkably changed. Though he still breathed with some difficulty, his face now had more color. He sat up, and his countenance was one of a normal man, not one about to leave this mortal realm.

"I am gladdened to see you so much improved," I told him.

"As am I to be so," he answered. "I am told you witnessed the unpleasantness below."

"Yes," I said. "Uncle, I cannot endure that this continues, yet I hardly know how to offer you relief other than by giving my full efforts to Cobb."

"You must for all the world make him believe you do, but you must never cease looking for advantage."

"I fear what happened today is but the beginning," I said. "Can we afford to play games with this man?"

"Can we afford to let him turn you into his puppet?" he asked.

"Both of us," my aunt said. "Both of us want you to fight him."

"But so that he suspects nothing," my uncle added.

I nodded. Heartened by his spirit, I told him I would do no less, and so I was determined, but I could not help but wonder how we would feel when my uncle was turned to a destitute man, homeless, broken, and without health. He was no fool and knew what bargain he made. I, however, was not certain I could endure it.

I SPENT WHAT TIME I could with my family, but at last I made to excuse myself, to return to my rooms, and change for the evening. Once I looked presentable, I hired a chair to take me across town and arrived with a satisfying promptness.

I could pretend to no surprise that Mr. Ellershaw's house on New North Street, not far from the Conduit Fields, was a fine one—a director of the East India Company ought to have a fine house, after all—but I could not recall that I had ever been invited in the capacity of a guest to a finer, and I admit I felt an unexpected apprehension. I had no Indian calicoes to wear, so I put on my finest suit of black and gold silk, woven, I could not but reflect, in the cramped garrets of Spitalfields or the dark hall of a workhouse. And though I knew I wore upon my back the labor of the cheated and the oppressed, I could not but reflect that I cut a fine figure in these fine clothes. We are all of us Adam's children, the saying goes, but silk makes the difference.

A polite if somewhat grave servant met me at the door and guided me inside and to a receiving room, where I was met shortly by Mr. Ellershaw, resplendent in his full-bottom wig and dressed in the height of imported finery. His waistcoat had quite obviously, even to my ignorant eyes, been woven in India, and was magnificent in its red and blue and black floral designs of indescribable intricacy.

"Ah, this is a very important evening, Mr. Weaver. Of the utmost importance, you know. Mr. Samuel Thurmond is here tonight, a Member of Parliament for Cotswold. He has been one of the great champions of the wool interest, and it is our role to convince him to back our proposal in the House."

"The repealing of the 1721 legislation?" I asked.

"Exactly."

"And how shall we do that?"

"You need not worry on that score for the moment. You need only follow my lead, and all shall be well. Now, as you are the last guest to arrive, you must follow me to the sitting room. I trust you will do nothing to embarrass me before my guests?"

"I will attempt to acquit myself to your liking," I assured him.

"Ah, good. Good."

Mr. Ellershaw led me through a maze of closely wrought corridors and into an expansive parlor where a number of guests were sitting upon sofas and chairs, sipping at glasses of wine. The only person in the room I knew was Mr. Forester, who did remarkably well at paying me no mind.

I was quickly introduced to Mrs. Ellershaw, a beautiful woman at least twenty years younger than her husband, though no doubt at least in her middle thirties. "This is my new man, Weaver," Ellershaw said. "He's a Hebrew, you know."

Mrs. Ellershaw had hair so pale it was nearly white, her skin was the color of porcelain, and her pale gray eyes were remarkably bright and lively. She took my hand and curtsied and told me she was delighted to meet me, but I could see that she was not. It took no great interpretive skills to see she was displeased by my presence.

Ellershaw appeared to have no recollection of having introduced me to Forester, and Forester showed no sign that he had previously met me. He too introduced his wife, but if Mr. Ellershaw held a winning ticket in the matrimonial lottery, Mr. Forester had drawn a blank. Though he was still a young man, and of a fine and manly appearance too, his wife was a great deal older than he was. Indeed, to call her elderly would not exaggerate matters. Her skin was leathery and hard, her muddy brown eyes sunken, her teeth yellowed and broken. And yet, unlike Mrs. Ellershaw, Mrs. Forester was of a jolly disposition. She told me she was glad to meet me and appeared to mean it.

I was then introduced to Mr. Thurmond and his good lady. The Member of Parliament himself was far older than Ellershaw, perhaps even a septuagenarian, and his movements were frail and uneasy. He walked heavily on his cane and shook slightly when he took my hand, but he appeared in no way lacking in his capacities. He made easy and intelligent conversation, and of all the men in the room it was he to whom I took the greatest liking. His wife, a handsome older woman dressed entirely in woolens, smiled kindly but said little.

Because the British dinner party cannot function without equity of the sexes, a fourth woman had to be presented to balance out my presence. To this end, Mr. Ellershaw had invited his sister, another older woman, who made it clear that she had been forced to abandon tickets to the opera in order to dine with us and was not at all happy about it.

I shan't bombard my reader with the tedium of the dinner itself. It was hard enough for me to endure, and I therefore have no desire either to relive the event or force my reader into a sympathetic misery. Much of the talk, as is the usual for talk at these sorts of events, revolved around the theater or the popular amusements about town. I thought to participate in these exchanges, but I observed that every time I opened my mouth, Mrs. Ellershaw eyed me with such evident disgust that I found it more agreeable to remain mute.

"You may eat freely," Ellershaw told me loudly, after he had helped himself to innumerable glasses of wine. "I have asked Cook not to present any pork. Weaver's a Jew, you know," he told the rest of the group.

"I daresay we do know," answered Mr. Thurmond of the wool interest, "as you have noted that point several times. And while our Hebrew friends are certainly in the minority on this island, I hardly think them so rare that they must be remarked on in such a way."

"Oh, but it is a remarkable thing for us. My wife does not think it proper to have Jews at the dinner table. Is that not right, my dear?"

I attempted to say something distracting, something that would change the subject away from this awkward business. Mr. Thurmond, however, decided that it was he who would rescue me. "Tell me," he said, too loudly, so that his voice would crush the discomfort of Ellershaw's comments, "Where is that charming daughter of yours, Mr. Ellershaw?"

Mrs. Ellershaw took on a high color, and Mr. Ellershaw coughed awkwardly into his fist. "Well, yes. As for that, she isn't my daughter. Bridget came with my marriage to Mrs. Ellershaw. A rather fair bargain, I think. But the girl's not about these days."

There was clearly more information regarding the daughter, and none was forthcoming. Thurmond could not have appeared more mortified to have stumbled upon so delicate a topic. He had attempted to distract from an awkward moment but had only succeeded in making the moment worse. His wife, fortunately, launched into an encomium of the pheasant on our plates, and in the end that did the business well enough.

After the meal had been completed and the ladies retired to the next room, the true business of the evening was at hand. Now that we were men only, the conversation turned at once to the East India trade and the legislation against it.

"I must ask of you, Mr. Thurmond," Ellershaw began, "that when Mr. Summers, a true patriot, introduces an act to repeal the 1721 legislation, as I believe he will do in the near future, you might consider lending your support to the effort."

Thurmond let out a laugh. His old eyes sparkled. "Why, that piece of legislation was an enormous victory. Why should I ever countenance its repeal?"

"Because it is the right thing to do, sir."

"Freedom of trade," chimed in Mr. Forester.

"That's just it," Ellershaw said. "Freedom of trade is the thing. Perhaps you have read the numerous works penned by Mr. Davenant and Mr. Child on the theory of free trade and how it benefits all nations."

"Both Davenant and Child were directly interested in the East India trade," Thurmond pointed out, "and can hardly be considered impartial advocates."

"Oh, come. Let's not be petty. You shall see for yourself if this wretched legislation is allowed to stand. The trade in calicoes here may cost some small number their employment, but its absence will diminish the available livelihoods as well. I believe that the East India trade offers far more opportunity than it takes away. What of the dyers and patternmakers and tailors who will be out of work?"

"That is not the case, sir. These people will earn their living through dyeing and making patterns for and constructing suits made of silks and cottons and the like."

"It is hardly the same thing," Ellershaw said. "There can never be the same enthusiasm for those clothes. It is not necessity that drives the market, sir, but fashion. It has ever been our way at the Company to introduce new fashions every season. We bring in new patterns or cuts or colors, and we put them upon the backs of the fashionable, and we watch while the rest of the nation lines up to get the newest thing. Our stock, not the desire of the people, must drive commerce."

"I assure you, fashions can and do exist in materials other than imported Indian textiles," Thurmond said, with great satisfaction, "and I believe the very notion of fashion will survive your ability to manipulate it. Allow me to show you something I brought along, suspecting as I did that the conversation might take such a turn as this." He reached into his pocket and pulled out a square of cloth about a foot in diameter. It was of a bluish base with yellow and red floral patterns upon it—remarkably handsome.

Forester took it from the old gentleman and looked it over, holding it in his hand. "An Indian calico. What of it?"

"It is no such thing!" Ellershaw barked. He snatched it out of Forester's hands and held it for less than two seconds before his face twisted into a grimace. "Ha, you clever dog! Indian calico, you say, Mr. Forester? This is spun of American cotton, I'll wager, by the coarseness of it, and printed here in London. I know every Indian print there ever was, and this is a London pattern if I've ever seen one. Mr. Forester is new to the India trade, for only an innocent could make such a silly mistake. Indian calico, indeed! What is your point, sir?" He returned the fabric to Thurmond.

The older gentleman appeared at least partially gratified. "Mr. Forester's mistake is an understandable one, for the cloth is very like an Indian one."

"That cotton is crude enough to rub the crust off a chimney sweep," Ellershaw called out. "Forester is an ignorant pup, I say. He knows nothing of textiles, just business. No harm meant, Forester. I have the greatest respect, and so on and so forth, but even the most remarkable intellect may be a dunce when it comes to textiles."

Forester had by now turned bright red with mortification, but he said nothing.

"As Mr. Forester has observed," Thurmond said, "American cotton can be spun with increasing skill to resemble Indian imports. This example may not deceive an aficionado such as yourself, but it may well fool the average lady in search of a gown. Even if it should not, new inventions are made all the time, and soon enough it will be impossible to tell the Indian from the American. Our native linens are being made with lighter threads, more like Indian fabrics, and wool and linen can be combined with great skill. Mr. Forester's mistake is an easy one to understand. The days of Indian imports are near over anyhow."

"I defy your argument. Mr. Forester may not be able to tell American cotton from his own shite, but there's not a lady of fashion or a clothes-loving beau on the island that would have been so fooled."

"As I say, perhaps not yet but soon."

"And what is to motivate these inventions?" Ellershaw demanded. "If people cannot have their India cloth, then the textile workers have no reason to improve their goods, for they own the market. It is the competition, you know, that will drive them."

"But they can't compete with these Indian workers, men and women who live as slaves, earning pennies per day at most. Even if we could produce textiles here in every way indistinguishable from the Indian, they would cost far more because we must pay our laborers more."

"The laborers must learn to do with less," Forester suggested.

"Fie, Mr. Forester, fie. Men must eat and sleep and dress themselves. We cannot ask them to make do with less because the Moguls of the Indies can demand that of their people. It is for that reason that we need the legislation. Is it not the government's role to step in and solve such problems?"

"It ought not to be," Ellershaw said. "I have spent my life in the trade, and if there is anything I have learned it is that government is not the solution to our problems. Rather, sir, government *is* the problem. A freely trading society in which the man of business is not taxed or burdened or hindered is the only truly free society imaginable."

"What freedom is this?" Thurmond demanded. "Sir, I know of your freedoms. I know that the East India Company controls more than one workhouse, and you conspire to have silk weavers arrested and put to work there, spinning without wages. And you, through your influence, have encouraged the growth of silk laborer colonies outside the metropolis, where wages are lower."

"What of it?" Ellershaw demanded.

"Do you think the world blind to your schemes? Why, I have even heard that there are agents of the Company among the silk workers. The men poor laborers often trust to look out for their advantage look out instead for the advantage of their oppressors. You contrive to lower the wages of silk workers so that silk working is no longer viable. You plan for the future, I see, to make silk so hard to come by at home that people will clamor once more for Indian imports."

I thought of Devout Hale's man, taken by the constable and thrown in the workhouse. Now it appeared he had been caught in a trap set by the East India Company with the goal of crushing the competition. And what chance did Hale and his men have? They were but people who had to live and eat and support their families. The Company had stood for a hundred years and would surely be standing a hundred years hence. It seemed to me that mortals did battle with gods.

Thurmond—who had, perhaps, made too free with his wine—continued to berate Ellershaw. "You do what you like, you harm whom you like, and yet you call yourselves the Honorable Company? Better to call yourselves the Devil's Company, if you are to put a true face on it. You imprison and break spirits and seek to contain all trade for yourself, and yet you speak of freedom. What freedom is this?"

"The only freedom imaginable, sir. A republic of commerce that spans the globe, in which we may buy and sell without regard to tariffs or duties. That is the natural evolution of things, and I shall fight to bring it about."

Thurmond gurgled doubtfully into his goblet. "A world controlled by those who care only for acquisition and profit must be a world of terrors indeed. Companies concern themselves only with how much money they can make. Governments at least look after the well-being of all—the poor, the unfortunate, and even the laborers, whose work must be cultivated, not exploited."

"You are a mighty fine man to speak of the laborers," Forester chimed in. "You own, sir, a vast estate in which the raising of sheep is your principal source of revenue. Is it not for your own benefit, your own investment in the wool trade, rather than the good of the laborers, that you seek to curtail the business of importation?"

"It is true that I earn my income from wool, but I do not see why I should be condemned for doing so. My lands bring in wealth, yes, but they also bring employment and substance to those who live on my lands, those who work the wool we produce, those who sell the products. There is a great chain of benefit that rises from natively produced goods. Imports, while they may benefit the few and indulge the tastes of the fashionable, do not contribute to the greater good."

"The wealth of the nation is the greater good, sir, the only greater good. And when the merchants and industrious men of the nation are wealthy, then those blessings will disseminate to all who live in the land. That is but truth, sir, and a simple one at that."

"I fear we will go round and round for an age and yet never convince our friend. Far better we understand that he has his position as we have ours," Forester proposed, "and we must live with one another accordingly."

"Yes, yes, very diplomatic, Mr. Forester, but diplomacy will get us nowhere, and it is, in my opinion, a sign of weakness. Still, I know your efforts are well intended. Spirit of friendship and all that."

"Indeed, and now if you gentlemen will excuse me, I am afraid I must depart rather early tonight." Forester rose from his chair.

"Somewhere more important to be, sir?" Ellershaw demanded, his voice not as unkind as his words. Still, there was no mistaking that he spoke with all the malice of a crouching predator.

"No, no, nothing of the kind. My wife mentioned to me that she was feeling unwell earlier, and I perceived she wished to depart early."

"Feeling unwell? Are you speaking against the food I've served?"

"Not at all. We have been delighted by your hospitality, but she has suffered from a bit of a chest cold of late, and I believe it may be returning."

"Hardly surprising, woman of her age. Marry younger, not older. That would have been my advice to you, Forester; had you asked, it could have done you some good. Yes, yes, I know your father made you marry that crone for her money, but you might have made a greater impression upon him had you refused to listen to his foul advice."

Seeing that Forester was too stunned to speak, Thurmond volunteered himself to throw some water on the fire of Ellershaw's discourse. "I see not what difference age makes to that happy estate, so long as it is a compatible match."

Forester said nothing, but the expression on his face evidenced that the match was by no means compatible.

Ellershaw chose to ignore this intervention. "Sit, Forester. There is still much to discuss."

"I should prefer not to," he said.

"And I tell you to sit." He turned to Thurmond. "The boy thinks to take my place at Craven House, you know. He must learn when it becomes a man to stay and when it becomes him to leave."

Thurmond could not much like the growing thickness of the air. He rose himself. "I believe I shall take leave as well."

"What is this, a mutiny? All hands on deck!" his host cried.

"It is late, and I am an old man," Thurmond said. "We shall leave you to your quiet."

"I require no quiet. Both of you sit that I may further entertain you."

"You are too kind. Nevertheless," Thurmond answered with a forced smile, most certainly having enjoyed more than his fill of Ellershaw's company, "I have had a long day, I'm afraid."

"Perhaps I have been unclear," Ellershaw said. "I must insist you not leave. We have not yet concluded our business."

Thurmond, who now stood by his chair, turned to study his host. "I beg your pardon?"

"You may not leave. Do you think I invite a pugilist Jew to dine with us because of his charming conversation and great learning? Don't be a blockhead. Weaver, be so good as to see that Mr. Thurmond returns to his chair."

"I must protest, Mr. Ellershaw," Forester said, "but I cannot think this is right."

Ellershaw slammed his hand upon the table. "No one," he roared, "asked what you think!" And then, as though a candle had been snuffed, his rage was gone; he went on with much gentleness. "There is much for you to learn, and I would fain teach it to you. Thurmond, I promise you, goes nowhere, and I think you should sit."

Forester obeyed.

Ellershaw turned to me. "Weaver, see that Mr. Thurmond puts his arse in his chair."

I saw that once again Mr. Ellershaw expected me to be his ruffian, and once again I wished no part of it. Nevertheless, I also understood that this was not like the incident in the warehouse. Refusing to follow his commands would not be met with a nod and a wink. No, this time I would have to buy time and see just how far this brute intended to push matters. Certainly, I told myself, he must understand that a man un-willing to beat a warehouse guardian will not be pushed to strike an elderly Parliamentarian. That was my hope.

Unable to find a better course, I rose to my feet and stood between Mr. Thurmond and the door. I folded my arms and attempted to look stoically strong.

"What is this, sir?" Thurmond demanded with a stammer. "You cannot keep me against my will."

"I'm afraid I can, sir. What might you do to stop me?"

"I can go to the magistrate, and you may be assured that I will do so if you do not let me depart this instant."

"The magistrate." Ellershaw let out a laugh. "Forester, he speaks of magistrates. That is a good joke. Indeed, you must first be permitted to leave for you to speak to the magistrate. But presuming I were to let you leave—say you were to make it out of my house without suffering from an apoplexy or fatal seizure, which no one would question in a man of your years—who would believe such a preposterous tale? And to whom do you think the magistrate owes greater fealty, sir? The East India Company, which rewards magistrates for sending silk weavers to workhouses, or you? Magistrate indeed."

Ellershaw rose to his feet and approached his guest, who had grown pale and trembling. His eyes darted back and forth and his lips moved as though mumbling a prayer, though I did not think he actually formed any words.

"I've asked you to sit," Ellershaw said, and he gave the old man a mighty push in his chest.

"Sir!" Forester barked.

Thurmond fell backward into his chair, knocking his head against the wooden back. I changed my position to get a better look at his face, and I observed that his eyes had gone red and moist and his lips continued to tremble. Then, mastering his emotions, he turned to Forester. "Do not trouble yourself. We shall be done with this indignity soon enough."

Ellershaw returned to his seat and met Thurmond's eye. "Let me speak plainly to you. This session of Parliament will see a repeal of the 1721 legislation. You will support the repeal. If you speak in favor of rescinding the act, if you become a spokesman for the freedom of trade, we will carry the day."

"And if I choose otherwise?" Thurmond managed.

"There is a man in your county, sir, a Mr. Nathan Tanner. Perhaps you know his name. I am assured he will win the election if something should happen to you, sir, and I can promise you that he will, despite all appearances, take the Company's side in things. We would much rather have you speak for us, I won't deny it, but we will take Tanner if we must."

"But I cannot," he said, spittle flying from his mouth as he blurted out the words. "I have built my life, my career, on protecting the wool interest. I shall be ruined, made a mockery."

"No one will believe such a shift in positions," Forester offered.

Ellershaw ignored the younger man. "You need not worry, Thurmond, about ruin or about what people believe. If you serve the Company, the Company will most assuredly serve you. Should your inclination be to remain in Parliament, we will find a place for you. If you have had a sufficient taste of public service—and, after all your years, certainly no one could find fault in that sentiment—we will find a very lucrative place for you in the Company—perhaps, if your enthusiasm be warm enough, even for your son as well. Yes, young Mr. Thurmond, I am told, is having a rather difficult time finding a place in life. A bit too fond of the bottle, they say. Surely he would like to inherit his father's sinecure with the East

India Company some day. I cannot but think that would put a father's mind at ease."

"I cannot believe I am hearing this," Thurmond said. "I cannot believe that you would stoop to force and threats of violence."

"I admire your zeal, sir," Forester tried, "but surely this is too much."

"Shut your mouth, Forester," Ellershaw said, "or you shall find yourself in that most uncomfortable chair next. Weaver shall not have a tenth of the disgust for using you as I may ask him to use Thurmond."

I was grateful that none looked upon me and no answer was asked of me.

"Believe what you wish," Ellershaw went on. "It is laid out before you, is it not? And you must understand there is a profound moral difference between the use of force for liberation and the use of force for conquest. I use force against you now to help to free the British merchant, lest he remain a slave forever to the tyranny of petty regulation."

"You must be quite mad," Thurmond managed.

Ellershaw shook his head. "Not mad, I promise you. I have honed my skills under the sun of the Indies, that is all. I learned much from the leaders of the East, and I know that decisive victory is achieved in different ways in different cases. I am not content, sir, to attempt to influence you and then hope for the best. I have made my case. You understand my intent and my willingness to do what is necessary. Now you must begin to work. You surely know that the Company has many ears in Parliament. If I do not hear, and hear soon, that you are beginning to discuss a repeal of the act in a favorable light, you will receive a visit from Mr. Weaver, who shall show none of the restraint he exercises here tonight."

Thurmond shook his head. "I will not brook such threats."

"You have no choice." Ellershaw rose from his chair and walked over to the fire, from which he removed a poker, now glowing red and hot. "Are you familiar with the particulars in which King Edward the Second met his end?"

Thurmond stared and said nothing.

"A burning poker was inserted into his intestines by means of his anus. Of course you know; the world knows. But do you know why it was done thus? The world generally believes it was seen as fitting punishment for his sodomitical inclination, so conceived by the wits of his day, and I do not doubt that his assassins appreciated the irony of so fatal a buggery. But the truth, sir, is that he was killed thus because it left no marks upon his body. If the poker is small enough and carefully inserted, there will be no signs upon the man to indicate how he died. Now, you and I know that the death of a king must be fully inquired into, but the death of a decrepit wretch like yourself—why, who should think twice on the matter?"

Forester now rose. "Sir, I can endure no more of this."

Ellershaw shrugged. "Leave if you like."

Forester looked at Thurmond and then at Ellershaw. He made no effort to look upon me. Eyes down, in the perfect manner of a coward, he accepted Ellershaw's invitation and went out of the room.

Ellershaw returned the poker to the fire and walked back to the table. He poured a glass of wine for Mr. Thurmond and then one for himself. Taking his seat, he raised the glass. "To our new partnership, sir."

Thurmond did not move.

"Drink the toast," Ellershaw said. "It would be the prudent thing to do."

Perhaps it was this gesture of kindness, no matter how grotesque, but something seemed to have shifted. Thurmond reached out for his glass and, refraining from raising it in a toast, he pressed it to his lips and drank greedily.

I must admit I felt some grave disappointment in his cowardice. Yes, he was an old man and scared, but how I wished he had summoned the courage to defy Mr. Ellershaw, to bring the matter to a head. I would refuse to harm the fellow, and perhaps that would have broken the ties between me and this brute.

"Now," Ellershaw said, after a moment of uncomfortable silence, "I believe our business is done here. You mentioned something of wanting to depart. You may now do so."

Recognizing a cue when I heard one, I returned to my seat and, somehow managing to keep my arm steady, drank greedily from my own glass.

Thurmond pushed himself to his feet, and was surprisingly steady. I expected a man of his age, so shocked as he must have been, to tremble prodigiously, but he appeared only mildly confused. He placed a hand upon the doorknob, looked back at Ellershaw, who waved him away with a flick of the wrist, and then he was gone.

I turned to Ellershaw, hoping for—I hardly know what—some sort of shame, I suppose. Instead I received a smile. "That went rather well, I think."

I said nothing. I attempted to have a look of no particular meaning upon my face.

"You judge my actions, do you, Weaver? A man of action like you? A hero of the pitched battle?"

"I do not know that the threats you have employed are in your own best interests," I managed.

"Not my best interests?" he answered with a sneer. "You are my club to wield, sir, not my master that I must answer to you. The Court of Proprietors meeting is upon me soon enough, and my enemies will attempt to destroy me. They have something planned. I know they do, and if I don't affect some change in the nature of things, I shall be quite ruined at Craven House. What is that against the rectum of an old man?"

Here was a question I felt best to consider of a rhetorical nature.

He nodded his head a single time, acknowledging my silence as accord. "Now off with you. I presume you can discover your own way out. And do take the back way, Weaver. I suspect my guests have had quite enough of you for one night."

—

CHAPTER THIRTEEN

*I*T STOOD TO REASON THAT THURMOND REQUIRED A BIT OF TIME TO collect himself before joining his wife, and I imagined he would have wandered off to some dark corner to stop shaking before cheerfully announcing his plans to depart. I, meanwhile, had been instructed to circumvent the parlor and make my way out. But to where?

It occurred to me rather alarmingly that Thurmond might not have been convinced to eschew a magistrate. It was certainly true that a justice would hesitate to pursue charges against a man of Ellershaw's stature, but it was possible, I thought, he might choose to pursue charges against me. He could, in fact, swear that I had gone rogue and threatened him independently. If I were Thurmond, I would consider such an action, if only as a means to regain my dignity.

It would be prudent, I thought, to follow the man and make certain he went home and not to a magistrate. To that end, I realized I must find my way out and then lurk in the darkness until gaining access to Thurmond's chaise.

I could only hope that Thurmond required more time for self-collection than I did for navigation, because it soon became apparent that I was lost in Ellershaw's massive home. Indeed, after several wrong turns through amply lit but deserted hallways, I began to grow anxious that I would miss my chance entirely to trail my prey.

However, after another fruitless turn I heard voices, which I approached with a great deal of caution lest I be discovered by the wrong person—I had Thurmond in mind, principally. I therefore stepped quietly on the balls of my feet, making as little noise as possible as I approached a nearly closed door from which I heard the voices I now identified as whispers. As I grew closer I understood them to be two voices, a man's and a woman's, but it was only when I came close enough to peer inside that I saw it was Mr. Forester and Mrs. Ellershaw, wrapped in an embrace, speaking in the hushed, hurried tones of secret lovers. She nuzzled her head into the nape of his neck while he explained that it was with the greatest sadness that he must depart.

This discovery, I believed, explained a great deal—certainly the animosity I perceived from both Forester and Mrs. Ellershaw. They could not but suspect that Mr. Ellershaw had obtained the services of a man skilled in drawing out secrets because he wished their own secret divined. I could not yet think how, but I felt I might be able to turn this new information to my advantage.

I examined the halls in both directions, preparing to make my departure, when Forester happened to turn in my direction. I could perceive no reason why he should have done it; rather, it was one of those unfortunate coincidences that can so upturn the life a man who dwells in secrecy and dark corners.

Forester turned and his eyes met mine. "Weaver," he breathed. "I knew it."

Having no reason to crouch like a sneak thief, I rose to my full height and approached boldly. I should hate for Thurmond to escape, but I would manage one matter at a time, and I should be foolish to let this beast unsnare itself because I hoped for better prey.

Forester, it was true, was a man of greater height than myself, and he attempted to use his stature to intimidating advantage, but I detected at once that he was not a man of action and he would make no efforts on my person. He merely wished to make me fear him. "Get inside the room," he hissed.

I obeyed with the easy air of a man who does the most agreeable thing he can imagine. Indeed, I stepped in, closed the door, and bowed most civilly. "I am ready to hear your commands."

"Don't play the jackanapes with me, sir. I can see you were sneaking about like the thief you are. And what now? Shall you go tell your master what you've seen? Shall you bring down upon this dear woman misery and shame and tyranny? And for what? Your thirty pieces of silver? I suppose that is the way with your kind."

"Perhaps if you refrain from spewing slurs against my people," I proposed, "you will dissuade me from my course."

"I know you shan't be dissuaded, so I shall spew what I like. That silk suit hides neither your beastly nature nor your uncouth experience, so I see no cause to treat with you like a gentleman. Think not I have any wish to berate you. I speak only so that when you hear of this lady's suffering, you will know yourself the cause, and I can only hope you will acquit yourself like your countryman Judas and take your own life."

"While I hesitate to deprive you of the joy of abusing my nature, my nation, and my appearance, I must inform you that Mr. Ellershaw has not asked me to discover anything of you. Indeed, I was told to show myself out, but as this is a large house, I lost my way and merely stumbled upon you by unhappy accident." I stopped short of promising to keep secrets, for I did not wish to remove the ball from the pistol just yet—if at all.

"Of course he isn't here about you," Mrs. Ellershaw snapped. She stepped forward. Though she was somewhat shorter than myself, she cut a more imposing figure than her paramour. She held herself erect, her bosoms thrust out, her chin high, her face radiant with color. Indeed, she squared her shoulders in the style of more than one fighter I've known from the ring. "Tell us the truth, Mr. Weaver," she said, her voice hard and angry. "You have no interest in Mr. Forester whatsoever?"

"Indeed I haven't," I told her, "though I cannot say why you should choose to frame my indifference to his actions with such rancor."

"Mr. Ellershaw has no concern for matters of the heart," she explained to her lover. "I should think he hardly recalls, if he ever knew, that men and women are disposed to have feelings for one another. If he were made aware of you, sir, he would keep his tongue until it served his interest. No, the thieftaker is here upon another matter."

"Out with it," Forester demanded of me, as though he had some means to compel me to say what I would not. The lady spoke into my silence.

"I hadn't believed he'd learn the truth, but clearly he has. It's Bridget. That wretched bargain she made was not good enough. Now he wants to end the threat permanently," she explained to Forester. Then she turned sharply back to me. "Were you to look through my things, my papers? You shan't find anything, I promise you. And you shall gain no intelligence from me. If you are half so clever as you seem to believe, you will return to Mr. Ellershaw and tell him you could learn nothing of my daughter's location, and you will tell him you are like to never learn, for indeed you shan't. I should rather throw myself 'pon the fire, in the manner of the Hindoo ladies, than give her to him."

What madness was this? It took a moment for me to recall where I had heard the name, but then I recollected it from dinner. Bridget was Mrs. Ellershaw's daughter from her first marriage. But why should she be hidden away, and why should Mr. Ellershaw care so much that his wife believed he might hire me to discover her?

"Madam," I said, offering another bow, "I cannot but be moved by your maternal sentiments, but allow me to state once more that I merely wished to discover the exit. I am upon no other errand than that."

She locked her eyes upon me for the better part of a minute and kept her face hard and unyielding. Then she spoke. "Follow this hall to the junction and turn to your left. Decline the stairs, and on your right you will see the kitchen. You may depart from there, which I believe to be more fitting for you than the front entrance."

I bowed once more. "As you wish," I answered, making no sign that this was the means of egress I should have chosen. "Sir," I said to Mr. Forester, as my awkward means of taking my leave. I then hurried in the direction given to me by the good lady and soon found myself in the cold of night.

I spared no time to consider the strange encounter I had just endured. Instead, I hurried around to the front of the house, where two chaises had been brought from the mews. Here was good news, for Thurmond had not yet departed, so I had not missed my chance, and in my delay I had gathered intelligence I hoped might help illuminate some of the darkness in which I dwelled.

My task now was to follow Thurmond, and to that end I studied the environment for some height I could scale that would enable me to drop down upon the coach as it passed. This was a skill I had mastered during my younger years, when I earned my living in not the most honest of methods. The top of a coach or carriage makes a wonderful starting point for any man seeking to surprise the inhabitants, particularly if he has an accomplice who will meet him with an extra horse for the escape.

There was, however, no way to gain purchase to an appropriate height and very little chance I might sneak inside the vehicle. The footman and the coachman were engaged in conversation, and while it was theoretically possible I might be able to creep past them and somehow avoid the inevitable creak of the door opening, I did not like to depend on such luck. And once inside, then what? How could I hope to go unnoticed by Mr. and Mrs. Thurmond?

As I considered my options—such as stealing a horse or following on foot in hopes they did not travel fast—a servant emerged from the house and darted over to the coach, instructing the driver and footman to spring into action. They did at once. The driver climbed up and took the reins, the footman hopped onto the back.

I followed through the shadows as they pulled directly to the door, and here I enjoyed a wondrous bit of luck, for the aged gentleman helped his wife inside but then declined to enter himself. Instead, he spoke a few words to her and gave some instructions to the coachman and then walked away from the house toward Theobald's Row. I followed at a safe distance, but I was close enough to hear when, at the corner of Red Lyon Street, he dropped a coin in the hand of another gentleman's waiting footman with the request to find him a hackney.

This was a far superior situation, for once the transportation was secured it was no difficult thing to hop on the back and remain crouched, that I might go unobserved. And so I did, clinging to the back as the carriage traveled at its snail pace through the filthy streets of the metropolis. My presence was remarked upon by a few of the whores and low men we passed, but the coachman failed to understand—or failed to care—and ignored the jeers until the conveyance arrived at Fetter Lane. Thurmond then departed and entered the Brush and Palette, a tavern favored by men of an artistical inclination.

I crawled down from the back, determined to wait a moment before entering.

The coachman then turned around. "Enjoy the ride, did you, my master?"

I knew too well the code of the streets either to ignore his meaning or to begrudge it. The metropolis inhaled knowledge and exhaled revelation, and if I did not wish this coachman to respirate to Thurmond, I would have to buy his silence. A sixpence, I was delighted to see, did the business, and the coachman and I parted friends.

I now turned to the matter at hand—principally the question of why Thurmond might choose to attend a coffeehouse of portrait painters—

but suspected the answer quickly enough, for I had done such tricks in my time. Why does a man ever go to a public house associated with men with whose business he has no contact? Because he wishes not to be seen.

Maintaining both distance and luck, I followed the worthy inside and was unobserved as he took a room in the back and left instructions with the publican. After a moment, I approached this fellow, a stooped fellow of about Thurmond's age. Rather than wasting time, I handed him a coin.

"What did the gentleman instruct you?" I asked.

"That when another gentleman should inquire for a Mr. Thompson, he be shown to that room."

I proceeded with another coin. "Is there a room adjacent to his?"

"There is indeed, and it is available for three shillings."

It was, of course, an absurd price, but we both knew I would pay without haggling, and so I was led to my own private space, where I waited, close by the wall, for something to happen. And something did. Within half an hour I heard another person enter the adjoining room. I pressed my ear to the wall, but I could still not make out the particulars of their conversation. Nevertheless, I recognized the voice of Thurmond's visitor. It was the second clandestine meeting I had seen the same gentleman engage in that very night.

Yes, Mr. Forester of the East India Company had come to meet with Mr. Thurmond of the wool interest, and I did not believe they met because of their many conflicts. With the meeting of the Court of Proprietors hard upon Ellershaw, it would seem his rivals had found much to discuss.

THERE WERE MANY QUESTIONS now before me. Ought I to tell Ellershaw of Forester's betrayal with Ellershaw's wife, his betrayal with his enemy Thurmond, with both, or with neither one? As near as I could tell, I gained no advantage in doing so. Sending Ellershaw, and perhaps the whole of Craven House, into chaos would not serve my ends, and I had nothing to gain by gathering for myself more of the gentleman's trust than I had already obtained. As for Cobb, I was determined to mention only Mrs. Ellershaw's indiscretion. Such intelligence would demonstrate to my overseer that I performed as he wished and would offer greater protection for my friends. At the same time I felt confident that Cobb would have no use for this information, and consequently there could be no risk in revealing it. As I knew not which was the greater villain in this conflict, I could not easily tell how best to disseminate my discoveries to full advantage.

The next morning, Ellershaw called me into his office, though he appeared to have nothing of import to say to me. I had the distinct impression that he wished only to test my mood following his cruel treatment of Thurmond the night before. I, for my part, kept quiet about what I had seen. Thus we spoke some time of my days as a pugilist. Ellershaw laughed at some of my stories, but after a quarter of an hour he informed me that I had wasted quite enough of his time and should go about my business, lest I waste his money as well.

"Of course, sir," I said. "But may I ask a question of a delicate nature?"

He waved his hand with grudging permission.

"It regards Mrs. Ellershaw's daughter from a previous marriage. Am I to understand there is something unfortunate that has transpired with her?"

Ellershaw studied me for a moment, his face remaining immobile and expressionless all the while. "The girl fled," he said at last. "She took a liking to a rogue, and, despite our promise that she would receive not a penny if she married him, there is every reason to believe she obtained a Fleet marriage. We have not received a word from her since, though you may depend upon it, we shall. They will certainly wait until they believe our anger has passed and then come calling, hat in hand."

"Thank you, sir," I said.

"If you think to earn for yourself a few extra shillings by finding the girl," Ellershaw said to me, "you must be disappointed. Neither I nor Mrs. Ellershaw cares if we never hear from her again."

"I had no such intentions. I was merely curious."

"You would be better served directing your curiosity toward the rogues of Craven House and less toward my family."

"Of course," I agreed.

"Now, as to Thurmond. He must know that he cannot be permitted to shrug us off so casually. It is time to make him fear us truly."

I considered Ellershaw's threat with the burning poker and trembled to ponder what mischief he had in his mind. "With less than two weeks left before the meeting of the Court of Proprietors," I said, "I hardly think it wise for you to have your strategy hinge upon frightening Mr. Thurmond."

"Ha!" he shouted. "You know nothing, and I have no intention that you should learn more. Do you think this my only avenue? It is but one, the only one that concerns you. Now, my informants within Parliament have told me that he plans to dine tonight with an associate of his near Great Warner Street. You must break into his home while he is out and await his return. Then, when he has gone abed, I wish you to pummel the scoundrel, Mr. Weaver. Pummel him within an inch of his life, that he might know that Craven House is not to be trifled with. Then, sir, I wish you to violate his wife."

I remained motionless. I said nothing.

"Do you not hear me?"

I swallowed hard. "I hear you, Mr. Ellershaw, but I am afraid I do not comprehend. You cannot mean what I think you to mean."

"Indeed I do. I have faced the resistance of such men before, I can promise you. In Bombay there were always chieftains and leaders among the blacks who believed they might stand up to the Company. They had to be made to see the consequences, and I believe Thurmond must be made to see too. Do you think this is a trivial matter? On what we do hinges the future of the Company, and upon that the world itself. The Company is the standard-bearer of free trade. You and I have a rendezvous with destiny, Weaver. We will preserve for our children this, the last best hope of man on earth, or we will sentence them to take the first step into a thousand years of darkness. If we fail, at least let our children and our children's children say of us that we justified our brief moment here. We did all that could be done."

I stifled my first impulse, which was to say I harbored grave doubts that our children's children should praise us for beating old men and violating old women. Instead, I took a deep breath and lowered my eyes deferentially. "Sir, you do not speak of a tribal leader among the Indians. You speak of a well-respected member of the House of Commons. You cannot expect the crime to go unreported. And even if you could be guaranteed of your success, I cannot condone such barbaric usage of anyone, particularly the aged—and I could most assuredly never participate in such a thing."

"What? You haven't the stomach for it? I thought you more of a man than that. This is the world we live in, Mr. Weaver, full of deceits and treachery. You must be the one to wield the club, or you will be thrashed by it. I have told you what I wish, and you are my servant; therefore, you will do as I say."

Once more I found myself faced with a conundrum: Actions that would preserve my place conflicted with actions that would preserve my soul. I might have had a difficult time convincing Cobb that I could not bring myself to beat a warehouse worker, but I would have to believe that even he could not expect me to engage in shameless violence and rape—if for no other reason than that such crimes must be pursued and, if traced to me, must surely be traced to him.

It occurred to me that this might be precisely a bit of curious luck. I had no choice but to walk away from Ellershaw, and Cobb could not blame me for doing so. Perhaps I indulged in unreasonable optimism, but such was all I had at my disposal.

Forcing my face into a cast of steely determination, I rose from my chair. "I cannot do what you ask, nor can I quietly countenance such a thing if you assign the task to another."

"If you defy me in this, you must lose your position here."

"Then I will lose my position."

"You do not wish to make the East India Company your enemy."

"Better the Company than my conscience," I answered, and turned toward the door.

"Hold!" he said, now rising from his chair. "Hold, do not go. You are right. Perhaps my methods are too extreme."

I cursed silently, for my hopes were cruelly, if not unexpectedly, dashed. Nevertheless, I turned. "I am glad to hear you rethink the matter."

"Yes," he said. "I believe you are in the right here. Nothing quite so brutal, then. But we shall think of something, Mr. Weaver. You may depend upon it."

ON MY WAY to the warehouses, I began to consider the larger situation. One moment I served Cobb, another moment Ellershaw, and a third myself. That is to say, I walked a precarious line, and though I would wish to have no master but myself, I understood that I must be a toad-eater, at least in some small degree, if I were ever to do any good. I loathed feeling powerless above all things and yet, with my friends' lives hanging by precarious threads, I must at least assume the appearance of subservience.

How to endure such a thing and not fall into despair? The answer, I believed, lay not in resisting my would-be masters but rather in setting out upon my own projects. I must learn what Forester hid in his secret warehouse. I must discover Ellershaw's plans for surviving the impending Court meeting—and very possibly discover more about Ellershaw's daughter. Such a path could be a blind alley, but many of the major actors in my little drama—both Ellershaws, Forester, and Thurmond—had spoken of her in ways that intrigued me, and though she appeared but an irrelevancy, I had long ago learned that pulling at loose threads could cause the curtain to unravel.

Mrs. Ellershaw appeared to believe that her husband wished to know her daughter's location, though he made precisely the opposite clear. It seemed to me likely that Mr. Ellershaw's interest in the girl must have been other than fatherly, and her marriage might have been an effort to escape as much as a pursuit of the heart. That being the case, her mother would clearly wish to protect her whereabouts.

One thing struck me, however. Mrs. Ellershaw feared that her husband had *learned the truth*. Not that he had discovered the daughter's address or wished to discover it. No, she believed there was a hidden truth of which Ellershaw was ignorant, which meant that the intelligence he had now provided me might well be false or incomplete.

As for Forester, it would seem he not only disliked Ellershaw but had reason to hate him—namely, his dalliance with Mrs. Ellershaw. Did he hate his lover's husband to the extent that he would betray him with Thurmond for the pleasure of it? I doubted it. Rather, it seemed to me that Forester had some business that depended on the failure of Ellershaw and perhaps even the Company itself—though I was at a loss as to what that might be. I did, however, suspect that it had something to do with the secret warehouse level Carmichael had spoken of, and I knew I would have to discover the contents of that room.

As always, Aadil kept a close watch on me throughout the day, his ugly scarred face studying my every move with Oriental single-mindedness. But toward evening I managed to remove Carmichael to a private corner on the pretense of scolding him for some imagined failure.

He was so earnest a fellow that when he obeyed my summons to meet in the back of the warehouse, he appeared downcast and apologetic before I even spoke a word.

"Have no concern," I said at once. "You've done nothing wrong. I merely set out the rumor in order to engineer our time together."

"That's a relief, Mr. Weaver, as I think well of you and would have you think well of me."

"Indeed I do. You've proved to be a diligent worker and a useful guide to the warehouses."

"I hope to remain so," he said.

"I hope you will remain so as well," I said, "for what I am now about to ask of you is not strictly within the bounds of your duties. I wish for you to show me the location of Mr. Forester's hidden cargo and to help me gain access."

His mouth parted slightly, but he said nothing for a moment. Finally, he shook his head. "It is a very dangerous thing you ask. Not only might I lose my place, but I should earn for myself the enmity of that beast Aadil. I don't want that, and if you are wise you won't want it either."

"I understand it is a risk, and yet I must see the contents of that room, and I cannot do it without your assistance. You will be rewarded for your efforts."

"It ain't about the reward, don't you mind that. It's about not losing my place. You might be the watchmen overseer, but if Aadil or Mr. Forester wants me thrown out without what they owe me, there's nothing that will stop them."

"I won't let that happen," I told him, wondering, as I spoke, precisely how I would prevent it. I told myself that if Carmichael's position should come under attack because of his assistance to me, I would make certain he would not suffer for it. I had enough friends and influence that, at the very least, I could secure him a position of equal income elsewhere.

He studied me, perhaps appraising whether or not my optimism was well founded. "To be honest, Mr. Weaver, I'm scared to go against them."

"I must learn what's in there. If you won't help me, I shall find someone who will, But I would prefer it to be you, as I believe I can trust you."

He took a deep sigh. "And so you can, sir, so you can. When shall it be?"

I had an appointment I would by no means wish to miss for that night, so we made plans to meet behind the main warehouse at the strike of eleven on the following night. Against his protests, I placed a coin in his hand, but in doing so, I feared I had only weakened his resolve. Carmichael, I recognized, wanted to help me because he liked me. If I became yet another employer, his trust diminished, and I needed such trust as I could muster wherever it would be found.

CHAPTER FOURTEEN

I DEPARTED FROM CRAVEN HOUSE THAT AFTERNOON, HOPING NO ONE would notice my absence and Mr. Ellershaw would not call for me again. As per my arrangements, I met Elias at the Two Schooners Tavern on Cheapside, where he had ordered a pot and a meal, which I presumed I would be called upon to pay for. When I sat down, he was wiping the last of the grease from his plate with the last of his bread.

"Are you certain this matter will not turn difficult for me?" he asked.

"Reasonably certain," I assured him.

I reviewed the plan, which I believed to be rather straightforward and easily accomplished—at least his end of it. Elias then wiped his face and departed to travel the short distance to Throgmorton Street, where the Seahawk kept its offices. I ordered a pot, which I allowed myself to drink over a third of an hour, and then paid the reckoning and made my way to the offices myself.

I entered the building and found myself in a large open room with several heavy writing desks where several clerks were currently at their labors. I noticed a door over to my left, which I believed led to Mr. Ingram's office. I had contacted him earlier that day—using Elias's name—to request an appointment. At that moment, Elias would be inside, attempting to secure insurance policies on several very elderly sea captains. Mr. Ingram, for his part, would be engaged in a rather lengthy effort to deny Elias, all of which gave me the time I required to attempt our scheme.

I approached the nearest clerk, a stooped-over gentleman of later year, his eyes obscured by bulky spectacles. He wrote in a hasty yet vastly neat hand in an opened ledger book, and he did so with such intensity that he failed to notice me as I approached.

"Ingram," I said to him.

He continued to avoid looking up at me. "Mr. Ingram is indisposed at the moment. If you wish to wait or leave your card, sir."

"No," I said quietly.

Perhaps it was too quiet, for he did not respond. I, in turn, thought it prudent to accentuate my displeasure with a slap to his desk. "Ingram!" I said once more.

He set down his pen and scratched at his nose with an ink-stained finger, flattened from years of scrivening. "Mr. Ingram is with a gentleman right now," he said, the concern evident in his voice. Indeed, his fellow clerks must have heard the concern as well, for they all ceased their labors and looked at me.

"I suggest you retrieve him," I said.

"'Tis not our style of conducting business within these walls," he answered.

"It ought to be your style when I come calling."

"And who are you?"

"Ah, it's Mr. Weaver, as I recollect."

I recognized the figure descending the stairs. It was none other than Mr. Bernis, the same prim little gentleman who had accosted me at the Portuguese eatery to inform me that my life was now fully insured. He hurried over to me and shook my hand—I say he shook it and not we shook, for I hardly participated in any manner.

"So very good to see you once more, sir. How may we assist you?"

"I have come to demand that you tell me the names of the men who have insured my life."

"As I explained to you earlier, we cannot reveal that information. There is an element of confidentiality that—"

"Confidentiality be damned," I answered, not a little harshly. Indeed, the clerk took a step backward, as though blown by the force of my vehemence. "I will know it."

"Sir," he said. I must give credit to poor Mr. Bernis. He was not a large man or overly inclined to the martial spirit, yet in the defense of his company he stepped forward and put a hand upon my arm.

I, in turn, picked up the poor fellow and cast him down upon the desk of the bespectacled clerk. The two of them tumbled together in a maelstrom of limbs and papers and spilled ink. I hoped most sincerely that I did not hurt the man, who was only doing his business, and I made a note that I must send him a gift in compensation, but there were more important matters to attend to than the delicacy of his feelings. "I *will* speak to Ingram!" I shouted, and made my desperation known by approaching another desk and wiping its surface clean with a great sweep of my arm.

As I had hoped, the room had now become a scene of chaos. Several of the clerks, one of whose face dripped with ink, ran toward the stairs. Papers were strewn here and there, and they all shouted at once, including poor Bernis, who had arisen from his sad tangle to call out Ingram's name most plaintively. I added my own voice to the chorus, shouting the name with far more malice.

My efforts had the effect I most desired, for the door to the inner office opened and its occupant emerged—a man of below-average height but trim of figure, with broad shoulders and a barrel of a chest. He was no doubt at least fifty years old, yet despite his age and stature, and indeed, despite the commotion, which must have come as a shock to his eyes, he held himself with a dignified bearing.

From behind him I saw Elias rise from his chair and move slowly toward the door, which he intended to close. I needed to make certain Ingram did not observe this effort, so I stepped forward, my index finger extended, and jabbed at him, coming just short of laying upon him a humiliating poke to the chest.

"My name is Weaver," I said, "and several men have taken out insurance policies upon my life. I demand to know their names and their business, or you will answer for it."

"Lewis," he shouted to one of the clerks, "fetch the constable!" A young man, cowering near the staircase—too afraid to move closer, too interested to retreat—scrambled to his feet, dashed past me as though I might bite him, and left the rooms.

It was no matter. There would be no constable present for another quarter hour at the earliest, and I had no intention of remaining so long. "All the constables in the world shan't help you, " I said. "I have made my demand, and I will be answered, one way or the other."

"You have been answered," he said. "You have my apologies, but we cannot give you the information you request. I desire you take yourself from here, lest your reputation be damaged by your actions."

"My reputation is secure," I answered, "and if I use it to level accusations upon you and your company, you will be the sorrier for it."

"I will be the sorrier," he informed me, "if I betray the confidence of those I serve by revealing what I have no obligation to reveal."

Our exchange continued in this manner for another several minutes until I noticed that the door to Ingram's office was once more opening. Here was the signal that Elias and I had agreed upon; it marked the time I must remove myself from the premises. I did so, with threats that they would not remain unpunished for these outrages.

Then I departed to the selfsame tavern where Elias and I had met earlier. I ordered another pot and awaited his arrival, which came far sooner than I had anticipated.

"I used the chaos of your visit as a reason to excuse myself," he told me, "but I cannot but suspect that Ingram or one of the clerks will realize my visit was in conjunction with yours and will understand our deceit."

"Let them understand it," I said. "So much the better. They cannot act upon it, for they shan't desire the world to learn their books can be so easily violated. Now, did you obtain the list of names?"

"I did," he said. "I know not what it means, but it cannot be good." He removed from his pocket a scrap of paper, upon which was written three names I had never before beheld.

Jean-David Morel
Pierre Simon
Jacques LaFont

"Perhaps you notice something about them," he said.
"These are all French names."
"Just so," he agreed.
"The French, I have been made to understand, are beginning to assert themselves within India, and it is not unlikely that, in order to achieve their ends, they must act against the East India Company. That

much I comprehend. What I do not comprehend is why they should believe their success depends upon mine—to such a degree that they must insure my life."

"That is but one interpretation. There is another, and I believe it may be far more likely, I am grieved to say."

"They know I will soon be dead, they see no reason not to profit from it," I said.

Elias nodded solemnly. "You had enemies enough before this, but I suspect, Weaver, that your situation has now been revealed to be even more dire than we had supposed."

—

CHAPTER FIFTEEN

*W*HILE DISSEMBLING WITH ELLERSHAW, CONCEALING FACTS FROM Cobb, plotting with Carmichael, and perfecting my schemes with Elias, it had never occurred to me that French knaves might be so confident in my impending doom that they should make wagers upon it. The thought was disconcerting to the least, but as I had discovered at Kingsley's Coffeehouse not long ago, even the most secure of wagers is never secure, and I had every confidence these foreign dandies would lose for their efforts.

I should have liked to have more time with Elias, for even though much of what we could puzzle out happened within the first five minutes of our conversation, there are, nevertheless, revelations that take time to sit and settle, like a good bottle of wine, before we are ready to consume them fully. This luxury of slow fermentation was not afforded to me, however, for I had an appointment to keep, and despite my uneasiness I would not be late.

It was the thing that had been in my thoughts all day, and it was now time to take myself to St. Giles in the Field. My reader certainly knows that this is not the most pleasant part of the metropolis, and while I am no stranger to the less delightful neighborhoods, this one offered particular difficulties, its winding streets and labyrinthine alleys designed to confound the most accomplished navigator. Yet I managed to find my way with reasonable alacrity, and a few coins in the palm of a garrulous whore helped direct me to the Duck and Wagon.

This was a tavern of reasonable architectural soundness, at least in light of its location. My entrance produced no considerable attention except among the gamers and whores and mendicants, all of whom sought fresh and unsuspecting purses. I have long plied my trade in these sorts of establishments, however, and I knew well how to wear a mask of menace. The unfortunates who prowled these waters in search of weak prey knew the scent of a fellow shark and accordingly kept their distance.

It took me little time to recognize that the Duck and Wagon fell into that category of tavern called a dive. Proximate to the kitchens, a massive pot, nearly large enough for a man to bathe therein, had been set forth, and surrounding it were half a score of men who had paid their three pennies for the opportunity to take two or three dives—dependent upon the rules of the house. In the hands of each was a long knife, which they plunged into this gustatory lottery, the winner to lance a piece of meat, and the drawers of blanks to find themselves impaling nothing of greater consequence than a carrot or turnip.

I took a table in a dark corner, far away from the excited and despondent shouts of the divers, and pulled my hat down, better to shade my face while sipping at a watery ale. It took two more watery ales before Miss Glade arrived, and I confess I did not know her at once. It was neither the darkness nor my slightly dulled senses that postponed my recognition, but her manner of dress. It would seem that the serving girl and the lady of business were not the only two disguises known to this intriguing creature. She came in looking like an aged and slovenly whore, so unappealing in her ersatz person that she might well have been invisible. There could be no better disguise, I realized, than to dress as a creature upon which no one wishes to gaze. These aging unfortunates, whose withered bodies are unfit for their trade, haunt the streets by the hundreds in hopes of finding a man too drunk or too desperate to care about the taint of his goods. Here was Miss Glade in tattered clothes and disheveled hair. Paint upon her face gave the illusion of age, and she had blackened some teeth and browned others, to create a sufficiently unsavory effect. But more than any of this, it was the way she carried herself. I had never before observed that old whores have a particular way of walking, but I now saw that it was so. Only her dark eyes, bright and alive and full of ravenous curiosity, betrayed her true nature.

At her request, no doubt to maintain the integrity of her disguise, she asked that I order a gin for her, and while a few of the patrons laughed at my taste in women, none thought any more of this arrangement than was natural. I was no longer fit in my senses, and this woman was lucky enough to find me.

"Very well, then," I said, feeling unspeakably awkward. "Your masquerade has quite astonished me, but it is no matter, for we have much to discuss."

"And yet it shall be hard to do so, for neither trusts the other." A smile, her true smile, emerged like the sun from beneath the clouded layers of paint.

"That, madam, is a sad truth. Perhaps you would care to tell me of your business at Craven House. And perhaps, while you are on that business, you might tell me how the silk workers' riots disturbed your plans the other night."

Something shifted in her gaze, and I knew I had struck home. "My plans?"

"When you saw me, you said, 'There you are,' or some such thing, and expressed a surprise that the uprising at the gates had not hindered me. It is clear you thought I was someone else, which was why you used your true voice with me rather than the one you deploy within Craven House. Had it not been for that understanding, I presume I would never have known you were anything but the creature you pretend to be when serving the East India Company."

"You presume a great deal," she said.

"I do. I will be less inclined to presumption should you provide me with facts."

"Maybe you should provide *me* with facts about your own doings."

I laughed. "We shall never achieve any goal at all if we play this game forever. Now, you invited me here; you must have given the matter some thought."

She pressed her lips together thoughtfully. "You are right, of course. There is no advantage in dancing about, and if neither of us dares to speak, nothing will get resolved. In truth, 'tis my greatest wish that we might find ourselves on unopposing sides."

"And why is that?" I inquired.

Her true smile emerged once more. "You must not ask a lady such questions," she said. "But I believe you know the answer."

Indeed, I hoped I did. And yet I could not allow myself to trust this woman. Yes, she had charm and beauty and good humor, a combination I could scarce resist, and in her all of these wondrous properties combined such that appeared nearly magical to me. Everything I had seen of her told me she had raised the art of dissimulation to new heights, so I must presume that any display of affection for me must be as false as one of her costumes.

"Sir," she said, "I must ask you a single question. Are you interested, in your business at Craven House, in harming or aiding the Company?"

"Neither," I said, without a moment's hesitation. I had not anticipated this particular question, but I saw there could only be one safe answer. A neutral position is more easily swayed. "I am indifferent to the fate of the Company and shall not allow its well-being, in one way or the other, to direct my actions."

The answer appeared to satisfy her. "I am pleased to hear it, for it means we shall have no cause to be at odds. Now, as to my business. Are you aware, sir, that unlike the other trading companies, the East India lacks a monopoly on its domain? Any company at all can trade with the East Indies if it has the capital and the means."

I laughed. "Yes, I have heard that. It seems to be a topic of perpetual interest at Craven House."

"As well it should be. The East India Company must always be on guard against those who would take what it believes to be its wealth. Consequently, it often takes actions to defeat potential competitors. But sometimes it does more than that. Sometimes it engages in unfair practices, outright thievery, in order to destroy some small venture that wants no more than a thimbleful of the great wealth of the East."

"And you represent such a venture?"

"I do," she said. "I am in the service of a trading gentleman whose ideas and contacts were stolen by East India agents. I am at Craven House to find evidence of this wrongdoing and to correct the injustice. Like you, I seek neither to harm nor help the Company, merely to see a wrong righted."

"I doubt the men of the Company would see things as you do, but that is no matter to me. The fate of the Company does not concern me, and if your patron has been wronged as you say, I certainly applaud your efforts."

"Thank you, sir. Now, perhaps you could tell me something of your affairs."

"Of course." I had given this a great deal of thought once Miss Glade had proposed our assignation, and I constructed a fiction I believed would serve my purposes admirably. "I am in the employ of a gentleman of more merit than means. He is, in truth, the natural son of Mr. Ellershaw. That worthy sired him some twenty years ago, but offered neither his child nor the boy's neglected mother the assistance that such ill-born children depend upon. Indeed, he turned away the just mother's calls for help most cruelly. I am there at his request, to help uncover some evidence of his patrimony so he may pursue a case against an unfeeling parent."

"I believe I have read of this incident," Miss Glade said.

"Indeed?" My face could not have hid my surprise.

"Yes. It was in one of those charming novels by Miss Eliza Haywood."

I let out a nervous laugh. A man at the next table looked over to see if I was choking to my death. "You are very witty, madam, but you know those novelists pride themselves on writing stories true to life. It therefore cannot surprise when a story from life in some way resembles the thing meant to resemble it."

"You are perhaps more clever than convincing." She spread wide her hands, not without a dose of good humor.

"But," I added, "if we are to be suspicious, let me inquire something of you. How does a young lady learn the considerable skills at disguise you possess? You are able not only to choose excellent costumes but also to alter the nature of your voice, even your bearing."

"Yes." She looked down. "I have not told you all, Mr. Weaver, but as we are in one another's confidence, and as I believe you mean me no harm, I shall endeavor to be more honest with you. My father, sir, was a tradesman of the Hebrew nation who—"

"You are a Jewess?" It took all of my will to prevent myself from shouting. It came out as a growling whisper.

Her eyes widened with amusement. "Does that so astonish you?"

"Yes," I answered bluntly.

"Of course. Our women must stay at home and prepare meals and light candles and sacrifice their lives to making certain that fathers and brothers and husbands and sons are well tended. Only British women should be permitted to roam the streets."

"I meant no such thing."

"Are you certain?"

Indeed, I was not, so I avoided answering the question. "We are not so populous upon this island that I should expect a charming stranger, such as yourself, to be among our number."

"And yet," she said, "here I am. Allow me, please, to continue with my story."

"Of course."

"As I said, my father was a tradesman—skilled in the art of stoneworking—who left the city of Vilnius when he was a young man and went out in search of a more prosperous life. Such men often find themselves in this kingdom, for it is surely the most agreeable place in Europe for Jews to live. It was here he met my mother, also an immigrant, who had been born into poverty in a place called Kazimierz."

"You are a Tudesco?" I said.

"So your kind chooses we should be called," she said, not without bitterness. "You do not love us."

"I can assure you, I am without prejudice."

"And how many of my species of Hebrew do you count among your friends?"

I found this line of questioning most unpleasant, so I suggested she continue with her tale.

"Owing in part to the bigotry of the English race, and in part to the bigotry of your own people, he found it excessively difficult to ply his trade here, but after many years of effort, he managed to earn a comfortable living. Sadly, when I was of only seventeen years, he died in an accident involving his labors. I am told that such accidents among men who work with stone are all too common. My mother had no means to support us, and we had no remaining relatives in the country. We thus came to depend upon the charity of the synagogue, but that institution, unlike your own, is so poor it could little afford to buy us bread or keep a roof over our heads. This shame was far too much for my mother, who had never been of a strong constitution, and she followed my father to the grave within six months. In my grief, I found myself alone in the world."

"I am very sorry to hear of your troubles."

"You cannot know my misery. Everything I knew had gone, and I had nothing to which to aspire but penury and illness. In such a state, however, I chose to narrowly examine my father's records and discovered that a man of some prominence yet owed him three pounds, so I traveled across the metropolis, making the journey on foot and enduring all manner of abuse you can imagine. I ventured out and suffered so, all in search of this debt, knowing the foolishness of the venture, for I had long since come to understand that such men will never pay when they can avoid doing so. I fully anticipated a rude refusal, but I met with something else entire. Despite the rags upon my back and disheveled appearance, the gentleman saw me himself and delivered silver into my hand at once with the most profound apologies and concern for my sorrows. Indeed, he paid double what he owed me out of consideration for my suffering. And he offered me more, Mr. Weaver. He suggested I might continue to associate with him in the form of his companion."

I struggled to keep my face from betraying emotion. "You must not be ashamed of doing what you must to survive."

"I have not spoken of shame," she told me, meeting my eyes boldly. "I had six pounds in my hand. I was in no danger of starving for months, perhaps. And yet I accepted his offer, for why, I thought, should I not have clean clothes, a place to live, and food enough to exist beyond the lofty state of eluding death? I know something of your story, sir, for it has been written of in the papers. In your youth, when you were penniless, you took to the ring. You lived, therefore, upon the merits of your body. I did the same, yet when women do so, they are called all manner of unsavory names. If a man takes it upon himself to care for a woman—attends to her needs, her clothes, her food, her housing, and in return she is obligated only to accept the attentions of no other men—in some lands they would style that arrangement marriage. Here it is called whoring."

"Madam, I assure you, I offer no judgments."

"You offer none with words, but I observe your eyes."

I could make no answer, for she had correctly observed my expression. I had lived upon the streets long enough to know the foolishness of judging a woman for using what advantages she has to keep from death—or from a state not much more desirable. I knew also that it was only because men wished to hold dominion over the behavior of women that we were so quick to give scurrilous names to their taking liberties with their own bodies. And yet I felt a disappointment, for I suppose I wanted her to be pure and innocent, and I knew this desire on my part was foolishness. It was, after all, her sense of freedom, her wit, her sense of being at ease in the world—nay, of being the mistress of the world—that so drew me to Celia Glade.

"Like you, I am but a product of the world in which I live," I offered. "I have been trained since my earliest youth to form such judgments upon women who make the choices you have. And if, in my more mature years, I wish to reject those ideas, there nevertheless remains within my mind a contrary voice."

"Yes," she said. "I have made decisions, and I knew they were the best decisions available, but I hear the contrary voice too. As I would have you not condemn me, I must not condemn you. Now, to continue with my history. I lived in a very high style while I was his favorite, and he very much enjoyed my natural tendency toward mimicry. At first he would only encourage me to imitate associates, but then he began to purchase disguises and have me assume all sorts of shapes; a gypsy mendicant, an Arabian courtesan, a peasant girl, even an old woman. For this gentleman's pleasure, I learned the skills you have observed. Then, as so often happens in these circumstances, he met another woman who was younger and newer and therefore more suited to his fancy."

"He must be the greatest fool in the world to have preferred another woman to you."

I saw a distant pleasure gleam in her eye, but she chose to ignore my flirtation. "Even though I was no longer his favorite, this gentleman, whom I shall not name, believed he understood his duty—unlike Mr. Ellershaw, as you describe it—and continued to assist me in my needs. And then, after some two years of this kind neglect, he contacted me and told me he wished me to apply my skills in his service. As he had been so kind to me in the past, I could hardly say no, particularly since to do so would be to sacrifice my future comfort. And so I have come to Craven House as his eyes and ears, to discover what I can about the Company's illicit practices, that the Eastern trade might be more open to all men of business. The night I met you, I thought you were one of my patron's servants come to collect some papers I had copied for his purposes, and that was why I inadvertently revealed myself."

I thought to say that I was not alone in telling fabulous tales fit for a novel, but I understood that to do so would be unkind. I merely nodded sympathetically. And then, when a hint of a tear appeared in her eye, I reached out to pat her hand. In so doing, I knocked over her tumbler of gin. It had sat neglected since arriving upon our table, and far from the fire as we were, I had every reason to believe it would grow enormous cold, in the way of such liquors. I could only imagine the startling sensation as it poured onto her lap.

"Oh, it's cold!" she cried out in her natural voice—not that of an aging whore at all—as she jumped back and began to wipe at the spilled drink. Fortunately, she was not too soaked, and though the other patrons of the tavern enjoyed the spectacle, no one seemed to notice that she cried out like a young lady, not like a used and withered baggage.

"I do beg your pardon," I said. I dashed at once to the counter, where I convinced the barman to lend me a relatively dry towel. I allowed Miss Glade to return to her seat thereafter.

"I am truly sorry for my clumsiness," I said, once I had returned the towel. "I must have been so dazzled by your beauty that I forgot to keep my wits about me."

"Your charming words would be more compelling were I not dressed this way," she said with a wry smile, but I knew I was forgiven. Indeed, the accident helped to leaven the tension between us.

I had much to think about, and I knew not how much of this discovery I should share with Mr. Cobb. It had been obvious to me that Miss Glade's story had been a lie—at least that part of attempting to aid a wronged merchant. Her narrative was too much like my own, a tale of minor justice pursued at no great cost. No one could object to or condemn her cause—no one but a Company man, of course—and whatever she suspected of me, she knew I was not that.

What of Miss Glade, though? If she was not what she said, what was she? I had my suspicions, for I had not believed her story of dressing up for her lover. I presumed she had not been upon the stage, for she would have said as much if it had been true. Then who would have the skills to so disguise herself?

It was in pursuit of such answers that I had spilled the drink upon her. The room was cold, and I knew the drink would be close to freezing, so I hoped she would cry out, and that her cry would be true and undisguised. It had been but three words, three syllables, but it had been enough for me to hear the trace of accent in those words. The *o* long and extended, the *h* clipped, hardly there at all, a period more than a sound, the *i* sounding more like an *e* than is common among the

British. It was neither the accent of a lady born on these shores nor the speech of one born to Tudesco Jews. Oh, yes, I knew that accent, even from so few words.

Miss Glade was a Frenchwoman pretending to be otherwise, and I could think of no reason why she should do such a thing if she were not a spy in the service of the French Crown, in service to the very men, I must presume, who had staked their wagers upon my death.

CHAPTER SIXTEEN

WHY WOULD THE FRENCH CONCERN THEMSELVES WITH MY ACTIONS at East India House? I was in no way equal to the task of pondering that question, and accordingly I chose to take my leave of the lady as soon as I possibly could, that I might contemplate this development in private. I forced myself to wait long enough, however, that she would in no way understand that her outburst had revealed anything of herself.

I accompanied her—or, I should say, she accompanied me, for she knew the warrens of St. Giles far better than I—to High Holborn, where I intended to procure a hackney for her. As we walked she began to remove pieces of her costume to a small sack she carried: her wig, her tattered gloves, replaced by fresh, a cloth that effectively wiped away all her paint. She still wore clothes hardly suited to accentuate her charms, and her teeth remained stained with paint, but by the time we emerged upon the busy street, she looked not like a crone but like a beautiful woman dressed rather shabbily.

"In what manner do you prefer me?" she asked.

"Allow me to ponder the question," I answered, "and I shall send you my response anon." I caught the eye of a coachman, who beckoned us forward.

"I shall ignore your teasing and accept your kind assistance with the hackney. But what of yourself?" she asked.

"I must first make sure you are safely away, and then I shall find my own conveyance."

"Perhaps we can share," she said, not a little vivaciously.

"I do not know that we travel in the same direction."

She leaned close to me now. "Surely we might arrange that the same direction is precisely where we go."

I do not know that ever in my life have I worked harder to master my passions. She looked up at me, her face slightly lowered, her dark eyes wide, her red lips slightly parted so I could observe the enticing pink of her tongue. It would have been easy, so easy, to follow her wherever she wished to lead, to allow her to take me in her arms. I could have told myself that I did it for the cause—by being close to her, I would learn more of her designs. Yet I knew all that to be false. I knew that were I to succumb to her advances, to my desires, I should not be able to trust my instincts from that moment. If it had only been my life, my safety, in the balance, I should have happily thrown the dice and accepted the wager. But my dearest friend, a kindly aging gentleman, and my infirm uncle depended on me to maintain my wits and my judgment. I could not stroll blithely to what might well be the most pleasant of gallows with the lives of so many others dependent upon my success.

"I fear I have an urgent appointment I must keep," I told her.

"Perhaps I could make an urgent appointment with you for another night," she proposed.

"Perhaps so," I managed, though my mouth grew dry. "Good night, madam."

"Wait." She very boldly took hold of my wrist with her hand. A jolt of excitement, hot as fire, passed through my flesh. I think she must have felt it too, for she let go at once. "I hope," she said, quite apparently stammering for words, "I—well, I know I can be playful, but I hope you have some regard for me. You do, don't you?"

"Of course, madam," I managed.

"And yet you are so formal. Will you not be at your ease with me?"

"I should very much like to," I said, "but I do not believe this is the time. Good night," I told her once more, and tore myself away hastily, hurling myself into the distance.

I had told her the truth. I should like to be at my ease with her, and this was not the time. No falsehood in that. I merely neglected to mention that I did not believe relaxing my guard around her would be beneficial to my freedom—or even my life.

—

A NEARLY SLEEPLESS NIGHT of confusion made matters no clearer to me, so it was my good fortune that I had the opportunity to encounter Elias that very next morning. It was distressing enough that the French wished to labor upon my death, but to learn that Miss Glade, a lady to whom I was forming an attachment of no small measure, might well be one of their number left me both confused and morose.

I had some business that morning with one of the clerks of Craven House, and after the meeting I was delighted to see Elias in the building's lobby, in close conversation with a woman. I momentarily wondered at his presence until I recollected he must be in the building on account of Ellershaw's malady. I hurried forward, but my eagerness dissipated almost instantly, for I saw that the person with whom he spoke was none but Celia Glade.

Before I was close enough to hear a word that came from his mouth, I recognized his posture: his tall form held ramrod straight, his smile wide and dazzling, one hand pressed to his chest in a continual performance of gentlemanly poise. Elias sought his prey as surely and as single-mindedly as any predator.

I divined that he had just spoken something meant to amuse, for Miss Glade put a hand to her mouth to stifle a laugh—a noise considered most inappropriate inside Craven House. It struck me as most inappropriate that he should try to charm her or, more horrifically, that she should be charmed by him. I told myself I could not trust Elias to maintain his defenses against such formidable female graces, but I knew better than to believe my own explanation.

Accordingly, I rushed forward, fully intending to break up this most unpropitious meeting. What, I wondered, did Miss Glade know? Was she aware of my friendship with Elias? Did she know that his fate was so closely bound to mine? The only thing of which I might be certain was that I wished she should learn nothing more than she knew already.

"Good morning, Celia," I said to her, ignoring Elias for the moment. "Do you think it wise to advertise to all of the Company that you have need to speak with a surgeon?"

In retrospect, I realized I might have chosen a less venomous method to end their discourse, one less suggestive of what I had learned of her—now likely false—history. At the time, I was pleased enough that it did the business. Miss Glade turned red and hurried off.

Elias narrowed his eyes and pressed his lips together, a sure sign of his irritation. "I say, Weaver, that was most unkind."

Given that I had much to discuss with him and could not do so here, I hardly hesitated before violating the rules and quitting the premises for a journey to a nearby tavern. The entire way, he complained about my ending his congress with Miss Glade.

"That girl was a delectable nugget, Weaver. I'll not forget this outrage soon, I tell you."

"We shall discuss it later," I grumbled.

"But I wish to discuss it now," he insisted. "I am far too irritated to discuss aught else."

I ducked my head to avoid one of the metropolis's many and notorious low-hanging shop signs we came hard upon. Elias was too distracted to see it, and indeed I was so angry I nearly let him strike himself, but in the end I could not see him take an injury, even a minor and comical one, so I reached up and pulled him down as he walked. He kept his balance and did not miss a stride.

"Oh," he said. "That was a good turn. But it does not excuse this outrage, Weaver. Outrage, I say. I shall order something very dear and insist you pay for it."

Once we were equipped with our pots and Elias had called for a plate of bread and cold meat, and then fortified himself with a pinch of snuff, he began once more.

"In the future, Weaver, when you see me with a pretty girl, I should very much like—"

"Your life and mine and the lives of my friends depend on what happens in Craven House," I said, not a little harshly. "As far as concerns you, I am the lawgiver there. You do what I say and when I say, and you do not grumble about it. I'll not let your insatiable appetites and inability to sense danger when it is under your nose lead the two of us and others into ruin. You may think being unable to govern your appetite for women is nothing but amusing, but in this case it may well prove to be nothing short of self-destruction."

He gazed into his pot, taking the time he needed to master his passions. "Yes," he said at last. "You are right. It is not the appropriate place to seek out pleasures, and you are right that I am not terribly good at making wise decisions when it comes to women, particularly the pretty ones."

"Good." I clapped my hand upon his shoulder, that he might understand it best to let the thing pass. "I'm sorry I grew so hot with you. I have been tried most sorely of late."

"No, you need not apologize. I require a good thrashing now and again, and better it be done by my friends than my enemies."

"I shall make an effort to recollect your words," I said with a grin, feeling much relieved that the discomfiture had passed. "Now, tell me about your more appropriate adventures."

I cannot say if it was with effort or if his mercurial nature allowed him to drop his resentment so readily, but he brightened at once. "Your friend Mr. Ellershaw is terribly afflicted." The news sounded grave, but he delivered it with a grin.

"The French pox?"

He shook his head. "Not the French pox but the English malady. Madness."

"What do you mean?"

"What I mean, Weaver, is that he believes he has an advanced and virulent case of syphilis—though at times he speaks of it as gonorrhea, not comprehending the difference—and yet he has not a single symptom. I can find no sores, pustules, rashes, or inflammations, nor can I find signs that there have ever been such."

"Are you certain?"

He took a long drink of his ale. "Weaver, I've just spent the last hour handling a deranged old fat man's privy member. Please don't ask me if I'm certain. I must obliterate the morning from my mind, and on the spur of speed too."

"What, then, did you tell him?"

"You know I am obligated by oath to treat my patients to the best of my ability."

"Yes, yes. What did you tell him?"

"As I'm under no obligation to refrain from pretending to treat a well man who believes himself ill, particularly if doing so will bring him peace, I informed him that I knew of some very particular cures, recently brought back from the Barbadoes, that I had no doubt would relieve his symptoms. I let a small quantity of his blood, purged his bowels, and left with him a rather violent diuretic. When I am done with you, I shall write my apothecary and have him send over a variety of mixtures that will have no other effect than to calm his agitation. And, as he appears to believe in my cure, perhaps it shall settle his spirits." He held up a shiny guinea. "Certainly he appeared most obliged."

"I should think. And will you continue to treat him?"

"As best I can, but he may grow agitated when I refuse to apply mercury, and I should rather avoid doing so since he does not require exposure to so strong a property as it contains."

"Give him whatever he likes, so long as it keeps you in his employ."

"Mercury is marvelous effective against the pox, but it has unwholesome effects. It is hardly ethical to give a man a cure he does not need that will engender a sickness he need not suffer."

"Is it ethical to allow you to spend the remainder of your years in debtor's prison to protect the health of a rapacious madman?"

"You make a compelling case," he said. "I'll consider my options when the time comes."

I nodded. "A wise course, though consult with me before doing anything, please."

"Of course. Now, if you'll permit me to bring up the matter of the girl one last time. Have you considered that if I could strike up an amour with her, it would give me a reason to return more often, and then there should be two of us inside who might more effectively than one—"

"She's a French spy," I said, ending his discourse with the suddenness of a fired pistol.

I regretted it at once. Even if my knowledge and his will could tame Elias's predatory impulses, I doubted he would be a match for the lady's own skills. If she pressed him, I feared his knowledge of her true nature would be legible upon his face as clearly as if written in ink.

Nevertheless, I had began and had no choice but to continue. "There is a French plot here somewhere, Elias. I know not if it be the most villainous of the schemes that surround the Company, but it is a plot. First we find that there are Frenchmen investing in my death as though it were a fund upon the 'Change, and now I find a French spy contriving to discover all about the Company and about me."

I proceeded to tell him of my encounter the previous evening with Miss Glade, and though I was careful to disguise the more amorous elements, Elias had known me too long and was too good a student of human nature not to suspect something.

"I say, have you an affection for this treacherous creature?"

"She wishes me to have one," I answered.

"And given that she is beautiful and charming, you find it difficult not to comply."

"I am master of my passions," I assured him, "and I have no desire to form a connection with a woman whose motives we must presume to be malicious. You need not worry about me on that score."

He took a moment to stare at his closely cut fingernails, a clear indication he wished to say something awkward. "I trust you have accepted that you shall never be successful with your cousin's widow."

I shook my head in disbelief. "Do you really believe that a longing for Miriam stands as the only obstacle between myself and true love with a deceitful spy?"

"I know you have long loved Miriam Melbury, and she has quite dashed your heart to bits, but I admit when you phrase it in such a way that my theory does not appear valid."

"I am relieved to hear you say as much."

"Still, you are reaching the age where a man ought to seek out a wife."

"Elias, if I wished to have this conversation, I might as well visit my aunt Sophia, who could make the case far more eloquently while irritating me far less and probably serving me something quite pleasant to eat. Besides which, I might make the same claim of you, yet I hardly see you seeking out a bride."

"Oh, I am not the marrying kind, Weaver, and if I were I should require a woman with a massive dowry who would overlook my relative financial difficulties. You, on the other hand, are a Hebrew, and your people cannot help but marry. If you wish to hear my opinion, I think a wife would do you good."

"Perhaps," I said, "I should ask Mr. Cobb to send you to debtor's prison now."

"Those who speak the truth must face the brickbats of resentment."

"Yes, and your lot in life is to suffer. May I suggest we confine our time to discussing the meaning of the French involvement?"

He let out a sigh. "Very well. I have never heard of the French sending agents to work against the great companies, but it does not surprise me that they would think to do so. After all, these companies produce prodigious wealth for the nation, and the East India Company is also an arm of exploration and expansions. There could be any number of reasons why the French should wish to infiltrate Craven House."

That, unfortunately constituted the extent of Elias's analysis. By this time I had finished my pot and thought it advisable to return to the East India yard, lest my absence be noted. I did not think any great harm would come of such an observation, but it served my interests well enough that I should draw no attention to myself.

I came in through the main gate, therefore, and proceeded to the warehouses, but I had not advanced more than a few feet before I heard my name called quite briskly.

"Mr. Weaver, pray you stop."

I turned to find Carmichael chasing after me. He ran forward, holding his straw hat to his head. "What is it?"

"Mr. Ellershaw come down here not half an hour past. He appeared most grieved that no one knew how to find you."

I nodded and headed back toward the main house and proceeded directly toward Ellershaw's office. He called for me to enter when I knocked, and when I stepped in, I found Mr. Forester sitting across the desk from him, several samples of cloth draped across the desk. Neither man, I soon observed, appeared happy to see me.

"Weaver." Ellershaw spat out some of the brown kernel on which he chewed. "Where have you been? Do I pay you for your leisure time or for your labors?"

"I'm sorry to have missed you," I said. "I was about an inspection of the warehouses when you called upon me."

"If you were inspecting the warehouses, how is it that no one knew of your whereabouts?"

"Because I did not wish for them to know. Inspections are most effective when they are a surprise to those inspected."

Ellershaw pondered this suggestion for a moment and then nodded slowly while he worked at the mass in his mouth. "Just so."

Forester held in his hand a piece of blue fabric, which he studied most attentively. Indeed, he tried most assiduously to keep his eyes from wandering from the cloth. I suspected he did not trust himself to contain his expression should our eyes meet, and I thought that a useful detail. Forester believed himself unskilled at dissimulation.

"What is it you want?" Ellershaw now inquired of me.

"I only wanted to attend to you, as you called upon me, sir," I said.

"I haven't the time for you now," he answered. "Can you not see that we are busy with things that are none of your concern? Is that not your opinion, Forester?"

Forester continued to cast his eyes downward. "It is. A man of his sort can have nothing to add to our discussion."

"I say," Ellershaw blurted out, "that is rather a harsh assessment. Weaver may not be a Company man, but he's a sharp fellow. Do you think you have something to say to us, Weaver?"

"I do not know what you discuss," I said.

"Nothing of interest to you," Forester murmured.

"Only these cloths. What you see before you, Weaver, are the fabrics the Parliament, may it rot in hell, will permit us to sell domestically after Christmas. As you see, it is devilish little. Most of our trade on these islands will now be in these blues"—he held up a piece of light blue cotton—"and I fear what trade we do with it will be a mere shadow of our former enterprise."

I said nothing.

"As you can see," Forester said, "he has neither the experience nor interest for these matters. I mean no insult to the fellow, but he is not a man whose opinion you must solicit."

"What is the cloth used for now?" I asked.

"Scarves," Ellershaw said. "Stockings, cravats, other such accessories, and, of course, dresses for the ladies."

"Then would it not be wise," I suggested, "to encourage men of fashion to mold their suits out of this material?"

Forester let out a loud laugh. "A suit, you say? Even the most absurd of fops would not wear a suit of so feminine a color. The very idea is laughable."

"Perhaps so," I said with a shrug, "but Mr. Ellershaw has observed that the key to success is to allow the warehouses to drive fashion and not fashion the warehouses. You may sell as much of this material as you wish, so ought not the Company work to change the public's perception rather than mold your product to *their* perceptions? As I have been made to understand it, you need only provide suits of this color to enough fashionable gentlemen in order for it to seem absurd no longer. Indeed, if you succeed, by next season no one will remember a time when suits of this shade of blue were unpopular."

"Nonsense," Forester said.

"No." Ellershaw let out a breath. "He is right. This is the very thing. Begin to send notes to your associates in the world of fashion. Make appointments to have a tailor pay them a visit."

"Sir, this is but the squandering of time and effort," Forester answered. "No one will wear a suit of so foolish a color."

"The world will wear these suits," he answered. "Well done, Weaver. With only two weeks left before the Court meets, I may yet preserve myself. Now, back to your appointed tasks. I shall have more to say to you anon."

I bowed to both men and departed, certain from the look on Forester's face that I had done nothing more than fan the flames of the hatred for which he bore me.

THAT NIGHT, AT THE APPOINTED time, Carmichael met me behind the main warehouse. The sky was unusually dark—cloudy and moonless with the occasional fluttering touch of snow—and though the grounds were well lit, there were ample swaths of shadow in which to make our silent way. The dogs, by now, knew my scent and would not remark upon it, and we knew well the times of patrols and the routes the watchmen would take, so it was no difficult thing to move unseen in the cold darkness.

Carmichael took me toward the northernmost edge of the East India yards, where stood the building called the Greene House. It was four stories in height, but narrow, and in none the best shape. I had heard tell that it was scheduled to be brought down some time in the next year.

The door was naturally locked, as the watchmen could not be entrusted with access to the interior, not when they would be tempted to help themselves to whatever they could find inside. But as master watchman I was granted full access, and after waiting for one of the patrolling men, who had the staggering gait of one who'd been drinking too much small beer while at work, we made our way inside.

I had taken the precaution of hiding candles and tinder where I knew I would be able to retrieve them, after which, in the dark and echoing space, I turned to Carmichael's flickering face.

"Where to?"

"Up," he said. "It's on the top floor, which has fallen into disuse because it's such horrible bad trouble to carry crates to and fro. And the stairs ain't great, so we'll have to be right careful. Also, stay away from the window with that light of yours. You don't want anyone to see. No telling who is Aadil's fellow and who ain't."

It was undeniably good advice, so I handed him the candle and determined to place my safety in his hands. It was entirely possible that Carmichael might not be what he appeared; that he might not be trustworthy or eager to help me at all. I had already encountered more double-dealing than was the norm, even in institutions like these companies, which bred backstabbing the way workhouses bred whores. For all that, I had no choice but to move forward, so I did, keeping close to my guide.

When we reached the top floor, Carmichael turned to me. "Here's where it gets a bit thorny."

When he held out the candle, I knew at once what he meant. The stairs were crumbling and broken, with no sign to indicate which parts would withstand the weight of a man and which would crumble under my feet. I presumed they could not be as fragile as they looked, for how else could Aadil and his followers haul crates up to the fourth floor? Nevertheless, I followed closely in Carmichael's footsteps.

When we reached the landing, he led me left, down a dusty corridor, until we stood before a door. I tried it and found it to be locked. I had come prepared, however, and removed from my pocket a set of picks that glistened in the light of Carmichael's candle. He, however, was not one to be outdone. In the spare light I saw the flash of a grin, and then he reached into his coat to hold up a key.

"I'm sure you're right skillful with those picks, sir, but this here will do our business a mite more simple."

I put the picks away, nodding in agreement. Taking the candle, I watched as he inserted the key and turned the knob and pushed open the door. Then with a grand gesture, originating in something I suspected other than politeness, he indicated that I should go first.

I did so, holding up my candle to illuminate a large, if not massive, room filled with crates of a variety of sizes. Some were stacked nearly to the ceiling; some lay scattered here and there as if with no reason. All were shut.

I set the candle down when I spied an iron bar, which I then gripped and approached the nearest container.

"Hold," Carmichael called. "You can't break it open. They'll know we've been here."

"They'll know someone's been here, that much is likely. But they won't know it was us. And we did not come up here to have an appraising look at the contents of the room. I must know what they are hiding."

He gave me an accepting but unenthusiastic nod, and so I broke open the nearest crate. Inside, it was full of thick rolls of cloths of bright floral patterns. I held the candle closer.

"What is it?" I asked Carmichael.

He took a piece of cloth in his hands, rubbed it between his fingers, stroked it, and put it near to the candle. "It ain't nothing," he said quietly. "It's just the same cloths they bring into the other warehouses."

We opened half a dozen more at random; again, nothing but standard East Indian cloth imports. Carmichael shook his head. "I can't make sense of it," he said. "Why would they go to the trouble of playing these freaks with hidden meetings and late night secreting away of deliveries. This ain't nothing but the ordinary."

I took a moment to consider why it was that a member of the Court of Committees would trouble himself to collect a clandestine network in order to warehouse goods that might as well be stored anywhere. "Is this a matter of stealing?" I asked. "Do they plan to sell the contents of this room for their own profit?"

"Stealing?" Carmichael let out a laugh. "To what end? In another month, the market for these cloths will be gone."

"A black market, perhaps? They mean to continue to sell the material clandestinely?"

Again, Carmichael shook his head. "No, the law don't forbid the trade in calicoes, only the wearing of them. If they wish to keep on selling the cloth, they can, but there won't be anyone to buy it. Come Christmas, they won't be able to give it away. Here in England, all this will be worth less than nothing."

"And you are certain that the cloth is ordinary?"

He nodded most solemnly. "'Tis but ordinary calico."

I felt certain I must be overlooking something of some significance. Carmichael, too, kept a puzzled look upon his face. "Maybe if you could get a look at the manifests," he suggested. "Could it be that there's some meaning not in the crates themselves but in from where they come or whither they're bound?"

It was a good suggestion, and I was about to say as much when we heard the unmistakable sound of a door opening on the first floor and muffled though agitated voices.

"The devil's arse," Carmichael cursed. "They must have seen the light through the window after all. You've got to get out of here."

"How?"

"The window. That one there. That side of the building has rugged stones, so that if you've got a good purchase you can get yourself up to the roof and hide."

"And what about you?"

"I'll have to close the window behind you. Now, don't worry about me, Mr. Weaver. I know these warehouses like a child knows his own street. They'll not find me, I'll warrant."

"I can't leave you to fend for yourself."

"There ain't no choice in it. We can't risk them finding you, for both our sakes. And trust me, they'll never know I was here. I've got a few minutes to put all back in order, lock the door, and slip into a crevice where they won't look. Come find me tomorrow, but for now you've got to get out that window."

I did not love to do it, but I saw the sense of his plan, and I understood Carmichael had proposed it not out of an altruistic impulse but because it was the soundest course. So I allowed him to lead me toward the window he had in mind. It was stuck with disuse, but I managed to pry it open and have a look out. The stones were, indeed, quite rough. A man afraid of heights or unused to handling himself in awkward situations—such as the uninvited entry or exit from premises not his own—might have trembled at this sight, but I could only think that, in the past, I'd managed far worse and in rain and snow too.

"I'll leave the window open just enough to give you something to grip when you return," he said. "But I'll have to lock the door behind me, so those picks of yours had better be good."

It was not the picks that would be tested but the picker, but I had my share of experience, so I merely nodded. "You are certain you wish to remain?"

"'Tis the best course. Now off with ye."

So I was off, out the window. Balancing on the thankfully ample ledge in the darkness of night, I caught hold of a jutting rock and forced myself up to a ledgelike protrusion, and then another, and then, with an ease I found almost troubling, I was on the roof. There I pressed myself flat where I might have a good view of the door. I could hear from the building a muffled commotion, but no more than that. And then nothing but the sounds of London at night: the distant cries of street vendors, the squawks of eager or outraged whores, the clatter of hooves on stone. Across the courtyard I heard the coughing and cackling and grumbling of the watchmen.

A light rain soaked my greatcoat and clothing through to my skin, but still I remained until I saw a group of men depart from the warehouse. From my lofty position I could not hear their words or determine who they were, except that there were four of them and one, from the size of the bulk under his coat, I believed must be Aadil. Another must have hurt himself on the stairs, I thought, because one of his fellows helped him along.

I continued to wait for some hours until I feared that light would soon destroy my cover, and so, with much greater difficulty and trepidation than on my ascent, I carefully made my way back down the ledge of the wall to the window sill and pried open the window—already ajar as Carmichael had promised. I then found that my picks were unnecessary, for the door had been left closed but unlocked. I knew not if my ally had done this by mistake, as an aid to me, or if the men come to inspect the premises had been careless. At the time I hardly cared. I should have cared, I later realized, but at the time I did not.

Now, without benefit of a candle, I made my careful way down the stairs, wondering all the while if Carmichael would rejoin me or if he had somehow managed to slip out without my noticing. There was no sign of him, however, and once on the ground floor, I studied the premises through a window until I felt certain I could leave undetected. It was then a matter of another half an hour of snaking through shadows to avoid the watchmen and make my departure. I arrived home in time to sleep an hour before rising once more to greet the day and the terrible news it would bring.

CHAPTER SEVENTEEN

—

ECAUSE I WAS TIRED AND SULLEN FROM MY DIFFICULT AND
ultimately unproductive night, I did not notice the dour mood when I
arrived at the warehouses in the East India yard—at least not at first. It
took me a few minutes to see that the watchmen and warehouse workers all were equally sullen and gloomy.

"What's happening?" I asked one of them.

"There's been an accident," he told me. "In the early morning. No
one knows what he was doing there; he had no business. Aadil thinks
he was stealing, but Carmichael was in the west warehouse—where all
the teas are kept, you know. And there was an accident."

"Was he hurt?" I demanded.

"Aye," the fellow told me. "He was hurt unto death. Crushed like a
rat under the teas he was aiming to steal."

TEAS.

A clever enough cover, I supposed, since whatever Forester and
Aadil were up to, it had nothing to do with teas. And as there could be
no defensible reason why Carmichael would have been moving crates
in a tea warehouse in the small hours of the night, the only available
conclusion was that he had been guilty of that most common of crimes,
pilfering from the warehouses to augment his meager income.

These transgressions were an open secret and were allowed so long
as no one grew too greedy. Indeed, the watchmen and warehouse work-

ers were paid poorly because it was understood that they would augment their income with a judicious amount of socking. If their remuneration was increased, the logic went, they would sock no less, so there could hardly be anything to gain by paying them a living wage.

I remained stunned for long moments, standing still while men rushed about me. I broke out of my malaise when I saw Aadil pass by: I reached out and grabbed his sleeve.

"Tell me what happened," I said.

He met my gaze and let out a laugh. How ugly his already unpleasant face grew when he wore a mask of cruel mirth! "Maybe you tell me. You overseer of watch."

"Pray, don't be petty. Tell me."

He shrugged. "Why Carmichael here last night, I wonder? He where he not supposed to be. He doing what he not supposed to do, taking tea for himself. Maybe in hurry, afraid he get caught. Take chances. Get crushed." He shrugged again. "Better than be hanged, yes?"

"Let me see the body."

He looked at me quizzically. "Why for you want see it?"

"Because I do. Tell me where they've taken it."

"Already carried away," he said. "I know nothing where. Coroner, maybe. Family? No one tell me. I no ask."

It was only with the greatest restraint that I was able to have this conversation. I had no doubt that Aadil had killed Carmichael, with Forester's implicit or explicit approbation. Yet these were suspicions, conjectures I could not prove, and in the end they mattered little. All I knew was that Carmichael had acted for me and had died for his trouble, and I was powerless to see justice served on his behalf.

Lest I betray my emotions or reveal that I knew more of the matter, I walked away, heading for the interior of Craven House.

Did Aadil suspect my involvement? He kept secrets from me, but that was to be expected. Still, Carmichael had violated the sanctum of the secret warehouse only after I had come to work there. Forester knew I was working for Ellershaw and he mistrusted Ellershaw. Why did they not come after me? There was certainly no good reason to believe they would not, simply because they had not yet done so.

It was now more urgent than ever that I find out what Forester was keeping in that warehouse or, since we had discovered the banality of the room's contents, why he was keeping it. Thus, with no useful outlet for my rage, I pursued the matter the only way I could imagine doing so—I went to speak to the accounts keeper, Mr. Blackburn.

He was in his office, scratching away at a piece of paper, hunched over it as his ink-stained hand whipped pen along page. He looked up after a moment. "Ah, Weaver. I presume you are come to inquire as to the means of replacing your lost worker."

I shut the door behind me. "I had nothing so mercenary in mind. Carmichael was my friend, and I am not so eager to see his place filled."

He looked at me with his puzzled expression, the one he always wore when not busy with his documents. It seemed to me that he could not imagine anything as uncomfortable or messy as friendship.

"Yes, well," he managed, after a moment, "even so, schedules have to be ordered, hmm? The yards must be watched. It would be a foolish thing to let sentiment interfere with what must be done."

"I suppose it would," I said, taking a seat without being invited to do so.

It was clear to me, painfully clear, that Blackburn wanted nothing so much as for me to leave, that he might go back to whatever banal task absorbed him, but I would not have it. Indeed, his discomfort might only serve to make him speak in a less circumspect manner than was, perhaps, his wont.

"May I speak to you in confidence?" I inquired. "It is of a delicate matter, and one that involves a particularly unorthodox use of Company grounds and Company resources."

"Of course, of course," he said. He had set down his pen and was absently blotting the page while he looked at me. I had as near his full attention as I could reasonably expect.

"I hope I might have your confidence, sir. I should hate if my interest in righting something sloppy should be visited upon me with something so unfair as losing my post. You understand, sir, I trust. I want to do the right thing and make sure there is nothing amiss in the warehouses. Still, when there are powerful men involved, it is not always easy to be sure the right thing is in one's best interest."

He leaned forward, stretching his narrow frame across the desk like a turtle stretching its neck out of its shell. "You need not worry on that score, Mr. Weaver, not at all. You may speak in the strictest confidence, and you have my word that I shall not speak of what you say to anyone, not without your leave. I trust that is sufficient."

It almost was. "I should very much like it to be," I said, with some uncertainty. "Still, there is a great risk to me. Perhaps it would be wise if I came back when I knew more. Yes, that would be better." I began to rise.

"No!" The word was not an order but a plea. "If you know something, we must resolve it. I cannot endure that there should be something amiss, some wound left untended, rotting upon the body of the Company. You do right, sir, in wanting to address it. I promise you, I shall do nothing you do not wish me to do. Only you must tell me what it is you know."

It was so very odd, I thought. Here this clerk doted upon the Company as thought it were a favored lapdog, or even a lover or a child. Had I not told him, he would have been driven mad by the unreachable itch, and yet he had nothing personal to gain from the intelligence, nothing personal to gain from correcting whatever impropriety to which I might allude. He was merely a man who liked to see geegaws aligned, be they his geegaws or a stranger's, and would stop at nothing to correct an aberration.

I cleared my throat, wishing to speak in a roundabout way so that I might make his torture all the more exquisite. "Last week, Carmichael spoke to me of an impropriety. I thought the matter of little urgency and would have pursued it at a more leisurely pace, but—as you can see—I am no longer free to pursue it with him at all. And while he considered the matter of little moment, I—well, I think you understand, Mr. Blackburn. I believe we are in that way alike. I do not wish this thing to go unattended forever."

I continued to avoid the topic, not only to further torment Blackburn but also because I wished to make it clear that I did not regard this issue too seriously. I in no way wanted to imply what I truly believed, that Carmichael had been killed over whatever I was about to say.

Indeed, he followed quite well. "Of course, of course," he said, waving his hand at me as I spoke to further my speed of revelation.

It was time to get to the meat of it. "Carmichael mentioned to me that there was a portion of one of the warehouses, I cannot recall which one"—again, this seemed to me the best course—"in which calicoes were being secreted away by one of the members of the Court of Committees. He said these crates arrived in the dark of night, and great care was taken to be certain no one knew about them: that they were there, what they contained, or in what quantity. Now, I am not one to question members of the Court, but as overseer of the watch, the practice of regularly superseding our scrutiny struck me as troubling."

It struck Blackburn as troubling as well. He leaned toward me, and his hands twittered in agitation. "Troubling? Troubling indeed, sir, most troubling. Secret stores, hidden quantities and qualities? That cannot be. That must not be. These records have three purposes. Three, sir." He held up three fingers. "The establishment of order, the maintenance of order, and the securing of future order. If some men think they are above documenting their actions, if they may take and add at their own whims, then what is this"—he gestured to the vast stores of papers about the room—"what is all this for?"

"I had not thought of it from that perspective," I said.

"But you must, you must. I do this work so that at any time any member of the Court may come here and know all there is to know about the Company. If someone chooses to run wild, sir, there is no point to it. No point to it at all."

"I believe I understand you."

"I pray you do. I pray it most earnestly, sir. You must tell me more of this. Did Carmichael say anything to you of which member of the Court might be acting so recklessly?"

"No, nothing of that. I don't believe he knew himself."

"And you don't know which warehouse."

Here I decided I would be wise to retrench. After all, I had to give the man something on which to base his inquiry. "I believe he might have mentioned a building called the Greene House, though I cannot be certain."

"Ah, yes. Of course. Bought from a Mr. Greene in 1689, I believe, a gentleman whose loyalties and preferments were too closely bound with the late Catholic king, and when he fled, Mr. Greene did not long linger. The Greene House has generally been used as a storage facility of, at best, tertiary importance. Indeed, it is scheduled to be brought down and replaced in future. If a devious man wished to hide something within the yard, that might well be the place to do it."

"Perhaps you can find some records," I suggested. "Manifests and such like. Something that will let us know who is misusing the system and for what purpose."

"Yes, yes. That is the very thing. It is the very thing to do. This sort of irregularity must not be countenanced, sir. I shan't turn a blind eye, I promise you."

"Good, good. I am glad to hear it. I trust you will let me know if you discover something."

"Come back later today," he mumbled, already opening a massive folio that spewed out a storm of papers. "I shall have this problem solved, I warrant."

IN CRAVEN HOUSE ITSELF, the mood was black among the servants. Carmichael had been well liked, and his death darkened everyone's spirits. I was passing through the kitchens to attend to my duties on the ground when Celia Glade stopped me by placing her slender fingers around my wrist.

"It's very sad news," she said quietly, not bothering to affect her servant's voice.

"Indeed it is."

She released my wrist now in favor of my hand. I confess I had a difficult time not pulling her close. The sight of those great eyes, her shining face, her scent. I felt my body rebelling against my intellect, and despite the cruel violence of the day I longed to kiss her. Indeed, I believe I might have done something as dangerous as that had not a pair of kitchen boys entered at that moment.

Celia and I parted wordlessly.

LATER THAT AFTERNOON, after a black day of grumbling among the men and of my having to resist the impulse to strike Aadil in the head each time his back was turned, I returned to Blackburn's office, hoping to find some useful intelligence. Alas, it was not so.

His face was pale and his hands trembling. "I can find nothing, sir. No records and no manifests. I shall have to order an inventory of the Greene House, discover what is there, and attempt to determine how it came and where it is destined to go."

"And by whom," I proposed.

He looked at me with a knowing expression. "Just so."

"Except," I countered, "do you really wish to pursue a general investigation? After all, if a member of the Court has gone to such lengths to hide his scheme, he may go one step further."

"You mean remove me from my place?"

"'Tis something to ponder."

"My services have never been questioned." A tone of desperation now entered his voice. "I have been here for six years, sir, working my way into this position, and no one has spoken anything but words of praise. Indeed, more than one member of the Court has wondered aloud to me how the Company functioned before my arrival."

"I doubt none of that," I told him. "But I hardly need tell you, sir, that a man of your position is at the mercy of those who stand above him. One or two unjust persons of power could undermine all you have done in the time you have toiled here. You must know it."

"Then how do we proceed?"

"Quietly, sir. Very quietly. It is all that can be done for the nonce, I'm afraid. We must both be determined to keep our eyes open, looking for any signs of deception, and perhaps then we will be able to link this aberration to its origins."

He gave a sullen nod. "Perhaps you are right. I will certainly do all I can to discover more, though I shall follow your advice and pursue the matter quietly, with books and ledgers rather than with words."

I commended him for his determination and left his office; indeed, I was out of Craven House and nearly at the main warehouse when I stopped in my tracks.

The idea came upon me all at once and in such a rush that I nearly ran back to Blackburn's office, though doing so was hardly necessary. He would be there, and time was certainly of no great issue. It was for myself that I ran, for I desired above all else to know at once.

I entered once more and, as was now becoming my habit, I closed the door. I sat down before Mr. Blackburn and offered him a generous smile. The impulse to bombard him with questions was strong, but I beat it back. To demand he tell me what I wanted to know might strike him as, in its own way, disorderly. I knew he did not like to speak of rough edges and puzzle pieces that did not fit, and I would have to approach the question with a certain amount of caution.

"Sir," I began, "I was halfway across the yard when I had a sudden desire to return and tell you that I have come to be a great admirer of yours."

"I beg your pardon?"

"Your gift for order, sir, and regularity. It is the very thing. You have inspired me in my work with the watchmen."

"I am flattered by your words."

"I say no more than what any man must acknowledge. I wonder, however, if there is more to know than what I have gleaned from our brief conversations."

"How do you mean, sir?"

"I mean, I wonder if you might spare a moment tonight, at an ale-house perhaps, to talk with me about your philosophy of order, if you will. Needless to say, as you are assuming the role of master and I the one of pupil, I shall pay your expenses most gladly."

Though he served the Company with his every breath, I believed Blackburn understood himself an object of some derision, so he observed me most skeptically at first, but as I spoke I believe I convinced him of the veracity of my words.

"You do know that it is not permitted."

"Not permitted?"

"The Court of Committees has forbidden clerks from attending taverns, brothels, and playhouses, for in the past they have observed that debauched behavior has led to a loss of productivity. If I were to be discovered in such a place, I should lose my position at once."

"But surely there is a place we might meet."

The hint of a wicked smile crossed his lips. "A tavern," he said in a very low voice. "These things may be arranged if ordered carefully. I know the very place where we can take a pot or two at our liberty."

I RETURNED TO MY DUTIES and observed the men of the India yards watch go about their work gloomily, as did I until three o'clock, when I received a summons from Mr. Forester. I was most unwilling to spend time alone with him, for I in no small way believed him to be responsible for Carmichael's death, though I knew not how or, to be blunt, why. Nevertheless, he appeared to me the most likely cause of this pretended accident, and I had no choice but to act ignorant. If I were to avenge my friend's death, I needs must play my part and let all out in the end.

I found Forester's door open; he bade me close the door and sit.

I looked up to find him smiling on me, looking rather like a man wearing a comical mask. "You have been in Mr. Ellershaw's personal employ about a week now, is that not right?"

"Yes, it is."

"It is a rather unusual arrangement, do you not think so?"

I attempted to appear confused. "I cannot say what is usual or unusual here, for I have not been in attendance long enough. I can say that at times unusual arrangements are all that we have available to us, and we must make do as we can."

Color rose to his face, and I could not but observe that he understood my allusion to his liaison with Mrs. Ellershaw. "I do not understand why your benefactor has taken upon himself and his own purse to have you manage the watch," he said.

"I know little of internal politics, but he is a member of the Court of Committees, and so the whole of the Company is his concern, or perhaps that is how he sees it. I hardly think it strange that he should take steps to aid the Company. And as I understand it, a man in my position could not be hired until after the meeting of the Court of Committees. If Mr. Ellershaw saw an urgent need, his handling of the matter appears to me quite ordinary."

"Perhaps so," Forester conceded. "It may well be that this is nothing more than a matter of Ellershaw's wisdom. I do have one difficulty with that theory, however, based on other actions, other inclinations, the man has adopted."

"And what is that?"

"I believe Ellershaw has grown quite mad. His mind is disordered with an amorous disease. I'm sure you have heard it. Everyone knows it to be true."

"Sometimes," I said, with deliberate caginess, "those things everyone knows to be true are the most false things of all."

"Play not such games with me. You've witnessed his behavior for yourself, I've no doubt. And even if you choose to ignore the signs of madness engendered by the French pox, you've seen that he is a slave to the betel nut, a most disgusting habit he learned from savages in India."

"Those brown things he eats?" I asked. I chose to let down my guard, for I truly had no idea of this food.

"Yes. I am told they are most addicting, and half of India is in the thrall of this poison. It affects the body, it is said, like coffee—only more strongly; once tasted, it holds its victim in its grip forever. And it produces another side effect."

"Madness?" I guessed.

"Precisely."

It took a moment for me to think how I should respond to these accusations. "You appear rather determined to believe that Mr. Ellershaw is mad, and you are most desirous that I believe it too. I wish to please all members of the Court of Committees, but in this I am afraid I cannot help you. You say my benefactor is mad, but I hardly know him well enough to ascertain such a thing, for I have only known him as he is now."

"Were you to come across a stranger howling at a flock of sheep, Mr. Weaver, you would not need to learn his life's story nor interview his friends to know the behavior was strange, only if it was unusual for this particular man. Similarly, you should have no difficulty in evaluation by observation, by placing it in context."

"I must restate my position that I think your observation flawed."

"Gad, sir, did you not hear him threaten to impale an old man with a burning poker? Is that not madness?"

"He would say it was naught but strategy, and I am new enough to Craven House to know nothing different. I have seen nothing to bring me to such a conclusion. I do know that such charges can be regarded with suspicion when the man making the accusations has much to gain from the ruin of the accused."

He leaned forward now, adopting an almost avuncular pose. "You have me at a disadvantage, to be certain, but I am not ashamed of what has transpired between me and that lady. You must not think that my accusations stem from my actions. Indeed, it is precisely the opposite. I first met that lady when I grew concerned about her husband's behavior."

"Again, I must tell you I have seen no just reason for these accusations."

"Hmm. And would you tell me if you did? Pray, don't answer. It is an unfair question, and Mr. Ellershaw is your patron. I know you to be a man of honor, sir, who does not like to betray a man who has helped you. But I beg you to recollect that your true business is to help the Company, not a single man within it. If you should see anything that would indicate that Mr. Ellershaw is not acting within the Company's interest, or perhaps is not capable of so acting, I hope you will come to me. That is the nature of a company, after all."

"I believed the nature of a company was making money regardless of the consequences."

"Nonsense. The word derives from the Latin, *com panis,* signifying the act of baking bread together. That is what we do. We are not individual men seeking our own fortune; rather we are a collective, baking our bread in union."

"I am delighted to learn that we engage in such useful and brotherly activities."

"Now that you have learned, I must beg you not to encourage him with any further nonsense. Blue cloth suits, indeed. Do you believe you shall further your cause here by making him the object of public humiliation?"

"I only made a suggestion. I hardly think it of such great import."

"Then you do not understand how impressionable his mind has become. Or perhaps you do not wish to. Mr. Ellershaw pays you, so you, I suspect, will feel an impulse to inform him of this conversation. I beg you not to do so. It is important you understand that I am not his enemy but the Company's friend, and if he were to believe I conspired against him, the Company would suffer in the ensuing confusion. And you must know I don't conspire against him, I merely work for the good of the Company. Someone must rise to his stature once he is gone."

"And that would be you, I suppose. An interesting thing to say, as he has made no suggestion that he wishes to be gone. Yet you claim to act only out of concern for the Company's interest." I chose to nock my arrow and let it fly. "In whose interest is your congress with his wife?"

To his credit, he did not look away. "Matters of the heart cannot always be controlled by will alone. You are a man, Weaver, and must know that."

I could not but think of Miss Glade, and for a moment I felt a true sympathy for Forester. I soon recollected myself, however, when I considered the death of Carmichael. Whatever sadness of the heart he might feel did not excuse his monstrous schemes. "I have already told you I should not like to be the one to make such a revelation to Mr. Ellershaw. And as to this conversation, I would hate to be the cause of discord within these walls, particularly while I inhabit them myself."

He smiled at me. "You show great wisdom."

"It is not wisdom, merely prudence. I hardly wish to involve myself in matters outside the purview of our bread-baking, despite what Mrs. Ellershaw believes. That lady accused me of involving myself in an inquiry about which I know nothing. What precisely does she think to be Mr. Ellershaw's interest in her daughter?"

He smiled. "You are sly, sir. You tell me you have no interest in the matter, and yet you attempt to trick me into revealing information of the most delicate nature."

"If you do not wish to speak of it, that is of no concern. I may choose to ask Mr. Ellershaw after all."

He half rose. "You must not. I believe Mrs. Ellershaw is wrong, and her husband does not pursue her daughter, but if you speak of this, it may well awaken the sleeping beast of curiosity."

"Then perhaps you should tell me."

He sighed. "I will tell you only this. The girl, Bridget Alton, was Mrs. Ellershaw's daughter by a previous marriage. Truly a striking girl, if I may be permitted to so observe. Very much like her mother—tall, with the whitest skin I have ever observed, and hair so blond as to be nearly white, yet her eyes are of the most remarkably dark brown. It made her most arresting, and we could take her nowhere without men stopping to stare. That she was attached to a family of some importance and possessed a significant settlement only increased her luster. Yet, despite these advantages, she chose to wed without her family's permission. It was one of those sordid clandestine marriages; you know the sort. Mr. Ellershaw, though he would hardly exchange two words with her at table, flew into a rage. He promised to track the girl down and punish her, so Mrs. Ellershaw has made every effort to conceal the girl from her husband's attentions."

"It is a private family matter, then," I proposed. "Nothing to do with the baking of bread."

"Precisely."

I thought it most expedient to act as though I believed him and thus rose and offered him an immediate bow. As I reached for the door, he called me once more.

"How much is it that Mr. Ellershaw pays you?"

"We agreed upon forty pounds a year."

He nodded. "For a man with your varied mode of income, the regularity of payment must be very pleasant."

I paused for a moment. Was he toying with me? Did he have some inkling that Mr. Ellershaw paid me only a fraction of what I might hope to earn if I practiced my usual trade? I had to presume not, so I merely assented and left the room.

I SUPPOSE THE DEVIL was in me, for I did not hesitate upon leaving Forester's office to pay a visit to Mr. Ellershaw. Perhaps I wished to punish the man I believed responsible for Carmichael's death, and perhaps I merely wished to stir up the hornet's nest to see what emerged. No matter, I decided; I had let things stand long enough, and if I were to make progress I would need to make a move, even if it be the wrong one.

I found Ellershaw alone, and he invited me in though he was busy reviewing some lengthy documents and appeared to resent the intrusion. "Yes, yes, what is it?"

I closed his door. "Sir, I have just come from the summons of Mr. Forester."

He looked up from his document. "Yes?"

"I believe, Mr. Ellershaw, he may mean you more harm than you know."

I now had his full attention. "Explain yourself."

"He wished me to confess your schemes and meanings." I took a deep breath. "He warned me from putting my faith in you and—well, sir, he told me you were mad."

"The devil take it!" he shouted, and slammed his hand so hard upon his desk that a bowl of tea rattled and spilled. "Damn you, Weaver, have I asked you to play tattler with my fellow members of the Court? What impudence is this? This damn Court of Proprietors meeting is breathing down my neck, I tell you. I am fighting for my very stature, and you bring me this nonsense!"

I confess his rage at me took me by the greatest surprise. For a moment, I felt the full force of his upbraiding. "I believe," I managed to say, "that you informed me of secret committees plotting against you and the need to discover this prior to the meeting of the Court. Surely Mr. Forester's efforts to undermine your work and reputation—"

"Quiet!" he shouted. "Enough of your palaver. I shan't endure such disloyal talk from a mere underling. If I were in India, I should have you thrown to tigers for what you say. Have you no knowledge of what a company is, what it means to be part of a company?"

"I understand you put much stock in the communal baking of bread," I ventured.

"Go see to your tasks," he said to me, his voice now more quiet, his temper more restrained, though he still appeared as though he might once more roar with the least provocation. "See to your duties and I shall see to mine, and trouble me no more with your theories of secret committees and plots. If you make trouble for me, Weaver, when there is so much to be lost, you will regret it, I promise you. And replace that damned dead man, I tell you. I shan't have any positions unfilled because there's a fool crushed by crates."

And so I was dismissed, that I might contemplate all the errors I had made during the day.

CHAPTER EIGHTEEN

—

*T*HAT NIGHT I MET WITH MR. BLACKBURN AT THE TAVERN OF HIS choosing. It was a neat place with many candles and lamps, in Shadwell near the timber yard, sufficiently far from Craven House for him to believe he was quite safe from discovery there. Inside, an unremarkable selection of middling men—tradesmen, small merchants, even a bespectacled clergyman—took their quiet drinks and meals. Blackburn and I found seats near the fire, for the warmth and because Blackburn explained that any accidental spills would dry more quickly there. Once we had sat, a handsome girl came over and asked us for our orders.

"Who are you?" Blackburn demanded. "Where is Jenny?"

"Jenny ain't well, so I'm here for her."

"That shan't do," Blackburn said. "I want Jenny."

"It must do," the girl answered, "for Jenny's got the flux and so shooting blood out her arse she's not like to live, so you'll have to make do with me, won't you, my sweet?"

"I suppose you will have to suffice," he said, with evident glumness, "but you must let her know I take this most unkindly. Very well, I shall have—damn it, be prepared to listen, I say. I will have a pot of ale, but I must make myself very clear. You are to wash the pot very carefully before I am brought it. Wash it, I say, and dry it with a clean cloth. There must be no dirt upon it, nor any foreign matter in the ale. You are to make very careful inspection before I am brought what I order. Mind me now, girl. If you don't, you'll answer to Mr. Derby."

She turned to me without pausing, as though such odd requests were best dismissed with no comment. "And you, sir?"

"Also a pot," I said. "But I shan't complain, if the amount of dirt is not above the usual."

The girl departed and came back in a few minutes, setting our pots down before us.

Blackburn took no more than a glance at his. "No!" he cried out. "No, no, this will not do! This will not do at all! Look at this, you stupid slut. There is a fingerprint made of grease upon the side of the vessel. Are you blind not to have seen it? Take this filth away and bring me something clean."

"It ain't going to be clean when you're wearing it 'pon your head, now, is it?" she asked.

My cooler temperament recognized her question as belonging to the rhetorical variety, but Mr. Blackburn seemed to take it rather more seriously. "I cannot abide such talk, for the thought of such an assault upon my person is an abomination."

"You're the balmy nation, not me," the girl answered, hands firmly on hips in a well-practiced attitude of sauciness.

This exchange had gathered the attention of the bulk of the room, and now, from the kitchen, came a rather portly man with an apron across his chest, no wig, and a shaved head. He pushed through the crowd and arrived at our table. "What is this? What's the trouble here?"

"Derby, thank Jesus," Blackburn breathed. "This impudent baggage is serving your drink in necessary pots and mixing the contents with night soil."

This struck me as a rather severe exaggeration, but I kept my council.

"He's right mad," the girl said. "It ain't nothing but a finger smear is all."

Derby struck the girl in the head, but not hard. In fact, he hardly hit more than hair and cap, and I knew at once it was for show. "Draw him another," he said, "and be sure it's spotless this time." He turned to Blackburn. "I am sorry about that. Jenny's got the flux, and this girl ain't familiar with your likings."

"I did instruct her," Blackburn said.

Derby held out his hands in a gesture of good-natured frustration. "You know how these girls are. They grow up in filth. You tell them clean, they think so long as it lacks a cat head floating upon the top, it will do. I'll go be sure she understands."

"You must make certain," Blackburn said. "Cleanliness of drinking vessels comes in three stages: the application of soap, the complete and entire removal of soap with clean water, and the drying with a clean cloth. Inside and out, Derby. Inside and out. Make certain she knows this much."

"I shall indeed." The fellow walked away, and Blackburn informed me that Derby was his sister's husband's brother, insinuating so that I could not but understand that the fastidious clerk had helped the publican out on an occasion or two when money had been hard to find. As a result, Derby indulged Blackburn's desires, making his establishment the only one in the metropolis in which Blackburn felt he might safely drink.

"Now, sir," he said, "as to your business, I believe you will find me your servant, and you will have just observed one of the most important principles of the orderly man's trade: the series. Once you inform your interlocutor there are to be three components to your discourse, you have established a series, and a series, sir, is undeniable. Once a man hears the first point, he shall long to hear the remaining ones. It is a principle I have often used to my advantage, and now I share it with you."

I responded with joy that he had been so good as to pass along this wisdom, and I begged to hear more of his philosophy of order. Thus began a long lecture interrupted only by my occasional comments of approbation. Blackburn spoke for well over an hour, and though I believed his notion of the series had some merit, it appeared to be the jewel in his intellectual crown. Rarely did his ideas transcend the matronly dictums of *A place for everything and everything in its place* and *Cleanliness is next to godliness.* Yet it was not only in these platitudes that Blackburn's peculiarity lay. As we talked, he aligned our pots of ale. He removed the contents of his pockets, ordered them, and replaced them. He tugged repeatedly at his sleeves, announcing that there was a formula, a ratio of coat to shirtsleeve, that must be observed at all times.

In short, I began to see what I had already suspected—namely, that if his concern with order was not a form of madness, it was, at the very least, a dangerous preoccupation, perhaps caused by some sort of humoral imbalance. It also became clear to me that when I pressed him for examples of Company errors, he declined to speak any ill of the doings at Craven House. He might well hate disorder when he found it, but his loyalty was fierce. I would have no choice, then, but to loosen his tongue some other way.

I excused myself, telling him I wished to relieve myself but hated to do so in public. I believe he understood and applauded my sentiments and so I left, not to make water but instead to make opportunities.

I entered the kitchen, where I found the serving girl assembling a tray of drinks. "I wish to apologize for my acquaintance's rude behavior before," I said. "He is rather taken with neatness in all things, and I am sure you meant no harm."

The girl curtsied. "You are very kind to say so."

"It is no kindness but only common manners. I would not have you think I approved of his treatment of you. Indeed, I know him from my business, and rather than being a particular friend, he is a kind of rival to me. Tell me, what is your name, my dear?"

"Annie," she said, with another curtsy.

"Annie, if you would offer me a favor, I am certain to reward your kindness."

She looked a bit more skeptical now. "What sort of favor have you in mind, then?"

"My acquaintance is of rather too sober a disposition. He judges his ale too carefully, and yet I should very much like to loosen his tongue. Do you think you might be able to add a bit of gin to his ale? Not so much that he might notice, but enough to give his spirits an encouraging nudge?"

She offered me a sly grin but immediately wiped her face blank. "I don't know, sir. It doesn't seem right to play so upon a gentleman's ignorance."

I held up a shilling. "Now does it seem right?"

She took the coin from my fingers. "It does indeed."

Back at the table the girl brought us our fresh pots. Blackburn and I talked more of indifferent matters, until he finished his tainted ale and began to demonstrate in his speech and movement that the gin was doing its business. I saw I had my opportunity before me. "For a man who has such a profound hatred of disorder, Craven House must be a difficult place to labor."

"At times, at times," he said, a slight slur coming over his words. "There are all sorts of wretched doings there. Papers filed in the wrong place or not at all, expenditures made without proper accounting. Once," he said in a hushed voice, "the night-soil man was murdered upon his way to perform his tasks, and the pots were not emptied that night. The lot of them were content to let their pots sit the next day without emptying. The whole lot of them, a bunch of filthy savages."

"Wretched, wretched," I said. "Is there more?"

"Oh, aye, there is more. More than you would credit. One of the directors, I won't say his name, but I've heard—mind you, I don't know that it's true—but I've heard he uses his shirttails to clean himself and then just goes about his business with them, all soiled as they are."

"But surely all of the Company men cannot be so terrible."

"All of them? No, not so terrible as that."

The girl came and took away our emptied pots, replacing them with fresh. She offered me a sprightly wink, so as to inform me she had plied the same trick with this as she had the last.

"I think that strumpet likes me," Blackburn said. "You saw that wink, did you not?"

"I saw it."

"Aye, she likes me. But I'd not lie next to that, not unless I could see her take a bath first. Oh, I like to watch a woman bathe, Mr. Weaver. That's what I like best of all."

While he drank, he continued to inform me of other crimes against hygiene. I allowed this to continue while he consumed the better part of his fortified drink, but hearing the slur in his voice grow increasingly more pronounced, and suspecting that the conversation might soon escape my ability to shape its contours, I pushed forward, I hoped not too forcefully. "What of other matters? What of the slovenliness you implied in areas beyond personal grooming? Matters of accounting."

"Accounting errors, indeed. Rampant, is what that is. Everywhere and all the time. You'd think they were possessed of invisible servants, magical ghosts to clean up their little messes, the way they act. And not always errors," he said, with an unmistakable twinkle.

"Oh?"

"Indeed, your very own man—but I say too much."

"You say too much not to continue. It would be the most cruel form of torment not to finish your thought. As we are friends, you must go on."

"Just so, just so. I take your point. It is like the series, is it not? Once begun, it must be concluded. I believe you have learned that lesson now."

"I have. And you must tell me more."

"You press me strongly," he observed.

"And you demur like a coquette, I think," I said, as good-naturedly as I could. "Surely you don't want to leave me upon the rack."

"Of course not. No, I suppose I may tell you a bit more." He cleared his throat. "Your patron—whose name I shan't mention for one cannot be too safe—once approached me with a scheme to liberate from the books a considerable sum for his own use. It was a scheme he had already managed, so he said, with the cashier general, and he required my assistance in disguising the sum from the eyes of posterity. He had some tale of its being for an important Company project, but as he could say no more than that, I knew at once that the project was surely gaming or whoring. Needless to say, I denied him."

"Why so?"

"Why indeed? In part because it would be a unspeakable crime to make free with the books. But there is another aspect to cooperation I found most instructive. The former cashier general, a fellow called Horner, aided your patron one too many times for his continued presence to remain comfortable. He therefore found his loyalty rewarded with an assignment to toil his remaining days in Bombay. To avoid such favors, I eschewed being so faithful a servant. I do not believe the Indies would agree with me."

"But what of this missing sum? Did Ellershaw do without?"

"Oh, no. I found the sum missing soon enough. A rather gross effort was made to cover the trail, but it could not fool me."

"Did you speak out?"

"In a company where loyalty is rewarded with exile to the most monstrous clime on earth, I hardly wished to evidence disloyalty. Rather, I took the opportunity to disguise the effort so well that no one else could ever find it. I would not willingly commit a crime, sir, but I saw no harm in smoothing things over once the crime had taken place."

I nodded thoughtfully. "Such entertaining tales!" I exclaimed. "Surely there must be more."

"Well," he said, "there *has* been a thing or two I haven't liked before now—before this Greene House affair, as I style it—but I can't say much on things of the past."

"I beg you tell me."

He shook his head.

I decided the time had come for a strategic disregard of Mr. Cobb's orders that I must inquire into the death of Absalom Pepper, yet never speak his name. He had said I must not raise the subject myself, but my interlocutor was now growing disoriented with spirits, and I believed I could disguise the matter should it come to that.

"Do you speak of the Pepper business?" I asked him.

His skin turned pale and his eyes widened. "What do you know of that?" he asked quietly. "Who told you?"

"Who told me?" I said with a laugh. "Why, it is common knowledge."

He now gripped the sides of the table. "Common knowledge? Common knowledge, you say? Who has been speaking? How did he learn of it? Oh, I am ruined, undone."

"Calm yourself, Mr. Blackburn, I pray you," I said. "There must be some misunderstanding here. I do not see why mention of the importation of pepper should cause you such distress."

"Pepper?" he said. "The spice?"

"Yes. I meant only that I believed the East India Company once traded nearly exclusively in pepper, and the change to textiles and teas must have been a true feat of organizational skills."

He let go of the table. "Oh. Of course." He took a hearty gulp of his ale.

I knew that now was my moment and I a fool if I did not seize it. "Yes, I meant only the spice, sir. Nothing but the spice." I leaned backward, letting my shoulders rest against the wall. "But tell me, pray. Whatever did you believe me to mean?"

NOW WAS THE MOMENT of greatest risk, I believed. I played a dangerous game, and I hardly knew the rules. He might realize I had deceived him, tricked him into an admission of knowledge—though of what, I was still ignorant—and turn against me. Or he might be drawn in.

He shook his head. "I am sorry," he said. "It is of no moment."

"No moment?" I returned, in as jovial a tone as I could muster. "No moment, you say? Why, you appeared monstrous distressed, sir."

"It is nothing, I tell you."

I leaned forward. "Come now, Mr. Blackburn," I said softly. "We trust each other, and you have sparked my curiosity. You can tell me what you believed me to reference."

He took another sip of his ale. I cannot say why he decided to speak—whether it was the spirits, the feeling of solidarity, or the belief that, as the matter was half revealed, it might as well be fully uncovered, that it could be better hidden away. I can only say that he took a deep breath and set down his pot. "There is a widow."

"What widow?"

"Not five or six months past, I received a sealed letter, marked with the imprint of the Court of Committees. The letter contained not a single name of a single director but only the seal of the Court itself. And it said I was to oversee an annuity to a widow—a hundred and twenty pounds a year, it was—and I wasn't to mention it to anyone, not even on the Court, for it was a great secret that the Company's enemies would use against us. Indeed, the letter informed me that, should this matter become public, I would lose my position. I had no reason to doubt the veracity of this threat. The payment, after all, was overseen by the same Horner, his last act as cashier general before he was shipped off to his Asiatic hell. Any fool might see that I was, through no fault of my own, at the center of a momentous and secret undertaking, and I had no choice but to comply if I hoped to avoid a most terrible fate."

"The widow's name was Pepper?"

Mr. Blackburn licked his lips and looked away. He swallowed hard of nothing, and then he swallowed hard of his pot. "Yes. Her name is Mrs. Absalom Pepper."

Despite my best efforts and two more pots of supplemented ale, I could not contrive for Mr. Blackburn to give me much more information. All he knew with any certainty was that Mrs. Pepper was a widow whose upkeep the Court of Committees had chosen to support. She lived in the village of Twickenham, just outside of London, where she had a house in the newly constructed Montpelier Row. Beyond that, he knew nothing—nothing but that her situation was unique and inexplicable. The Company paid no such annuities, not even to directors. Pepper appeared to have had no connection with the East India Company whatsoever, yet they regularly sent his widow a handsome allotment and regarded the matter as being of the most delicate variety.

I continued to press as forcefully as I dared, but it soon became apparent that I had reached the limits of his knowledge. Yet here was the path that would lead to the secretmost desire of Cobb's heart and very possibly to the freedom of my friends. I did not dare hope that I might soon be free of this troublesome enterprise, but perhaps I could use the discovery of Absalom Pepper, once I had learned something, as a means of alleviating the burdens set upon my uncle.

By the time I concluded my interrogation, Mr. Blackburn was too inebriated to make his own way home—quite near too inebriated to stand, in fact. I placed him in a hackney and sent him on his way, reasonably hopeful that the coachman would do as I had paid him and not merely rob the poor fellow.

Though I had myself taken a bellyful of drink and was not the most clearheaded, the hour was not yet late and I thought I might still pay a visit to Mr. Cobb and inform him of this latest intelligence. I first needed to think matters through and determine if such was my best course, so I returned inside to sit by the fire of the tavern and sip the remains of my final pot. As I did so, I thought better of such an excursion, for I regained enough of my senses to recall that I did not work for Mr. Cobb any more than I worked for Mr. Ellershaw. I worked for myself, and my primary employment was to disentangle myself from this opaque web. I would say nothing for so long as I could.

I called over the pliable young Annie and requested a pen and some paper, and then I wrote two notes. The first was to Mr. Ellershaw, explaining that I should not be at Craven House the next day, for I had been laid low—inspired by the plight of the unfortunate serving girl—with a bloody flux. When a man has a cold or a debilitating ache of one sort or another, he often invites unwanted unsolicited medical advice, so I pretended to a more unpleasant ailment, believing it would preclude further inquiry on his part.

My second note was to Elias Gordon, asking that he meet me in such a way that our movements could not be observed. I gave these missives, along with another coin, to Annie, who promised that the kitchen boy would run them immediately.

It was then that I caught, if only fleetingly, the eye of a smallish fellow of middle years who sat huddled in the far corner. I had seen him upon my entrance and thought nothing of him, and I would have thought nothing of him now, except that in the instant he looked away from me he looked toward Annie. It might have been of no moment, mere tavern curiosity, but my suspicions were now aroused and I performed a subtle examination of this man.

He was dressed in a disheveled brown suit, and his old outdated wig shed like a sick lapdog upon the tattered shoulders of his coat. He wore small spectacles halfway down his nose; I could not tell much of the cast of his face because of the poor lighting, yet from what I did observe he seemed nothing so much as a poor scholar. It was entirely possible that the man was an agent of some force or other and merely used the visage of an impecunious university man as a disguise. I must also consider the possibility that the man was no more than he appeared and that circumstances had conspired to make me overly uneasy.

This option sat ill with me, however, for the scholar held open before him an open octavo of black binding, at which he spent most of his time glancing. A man could avail himself of far superior lighting than where he had lodged himself, and even a man whose eyes wanted no spectacles should have a hard time reading amid the gloom this man inhabited. I could not but conclude that he was a spy, though for Cobb or the Company or some other power, I could not say.

I therefore elected to remain where I was. If he wished to follow me when I departed the tavern, I could certainly take my chances. I would either lose him entire or he would follow me back to my lodgings with no harm done. But if he rose and attempted to stop the boy, I would have to follow, because I could not allow my letters, particularly the one to Elias, to fall into the hands of some unknown enemy.

Once more, I called Annie over, and bade her bend down low and close, and I set a hand upon her inviting bottom. "Laugh," I said, "as though I had just said something of the greatest amusement."

To my great surprise, she let out a laugh without further question.

"Now, pray don't turn around, but there is a bookish sort of fellow in the far corner. Do you know who I mean?"

"What's this about, then?"

"It's about you earning another shilling."

"Oh, all right then. Aye, he's been here all night, that one. Same as you."

"And what's he been drinking?"

"Nothing but milk, if you can credit such a thing. A grown man, him, drinking milk with no bread, like he was a child."

I could believe it indeed. The boy to whom I had entrusted the letters no doubt had other chores to complete before setting out, but I now saw him leave the tavern. In an instant, the scholar rose to follow. I waited a moment, until he was just stepping past the door, and, even as I put another piece of silver in the girl's hand, I took to my feet and after the sham academician.

When I came out to Market Hill, the scholar was already coming up hard by the boy. The ground was hard with packed snow and I should hate to have to run upon it, but run I would, if it were required.

"Hold there," the scholar called after the boy. "Hold there, my fine young man. A word with you, and a reward for it too."

The boy turned to look and saw, instead of a smiling and harmless fellow, a pained face as I struck the man in the back of his head and sent him down into the muddy street.

"He meant you no good, but only injury," I told the boy. "Go deliver your messages. I'll take care of this rascal."

The boy continued to stare, however, fascinated by the raree-show before him, but, the villain being quite incapacitated, I thought little of the delay. The scholar, for his part, was in discomfort and disoriented but still quite alert. I stood over him, putting one of my shoes upon his hand so he would not be tempted to rise. Though I offered no instructions, he quickly observed that any movement he made met the response of added pressure.

"Now, sir, tell me for whom you work."

"It is an abominable thing to strike a man of the universities. Once the world learns this crime was done by a Jew, there shall be terrible consequences for your fellows."

"And how would you happen to know I'm a Jew?"

The scholar said nothing.

"Whether you are a man of one of the universities or no is not my concern. It is my concern that you have been observing me and that you meant to stop that boy from delivering my correspondence. Now, will you tell me who employs you?"

"I shan't tell you anything."

As it happened, I believed him, nor did I particularly think that knowing it was Cobb or Ellershaw or anyone else would much change my plans, so rather than try to force him to speak, I knocked his head against the ground until he was unconscious. I then searched his things and found little except for a ten pound note issued by the very same goldsmith whose notes Cobb used to pay me.

I looked up and saw the boy had not yet departed but stood still in fear. "Give me the notes," I said. "If there's one villain about, there may be another. I shall arrange to have them delivered differently."

The boy gave the notes to me and ran off, leaving me alone in the street. I held them in one hand and continued to stare at the still form of the scholar, wondering if I had lost my temper too soon with him and whether he might have had more to tell me. The subject was perhaps moot, however, for in an instant I felt a hand upon the back of my head, pushing me hard into the snow and sludge of the road. I went down, though not hard, and recovered myself in a moment, though a moment too late. When I looked up I saw the figure of a man running off with my notes in hand.

IN AN INSTANT I was on my feet and after the thief, but he had already gained a considerable advantage. I could see him far ahead, a bulky man who moved with improbable grace. I, on the other hand, having years before broken my leg most severely, could not run with the same speed, and I feared that, despite the most diligent effort and my determination to ignore the pain of my old wound, the villain would escape.

He turned and ran to Virginia Planter Hill and was about to enter upon the Shadwell, which I considered a stroke of good fortune. The street was wide and well lighted but would be largely deserted this time of night and I might have some small chance of overtaking him there.

As I struggled to gain upon him, or at the least not lose him entire, he ran onto Shadwell but in an instant threw himself back, nearly toppling over, as a speeding phaeton barreled past him, its driver shouting an insult at the man he almost destroyed.

Now again on his feet, he crouched like a great cat, and when another phaeton had nearly passed him, he leaped out and into it, giving the driver cause to let out a startled cry, just audible over the trample of hooves and the roar of wheels. What manner of man, I wondered, is so reckless with his life that he would attempt to leap into a speeding phaeton? It enraged me, for his having done so necessitated that I do the same.

I redoubled my efforts for speed as another phaeton passed, and another yet; it seemed to be as many as eight or ten involved in this race. Reaching Shadwell just as the straggler of the group came upon me, I was determined not to lose it. In the dark I could see it was green with gold stripes, one in the symbol of a serpent. I had just time enough to realize that this was the same machine that had run down Elias's accuser some days ago, a man who would have run down a child if not for that worthy's intervention. The phaeton was driven by a self-absorbed coxcomb, a man who considered his foolish race more important than human life. And he must be my companion, for I hurled myself in the air, hoping most earnestly to land inside and not be caught under his wheels.

In that, at least, I was successful. I landed hard in the phaeton, crashing into the driver, who let out a little shriek.

"What madness is this?" he demanded, his wide eyes reflecting the light of street lanterns.

I stood quickly and took the reins from him. "You are a fool, a monster, and a poor driver as well," I said. "Now be quiet lest I shove you out."

I spurred the horse hard with the whip and discovered it was capable of greater speed than its owner would allow. The man suffered, I saw, not from a lack of power but a lack of courage, for as the horse increased in its velocity he let out another little shriek.

"Slow down!" he cried, in a voice that cracked like dropped crystal. "You'll kill us!"

"I observed you run down a man a fortnight ago and respond with nothing more than a laugh," I called to him, making myself heard above the hooves and the rush of cold air. "I hardly think you deserving of mercy."

"What do you want?"

"To overtake another man," I said. "And, if time permits, to punish you."

I raced hard and recklessly, urging the horse on to speeds most unsafe, but I had little choice. I passed one of the other phaetons, whose driver looked upon me and the cringing man at my side with the greatest confusion. I passed another after that, and then a third. If I had a mind to, I thought, I might win this race.

Ahead of me, the phaetons turned the corner onto Old Gravel Lane and slowed accordingly. If I were to overtake my letters, however, I would have to set aside my concern for safety, so I slowed hardly at all as we turned. As the phaeton turned up on one side, I clutched the reins with one hand, reached out with the other, and grabbed my unhappy passenger, pushing him toward the elevated side of the conveyance. This had little effect, but little was enough, for though we came close, we did not tip. In the process of rounding the turn, we passed three more of the racers, so that there were now only three ahead of us.

The horse appeared to be as excited as I that we had survived my foolish maneuver, and it found more reserves from which to draw as we began to close on the remaining racers. As we narrowed the gap, I saw that it was not the lead phaeton but the one behind it that contained two men. Knowing I would do what was required to stop it, I hit the reins again, hoping the horse would obey—or could obey, for that matter. I knew not what capabilities the horse yet possessed, but while the first phaeton increased its lead, the one with two men began to slow, so that I raced alongside it. I moved us closer, and though it changed with each bumpy instant, the space between us varied from as much as four feet to as little as two.

The men in the opposing phaeton shouted at me, but I could not hear them and had no desire to take time to try to understand. With the cold wind blowing hard against my face, I once more put the reins in my left hand and reached down with my right, hoisting the coward to his feet.

"Take the reins," I shouted, so he might understand me. "Keep as close to him as you can. If you fail or defy me you shall answer for it. If I wish, I can find you by the marks on your phaeton, and I promise you do not want me to come looking."

He nodded. Once too afraid to drive recklessly, now too afraid not to, he took the reins and attempted to hold the horse steady. I crept toward the edge of the phaeton, bracing myself as best I could. I knew I ought not to try it. The two phaetons moved too rapidly, the distance between them changing each instant. I have done many foolish things over the course of my life, I thought, but nothing so foolish as this endeavor, destined to fail, destined to end in my destruction. And yet if I did not do it the enemy would escape with my notes, and he would know far more than I wished him to know. I could not let my schemes turn to dust and see my uncle in debtor's prison, so I sucked in a breath of air and leaped into the void.

Why I did not die, trampled under hoof and wheel, remains a mystery, but somehow, at the very moment of my leaping, my phaeton lurched toward the other, giving me extra power, and the other lurched toward mine, giving me less distance to cross, and so it was that I landed hard in the conveyance alongside, crashing hard into the man holding the reins.

I presumed him to be the letter thief and knocked him aside, grabbing the reins and forcing the animal into as sudden a stop as I might contrive. Only by bracing my feet against the bottom did I keep myself from flying forward. My fellow passengers were not so well prepared, however, and they went flying from the machine.

It was again thanks only to the ordering of providence that neither was trampled by the other racers, and it was owing only to the callousness of these men that none of the other contestants thought to stop and help their fellows. Once the horse had ceased its motions, I jumped out and ran back some twenty feet to find the two men huddled close together by the side of the road. A crowd had gathered to jeer at them, having no love for phaetoneers.

They appeared pathetic and bloodied but to my best guess not seriously hurt. However, I did not know how long that state would last.

I reached into my pocket and pulled out a pistol. A light snow had begun to fall, and I feared that even such moisture as that might ruin my ability to fire, but I hoped that in their state they would not think of such things. "Which one of you stole my papers?" I demanded.

"It wasn't us," one of them shouted.

"It was one of you. Yours was the only phaeton with two men aboard. Now, who was it?"

"It wasn't us," the other one echoed. "He's telling you the truth. The other fellow was as strong as Hercules. He tossed me from my phaeton into Johnny's, here. We tried to tell you. If you hadn't ruined everything, we'd have caught him."

Silently I replaced my pistol, hardly able to believe I had gone to such lengths for nothing. I had risked my life to stop the wrong carriage, and now the villain had escaped with my letters.

"He was a Hercules!" The man repeated, wiping the blood from his nose with his lace sleeve. "A great black-skinned Hercules with scars upon his face. I've never seen anyone like him."

I had. I had seen someone like him far too recently, and before this affair was over, I would make Aadil pay. In the meantime, he knew far too many of my secrets and he had got the better of me, and I knew not which upset me more.

—

CHAPTER NINETEEN

*T*HE MESSAGE SENT TO ELLERSHAW WAS OF NO CONSEQUENCE, BUT the information that I intended to meet with Elias was of far greater moment. I had to make a decision. My enemy knew what I planned, which thus far was not much. Did I lie back and wait, in hopes of catching him at his tricks, or did I strike first and thereby hope to gain the upper hand? Had I the twin luxuries of time and freedom I might have opted for the former, but I could not be away from Craven House as long as I wished, and therefore chose the latter option. I would act on the information I had gained by meeting with Blackburn, and in doing so I would hope that primacy of acquisition afforded me some advantage. I therefore sent my messages again, more successfully, and attempted to get what little sleep I could.

The next morning, after taking great pains to see that no one followed me, I took an early coach to Twickenham, a journey of some two hours, and then waited two hours more in a public house for the second coach to arrive, this one carrying Elias. It was certainly possible that an enterprising villain would have someone keeping an eye on my friend, and as Elias would not be quite so quick as I to observe such a person, I thought it safest if we did not travel together. Once he walked into the tavern, I felt reasonably certain that we had arrived safely.

He insisted upon a meal and a few drafts of beer to help shake off the lethargy of the journey, and once he had satisfied himself we asked directions and headed for the home of Mrs. Absalom Pepper. Everyone was familiar with the new homes on the graciously tree-lined Montpelier Row, and we found her with little difficulty.

Here our journey required some luck, for I had not sent a note ahead, and there were no guarantees that Mrs. Pepper would not be out upon visits, or making purchases, or on a journey for all I knew. But these anxieties, to my relief, were unfounded. Heloise Pepper was indeed home. Our knock was met by a quiet and unattractive girl of some sixteen or seventeen years who suffered from plain equine features and disfiguring scars from the smallpox. She led us into a sitting room, where we were soon met by a handsome woman of some twenty-five years, dressed in widow's weeds, to be sure, but rarely has anyone donned the garb of mourning to greater advantage. The black of her attire was offset by the matching raven hues of her hair, arranged in a comely if slightly disarrayed bun, and through the darkness of cloth and tresses shone a face of porcelain and bright eyes of a remarkable mix of green and brown.

Elias and I both presented our most polite bows, his deeper than mine, for he offered her the very special bow he reserved for pretty widows with large annuities.

"My name is Benjamin Weaver and this is my associate, Elias Gordon, a noted surgeon of London." I added that fact in the hopes she would think we were here upon some medical matter. "I pray you forgive the intrusion, but we have rather urgent business, and it is our hope that you will be willing to answer some questions concerning your late husband."

Her face brightened considerably, and her color rose with pleasure. It was as though she had been waiting, hoping against hope, that someday strangers might knock upon her door wishing to ask about her husband. And now, here we were.

Yet there was a hesitation too. A calculated caution, as though she had to remind herself to be careful, the way a child must remind himself to fear the fire. "What do you wish to speak of regarding my dear sweet Absalom?" she asked. She held to her chest a coat that she was in the process of mending, but I observed that she now gathered it in a bundle and appeared to rock it as though it were an infant.

"I know his death must be painful for you, madam," I continued.

"You cannot know, sirs," she said. "No one who wasn't married to him could know what it is to lose him—my Absalom, the best of men. I can tell you as much as that. If that is what you wish to know—was he the best of men?—then you have your answer. He was."

"Indeed, the nature of the man is part of what we wished to ascertain," Elias offered, "but not the whole."

Cleverly done, I could not help but silently observe. In so praising the man and hinting at some purpose designed to celebrate his grandeur, Elias had effectively flung wide the gates for inquiry.

"You gentlemen must be seated," she said, gesturing to her moderately appointed sitting room. The furnishings were not the best, but they were neat and well looked after. She then asked the dour serving girl to bring us some refreshment, which turned out, much to Elias's pleasure, to be a sprightly wine.

I took a small sip but no more. I had already had my fill of drink and did not wish to allow my thinking to become clouded. "Madam, what can you tell us of your late husband, of your lives together?"

"My Absalom," she said, rather dreamily. She set down her glass so there would be nothing spilled by the force of her sigh. "You know, my father did not wish me to marry him. He could not see him as I did."

"And how did you see him?" Elias managed, setting aside his wine for a moment.

"As beautiful. My mother saw it, mind you, but she also wished me not to marry him, for she was jealous of his beauty. Absalom was the most beautiful man there ever was, and he was full of kindness and goodness. My father said he only wanted to marry me for my dowry, and it's true that the money didn't last long, but only because Absalom had great dreams."

"What sort of dreams?" I inquired.

She smiled at me in a way both tender and pitying, a smile a clergyman might give to a simpleton who had inquired of the nature of God. "He was to make us rich," she said.

"In what way?"

"Why, with his thoughts," she informed us. "He was always thinking, always working something out upon his papers. And surely he must have had some important thoughts, for that is why I have the annuity. Even my father would be impressed by it, if he would but speak with me, but he has not endured a word from my lips since Absalom lost the dowry money. Then all he said was that he knew this and would have told me that, but surely Absalom was right and he can look down with forgiveness from heaven."

"As it happens," Elias said, "it is in part because of this annuity that we have come to see you."

The smile dropped from her face. "I see what this is then. But I must tell you gentlemen that I have no shortage of suitors already, and none are wanted. A widow with an annuity is like an untended sweet-meat for the flies, if you will pardon me for being so blunt, but I am not here to be picked at. I have been married to Absalom Pepper, you see, and I cannot endure the thought of being married to another. I know how you gentlemen are. You think an annuity that goes only to a widow is money wasted. To me it is a celebration of Absalom's life and spirit, sirs, and I shan't see it soiled by giving my hand to another."

"You quite misunderstand us," I offered in a hurry. "Though I cannot blame any man for seeking your attention, annuity or no, such is not our business. We are here to discuss the business of the annuity, madam. You see, we wish to know of its origination."

Here the beatific glow of self-satisfaction, the radiant power of one who has touched the hem of a saint, dissolved at once. "Do you mean to say there is some difficulty? I was assured that the annuity would last for the duration of my years. It is not right that it should change now, sir. It is not right, and you may depend upon it. One of my suitors is a man of the bar, and though he has no chance of winning my favor, I know he will go to any lengths to serve me. I promise you, he shall see to it that no crime of this sort is countenanced."

"I do beg your pardon," Elias cut in. "I regret to have given you cause for alarm. My associate meant nothing of the sort. We have no power over your annuity and wish you no harm on that head. We merely wished to see if you could explain why you are entitled to it. Why has this money been settled upon you?"

"Why?" she asked, growing ever more agitated. "Why? Why should it not? Is that not the way of the silk weavers?"

"The silk weavers?" I burst out, though I knew I should have held my tongue. "What has this matter to do with them?"

"What has it *not* to do with them?" Mrs. Pepper retorted.

"Madam," Elias cut in, "we were under the impression that your annuity originated with the East India Company."

She stared as though we had offered her the gravest insult imaginable. "Why ever would the East India Company pay an annuity to me? What had Mr. Pepper to do with such men as those?"

I had thought to say this was what I hoped she could tell us, and I believe the words were upon Elias's lips as well, but he too refrained. What, after all, could be gained by asking a question so obviously answered?

"Madam, we are clearly operating under a false impression," Elias said. "Can you tell me whence the annuity does come?"

"I told you, didn't I? It's the silk weavers' guild. After Mr. Pepper died, they sent a man to me who said that, as Absalom was a member of the guild and as I was his widow, I was entitled to a death benefit. You must swear you ain't taking it away."

"Allow me to explain," I said. "You see, madam, we represent the Seahawk Insurance Office, and there was a clerical error with one of our claims relating to the East India Company. I will work with all my efforts to make certain the claim does not come into jeopardy, you understand. It is merely a matter of remaining orderly with the records. In any event, we believed the annuity came through the Company, but our records may be even more confused than we thought. Let me assure you that nothing you say will harm the security of the annuity. You can only aid us in better organizing our management of it."

Now she appeared somewhat mollified. She took from her breast a locket and studied the picture inside, a picture of her late husband I could not doubt. After whispering a word or two in the jewel's direction and placing a loving finger upon the image, she replaced it and turned to us. "Very well. I shall try and help you."

"I thank you," I said. "Now, if I understand you, you say this annuity is part of a common benefit provided for members of the silk weavers' guild?"

"That is what I was told," she said.

The very notion stretched the boundaries of the absurd. One hundred and twenty pounds a year for the widow of a silk weaver? Such men were lucky to earn twenty or thirty pounds a year, and while I knew the linen men formed combinations and looked after one another, they had no guild that I had ever heard of. It was good for me, however, that I had a contact among their number, the very same Devout Hale whose riotous impulses I had put to work in first getting me inside the East India Company. I could only hope he would be able to serve me once more—this time with information.

"Just so the matter may have no more confusion," I said, "your husband was a silk weaver in London. Is that right?"

"That's right. Aren't you one as well? You said you were a weaver, did you not?"

I chose to disregard the question and allow her to continue with her misunderstanding. "Madam, you must know what your husband earned in his trade. Did it not surprise you that he would have a death benefit worth so many times his annual income?"

"Oh, he would never discuss anything so base as money," she said. "I only knew that he earned enough for us to live well. My father persisted in his belief that a silk worker was no better than a porter, but did not my Absalom buy me clothes and jewels and nights at the theater? A porter indeed."

"There are many degrees and levels of expertise among the silk workers, of course," I said. "Perhaps you could tell me more of the capacity in which Mr. Pepper worked in the silk weaving trade, so I might—"

"He was a silk worker," she said, with brusque finality, as though I somehow soiled his name by making such inquiries. And then, with a lighter tone, "He would not trouble me by speaking of his labors. He knew he did rough work, but what of it? It earned our bread, more than our share for our happiness."

"As to the East India Company," I said, "you know of no connection with your husband?"

"None. But as I said, I did not pry into matters of business. It would not have been seemly. You say there is no danger to my annuity?"

Though I hated to cause so agreeable a lady distress, I knew I had no choice but to present myself as her ally against possible attack, for if I wished to speak to her again, I wanted her to speak with eagerness and honesty. "I hope there will be no danger, and I can assure you I will do all in my power to make certain you continue to receive the sum."

ON THE COACH on the way back, Elias and I spoke in quiet voices, for we shared the vehicle with two older tradesmen of unusually severe countenance. They smoked me for a Jew almost at once and spent the bulk of the trip staring malevolently. On occasion, one of them would turn to his companion and say something along the lines of, "Do you like sharing a coach with a Hebrew?"

"I never love it," his friend would respond.

"It does not answer," the first would say. "It is a low way to travel, indeed."

They would then return to their malevolent staring until enough time had passed to engage in another terse exchange.

After perhaps three or four of these exchanges, I turned to the gentlemen. "I make it my habit never to toss from a moving coach a man who is above forty-five years of age, but each time you open your mouths, you cushion that scruple by approximately five years. By my calculations, and based upon your appearance, the next time you speak so rudely, I will be fully empowered to toss you without a second thought. And as for the coachman, you need not worry about his interfering. A few coins will answer his concerns, and as you know, we Hebrews have no shortage of the ready."

Though it was unlikely that I would actually throw a man hard by seventy years onto the road, the threat of such a punishment rendered these wits silent. Indeed, they appeared thereafter reluctant even to glance at us, which made conversation somewhat easier.

"Heloise and Absalom," Elias mused, directing my attention once more to the matter at hand. "It is a most unpropitious conflation of names, and a poem I should hate to read."

"Mrs. Pepper hardly seemed to note the evil omens, so enchanted was she with her late husband."

"One wonders what sort of man he must have been," Elias mused. "Indeed, beyond his personal charms, I cannot think why the Company would pay his widow so handsomely."

"It seems to me rather obvious," I said. "They have done something horrific, and they wish to keep the widow quiet."

"A fine theory," Elias agreed, "but there is a problem with it. You see, if the Company had offered her ten or twenty or even thirty pounds a year, the story of a guild annuity might have been creditable. But one hundred and twenty? Even blinded by an inflated sense of her late husband's worth, as is surely the case, the widow cannot truly believe that such beneficence is standard. So if the Company has somehow engineered the death of that fellow, why would it behave now in such a way as to draw attention to the very irregularity of it?"

His question was a good one, and I had no easy answer. "Perhaps the Company's crime is so great that it favors a smothering benevolence to any masquerade of veracity. Perhaps the widow knows this guild is not the source but wishes to perpetuate the fiction of Mr. Pepper's superiority to all other men."

Elias mulled upon the notion but had no sound conclusions, and we agreed that we would see no logic of it until we were able to learn more.

BACK IN LONDON, I sought out Devout Hale, for he, I hoped, could clarify the role played by Pepper among the silk weavers, but I could find no trace of him at his usual haunts. I left word everywhere and then returned home, where I found none other than the duck-faced Edgar awaiting me. Many of his wounds had begun to heal, though his eye remained blackened and, of course, the gaps remained where his teeth once stood.

"I'd like a word with you in your rooms," he said.

"And I'd like you to leave," I countered.

"I won't, and you can attempt to shove me off if you like, but I suspect you don't want to draw attention to yourself in your own neighborhood."

He had the right of it, so I reluctantly permitted him to come in, where he informed me that Mr. Cobb had reliably heard that I had not attended Craven House that day. "The word is that you claim ailment, but you look quite well to me. I see no sign of blood flowing from your arse."

"Perhaps you would care for a closer inspection."

He made no response.

"I was indisposed," I now attempted, "but I have begun to feel better, and I went for a walk in the hopes of clearing my head."

"Mr. Cobb wishes me to assure you that no clever tricks will work upon him. You'll be at Craven House on the morrow, sir, or he'll know why. You may depend on it."

"You've delivered your message. Now be off with you."

"Mr. Cobb also commands that I ask if you have grown any closer to discovering aught of the name he gave you."

"No, I have learned nothing." I knew well how to look like the very model of veracity when telling the greatest of lies. I had no concerns of having betrayed myself by my demeanor, but if Aadil worked for Cobb, and the somewhat veiled contents of my message had been understood, it was possible that my enemy had spoken with the Widow Pepper and knew what I knew. Possible, I thought, but unlikely. I knew not what Aadil was nor to what end his allegiances stretched, but I did not believe they were to Cobb.

"It had better be so," Edgar said. "If he learns that you withhold information, there will be terrible consequences, and you'll have cause to regret them. I don't doubt it, and neither should you."

"Get on with you then. I've heard your message."

Edgar did, indeed, depart. I was both relieved and disappointed to have an encounter with him that did not conclude with violence.

I HAD THOUGHT MY DAY ended and indulged myself in a glass of port by my fire, attempting, as best I could, to think of nothing—to forget the day's events, revelations, and questions, that I might better prepare my mind for sleep. It may well be that I dozed off in my chair, but this slumber was abbreviated by a knock upon the door. My landlady informed me that there was a boy below with a message, and he believed its contents could not wait.

With some consternation I arose, angry that what little quiet in which I might indulge had been so destroyed, but when I descended the stairs I saw at once that the boy was of the Hebrew nation. I recognized him from my uncle's warehouse, and by the reddening of his eyes I knew without looking what his note said. I nevertheless took it with a trembling hand and read its contents.

It came from my aunt, written in her native Portuguese, for in her hour of despair her uncertain English had perhaps abandoned her. And it said what I most feared. My uncle's pleurisy had struck him another blow, and from this one he had not recovered. It came hard and fast, and though for an hour he had struggled most heartily to breathe, his strength could not match the power of the affliction. He was dead.

———

chapter twenty

WILL SPARE THE READER AND MYSELF FROM THE SCENES OF SADNESS I was forced to endure. I will say only that by the time I reached the house, much of the neighborhood was already in attendance, and the ladies of her acquaintance labored to give my aunt what little comfort can be had in such times. My uncle had been ailing, yes, and his days had plainly been limited, but I now understood that my aunt had never believed the end to be imminent. Eventual, certainly, and more quickly than she would have considered just, but not this year, or the next, or, perhaps, the one after. And now her great friend and protector and companion, the father of their lost son, was now himself lost. Though I have many times been despondent in my solitude, I cannot say that I have ever been so alone as she was without her husband.

The men of the burial society had already sequestered my uncle's body to prepare it by washing and then placing the lifeless form in a burial shroud. One of these men, I knew, would by custom be asked to stand guard to the body, that it might not be left alone at any time. It has ever been our custom that the body be buried quickly, within a day if possible, and after making inquiries I learned that arrangements had already been made by several of my uncle's associates, including Mr. Franco. A representative of the Ma'amad, the ruling council of the synagogue, informed us that the funeral would be scheduled for eleven the following morning.

I sent a note to Mr. Ellershaw, informing him that I would be absent from Craven House the next day and explaining the reason. Mindful of

Edgar's warning, I sent a note to Mr. Cobb, informing him as well. I would be indisposed for the next day or two, I told him, and given that I believed his actions had accelerated my uncle's decline, I advised that he would be wise not to trouble me.

The long night somehow passed. Mourners faded away, and I remained in the house, along with several of my aunt's closest friends. I begged Mr. Franco to stay but he declined, saying he was too new to the family's friendship and had no wish to impose himself.

As has ever been the custom, friends brought food the next morning, though my aunt ate little, partaking only of some thinned wine and a piece of bread. Her friends aided her in dressing, and together we walked to the magisterial Bevis Marks synagogue, that great monument to the efforts of Portuguese Jews to establish a true home in London.

Though she was in the horizonless darkness of grief, I must believe that it was some consolation for my aunt to see how full that building was with mourners. My uncle had made no small number of friends among our community, but here too were members of the Tudesco race and even English merchants. If there is one feature of Christian worship I admire, it is that women and men are suffered to sit together, and never have I more lamented our synagogue's separation of the sexes than that day, wishing to remain with my aunt and give her comfort. Perhaps the need for comfort was my own, however, for I knew she sat with her friends, women who offered her what friendship she desired and who, I must admit, knew her far better than I. To me she had always been a quiet and congenial lady—when I was a child, quick with a sweet or pastry; as an adult, equally quick with a kind word. Her friends would know her inner heart; they would know what to say while I remained too torpid of mind to find the right words.

I, too, had the comfort of friends. Since my return to the neighborhood of Duke's Place I had been warmly embraced, and I sat with many well-wishers. Also by my side was Elias. I had neglected to inform him of the event—out of pride, I suppose, not wishing for him to see me in my sorrow—but my uncle was well known about town, and he received word in very little time. I must say he surprised me by knowing enough of our traditions to refrain from bringing flowers, as he would to a Christian service, and spoke instead to the beadle of the synagogue about a gift to an appropriate charitable cause in my uncle's name.

The day was cold and crisp, full of dark clouds but surprisingly free of wind, rain, or snow, and so when we retired to the nearby grave site, the weather seemed to me fitting—hard and cruel without being punishing. It accented our sorrow without distracting us from it.

After the conclusion of prayers, we took turns tossing a shovelful of earth upon the plain wooden casket. Indeed, here was one area in which I believed absolutely that Jews have the right of it over Christians. I do not understand why members of their churches insist on dressing their dead in finery and burying them in ornate coffins, as though they subscribed to the superstitions of the Egyptian kings of old. The body, it seems to me, is a thing without life. The commemoration should be of the ineffable thing that has passed, not the material thing that remains, and such showy ostentation is a product of earthly vanity, not the hope of heavenly reward.

The service concluded, we made our way slowly back to my aunt's house, where we would begin the traditional seven-day period of mourning. It is the custom of my nation that in this time the mourner is not to be left alone but rather visited throughout the day and given gifts of food and other provisions so that the necessities of life need not trouble her. Here I felt great consternation, for I believed it my responsibility to tend to my aunt's needs, yet I could not stay away from Craven House and Cobb for seven days. There would be too much to do during those days of mourning, and if I was to aid Ellershaw, as was indeed my task, I could not retire from my duties now without endangering Elias and Mr. Franco. Cobb might grant me a day or two, but more than that, I knew, would push the limits of his humanity.

As I walked among the swirling crowd of friends and mourners, I felt a hand upon my arm and turned to see Celia Glade walking beside me. I confess I felt my heart leap, and for a wondrous fleeting moment I forgot the depths of my sorrow and felt joy, unambiguous joy, at her presence. And though the recollection of grief soon returned to fill my heart, there was another moment, a more deliberate moment, in which I allowed myself not to dwell on the disturbing truths of this lady—that I knew not who or what she truly was, if she was a Jewess as she claimed, if she was in the service of the French Crown, and what she wished of me. In that moment I allowed myself to think of those questions as mere trivialities. I allowed myself to believe she cared for me.

I stepped aside, under an awning, and she came with me, her hand no longer upon my arm. Several of the funeral procession studied us with interest, so I entered an alley that led to an open courtyard, a place I knew to be clean and safe and where she followed me.

"What are you doing here?" I asked her.

She had come dressed in black, and these colors showed off the dark of her hair and eyes and the light of her skin to advantage. A slight wind had picked up since the burial, and it blew strands of hair about her dark bonnet. "I heard the news of your uncle. There are no secrets among Jews, you know. I came only to tell you of my sorrow for you. I know you and your uncle were very much attached, and I feel for your loss."

"It is interesting that you know of my feelings for him, as we have never spoken of it." My voice was low, steady. I could not say why I took this tack with her except that I so wanted her to be someone I might trust that I could not stanch the urge to thrust all doubt forward.

She bit her lip, caught herself, and closed her eyes briefly. "You must know, Mr. Weaver, that you are something of a public figure, among the Jews and among the English too. Your friends and relations have all been noted by the men of Grub Street. I cannot stop you from assigning sinister meaning to my visit, but I wish that you would not."

"And why do you wish it?" I asked, somewhat softer.

She reached out once more and put her hand on my upper arm—but only for a moment. She thought better of it, of the circumstances, of where we were. "I wish it because"—she shook her head gently—"because it is what I wish. I can think of no better way to express it."

"Miss Glade," I said. "Celia. I know not what you are. I know not what you want of me."

"Stop," she said, her voice soft as a mother quieting an infant. She raised two fingers and gently brushed my lips. "I am your friend. You know as much as that. The rest is but details, and they will out in time. Not now, but in time. For this moment, you know what matters—you know the truth in your heart."

"I want to—" I began, but again she would not have it.

"No," she said. "We will speak of it later. Your uncle has died, and you must mourn. I did not come here to push you to anything or ask you questions or make you explain your sentiments. I came only out of respect for a man I never knew but of whom I have heard great things. And I came to offer you what I can and to tell you that you are in my heart. That is all I can do. I can only hope it is enough, and not too much, and I will leave you to your family and Portuguese friends. If you find you wish to say more—well, you may seek me in the kitchen."

Her lips turned into a sardonic smile. She leaned forward and kissed me, soft and fleeting, upon my lips, and then turned to make her way from the alley, and I turned to watch her go.

While we had been in this conversation, the sun had emerged from a small gap in the clouds to shine down upon the very spot where the alley opened to the courtyard. As we turned we both saw a figure there, silhouetted against the sunlight—a woman, tall and finely shaped, garbed in black, her gown rippling in the growing breeze, her hair fluttering against her bonnet.

"I am sorry," she said. "I saw you enter the alley but did not know you were not alone."

I could not see the face, but I knew the voice at once. It was my cousin's widow, my uncle's erstwhile daughter-in-law, the woman I had sought to marry. It was Miriam.

HERE WAS A WOMAN who had chosen not one other man over me but two. She had rejected my proposals of marriage more times than I could count without making an effort. And yet for a moment I believed I must say something to explain what I was doing with Celia Glade, apologize, offer a false and convincing story. Then I recollected myself. I owed her no explanation.

I owed her something, however, for she had vowed never to speak to me again and yet here she was. Miriam had believed herself unequal to the task of being a thieftaker's wife and had instead chosen to marry a Parliamentarian named Griffin Melbury and convert to the Church of England. Sadly, Melbury had been not a little involved in the scandalous affairs of the late Westminster election, and though I at first had been grudgingly inclined to accept his worthiness, his true and scurrilous nature ultimately became undeniable—to me if not to his wife. Miriam held me accountable for that man's ruin and death, and though I had made it a policy not to accept or deny responsibility, she knew well that I did not love him and could feel no sorrow over what had befallen him.

Miss Glade, I soon realized, was ever the most useful person to have around at such awkward moments, for she did not seem to feel or fall prey to their difficulties. She stepped forward and took Miriam's hand. "Mrs. Melbury," she said. "I have heard so much about you. I am Celia Glade."

What, I longed to ask, had she heard about Miriam? Unlike my dealings with my uncle, here was something that had never made the papers. Celia might tell me to trust my heart, but how could I when I could not trust its object? She knew too much of me.

Miriam took the hand briefly and half curtsied. "A pleasure," she said. She turned to me. "I cannot attend the house. I wished only to say that I am sorry for your loss. For our loss. I did not always agree with your uncle on all things, but I knew his worth and I shall miss him. The world will miss him."

"You are kind in your sentiments," I told her.

"'Tis nothing but the truth."

"And now I expect you will go back to not speaking to me," I said, attempting some levity in my manner of speech.

"Benjamin, I—" But whatever she had to say, she now thought better of it. Instead she swallowed hard, as if forcing down her words. "That is precisely what I shall do," she told me, and so turned away.

I remained there, watching her go, watching the space where she had stood, trying, as Celia insisted, to listen to my heart. Did I still love her? Had I ever loved her? In such moments, one begins to wonder about the nature of love, if it is real or an illusion of indulgence, of fancy and self-importance, of assigning a condition or state of being to ghostly and intangible impulses. Such musings can lead to no conclusions but only more confusion.

Celia shook her head, as though contemplating something of the greatest import, measuring the nuance in her mind, taking stock of all before making free to speak. Then she turned to me. "I believe the winter has been hard on her skin. Did you not think so?" Wisely, she departed rather than await an answer.

AT THE HOUSE, the wine poured freely, and the mourners drank freely, as has always been the custom for funerals in our community. I shook more hands than I could count; I accepted more condolences than I can remember. I heard countless stories of my uncle's kindness, his charity, his cleverness, his resourcefulness, his good humor.

At last Mr. Franco took me aside to a corner where Elias awaited. "Tomorrow you must set aside your grief and return to Craven House."

"Listen to him," Elias said. "We discussed this together. Neither of us wishes to appear to act out of self-interest. I, for one, would applaud your defying Cobb and telling him to go to the devil. I've been arrested for debt before and one more time shan't hurt me, but I believe this conflict has escalated. Great and unforgivable harm has now been done, and telling Cobb to go to the devil may bring you satisfaction but it cannot bring you revenge."

"You can strike back," Franco said, "only by discovering what he wants, by following the trail he sets out for you, by making him believe his designs are within reach of completion and then taking everything away. Like Mr. Gordon, I should go to prison with a heart full of gladness if I believed it would accomplish some good, but it can only mean the delay of Cobb's goals, not his destruction."

I nodded. I wished to defy Cobb, to beat him, to put a blade in his back, but my friends had seen through the murk of my anger and gone to the heart of the matter. I had to destroy him for this, and I could do it only by learning what he wanted.

"I shall make myself available to your aunt," Franco said. "I live in retirement, and I have no other duties. I will make certain she wants for nothing, Mr. Weaver. And she has a dozen friends and more, people who know nothing of these events, who are willing to do the same out of love. You may *wish* to be here, but you do not *need* to be here."

"I know you are right," I said, "and I would do what you say, but I fear the sadness it will engender. How must my aunt feel when I abandon her in this dark hour?"

The two men exchanged looks. Then it was Mr. Franco who spoke. "You must know that in this we follow the lady's instructions. She approached me and bade me tell you as much. Seek revenge, therefore, not for your sake or ours but because the grieving widow asks you to do it."

IT WAS NEAR MIDNIGHT when I made to leave the house. Some of my aunt's friends had agreed to spend the night, even though she told them she did not require it. It was time, she said, to learn to live alone. She must spend the rest of her life in such a state.

Other than these friends, I was the last to remain, and so at last I arose to kiss and hug the lady and take my leave. She walked me to the door, and though her face was drawn and her eyes red from tears, I saw in her a determination I had never before observed.

"For now," she said, "Joseph will order the operations of the warehouse. For now."

I feared I understood her meaning only too well. "My dear aunt, I am unequal to the task—"

She shook her head and attempted a sad imitation of a smile. "No, Benjamin. I am not your uncle, to ask you to do what is not in your nature. Out of love he wanted to make you something you are not. Out of love, I will not ask it. Joseph will manage while I mourn. Then I will handle the business myself."

"You?" I spoke louder, faster than I had intended, but I could not contain my shock.

Again, another pale smile. "You are so like him. When he discussed what would happen after he was gone, he spoke of you, he spoke of Joseph, he spoke of José. Never once did he speak of me. I come from Amsterdam, Benjamin, where there are many women of business."

"Dutch women," I observed. "There are no Jewesses of business."

"No," she agreed, "but this is a new land, a different time. To Miguel, to the world, to you, Benjamin, I have been all but invisible because I am a woman. But now he is gone, and there is no one to obscure your view of me. Perhaps you will discover me to be something other than what you have supposed all your life."

I returned her smile. "Perhaps I will."

"Mr. Franco and Mr. Gordon spoke to you?"

"They did."

"Good." She nodded heavily, thoughtfully, as though completing an idea in the privacy of her mind. "You can do what you must? You can go back to this man, this Cobb, and do as he asks long enough to learn of his designs?"

I shook my head. "I don't know. I don't know that I can contain my anger."

"You must," she said softly. "To hurt him is not enough, you must do more. You must take your anger and separate it from yourself. You must place it in a closet and shut the door."

"And when the time is right, open it," I said.

"Yes," she agreed. "But only when the time is right." Then, she leaned over and kissed me on the cheek. "You've been a good nephew today—to me and to Miguel. Tomorrow you must be a good man. This Jerome Cobb destroyed your uncle. I want you to destroy him in return."

—

CHAPTER TWENTY-ONE

WOULD HAVE SPENT ANOTHER RESTLESS NIGHT, BUT FOR THE exhaustion that so encumbered me it felt near a palpable burden. Somehow, as the day progressed, I had moved beyond grief and sadness and anger into a numb dispassion. I would wake up on the morrow, and my life must continue, much as it had been before. I would have to return to Craven House, I would have to speak with Cobb, and I would have to continue to do his bidding and to work against him.

And so, the next morning, I prepared myself to do all of these. Sleep had returned some blood to my sadness, but I thought too of my aunt, of her strength and iron determination to come out from my uncle's shadow. She would manage the business, she said, and she appeared as willing to manage me and offer me direction as my uncle Miguel had. I could not but honor that fortitude and attempt to emulate it.

I therefore cleaned myself at my washbasin, dressed, and took myself to Cobb's house, arriving there shortly after the clock had struck seven. I did not know if I should find him awake or not, but I would find his bedroom and wake him myself if necessary. Edgar answered the door, now deferential and distant. He would not meet my eye, and I believe he understood that on this day, on this occasion, he must offer me no resistance.

"Mr. Cobb has anticipated your visit. He is in the parlor."

So I found him. He rose when I entered and took my hand as though we were old friends. Indeed, from the look upon his face a stranger would think that it had been his family to suffer a loss and I merely paying a consolation visit.

"Mr. Weaver," he began, in a tremulous voice, "allow me to say how very sorry I am to hear of your uncle's death. It is a tragic thing, though of course pleurisy is a terrible business, and a physician can do so little."

He made a few more noises, inchoate words, but ultimately he said no more. I believe I understood his struggle. He wished to articulate the idea that my uncle had died of his illness, rather than from any distress caused by his debts. However, he must know the act of making this observation would almost certainly anger me, and he could not bring himself to speak further.

"You wish to avoid all responsibility," I said.

"I only mean to say that no one thing . . ." He stopped there, not knowing how to proceed.

"I shall tell you what I have considered, Mr. Cobb. I've considered telling you to go to the devil and allowing the consequences to fall as they might. I have considered killing you, sir, which I believe would release me of any further obligation to you."

"I have taken measures, you must know, that should anything befall me—"

I held up a silencing hand. "I have not chosen that option. I shall only tell you to release my aunt from the burdens under which my uncle suffered. If you cancel those debts, return to her the goods withheld from my uncle, and do not force that lady, in her grief, to meet the demands of rapacious creditors, we can continue as before."

He was quiet for a moment. Then, at last, he nodded. "I cannot do what you ask," he said, "but I can stay hands, sir. I can hold back the tide of collection and make certain the creditors do not trouble her until, let us say, after the meeting of the Court of Proprietors. If we are satisfied with your work to that point, we shall release the lady, and only the lady, from those confines. If not, there can be no call for lenience."

In truth, it was a better arrangement than I anticipated, so I nodded my assent.

"While you are here," Cobb said, "have you any news to report? Any progress?"

"Do not tempt me, sir," I said, taking my leave at once.

—

AT CRAVEN HOUSE, the men with whom I worked, including Mr. Ellershaw, were polite and deferential upon first seeing me, but, as is the way with such places, they soon forgot my grief, and matters had returned much to their usual courses by the end of the day. I had occasion to pass Aadil several times, and he grunted his usual sullen comments at me, and I responded much as I always did. He had cause to believe I did not suspect him in the theft of my notes, and I saw no need to yield the one advantage I might have over him. Indeed, before long, I found myself settling into my usual suspicion of him, thinking of him not too differently than I did before the phaeton race.

Yet there was a difference, for he remained for me a constant reminder of the many difficulties I faced and the burdens under which I labored, and this spurred me from my malaise and toward action. I might lament my uncle's passing in private moments, but I had much work to do in the service of the living, and the recollection of my aunt's fortitude and determination drove me onward.

Toward the end of the day, I contrived an excuse to pay a visit to Mr. Blackburn's office. I was curious as to what, if anything, he would recall of the intelligence he had given me, and if he believed he had cause to resent my usage. To my great surprise, I found him not at work but rather collecting his private effects and ordering his space.

"Mr. Blackburn," I said, getting his attention, "what happens here?"

"What happens," he said, in an uneven voice, "is that I have been dismissed. After my many years of faithful service, they have chosen to send me on my way."

"But whatever for?"

"They claim, sir, that my services are not equal to the payment I have been used to receiving. That I must leave, for they would not have a man who believes himself worth more than he is earning, nor should they pay him more than he is worth. And with that, I am gone by day's end."

"I am full of regret for you," I said. "I know how much you value your place."

He approached now, keeping his eyes and his voice low. "You have not said anything of our conversation? You told no one we spoke?"

"I have not. I would not betray you in that way."

"It is no matter. I believe we were watched. I believe they saw us together at the tavern, so I am to be set upon my way."

"I am very sorry."

"I am sorry for it too. I ought not to have been seen with you," he said, though utterly without resentment. He did not seem to blame me but rather to regard the mistake as his own, as though he had taken a foolish jump upon a horse and hurt himself accordingly.

"I regret being the cause of mischief for you," I said. It was true enough, though I refrained to add that he ought to count himself lucky that he was only deprived of his place and not his life, like the other unfortunates who had come to harm through my efforts to learn from them.

He shook his head. "Yes, I regret it. I regret that the Company shall come to ruin without me. Where, sir, shall they find a man of my talents? Where?"

I had no answer, and neither did Mr. Blackburn, who had begun to shed tears of grief.

"If there is anything I can do to aid you, sir," I said, "do not hesitate to call upon me."

"No one can aid me now," he lamented. "I am a clerk without a position. I am like a ghost, sir. A living ghost, left to wander the earth without purpose or pleasure."

I had no response to this so I left him, struggling to replace my feelings of guilt with feelings of rage. I will not blame myself, I vowed, but Cobb. Cobb will answer.

AT MY HOME THAT NIGHT I found that Devout Hale had returned my messages, and I could think of no better way to occupy my time in the service of making Cobb answer than to pay Hale a visit. He had informed me I might find him that very night at one of the Spitalfields coffeehouses, and so, after a brief visit to my aunt, I took myself thither.

I arrived on time, and Hale put his arm around me and took me to a secluded spot. "So, what is so urgent, then?" he asked. He looked more wretched than the last time I saw him, as though his scrofula had progressed with my own troubles at Craven House. He folded his reddened hands one on the other and stared at me with veined and deep-set eyes.

"You left messages everywhere, and you have the appearance of alarm upon you. Have you some news about the king?"

"I have been unable to make progress on that score," I said. "I am sorry, Devout, but I told you I am not so well affixed as you think and I have been consumed with my East India troubles."

"As have we all. Well, for the moment I will only ask you to keep your promise in your mind. Now, tell me what you need of me."

"I must ask you about someone. Have you ever heard the name Absalom Pepper?"

"Course I have." He ran a hand though his thinning hair, and an alarming cluster of it came out on his fingers. "He was one of my men. He worked the loom."

I paused to consider this confirmation. "Did he have, to the best of your recollection, any dealings with the East India Company?"

"Him? Hardly. He wasn't built for it, you know. He was a slight fellow, small and pale, more of a girl than a man to my mind. Pretty as a girl, too. Now, women of a certain type like a man with feminine beauty, but I'm always a bit suspicious of the type, if you take my meaning. As to your question, he wasn't one for Craven House dealings. The rest of us would go to tear up the evil place, and he'd send us his good wishes but no more than that. Still, he was quick with the loom, that one, and very clever. The most clever of us all, I thought, though you'd hardly know. He kept his own council, and in his free time he'd always be writing this or that in his little book. Most of the boys here, you know, can't read or write, so they just looked at him like he was the very devil himself, and he would sniff right back at them with the devil's own contempt."

"What was he writing in this book of his?" I asked.

Hale shook his head. "He never told me and I never cared enough to ask, to tell you the truth of it. He wasn't my friend, and I wasn't his. Not enemies, mind you, but not friends either. He did his work and was more than worth the space he took, but I didn't much care for the airs he put on. That's fine for a worker, but it don't answer in a friend."

"And when he died, did you offer any compensation to his widow?"

"Compensation? Ha! That's a mighty good one. Sometimes when a fellow dies, there will be a contribution of some sort, but that's usually when a fellow perishes in some accident related to the work. Or, at the very least, when it's a fellow the boys like. But Pepper—I heard he got drunk and drowned in the river one night. Just as like made to fall, I would think, with his lordly disposition and all. He might have pushed some rough too hard, and—well, that rough pushed back, so to speak."

"So, there is no way that you and your combination pay an annuity to his widow?"

"An annuity? That's a right fine joke. You know full well we can barely pay the baker. An annuity indeed. Like I said, we take care of our own. Last year, when Jeremiah Carter died of the rot after an accident that took his fingers, we collected more than two pounds for his widow, but Jeremiah was always very popular, and his wife was left with three little ones."

I made no comment on that sum and the small fortune provided by the Company for Pepper's childless widow.

"So, I've been forthcoming, and I reckon it's your turn, Weaver. What's this about?"

The truth was, I did not know. "It is too soon to say." I formed my words slowly, still attempting to decide how much information I could safely pass along. The great danger that loomed above me and my friends made me reluctant to speak at all, but I also knew that Hale had been kind to me and trustworthy—and, perhaps more important, there might be more information unearthed by informing him of what little I knew. I therefore swore him to secrecy and proceeded to tell him what I thought safe.

"What it's about I don't know," I said. "I do know that the East India Company has contrived to pay his widow an annuity of a considerable sum and then credit some sort of fictional silk weavers' guild with the generosity."

"A considerable sum, my arse!" Hale cried. "Why, the poor girl is living in squalor."

"I think you must be misinformed. I have been to Twickenham and saw the lady lives remarkable well for a silk worker's widow—or anyone's widow, for that matter."

"Weaver, I should never have taken you for so great a dunce. His widow don't live in Twickenham. She'll never dream of living in Twickenham. She's in a run-down old house off Little Tower Hill, and I can promise you she ain't got no annuity of any sort. What she's got is gin, and counts herself lucky when she's got a great quantity of it."

There was some more back and forth of this sort, but once we established the credentials of both ladies, it became increasingly clear to me that Mr. Absalom Pepper may well have been guilty of that crime, too common among the lower order of men, of being married to two women at the same time. For that reason, and many more, he was beginning to strike me as a very interesting personage indeed.

IN THE HACKNEY on the way to the second Widow Pepper's house, Hale mused incessantly. "There's something amiss here," he said, with a low growl. He sounded like a dog perceiving footsteps on the outer boundary of its hearing. "There's never been a more heartless or penny-pinching bunch of thieves in all the world than the East India Company. They are for nothing but their own profit, and if they are paying this alleged Pepper widow money, it is to buy her silence. They have done something despicable. Indeed, they have taken his life, you may depend upon it. How much do they pay her?"

Against my better judgment, I informed him of the sum.

"By Christ," he swore, "that's blood money if I ever heard of it. It's absurd that they should pay so much, and its absurd that she should believe the money comes from us. It makes no sense, Weaver."

He was right, of course. Elias and I had already arrived at the same conclusion. The sum drew attention to itself, and it was no sound part of an effort to conceal a crime.

"The lady I spoke to told us that Pepper was always taking notes upon things. Did he leave any of his writings about with you?"

"I have other things to concern me than idle scribblings."

"Did you ever chance to observe what he wrote?"

"As a matter of fact, I did, but it didn't much answer, as I never learned my letters." Seeing my eyes widen and then a crestfallen expression overtake me, Hale hurried to add a further detail. "I can't read, it's true, but I know what letters look like, at least, and Pepper's writings were not made of them entire."

"Not made of letters?"

"Well, there were some, but there were drawings too. Pictures of things."

"What sort of things?"

"It was hard to say, given that I only caught a glimpse. When Pepper saw me gazing at his papers, he snatched them away and glared at me something fierce. I tried to laugh it off, pointing out I could no more read what he'd written than the newspaper, but his mood didn't lighten none. Said I was trying to steal from him. I told him I had no interest in stealing his papers and no notion of who should want them."

"But what did the drawings contain?" I asked again.

"From the quick look he afforded me," Hale said, "it looked like he was drawing pictures of us."

"The silk weavers?"

"Not the men themselves, but the room and the equipment, the looms. Like I told you, it was only a quick glance, but that was the impression I got. Though I couldn't guess why someone should care to steal a picture of a bunch of silk workers and their things. Who could care to look at something of so little import?"

The only answer that came to my mind was an organization that had been harmed by the will of the silk weavers: the East India Company.

Hale told the hackney man where to stop. I jumped out and offered my ill friend a hand, but he shook his head. "I took you here, Weaver, but that's as far as I go. I knew poor Jane Pepper when she was a girl, and I've no heart to see her as she is now. Her father, rest his soul, was a friend of mine, and it burns me up to think he saved his whole life to put together twenty pounds dowry on his little girl. At the time I thought he was throwing away the money, letting her marry Pepper, and now I know it." He shook his head again. "There's some things I cannot choose to see."

I understood this reluctance only too well. I never wanted to be in St. Giles after dark, and after Hale's ominous warning I wanted it even less. Nevertheless, I followed his directions and soon found the house to which he had directed me. My knock was answered by a very old woman wearing a dress in a very poor state of repair. When I told her I wished to speak with Mrs. Jane Pepper, she let out a sigh of exasperation, or perhaps sadness, and directed me up the stairs.

Mrs. Pepper met me at the door in such a state of undress that it was no longer possible to pretend I did not suspect that her place in the world had fallen considerably since her husband's death. She wore her hair and her gown loose, with the better part of her ample bosoms exposed. And she smelled of gin. Indeed, I could see, in the hard lines around her eyes and the way in which her cheekbones jutted out against the tight skin of her face, that in defiance of natural order it was the drink that owned the drinker. And yet, under the hard crust of misery and desperation, I could see the remnants of a lovely creature. There could be no doubt that Absalom Pepper had an eye for beauty.

"Hello, my dear," she said to me. "Please come in."

I accepted her invitation and took a seat, without waiting to be asked, in the room's only chair. She sat across from me on her bed. "What's it to be tonight, then, dearie?"

I reached into my purse and retrieved a shilling, which I handed her. "Some questions, only. That's for your time."

She snatched up the coin the way I've seen monkeys snatch at sugar plums meted out by their masters. "My time," she told me in a steady voice, "is worth three shillings."

I could little credit that she had ever been paid so well for any favor, let alone one as gentle as that I sought, but I hadn't the spirit to argue with the poor creature, and I provided the coin she required.

"I wish to ask you of your late husband."

"Oh, my Absalom," she said. Her eyes became moist, and some of her icy hardness appeared to melt. "Was there ever a dearer man?"

I was struck at once by such similarity of devotion in the two Mrs. Peppers. I knew not how the late Mr. Pepper had so charmed the ladies, but I could only wish I knew a small fraction of his secrets.

"He was a good husband, then?"

"He was a good *man*, sir. The best of men. And it is often true that a good man does not always have the leisure to be a good husband."

Particularly if he is busy being someone else's good husband, I thought, though I would not dream of giving voice to such a comment. "What can you tell me of him?"

"Oh, he was good to me, sir, very good to me. When he was with me, I should have never suspected there were even other women in the world, for he only thought of me, only saw me when we walked down the street together. We could be in St. James's with the fanciest folk in the metropolis, and he would not notice a one of them. And he would—" She stopped herself now and gave me a critical glance. "Why is it you wish to know? Who are you?"

"I do beg your pardon, madam. My name is Benjamin Weaver, and I have been charged to inquire into the affairs of your husband in order to determine if he may have been owed some money prior to his death."

It was a cruel trick and I knew it, but there was little I could do to aid this Mrs. Pepper, and much I would have to do to aid those who depended upon my labors. Besides, a little hope might, in her case, be more of a kindness than a cruelty.

"Money? Who from? How much?"

I held up my hands, as if to say, How can such powerless people as ourselves fathom the ways of the great? "Indeed, I cannot say how much, nor exactly who from. I have been hired by a group of men inclined to invest in projects, and they have asked me to inquire into Mr. Pepper's affairs. I know nothing beyond that."

"Well," she said thoughtfully, "he had more going on than silk weaving, I can tell you that. He always had money in his pocket, which none of the other silk weavers did. And I wasn't to say anything to Hale and the others about it neither, because they wasn't to know about it. On account they would be jealous of Absalom, what with his being so very clever and handsome."

"And what did he have going on, other than silk work?"

She shook her head. "He would never tell me. Said I shouldn't concern myself with such dry matters as that. But he swore we would be rich one day soon. And then he died, all tragic like, falling into the river. It was a cruel thing for fate to leave me so, alone and penniless."

She leaned forward in her distress, and this gesture further exposed the barely hidden swell of her breast. I could not fail to understand her meaning, though I was determined to pretend to misunderstand it just the same. She was a beautiful woman, but a hardened one, a destroyed one, and I could not so debase myself by taking advantage of her misery. I might be tempted, but I would not do it.

"It is very important," I said. "Did Mr. Pepper ever tell you *anything* of his aspirations? Did he mention names, places, anything of that sort, which could help me to figure out what it was he worked upon?"

"No, he never did." She stopped still for a moment and then looked hard upon me. "Do you mean to steal his ideas, the things he wrote down in books?"

I smiled at her question, as though it were the silliest thing in the world. "I have no interest in stealing anything, madam. And I promise you, upon my honor, if I discover that your husband stumbled upon something of note, I will make certain you receive what is yours. It is not my task to take anything from you, only to learn and, if possible, restore to your family something that may have been lost."

My words so succeeded in assuaging her concerns that she rose and rested a hand upon my shoulder with a gentleness I would not have expected from a woman to which the world had not been gentle at all. She looked at me in such a way that let me know in no uncertain terms she wished for me to kiss her. I confess I was flattered, and it is a testament to her charms that I was, for why, my perceptive reader will wonder, should I be flattered by the willingness of a whore to whom I had already given money and made a vague promise of future wealth? Nevertheless, I felt my previous resolve begin to dissipate. I cannot say with any certainty what would have transpired had not something most unexpected happened.

The Widow Pepper began to move her fingers to my face, but I held up a hand in a halting gesture and raised a finger to my lips to signal silence. As quietly as I could manage, I moved over to the door of her chamber. Alas, ever mindful of her safety, Mrs. Pepper had locked it, which would detract precious seconds from the advantage of surprise, but it was what I had been given, so, quickly as I could, I turned the key in the lock and flung the door open.

As I had feared, whoever had been lurking outside had determined my movements sooner than I would have liked, but I caught the glimpse of a man running, nearly falling, down the stairs, and at once I charged after him. I lacked my quarry's grace, I suppose, because the stairs took me more time than they did him, and by the time I reached the ground floor, he had already flung wide the front door and was out upon the street.

I followed hard behind him, and when I came out of Mrs. Pepper's house, I saw the figure heading down the Tower Hill Pass toward East Smithfield. He moved swiftly, but without the disadvantage of stairs I could hope at least to match his pace, and I had a great deal of faith in my endurance. One thing a man who has fought in the ring must know is how to continue to exert himself even when his stores of energy feel depleted. Even if I could not overtake him at first, I reasoned, if I could but keep pace, I should catch him in the end.

As it happened, the grace he had shown upon the stairs did not manifest itself in the dark of the streets. He stumbled in a slick pool of dark filth and went sprawling forward. But as quickly as he went down, he was up again, springing to his feet with the alacrity of an Italian acrobat. He then made a quick turn down one of the dark alleys for which St. Giles is duly notorious. These streets are winding labyrinths without lights, and unless one knows his way, he may well depend on losing it. I, however, did not even have that opportunity, for I lost my man first. Once I rounded the first corner, I was met only with the distant patting of footsteps, but from which direction and to what direction I could not say.

I had no choice but to abandon pursuit. And though I regarded this decision with the melancholy that comes with failure, I attempted to comfort myself by saying that I could have done little had I actually captured him. Besides possessing an unexpected quickness, the man was larger and almost certainly stronger than myself. Overtaking him might have been more dangerous than informative. Besides, in the moment he stumbled, I was able to observe his form with a flash of clarity. I could not be entirely certain, and I would have been hesitant to swear in court to his identity. Nevertheless, I was near certain.

The man who had been outside Mrs. Pepper's door, spying on me, or perhaps her, had been, I was almost certain, none other than the East Indian, Aadil. He continued to dog my steps and to keep an eye upon me, and I knew not how long I could pretend not to know it.

GIVEN EDGAR'S WARNING, I was in no way eager to take another day away from Craven House, but I believed myself close to an answer and wished to push forward. The next morning I therefore sent another note to Mr. Ellershaw, informing him that my aunt required some service of me and I would be late in arriving to work.

I advised him that if he had further questions, he might communicate directly with my surgeon, and then I wrote Elias informing him of the lies I had told and leaving him to clean up the mess. That concluded, I took the coach out to Twickenham, once more to visit with Mr. Pepper's widow. She received me again, but this time less civilly than before. Perhaps she had now begun to fear for the future of her annuity.

"Again, madam, I have no wish to cause you dis-ease, but there are some questions. The gentlemen of the Seahawk Insurance Office wish to assure you that your annuity is very likely in no danger whatsoever. We cannot oblige you to answer our questions, but I believe your funds will be far better secured if you choose to be of help."

These words appeared to promote precisely the alarm I wished, and she told me she would help as best she can.

"You are too kind. Now, you must understand, as we discussed yesterday, that one hundred and twenty pounds per annum is an unusual amount for a man of your late husband's income. Have you any idea why you should have been designated for such generosity by the guild?"

"Surely you have already asked these questions. I do not love your taking liberties with Mr. Pepper's memory in this way."

"I have indeed already asked these questions," I admitted, "but having not yet received sufficient answers, I find I must ask again. As for the matter of Mr. Pepper's memory, I hope you will allow me to point out that in these inquiries we have a much greater opportunity to honor his memory by discovering the lost instances of his cleverness."

It was my own cleverness I now celebrated, because I saw my words had the desired effect upon the affectionate widow. She appeared no less skeptical, but I observed that she could not allow any opportunity to celebrate the saintly Mr. Pepper to pass.

"I don't know much about it, except that he was always at his books, reading and making notations of one sort or another and making his drawings."

I thought it highly unusual that a silk weaver would have books, let alone many books, in his possession. Books cost a great deal of money, and a silk weaver has little enough of that, though I had learned enough of Mr. Pepper to see that he was an exception to virtually all rules. Whatever his interest, it must have been more than an idle curiosity. It must have been something he believed would return the investment of time and money. "How did he afford the books?" I asked.

"We never suffered for them, I assure you. Important though his learning may have been to him, he would not have been able to endure it if it had resulted in my doing without what I needed or desired."

"And his drawings: Did you know their nature?" I pressed on.

"He didn't share that with me. He said it wouldn't answer to trouble a woman with what he had in mind."

"So your husband never spoke to you of his intentions?"

She shook her head.

"You mentioned he kept books. May I see them?"

She shook her head once more. "When the man from the silk weavers' guild came, he said those books and papers and such would be of the greatest good to the guild and offered to buy the lot of them for another ten pounds. They weren't of any use to me, and I would have sold them anyway. I don't know if ten pounds was a good price, but I reckoned that even if it weren't they had been so good to me it might be uncivil to resent them over such a thing."

"They took everything, then."

"I said they did," she answered, irritation peaking through her voice.

Now I understood why it was that this particular Widow Pepper should be the one to receive compensation. The Company had paid her for Pepper's books and papers. "Tell me, Mrs. Pepper. I understand that your husband never discussed his researches with you directly, and such arrangements are certainly common among husband and wife, but it is an unusual household in which information does not seep through the cracks, the way the smell of a soup wafts from the kitchen to the adjoining rooms."

She nodded, and I waited, but she did not follow my lead any more than to comment that she did not like for the smells of her kitchen to infect the rest of the house.

"Is it not possible," I continued, "that you overheard Mr. Pepper speak of his business to friends and associates? I cannot emphasize how important it is that we learn of his work. It may be the very thing," I added with a deliberate twinkle in my eye, "to lay to rest any questions regarding this annuity."

"Why must there be questions?" Her voice was now several pitches higher than its usual.

"Indeed, my most earnest desire is to lay such questions to rest and to leave your arrangement unperturbed. You will help me to do so, will you not?"

It was abundantly clear that she would. "He never much talked about his researches, as he styled them, with me, but he did have one particular friend with whom he did discuss such things. I never met this gentleman, for he was never invited to our home, but Mr. Pepper used to mention him in the loftiest terms as a fellow who could appreciate and encourage and aid his researches. He would go off to spend great amounts of time with him and their books, learning whatever it was they wished to learn."

"Did you learn this gentleman's name?"

"Aye, but not the name entire. Mr. Pepper only referred to him as Mr. Teaser."

It took a great deal of will to stifle a grim smile. Mr. Teaser sounded like nothing so much as a character from a stage comedy. I began to suspect that he might not have been so much a he as a she, and that when Pepper met this particular friend, little in the way of research was conducted. Nevertheless, I had no choice but to inquire fully into the matter.

"What can you tell me of this Mr. Teaser?"

"Very little, I'm afraid. He spoke of him infrequently, and when he did so it was with a strange mixture of satisfaction and something like contempt. He would praise Mr. Teaser's perspicacity but at the same time laugh at him, saying he was as simple as a child, and that he—my husband, the late Mr. Pepper—might lead that poor man where he wished."

"Is there any hope," I inquired, "that you chanced to overhear the location of these meetings?"

"In that I may assist you. On one occasion, I did chance to overhear Mr. Pepper speaking to a friend of his, describing a forthcoming meeting, and he identified the location as a house on Field Lane, bordering a tavern called the Bunch of Grapes, if I recall. I cannot say if this is a public house or a private one, but I do recall hearing him give that direction."

"Did you ever follow that direction yourself?"

"No, why should I?"

Because you were curious, I thought. Because you would never have recalled the location if it had been of no consequence to you. Nevertheless, I held my tongue, for I had nothing to gain by exposing that I knew more of her heart than she wished to allow, and it would little serve my ends to demonstrate that I saw she was, in a very strange way, jealous of this Teaser.

Further inquiry revealed that Mrs. Pepper had nothing more to tell me, so I thanked her for her time.

"And what of my annuity?" she asked me. "Is it safe?"

Having no desire to eliminate what I believed might still be a useful fount of knowledge, I chose to remain vague. "I shall do all I can to serve you," I said, with a bow.

She bit her lip in clear distress. "If I show you something," she said, "if I let you look at it, you must accept that I do it in the spirit of co-operation and you will do what you can to help me."

"Of course," I promised, making all possible efforts to banish from my mind the hypocrisy of words. I could not say to what ends the East India Company paid this lady an annuity, but should I expose their se-crets, in all likelihood the money would run dry. In short, I made every effort to convince this woman to aid in her own ruin.

She bade me wait and then disappeared for a moment, returning with a thin calfskin-bound quarto in her hands. She clutched it to her bosom so that I could observe a large discolored streak along the front of the book.

"It was always a peculiarity with my husband, the late Mr. Pepper, that his books were his memory—or so he told me several times. He had to write down his ideas, nearly at the moment he had them, lest they be gone in an instant, never to be recovered. Indeed, he believed he had forgotten more fine notions than a whole army of men will enjoy in their lives. So it was that he kept books about him at all times and took notes incessantly. Many of these books, he believed, had fine ideas, many others, nothing of note. When the men of the guild came for his books, they said they wanted everything. And yet I held some-thing back. Just this one volume, and only because he told me it was a book of false starts, terrible ideas. It was a book he once told me he would never care if he lost. I recollected this volume, for it had the im-perfection in the calfskin that looks almost like a letter *P*—for Pepper, you know. In any event, I dared to keep it for myself."

I held out my hand. Reluctantly, she delivered the goods. Page after page was full of cramped, slanted writing, so small I could hardly read it. The letters ran together, and my head began to ache from the effort to decipher. In addition to these passages were, as Hale had told me, drawings—drawings of what looked like the equipment and materials for silk weaving.

Mr. Pepper believed the book to be of no value, but I could not be so certain. "May I take this with me? I promise to return it to you."

It pained her, but she granted me a reluctant nod.

Now confident that my efforts could hope for no further reward, I bade her farewell, once more promised to diligently pursue her case, and went to find the return coach. Alas, it was a longer wait than I should have liked, and I did not return to the metropolis until nearly dark. Then, once upon my familiar streets, I had to make my way home, so a dark gloom cast itself over Duke's Place as I approached my home.

I had grown very hungry during my travels and considered stopping to eat before retiring, but there is nothing like travel to make one wish for rest, and even if my landlady should not have a light supper at the ready for me, I preferred a meal of bread and cheese in my room to one of cold meats and peas in an eating house.

But as I approached my house I felt a rough hand land upon my shoulder. When I turned, I could not say I was entirely surprised to find the very faithful Edgar at the ready to deliver a sneer.

"You been smoked, Weaver," he said, pressing his lips together in his duckish way. "You thought to hide like a coward under cover of your uncle's death, but we are not so foolish as you think. Did you believe Mr. Cobb would not discover your double-dealing?"

"What double-dealing is that, you rascal?" I managed. I tried to sound indignant, but in truth I wondered which particular bit of deception had been uncovered.

He barked out a laugh, for clearly what he felt was satisfaction and not mirth. "It is one thing to believe you might play us for fools. It is quite another to feign ignorance once you've been caught. There is nothing in it for you, so you may as well accept that you've been discovered, and you had better be more forthcoming lest you do more damage to your friends."

"More damage? What is it you mean?"

"What I mean is that Mr. Cobb has been generous with you, far too generous in my opinion, but your foolishness has now caught up with you. You were told that, should you defy us, should you refuse to deal with us like a gentleman, then your friends would suffer. It became clear, all too clear, that you would not believe us unless you were shown a measure of our determination, so Mr. Cobb has decided it is time to show you he means what he says."

I lashed out without giving the matter a moment's thought. I grabbed the unctuous fellow by his cravat and twisted that instrument, turning his face, almost immediate, a dark color, the precise shade of which was impossible to determine in the darkness. "What have you done?" I demanded, though it quickly became clear that he would not answer so long as I strangled him. Reluctantly I let go and allowed the wretch to fall to the ground.

"What have you done?" I asked again, delivering a kick that he might understand the earnestness of my question.

"It's your friend Franco," he told me, after a series of histrionic flailing gestures. "Franco has been taken away. And if you don't begin to follow orders, he will be but the first."

CHAPTER TWENTY-TWO

*W*HAT CAN I SAY OF MY CONSTERNATION AT THIS MOMENT THAT my reader cannot, for himself, imagine? Moses Franco, a man to whom I was kindly disposed, one who had never done me harm and had only meant me well, was now thrown into a dark dungeon because of my actions. I told myself that I must refuse to shoulder the blame. It was, after all, Cobb and Hammond, his vile lapdog nephew, who had taken these actions. I had never sought harm for Mr. Franco. Nevertheless, I could not entirely convince myself that I spoke the truth. After all, I had been heedless with my investigations, and I had not reported my discoveries to my unwanted overseers. I had tried to serve many masters, none more than myself, and now it was for Mr. Franco to pay the price.

I thought to take myself to the prison at once, but it was late, and I had no desire to disturb whatever rest and quiet he might find in that place. Instead, I spent a night of restless sleep and left early the next morning to confront my tormentors. It being Sunday, I was not expected at Craven House, and was at liberty to indulge myself in a day of not pretending to serve the East India Company.

I arrived before eight o'clock, an unreasonable hour, but I had little concern for the comfort of Mr. Cobb's household. In fact, I wished to wake them early, and I had every intention of arriving before they left for Sunday worship, presuming, of course, that these were the sort of men who might spend six and a half days indulging in every villainy imaginable and believe it justified by a few hours of hypocritical repentance.

I was surprised to find I needed to pull the bell cord but once to be received by a dressed and ready Edgar, regaled in full livery and without a hint of sleep about him. "Weaver," he said. "Why does your appearance not surprise me?"

I pushed past him, and he snorted at my rudeness. He little understood, however, that the very fact of his life, the terrible truth that he dwelled upon the same world as beautiful women and laughing children and prancing puppy dogs, filled me with such disgust that had I not brushed past him I should have been forced to strike him. I do not mean a manly challenge and round or two of fisticuffs, either. No, had I remained in that hallway another instant, I should have stomped hard upon his foot, driven my elbow into his nose until it blossomed with blood, battered my knee into his manhood—I hardly know what.

I followed the sounds of silver making music against porcelain and soon walked into a small dining room—not the capacious grandeur of Ellershaw's but a much smaller and more intimate space. I presumed Cobb to be possessed of a second dining room where he could entertain in high style, should he ever wish to do so. Still, this room had the pleasures of comfort, though its Turkey rug was of all dark blues and browns, its furnishings a near black in color, and the walls a green so gloomy it might well have been the color of a cloudy moonless night. There were, however, high windows that sent in lances of light, giving the impression that the room was crisscrossed with the filament of a spider's lair, and there, at breakfast, were the spiders.

Cobb and Hammond sat across from each other at a rectangular table, not so large as to impede conversation. The table itself was filled with enough food to satisfy a company five times their number: breads and mushrooms and cakes. And while I stood there, squinting in the streams of encroaching sunlight, the two men filled their plates with every imaginable manifestation of pig flesh: rashers of bacon, links of gray sausage, slivers of ham cut so thin as to be nearly translucent, their fat glistening in the candlelight. Though I now essayed to adhere to the dietary laws of my people, I had not always done so. Nevertheless, in recent years, since my return to Duke's Place and the eateries of the Hebrews, the smell of pork had become unpleasant to my nostrils, but that was not what filled me with such disgust. Rather, it was the carnivorous pleasure with which these men ate. Indeed, watching them put the meat in their mouths, I sensed that, had they their way, they would have preferred to rip suckling piglets from their mother's breast and devour them alive.

Cobb looked at me, nodded, and washed down whatever was in his mouth with a reddish-yellow liquid that sloshed in an oversized crystal goblet. I took it for some sort of thin arrack punch. "Weaver," he said, once he had swallowed and set down the goblet. "This is not entirely a surprise. Shall I have Edward set a place for you?"

"Oh, let's not be excessive," Hammond said, snapping upright from his plate, which he had been studying with rapt attention. Less fastidious than his uncle, he did not wait to swallow his food entire, and shards of pink ham exploded across the table. "He has no desire to eat with us, and we none with him. Let him stand there if he has something to say. And better yet, let him stand there while he listens to what we have to tell him."

"I wish Mr. Franco released from the Fleet," I said.

"I can understand how you must feel, Mr. Weaver," Cobb said, "but surely you must understand our position. You have not been entirely forthcoming with us."

"And we have been paying him. That's the very devil of the thing, you know," Hammond announced. "It isn't as though we've simply been forcing him to do our bidding, now is it, Uncle? No, he's received coin, and good coin too. And from the East India Company as well. And now he has the audacity to accuse us of wrongdoing because we penalize his failure to perform his duties. I daresay he's lucky he's not the one languishing in there, waiting to die of jail fever before Parliament can enact some foolish relief law."

Cobb coughed gently into his fist. "You must understand my position, Mr. Weaver. Mr. Hammond is inclined to excess. I, however, am not. Nevertheless, even a patient man has his breaking point. Surely you can see that. You have been running inquiries all over London, learning we hardly know what, and you have not reported a single fact to us. You have attempted to interfere with my own communications network, and that is a very bad business."

"The man who tried to take my letters?" I asked.

"Indeed. You treated him rather roughly, and I resent it."

"How could I know he was in your employ and not someone with a loyalty to Craven House?" I ventured, but rather feebly, I thought.

"Oh, that is very poor," Hammond said. "Very poor. He is like a child caught with one hand in the larder, saying he was merely attempting to slay a mouse."

Cobb bit into some sort of apple pastry and chewed methodically. After he swallowed he looked at me very gravely, as though he were a schoolmaster scolding a favorite student for form's sake. "I think, Mr. Weaver, that you had better tell us everything that you've discovered thus far. And from this moment, I'd like you to send us regular reports. I wish to hear about all elements of your dealings at the East India Company, and I wish to hear all the details of your inquiry, even those aspects which yield no results. If you spend the day inquiring of a tailor you think can tell you something and then discover he knows nothing, I wish to hear his name, his address, what you thought he knew, and what he actually knew. I trust you understand me."

I clenched my fist and could feel my color rising, but I nodded all the same. There was still Elias, still my aunt. And there was, of course, still Mr. Franco, whom I hoped to see set at liberty. Thus it was that I followed my aunt's advice: I took my anger and set it aside; I placed it in a closet whose door I would open someday but not now.

"I fear I have been too busy to report with any regularity," I said, by way of an apology, "but if you wish to work out a system by which I might, to your own satisfaction, send you communications, I shall certainly endeavor to comply. As for what I can now report, I trust once I do so, Mr. Franco will be released."

"I should think not," Hammond burst in, having no desire to let his uncle answer this question. "We cannot let such a thing be. Weaver has defied us, so we punish his friend. If we now release the friend once he agrees to make everything right, he has no incentive to remain honest with us. He may do as he likes and think he will tell us if he must but deceive us so long as he can. No, I must insist that Franco remain imprisoned for the duration, as a reminder of what awaits the others should Weaver think himself too clever once more."

"I fear I must agree with my nephew," Cobb said. "I am not angry that you have attempted to deceive us. It is only natural for you to do so. You do not like this situation, and that you would press to see what you might hope to get away with is entirely understandable. But now you must learn that, though I wish you no harm, I must be resolved to do harm if that is the only way. No, Mr. Weaver, your friend must remain in the Fleet, though perhaps not forever. If, after some time has passed, I believe you have been dealing fairly with us, I will consider seeing to his release. He must remain there long enough, you understand, for his imprisonment to be undesirable. Otherwise the effect will be as my nephew has stated, and you will have no reluctance to, shall we say, do things in the manner of your choosing rather than ours. And now, sir, I must beg you to tell us precisely how you have been using your time and what it is you did not wish us to know. In other words, I would very much like to hear what you thought so interesting that you would rather withhold it than protect your friends."

"Stop coddling him, by gad," Hammond said. "The devilish Court of Proprietors meeting is hard upon us, and we have no notion of what Ellershaw has planned. No notion of Pepper or his—"

"Weaver," Cobb broke in, "it is time to tell us what you know."

I had no choice. I had to stand there, again feeling like a schoolboy, this time one brought to the front of the class to conjugate Latin verbs or read a composition. And I had a difficult decision to make while I did so, for I had to determine what, if anything, of Absalom Pepper I would reveal. This dead scoundrel, I knew, was the key to what Cobb wanted, and if I could but find the truth at the end of this dark and meandering path, I might be able destroy my taskmasters. If I was not careful, I could not believe with any confidence that they would decline to destroy me.

I therefore recited my lessons. I told them of Ellershaw and his phantom illness that bordered on madness. I spoke of Forester and his secret relationship with Ellershaw's wife, and of my strange evening at Ellershaw's house. All the sordid details came tumbling out of me as I attempted to use smoke and confusion to hide what I did not want to reveal. So I described how I was made to threaten Mr. Thurmond of the wool interest, of the general awkwardness of Mr. Ellershaw's domestic situation, and even of the sadness of a lost daughter that Mrs. Ellershaw was forced to conceal. I told them about Aadil, only to say that he was hostile with an air of danger and that he very clearly wished me harm. At that point I appeared to falter, for I meant to appear to falter. I had one more piece to deliver, and I wished to appear reluctant if not entirely unwilling give up my final treasure.

"Explain, if you will be so kind," Hammond said, "what was in the letter you sent to your surgeon friend, and what it has to do with your frequent visits to the silk-working taverns."

"Yes," I said. "I was coming to that. Indeed, I saved it for last, because I believe it is the final piece of the puzzle—at least, as much of the puzzle as I've yet divined. You see, I learned that Forester maintained a portion of one of the warehouses for a secret holding, though of what no one knew. With the help of one of my fellow watchmen, I made my way into this secret room to learn what Forester stored for himself. While we were inside, we were discovered. I escaped undetected, but my companion was caught and killed, though his death was made to look like an accident. I very much believe that it was this East Indian, Aadil, who killed him."

"Cease your pausing for effect," Hammond boomed. "This isn't a dramatic reading of *Gondibert*. What was in the secret store? Had it anything to do with Pepper?"

"That I cannot say. But the secret store was the purpose for my meeting with the silk workers. You see, I didn't entirely know myself, nor did I understand why it should be worth hiding, would be worth protecting with murder."

"Out with it!" Hammond boomed.

"Raw silk," I lied, hoping that this would be enough to set them on a wrong path. "Raw silk produced in the southern American colonies. Forester and a secret group within the Company have found a way to produce silk cheaply on British colonial soil."

Hammond and Cobb looked at one another in amazement, and I knew my lie had struck home. I had replaced Forester's inexplicable stash of ordinary calico with something that I knew from Devout Hale to be the holy grail of British linen production—silk that required no trade with the Orient. I could only presume that my deception had been sufficiently fabulous to blind them.

ONCE I HAD PRESENTED my story to Cobb and Hammond, I ceased to exist. I faded into nothingness as they argued bitterly in whispers—one of the first signs that my company was no longer desired—about what this intelligence might mean and how they must deal with it. I therefore muttered a few polite words of farewell and departed unnoticed, leaving them to solve their puzzles and go chasing after fictitious quarry. As for the potential consequences of my actions, I told myself it little mattered. Should they discover I had not told them the truth, I would merely blame the false intelligence upon the silk workers. Let Hammond go after the men who rallied to Devout Hale's flag if he dared. He would not dare, I was certain.

My next unfortunate stop was to be none other than to see Mr. Franco, so I took myself to Clerkenwell and that notorious debtors' hell known as the Fleet Prison. This great redbrick structure might have looked stately from the exterior, but it was a most wretched place for the poor. Even those with some cash about them would find only tolerable comforts inside, and any man who was not indebted going in must become so once inside, for the smallest morsel of bread was sold for a fortune. In that way, debtors, once captured, could hope for no release without the intervention of friends.

As I had, on occasion, business at that institution—though fortunately none of it involving my own insolvency—I was able to find one of the wardens familiar to me and locate Mr. Franco with little difficulty.

With some relief I discovered that his state of penury was not so dire that he was unable to afford decent lodgings for himself, and so I found my way to one of the better quarters of the prison. Here I found a dank hallway, flooded with dim light from the overcast skies trickling in from high barred windows. The halls smelled of beer and perfume and roast meats, and there was a busy trade taking place as peddlers and whores and hawkers pushed their way through, selling their wares to whoever would have them. "Best wine in the Fleet," one man called. "Fresh mutton pies," cried another. Off in one darkened corner, I saw a grotesquely fat man whose lips had long since been cut off sliding his hand into the bodice of an equally unsavory woman.

Soon enough I found Mr. Franco's room, and my knock was answered at once. Mr. Franco stood with a book of Portuguese poetry tucked under his arm. He appeared to me a worried man, with eyes both reddened and propped up by black rings, but otherwise himself. He had taken great pains to keep himself neat and dignified: a heroic effort, surely, under such difficult circumstances.

To my great surprise and mortification, he embraced me. I should have preferred, I then realized, his anger. After all, did I not deserve as much? His friendship pained me more than any outrage he could deliver.

"My dear Benjamin, how very good of you to come. Please, please, do make your way inside. I am sorry I have such awkward accommodations, but I promise to do my best."

The room was small, some fifteen by fifteen feet, with a narrow bed and an old writing table with one leg so much shorter than the others that it appeared it would totter should the slightest breeze come through the chamber—though none ever did, for it was cold and stagnant and smelled of sweat, old wine, and the sour tinge of a dead mouse rotting off in some undiscoverable crevice.

Mr. Franco gestured for me to sit in the only chair while he walked over to his writing desk—surely the most important furnishing in such a place, for it provided a venue for the composition of degrading letters to one's friends, begging for what they might spare. His desk contained no papers but books, and there were three bottles of wine, a few pewter tumblers, a half-eaten loaf of bread, and a large chunk of very pale yellow cheese.

Without asking if I desired refreshment, he splashed some wine into one of the cups and handed it to me. He took one as well, and after he said the blessing upon the wine, we both drank deep.

"You must know," I began, "that no amount of money I could raise would free you from these walls. My enemies have contrived you must stay here, and I believe they will make certain it remains so. Nevertheless, they have indicated that if I behave as they wish, they may release you in a few weeks."

"Then I must prepare myself for a long stay, for if I can have any influence upon you at all, I will keep you from behaving as they wish. They punish me to make you pliable, Benjamin. You cannot give in to them, not now. Do as you must. I shall remain here. Perhaps you will send me some books and make certain I have acceptable food, and I shall be well. May I impose upon you by making a list of what I should need?"

"It is no imposition. I would take the greatest pleasure in providing for you."

"Then do not trouble yourself about my confinement. This room, while not the finest I've inhabited, is no torment, and with your help I will have nourishment for body and mind. As it is no difficult thing to take exercise, I shall find it no task to maintain body and spirit. All will be well."

I admired beyond words how philosophically he accepted his fate, and I was grateful that he had asked me to bring him some little things, for in so doing I would assuage my guilt.

"Is there anything else I might do, that I have in my power, to make your imprisonment less odious?" I asked.

"No, no. Except, that you must tell me all, for there is no risk now in doing so. No more harm can befall me. Perhaps, locked away as I am now, I may be able to do you and myself some good."

I could not deny the truth of his words, and I feared always that if he were to learn something on his own, he would feel himself compelled to act upon it, heedless of his own good. Instead, I chose to filter the information—for my sake and his.

Thus I told Mr. Franco not precisely everything, but near enough— all that I had told Cobb and Hammond, and much of the rest as well. I told him I suspected Celia Glade to be a French agent. I told him about Absalom Pepper and his two wives. The only thing I held back was the truth about what Forester kept in his secret warehouse. In part, I worried that, even here, the walls might hide the watchful presence of the enemy, and I also feared that we had not seen the worst of what Cobb and Hammond had to offer. How could I be certain they were not above cruel forms of questioning? It would be best, I decided, to keep some things close, even from my friends.

Mr. Franco listened with particular interest to my description of the mystery surrounding Ellershaw's stepdaughter. "This is the perfect place to find out," he said. "If she engaged in a clandestine marriage, she would do so within the Rules of the Fleet."

"Very true," I said, though without enthusiasm.

"As you are here, perhaps it would be wise to pursue that line of inquiry."

"I should prefer not to. I am sufficiently aggrieved that I must inquire into the Company. I have no desire to upturn personal lives and heap miseries upon Mrs. Ellershaw or her daughter."

"Often, in business, it is the circuitous path that is the most expedient. That matter has been raised, and you tell me that this Forester appears to be concealing something from you."

"Yes, but as he has tender feelings for Mrs. Ellershaw, it seems likely that he conceals to aid her."

"I see no harm in pursuing the matter, in the event you are mistaken. I do not wish to use my position to influence you, but I would hope you would use every advantage possible to influence those who hold all our fates in their hands."

It was true enough. The investment of a few hours might yield nothing, and if that were the case I could easily forget I had pursued this course. "Perhaps you are right."

"Indeed, I may save you some time. I met this morning a priest by the name of Mortimer Pike who told me he lives within the Rules, on the Old Bailey, and he, at least according to his own declaration, is fairly the king of Fleet marriages. He appears rather proud of the claim that he has performed more of these ceremonies than any other man alive. I cannot speak of his veracity, but he does appear to do a brisk trade and, what's more, knows the other priests."

I thanked him for the intelligence. And, after visiting for some half an hour more, I set off in search of this servant to Hymen.

IT HAS EVER BEEN one of the most curious aspects of the city that there are small sections in which the normal laws that govern our lives do not apply, almost as though one might stumble into a neighborhood where a dropped object would fly upward rather than downward or in which the old turn young rather than the young old. The Rules of the Fleet, the dense and tangled quarter surrounding the prison, was such a place, for therein a man could never be arrested for debt, and so the most desperate debtors in the city would make it their home, never venturing away except on Sundays, when no man can be arrested for debt anywhere. By similarly curious tradition, marriages can be performed within the Fleet, even marriages of the underaged, without permission of parents or the traditional reading of banns.

Thus I walked the streets of the Rules, in the shadow of St. Paul's Cathedral, and listened to the cries of the boys in employ of priests—every one of them impecunious, defrocked, or false. "Marriage, marriage, marriage, marriage!" called out a young fellow from under a shop sign. Another tugged at my pant leg with dirty hands. "Get married, sir?"

I laughed. "To whom? I have no lady with me."

"We can answer that, for we've no shortage, sir."

Was marriage now like a good meal, something a man must pursue when he felt the need, and if only indifferent offerings were available, he must make do? I told the boy I searched for Mr. Pike's marriage house and he brightened prodigiously.

"I work for him, I do. Come on, then."

I could not help but feel equal amounts of amusement and sadness at this mode of commerce, but such is the nature of marriage in our kingdom. Indeed, it is said that fully one third of all marriages that take place are of a clandestine nature; that being the case, it is surely cause to wonder if the rules governing the institution require some revision when so many people are unwilling to comply. Granted, many such marriages were of a kind that no just law could endorse—those between siblings or other near relatives, those between parties already married, those between children or, worse yet, adult and child. And yet the greater part of these secret marriages stood between young people who simply cared not for the lengthy process required of them by canon law.

In light of this demand, it is hardly surprising that officiating over marriages should become a popular means of generating income among indebted priests and, indeed, indebted men who are capable of performing a tolerable impersonation of a priest.

I could not say into which category Mortimer Pike might have fallen, but he clearly operated a profitable business at the Queen's Fan, a tavern close enough to the Fleet Ditch to be permeated with the stench of that river of offal.

When I walked inside, I observed that the building was no place in which to make one of the most solemn decisions in the life of a man. Here was a poor sort of tavern, an old wooden structure with a low roof, smoky, crowded, and all surfaces sticky. The clock on the wall read shortly before nine, for by law a marriage must take place between 8 A.M. and noon, so here the world was always frozen between those hours.

A goodly number of prospective spouses drank while preparing themselves to enter Hymen's temple; toward the back, the good priest performed his services in a little alcove decorated with tarnished church vestments. I heard his words before clearly observing the wedding party, noticing he hurried through the service in a haphazard manner, and though I am no expert in Church doctrine, I could not but suspect he read the text unexactly. This little confusion was made clear when I noted a distinctive drunken slur to his voice and saw that the book he held was not precisely ecclesiastical but rather a collection of the plays of John Dryden, and held upside down too.

This little impropriety did not long hold my attention, however, for I noted something far more amiss. The bride was dressed in a most exquisite blue silk gown with a gold bodice and ivory stomacher. She wore about her graceful neck a chain of gold and had all the appearances of a lady of some worth. The groom, however, was dressed in plain undyed wools, was possessed of many scars upon his face, and had the general appearance of a rude fellow. Indeed, the clandestine marriage had been invented in large part to facilitate the unions of those unequal in rank, but something of far greater import transpired here. The bride, elegant in dress though somewhat unlovely in her face, could not stand of her own accord and was held in place by two fellows as rude as the groom. These men laughed to each other and made a great joke of attempting to hold the bride's head upward, because it was clear to me that she was entirely disordered with drink or some other potion.

Drunkenness at these affairs is to be expected, though not always for the clergyman, and I might not have been alarmed had not, when the good priest asked the lady if she willing accepted her vows, one of the rude witnesses took her head and puppeted a nod, which produced general laughter among the men.

"I shall accept that," the priest announced, and then turned to the groom.

Perhaps the priest could accept it, but I could not. Hardly taking the time to consider the prudence or consequences of my actions, I lunged forward, drawing my hanger as I did so. In an instant I stood among the wedding party, but I differed from the others in the gathering in that I had a blade pressed to the groom's throat.

"Speak a word," I told him, "and it will be your last."

"By Mary's cunny, who are you?" he demanded, in violation of my orders, though not significant enough a violation for me to follow through with my threat. I had, after all, only intended that the ceremony not be completed.

"I am a stranger who has happened upon what appears to me an abduction and forced marriage," I said. Such crimes, sadly, were another consequence of the ease with which clandestine marriages were carried out. Young women of considerable portions might be abducted and made insensible one way or another, so that they would awaken to discover themselves wedded, their bodies violated, and their new husbands demanding dowry.

"A forced marriage!" the priest cried, in a poor imitation of alarm. "Sirs, you scandalize me!"

"Give us a moment to make this spark mind his own affairs," one of the witnesses said, and the two men put the bride down upon the floor as though she were a sack of flour. They turned toward me, indicating with raffish grins that they were more than ready to answer what I should demand. I turned from the groom and quickly struck with my blade. It had ever been a maxim of mine that the removal of an eye is the fastest way to discourage a villain from further mischief, and here I found it a means by which two men could be dispatched. No sooner had I slit one of the fellow's eyes, and he cried out and dropped, than his companion fled the premises without further complaint.

Allow me to say, lest I be accused of excessive cruelty, that I reserve such tactics for when I believe my life to be at risk—which was not precisely the case here—or when I deal with men I think deserving of more than a sound beating. Anyone who would say I am cruel must consider that here was a man who would take a young lady from her family, ply her with drink, force her to marry a monster she knows not, subject her to rape, and then demand that she ask her family for her marriage portion. If he does not deserve the loss of an eye, I am hard-pressed to consider who might.

The rascal was now on the floor, rolling and shouting most pitiably, so I turned to the groom. "He was only the assistant, so I believe one eye sufficient. You are the perpetrator, and so you shall lose both. Alas, my code of honor demands that you threaten me before I can, in good conscience, deprive you of your vision."

His unwashed face had gone white, and I understood he meant to make no fight of it. He backed up and away and then around me, collected his friend from the floor, and dragged him from the marriage house with all the dispatch at his disposal.

I, the priest, and those awaiting marriages watched the slow exodus in silence. When it was over, the priest turned to the boy. "It is well we ask for payment in advance," he said. Then, to the crowd. "Who is next?"

By now I had picked up the unconscious bride and held her by keeping one of my hands under her armpit—not the most gentlemanly means in the world, but the best at my disposal. I was grateful she was slight of build.

"I am next," I growled to the priest. "You will deal with me."

"Ah, you wish to marry the lady yourself?"

"No, I wish to make you account for your actions. How could you allow such a crime to take place?"

"It is never my business to inquire into why couples wish to marry, sir. I merely provide a service. It is business, you know, and business has nothing to do with right or wrong. People must take responsibility for their own lives. If the lady did not wish to marry, she must say so."

"She does not appear to me in a condition to say anything."

"Then she had a responsibility not to find herself in so poor a condition."

I sighed. "She is heavy. Have you a back office where I can set her down and deal with you as I see fit?"

"I have marriages to perform," he said.

"You'll deal with me first, or I promise you will never perform another marriage again."

He knew not what I meant, for neither did I, but as he had seen me run my blade into a man's eye not minutes before, he understood I meant something unpleasant and complied accordingly.

"Come with me then." Mortimer Pike was some five feet in height and fifty years of age, with a face lined and weathered, but handsome and charming for all that, and he had a pair of sprightly grass-green eyes as dull with drunkenness as his movements.

We moved slowly because of my burden, but once in his office, I set the lady down in a chair, where she slumped like an enormous doll. Making certain she would not topple, I turned to the drunken villain of a priest.

"I want to review your marriage records."

He studied me for a moment. "My primary purpose, good sir, is to marry those in search of happiness, not the distribution of records. I cannot even consider aiding you while couples await my services."

"Please don't make me threaten you more. Or, worse, act upon threats. If you do as I ask, you may then leave me be to examine the books, and I will need disturb your work no further."

"It is hardly work to provide happiness," he said. "No, it is a blessing. The greatest blessing a man can know."

"Knowledge is a blessing too, and I wish to be blessed with the record of a marriage of a Miss Bridget Alton. I had hoped I might be able to review your book for such a record."

"The book," the priest repeated. The moment I mentioned his volume he picked it up and, though it was a large and heavy folio, clutched it to his bosom as though it were a beloved infant. "You must understand that the registration of a marriage is a sacred and private business. I am afraid it is quite against the laws of God and man to show this book to anyone. And now, if you will excuse me."

"Begging your pardon." I took a gentle hold of his arm to make certain he did not truly abandon me. "Is not the very purpose of that book to provide a record so that men upon the very sort of errand I am performing may have an opportunity to do their researches?"

"It is commonly believed to be so," he said. "But that belief, as you have just now discovered, is a false one."

"You will let me look at the book, or I shall take this lady to the magistrate and make certain you hang for what happened today."

"Perhaps if I let you look at the book you will spare my life *and* give me two shillings."

In a way, I could not but admire his audacity, and accordingly I accepted his offer.

THE YOUNG LADY's still slumber improved into a dull snore, which I took to be a good sign that she might recover soon. I certainly could not take her home until I knew who she was and where she made her home, after all, so I kept her as my companion while I did my work.

After agreeing to let me see his books, Pike led me to a shelf where were stacked numerous folios. "I have been providing happiness to men and women for some six years now, Mr. Weaver. It has been my privilege to serve the poor and the needy and the desperate ever since I made some rather foolish investments in an affair of sheep raising. My very own brother-in-law, if you can credit such a thing, neglected to mention that he had no particular plans to buy sheep. The money was all lost, and I could not pay quite what I owed. And, if I am to be honest in the eyes of God, I must also mention that I did not precisely end my spendings once this disaster had taken place. And so, for the matter of a mere few hundred pounds, left to rot for all eternity. Most men would turn to despair, don't you think?"

"Perhaps so," I agreed.

"You are right. They would. But not I. No, I have turned to serve the Lord here in this hell of desolation. And in what better way can the Lord be served than by performing that most holy of sacraments, marriage? Did not the Lord advise us to be fruitful and multiply? My own wife, sir, has been a blessing to me these many years. Are you married, Mr. Weaver?"

Because I could not be entirely certain I would be permitted to leave there in a state unblessed by matrimony, I thought it prudent to lie and say I was.

"Ah, very good, sir, very good. I can see it upon your face. There is no state happier than the married state. It is the very ship of good fortune, which every man must pilot for himself. Don't you agree?"

I said nothing, lest he once more try to convince me to marry the sleeping lady.

Seeing that I would not answer, he gestured toward the books. "These go back six years, sir. As many as a hundred marriages a week, and the names do begin to compile. Now, when was this marriage you mention?"

"Not six months ago," I said.

"Very easy, very easy indeed. It is the very book I hold in my hands."

When he made no gesture to hand it over, I reached into my purse and pulled out the coins he had mentioned. The book, now liberated, was set before me.

"Perhaps you might recollect the woman I seek," I attempted. "I am told she is very remarkable in her unusual beauty. A tall creature, very pale, with white skin and hair. What is most astonishing, they say, is that in spite of her pallor, her eyes are most dark. Have you seen such a woman?"

"I may have," he said thoughtfully, "but in my penury, my memory is not what it once was. It is a sad thing for a man's thoughts to be so distracted by wondering whence his next meal might appear."

I handed him another coin. "Does that aid your memory?"

"Indeed it does, and I can now definitively report I have not seen the girl you seek."

—

GIVEN THAT THE GIRL had come from a respectable family, I could be fairly confident, if not absolutely certain, that she would write with a good hand. That fair confidence, however, did not allow me to feel free to pass over the unintelligible scrawls in the book without a second glance. It therefore took me better than two hours to make my way through the last six months' worth of names, and I had nothing to show for my labors. No sign of the lady in question. Certainly it was possible that she might falsify her name, but that was the sort of trick used by a man who wished to be married in the most physical sense but perhaps not the most legal. A woman, I believed, even a young and love-struck woman, would be less eager to cheat herself out of the slim legitimacy converged by a Fleet marriage.

When I closed the book, the Reverend Mr. Pike emerged from whatever shadow in which he had been lurking. He shook his head sadly. "You've met with no luck, I see. It is a very sad thing. I do hope you will come back should you ever again be in need of matrimonial records."

"Certainly," I said, though I thought it an odd suggestion that I should pursue such things on a regular basis the way a man might be asked to come again to a shop selling snuff or stockings. I looked over at the sleeping woman, thinking I might now try to rouse her and discover where she belonged. Before I could do so, Pike ahemmed behind me.

"If you will allow me." He opened the door to his office and I observed that the tavern contained a queue of priests awaiting me, an army of shabby men dressed in soiled black suits and yellowed cravats, once, no doubt, in some earlier and unimagined time, a pristine white. Each of these men held, in a variety of styles—clutched to their breasts, crooked under their arms, held in both hands like offerings—volumes of a variety of sizes and girths.

"What is this?" I inquired.

"Ho-ho," Pike said, with a hearty laugh. "You thought the word would not get out, did you? It spreads like fire, you know. All these men have heard I've been entertaining a gentleman willing to pay two shillings for the right to peruse a registry book."

—

I SHOULD HAVE BEEN perhaps a bit more cautious with the money, had I not intended reimbursement from Cobb, so I agreed to the avaricious terms set out by the good Reverend Pike. Another shilling for the use of his room, another again for more candles to illuminate the pages as my eyes grew fatigued. Never, I must admit, have I had such good service. At the first sign that my lips had grown dry, he offered to send out for beer, and when my stomach made a large rumbling noise he sent for bread and cheese—all provided, of course, at outlandish prices.

In the end, I toiled for more than two hours, feeling the dust accumulate under my nails, in my nostrils, along my tongue. I was fairly sick of the books but I vowed to review them all. And so it was not until the seventh or eight priest, a slight man with a hunched back and a crooked smile, presented me with his little quarto registry that I struck gold. While this strange fellow hovered over me, I could not believe my astonishing luck. There it was, the girl's name, *Bridget Alton,* in undeniable clarity.

The happy groom's name was there as well, though this was harder to make out. It took some scrutiny before I could read it, but once I did there could be no doubt that it was a false one: Achitophel Nutmeg. And it hardly took a man of rare perceptive powers to divine this worthy's true identity, for the first names were both from the biblical tale, not to mention the Dryden poem, "Absalom and Achitophel," and the last names both staples of the spice trade.

Once more, I had stumbled upon the considerable persuasive prowess of Absalom Pepper, the very man Cobb claimed had been killed by the East India Company. Now it appeared he had married Ellershaw's stepdaughter.

CHAPTER TWENTY-THREE

I WAS FORTUNATE THAT MY MOTIONS, AS I WALKED ABOUT EXCITEDLY after making this discovery, awakened the young bride, who after much confusion told me her name and where she lived, explaining that she had been lured away from her home by a piteous cry for help from an old woman. Once out upon the street, she had been abducted by the three gentlemen I'd engaged with earlier and thence taken to a tavern, where she was made upon threat of injury to ingest large quantities of gin.

Though she listened to my tale of her rescue with gratitude, she declined to travel anywhere with me—a precaution I could not object to, since, had she taken it earlier, she would not have found herself so trepanned—so I sent a note to her family. Within the hour, a coach arrived, and she was escorted to it by a footman, who assured me I had his master's gratitude and would be handsomely rewarded for my efforts. (Though I write this memoir some thirty years later, I still await that reward.) In any case, once the girl was gone from the marriage house, I was merely relieved to be well rid of the burden.

This liberty rendered me free to consider the marriage I had late uncovered. The marriage book listed an address for the happy couple, and while I had little expectation that the information would prove accurate, here was a case in which I found myself most pleasantly surprised, for without difficulty or mayhem I located the daughter Mrs. Ellershaw was so desirous to keep hidden.

Unlike the most recent Pepper widow I had discovered, I was somewhat relieved to find that Mrs. Ellershaw's daughter lived in a respectable set of rooms on Durham Yard, a pleasant street enough, though certainly far below the grandeur in which her mother and stepfather lived. Her furnishings, however, were of the most elegant sort, for she had fine wood chests and shelves and tables, handsomely upholstered chairs, and a thick rug from the Orient. Both she and her maid were dressed quite modishly, with wide hoops, and the lady, at least, lacked not for embroidery and lace and fine ribbons in her bonnet.

The lady received me in the parlor of her landlady's house. Her serving girl provided wine and then sat primly in the corner, concentrating most amiably upon her sewing.

"I am very sorry to disturb you, madam, but I must ask you some questions about your late husband, Mr. Pepper."

Ellershaw's stepdaughter, whom I must call Mrs. Pepper, despite her being now one of a small army of women bearing the name, appeared most distressed at the mention of her late husband. "Oh, Mr. Pepper. He was the best of men, sir. The very best of men."

I could not but note the unlikelihood that three such different women should deliver their observations of the same man in precisely the same words. "Madam, begging your pardon, but did the late Mr. Pepper ever describe himself in those very terms?"

Her color heightened prodigiously, and I knew I had struck the nail true. I could hardly be surprised, however, that a man who should think so well of himself that he might marry three women (at the least) should be freighted down with vanity. "Mr. Pepper," she explained, "was a most remarkable man, and he would have been less remarkable had he not possessed the insight to witness his own superiority."

I bowed from my seat, for I could not but applaud her sophistry. "It must have been a great blessing to him to be possessed of so devoted a wife."

"I pray it was so. But tell me, sir, how I may be of service to you and what your business might be with my late husband."

What indeed? It occurred to me that I should have thought this matter through with greater care, but I had grown so comfortable with interrogating the widows Pepper that I had not rehearsed to myself the very particular difficulties of this particular interview. I knew nothing of the light in which Mr. Pepper had represented himself to this lady, so I could not take that approach, nor could I enter the harbor from the

THE DEVIL'S COMPANY | 271

angle of my position at Craven House, for I presumed that my connection to Mr. Ellershaw could run the ship aground. The previous two widows had been, at least to my opinion, unsophisticated enough that I could paint my fictions with broad strokes, provided they were confident. However, I could not but perceive at least some cleverness in this lady's eyes.

I therefore chose to adopt a course as close to a probable truth as I could easily devise upon such short notice. "Madam, I am something of a private constable," I began, "and I currently conduct an inquiry into the untimely death of Mr. Pepper. There are those who believe his drowning not to be an unfortunate accident but rather an act of unspeakable malice."

The lady let out a gasp and then shouted for her girl to bring her a fan. At once a marvelously painted gold and black fan of oriental design was in her hand, waving back and forth most violently. "I won't hear of it," she said, her voice an urgent staccato. "I can accept that it was the will of providence that my Absalom might be taken so young, but I cannot think it would be the will of a human being. Who could hate him so?"

"That is what I wish to learn, Mrs. Pepper. It may be that there is no more to this than meets the eye, but if someone has harmed your husband, I believe you would rather know the truth."

She said nothing for a long moment and then abruptly ceased her frantic fanning and set that agent upon her side table. Instead, she picked up my card and examined it once more. "You are Benjamin Weaver," she said. "I've heard of you, I believe."

Again, I bowed from my seat. "I have been so fortunate as to receive some public notice. At times, sadly, the notice has not been laudatory, but I flatter myself that, on balance, I have been treated kindly by the Grub Street tribe."

She worked her jaw slowly, as though masticating my words. "I am hardly familiar with these matters, but I cannot believe that a man of your skills can be retained cheaply. Who then inquires into Mr. Pepper's death?"

I saw now that I had been right to be wary of her intelligence. "I serve both the great and the low. Though not averse to earning my bread, neither do I shy away from righting wrongs perpetrated against the poor."

This bit of puffery mollified her not at all. "And whom, in this case, do you serve?"

It was time to put my plan to the test. I should either be struck dead upon the battlefield or carry home the victory. "It is ever my policy to keep such matters private, but as the man in question was your beloved husband, it would be inexcusable to stand upon ceremony with you. I have been hired by a gentleman of the silk industry who believes that Mr. Pepper may have been struck down with malicious intent."

"The silk industry?" she asked. "What concern can his fate be to such as they?"

"Mrs. Pepper, forgive the delicacy of this question, but in what manner did your late husband make his way in the world?"

Her color rose once more. "Mr. Pepper was a gentleman," she said with great force.

"He had no—?"

"He was to come into money of his father's estate," she said, "had not a pack of rapacious solicitors conspired to convert his inheritance into a private pool of wealth from which they might dip." She once again worked the fan mightily. "He applied all the money of my dowry to his legal fees, but they would not give him justice, and since his death they have been so bold as to deny the very existence of the case."

"Forgive me once more for the indelicacy of the question—"

"Let us say that you will know I have forgiven the indelicacy of *all* your questions unless I ask you to leave, at which point you will know that no further forgiveness is forthcoming. In any event, if you truly mean to find justice for Mr. Pepper, then you ask these questions for my own cause as well."

"You are too kind, madam. As to my question, I have made some inquiries about town, and I have heard the sad rumor that your marriage was not approved by your family."

"There were those in my family who forbade the marriage, but I had allies as well, who provided me my dowry secretly that Mr. Pepper's cause might be best pursued."

I nodded. If Mrs. Ellershaw had taken her daughter's side in this clandestine marriage, it might explain at least a portion of the rift between that lady and her monstrous husband.

"Again, a most delicate question, but may I inquire into the worth of the dowry?"

From the look upon her face, I had no doubt that our interview came very close to ending precisely there, but she apparently thought better of it. "I hate to speak of such things, but the amount was fifteen hundred pounds."

With some effort, I kept my face impassive upon hearing this massive sum.

"And this amount was lost to legal fees?"

"As vile as it sounds, so it was. These solicitors are skilled at nothing but lies and tricks and delays."

I made some sympathetic comments meant to mask my disbelief. "Can you not conceive of any reason why the silk workers of this city might take an interest in the cause of your husband's unfortunate accident?"

She shook her head. "I cannot think of it."

"He never spoke to you of silk engines? You never observed him making notes upon such things, contemplating projects, anything of that nature?"

"As I have said, he was a gentleman born, pursuing his just inheritance. I believe you mistake him for a 'Change Alley projector."

"Then the error is mine," I said, with my third bow of our session.

"What did these men tell you, sir? Why should they take an interest in Mr. Pepper?"

I could only hope that she knew so little of how these affairs were conducted that my untruth would not surprise her. "I have not inquired into that."

"And do they believe they know who would do him harm?"

Here I decided to take a considerable risk. If this lady chose to take my accusations to her stepfather I would have exploded my disguise, and I shuddered to think of the consequences for my friends. "Out of respect for you and your loss, I shall tell you, but I must have your word that you will tell no one. There are networks of communication and rumor, channels of intelligence that will undermine my pursuit of justice, perhaps even endanger my life, if what I tell you now is revealed prematurely. No matter the anger this accusation engenders within you, you must keep it locked in your breast."

Her head snapped violently to her left. "Leave the room, Lizzy."

The maid started in her chair. She ceased her sewing but did not otherwise move.

"Go upstairs now, I say. If I don't hear the creaking of the upper stairs in a moment's time, you can seek another position and without a reference from me."

This threat provided the girl with the incentive she needed, and she fled the room.

I took a sip of my wine, now grown cool, and set it back down. "I beg you to recall this is but an accusation. Nevertheless, there are men among the silk workers of this metropolis who believe that Mr. Pepper's death was arranged by the East India Company."

The color at once drained from her face, and her limbs began to tremble violently. Her eyes grew red, but no tears emerged. Then, at once, she propelled herself to her feet so violently that I feared she might hurl herself at me. Instead, she left the room, shutting the door hard behind her.

I hardly knew how to conduct myself. Had I been excused? I rang for the servant, but no one answered. Then, after what felt like an interminable period, but might have been no more than five minutes, Mrs. Pepper reappeared. As she did not sit, I rose to meet her gaze from across the room.

"They brought him here, you know," she said. "They dragged his body out of the river and brought him to this house. I held his cold hands in my own and wept over him until my physician insisted I withdraw. I have never known such sadness and such loss, Mr. Weaver. If Mr. Pepper was killed by a malicious agent, I want you to find him. Whatever these laborers pay you, I shall treble as your reward. And if you find that it was the East India Company, I shall stand by your side and make certain that they pay for their crimes."

"You have my word—"

"Your word is nothing to me," she said. "Return when you have something to tell me. Trouble me no further with idle speculations. I cannot endure the pain."

"Of course, Mrs. Pepper. I shall endeavor—"

"Endeavor to show yourself out," she said. "For now that must suffice."

—

CHAPTER TWENTY-FOUR

I HAD NO NOTION OF WHAT TIME IT WAS WHEN I EXITED THE WIDOW'S house, only that the world had gone dark and the streets were full of the drunken shouts and shrill laughter of nighttime. When I removed my watch—guardedly, of course, for at such a time it only took but one tick of a timepiece for those items to be lost to artful hands—I saw that it was not yet seven o'clock, though I felt as though it were past midnight. At the nearest opportunity, I found a coach to take me home.

I had much to do. I knew of Pepper's dealings with the mysterious Mr. Teaser, as I knew him to be married to three different women—and I should hardly have been surprised if I were to find more. But why did Cobb care about Pepper? What was Pepper's relationship with the East India Company—or with Cobb, for that matter? How was this all connected to Forester's plot or Ellershaw's need to overturn the 1721 legislation? Did Celia Glade's presence mean that the French had a hand in all of this, or had I merely stumbled upon a spy—no doubt one of hundreds scattered across the metropolis—who collected information and sent it home, where wiser heads would determine if it had merit?

I had no answers and threatened to find no answers. I only knew I was tired and that an innocent and helpful man, the good-natured Carmichael, had died because of all this double-dealing. I wanted no more of it. Perhaps it was time to cease resisting Cobb. My efforts to undermine him and find his truths for my own purposes had granted me nothing but the imprisonment of one friend, and I would not risk the imprisonment of more.

I had been considering these matters and working myself into a very high state of agitation and anger. It was for this reason, then, that I could hardly understand, let alone manage my emotions, when I entered my house and found a visitor awaiting me in the drawing room.

It was Cobb.

I FELT NO GREAT CONCERN for his well-being, but I immediately noted that he looked unwell. He appeared drawn and quite agitated. He rose as soon as I entered the room, and, holding his hands together, he took a few tentative steps toward me.

"I must speak with you, Weaver. It cannot wait."

I will not say the rage I felt toward him disappeared, but curiosity stayed my temper. Edgar, after all, had been ready to thrash me for sending a boy to Cobb's house. Now Cobb himself appeared at mine.

I therefore directed him to my rooms, that we might enjoy privacy, and there, once I had lit my candles, I poured myself a glass of port, and chose not to invite him to join me, though his hands twitched and his lips trembled, and I saw he wished for a drink of something bracing above all things.

"Your presence here surprises me," I told him.

"It surprises me as well, but there is no helping it. I must speak with you man-to-man. I know you have had cause to feel anger toward me, and you must believe I wish things could have been otherwise. Hammond suspects you are holding back, and so do I. But I come here without him to plead with you to tell me what you have not already told us. I do not threaten you or your friends. I just wish for you to tell me."

"I have told you all."

"What of *him*?" he asked, and whispered the name: "*Pepper.*"

I shook my head. "I have learned nothing of his death."

"But what of his book?" He leaned forward. "Have you learned anything of that?"

"Book?" I asked, rather convincingly, if I may say so. Cobb had made no mention of the book, and I thought it wisest to feign ignorance.

"I beg of you. If you have any idea where it can be found, you must get it to me before the Court of Proprietors meeting. Ellershaw cannot be allowed to have it."

It was a convincing performance on his part, and I confess I felt a moiety of compassion for him. But a moiety only, for I did not fail to recollect Mr. Franco in the Fleet, and though Cobb might be a pathetic figure at the moment, he was still my enemy.

"You must tell me about this book. I know nothing of it. Indeed, sir, I resent you sending me upon this quixotic quest, chasing after a man of whom I may not speak, and now, I discover, in search of a book no one has mentioned. Perhaps I might have been done with you already if you had only told me of this book."

He looked into the black of my window. "The devil take it. If you have been unable to find it, it cannot be found."

"Or," I suggested, "perhaps, if Ellershaw knows what this book is and why you value it, he has it already, possessing the advantage of knowing it when he sees it. I cannot even say that I have not held this book in my hands, for I know nothing of it."

"Do not torment me so. Do you swear you know nothing of it?"

"I tell you I remain ignorant." It was an evasion, but if Cobb noticed it, he gave no indication.

He shook his head. "Then that will have to do." He rose from his chair. "It will have to do, and I will have to pray that things stand as they are until the Court meeting."

"Perhaps if you told me more," I suggested.

He either did not hear me or could not. He opened my door and took himself from my home.

WHEN I ARRIVED at Craven House the next morning, I was informed at once that Mr. Ellershaw wished to see me in his office. I was fifteen minutes late, and I feared he might use the opportunity to chastise me for my failure to observe form, but it was nothing of the kind. He was in his room with an officious-looking younger man who held a measuring tape in his hands and a dangerous-looking bunch of needles in his mouth.

"Good, good," Ellershaw said. "Here he is. Weaver, be so kind as to let Viner here measure you, would you? This will be just the thing. Just the thing for the Court."

"Of course," I said, stopping in the middle of the room. In an instant, the tailor was whipping the measuring tape about me as though it were a weapon. "What is this for?"

"Arms up," said Viner.

I raised my arms.

"Worry not, worry not," Ellershaw said. "Viner here is a miracle worker, are you not, sir?"

"A miracle worker," he agreed, mumbling the words through his pins. "All done here."

"Very nice. Now be off with you, Weaver. You've something to do, haven't you?"

AADIL DID NOT SHOW himself that day, and I began to wonder if he would show himself at all. He must have known I had seen him, and now he could no longer pretend to be a disinterested if hostile worker and no more. He had played his hand too openly, and while I had no doubt he would continue to serve Forester, I suspected his days of doing so at Craven House had come to an end.

I planned that night to pursue my final unexplored link to the seemingly charming Pepper—that is to say, his Mr. Teaser, whom his Twickenham wife had set me upon. I no sooner was ready to leave the India yard when Ellershaw, once more, requested me.

In his office, again, was the very efficient Mr. Viner. Efficient, I say, because he had already managed to construct a suit based on the measurements he had taken that morning. He held out to me a neatly folded pile of clothes of light blue cast, as Mr. Ellershaw stood observing in an absurd posture, showing off a suit of exactly the same color.

I understood at once, recalling—and regretting—my own suggestion that this feminine cloth be turned into masculine suits. Ellershaw had taken my notion to heart and chosen to grab the domestic market in the only way possible, should his efforts fail.

"Put it on," he said, with an eager nod.

I stared at him and I stared at the suit. It is difficult for me to explain just how precisely absurd he looked, and how absurd I was sure to look by his side. These cottons would surely make pretty bonnets, but a suit of robin's-egg blue for a man—a man who was not the most absurd dandy—could hardly be imagined. And yet, as I stood there, I knew I could not very well say that such a thing was not to my taste. I could hardly turn my nose up at it, however aesthetically practical but socially and morally abhorrent.

"It is very kind of you," I said, hearing the weakness in my own voice.

"Well, put it on, put it on. Let's see if Viner is up to his usual good work."

I looked about the office. "Is there some place for me to change?"

"Oh, don't tell me you're bashful. Come, come. Let's see that suit on your back."

And so I stripped to my shirt and stockings and put on over them this monstrous blue suit. And as much as I disliked the thing, I had to be impressed with how well such a hastily constructed thing fit.

Viner circled around me, tugging here and pulling there, and finally turned to Ellershaw with evident satisfaction. "It's very nice," he said, as though praising Ellershaw's work rather than his own.

"Oh, indeed. Very nice indeed, Viner. Your usual fine work."

"Your servant." The tailor bowed deeply and left the room, dismissed by some unseen cue.

"Are you prepared to go?" Ellershaw asked me.

"To go, sir?"

"Oh, yes. These suits are not meant for private enjoyment. Hardly does us any good at all, now, does it? We must be seen. We are going out to let London have a look at us in these clothes."

"I had a rather urgent appointment tonight," I began. "Perhaps if you had mentioned this earlier, but as things stand now I'm not sure I can order—"

"Whatever appointment you have, you should be delighted to miss." He said it with such confidence that for an instant even I didn't doubt it. "Good, then. Let's be off."

I nodded and affected an enthusiastic smile, though I felt absolute certain that I resembled a man choking to his death.

IN HIS EQUIPAGE, Ellershaw explained that we were heading for Sadler's Wells to feast upon food and the gaze of others. He cryptically warned that I must expect there an unpleasant surprise, but when we arrived I could divine nothing unpleasant about the gardens except our own attire and the stares and sniggers we drew. Great fires had been set outside to make dining al fresco possible in the cold, but everyone chose to stay in the main house.

It was still early, but there were a fair number of people already in attendance, enjoying the expensive and not particularly good food served at such vivacious places of entertainment. I must say that our entrance sparked a great deal of notice, but Mr. Ellershaw met each open stare and sneer with a good-natured bow. He led me to a table and then ordered wine and some cheese pastries. A few gentlemen came over to greet him, but Ellershaw made no return of any friendly nature. He merely exchanged platitudes and, without bothering to introduce me, sent them on their way.

"I wonder," I said, "if this was a terribly good idea."

"Don't you worry, my good man," he said. "All will be well."

We sat there for an hour or more, listening to a group of musicians whose bare competence strained the imagination. I lost myself in a silent reverie of discomfort until a shadow crossed over me, and when I looked up I was astonished to find none other than Mr. Thurmond before us.

"You both look absurd," he said.

"Ah, Thurmond." Ellershaw shifted in his seat, clearly delighted. "Please, join us."

"I think not," he said, but he nevertheless pulled out a chair and sat at our table. He reached over and poured a healthy quantity of our wine into his own glass. I must admit I was somewhat impressed by his casual air. "I really can't think what you hope to accomplish. Do you imagine that the two of you can, single-handedly, create a fashion frenzy? Who among the bon ton would wear such a suit?"

"As to that, I cannot say," Ellershaw answered. "Perhaps no one, perhaps everyone. But if you and your kind are determined to limit what we can import into this country, I think you will find that I am equally determined to prevent your measures from having any effect. It is a new kind of world trade, Mr. Thurmond, and you can no longer pretend that what happens in London shall have no influence on Bombay—or, perhaps more importantly, the other way around."

"You are nothing but fools," Thurmond said. "You think to save yourself with this nonsense? It shall never happen. Even if these liveries of yours were to be popular, blue suits would rule the day for but a season or two. You would have a few good years and then be no better off than you are now. You might have gained some time, but nothing more."

"In matters of trade, a season or two is an eternity," Ellershaw said. "I disdain to look farther ahead than that. Indeed, I live from one meeting of the Court of Proprietors to the next, and if the world be damned in six months, I care nothing for it."

"That position," he said, "is an absurdity—much like your suits."

"Think what you like, sir. You may choose to defy the Company if you wish. For all I know, that is the only thing that will continue to get you elected to your seat. But we shall see who survives longer, the East India Company or your desiccated wool. Oh, I daresay. Is that young man coming in not the duke of Norwich's heir? And, I do believe those cheerful friends he's with are the very toast of the world of fashion."

Thurmond turned to look, and his jaw fell open with surprise and even something like horror. Here came Ellershaw's Holy Trinity, his fashionable cadre—all handsome and self-satisfied young men—with an equal number of young ladies about them. Each one wore a suit made out of blue India cotton. The ladies, too, wore gowns of blue India cotton, so that they moved together in a great azure swirl. The entire assembly hall glanced over to them and then back to us, and I understood at once that though we were regarded as objects of derision when we first entered, we now became objects of envy.

Ellershaw nodded with satisfaction. "Every man in this room is now thinking of how he can best reach his tailor to have one of these suits made up."

Thurmond pushed himself away from the table. "It is but a temporary victory," he said.

Ellershaw smiled. "My dear sir, I am a man of business, and I have spent my entire life with the knowledge that there is no other kind."

THE REST OF THE EVENING, Ellershaw remained in high spirits, claiming that this was the very thing, that the Court meeting would present no obstacles now. I thought it rather optimistic, but it was nevertheless easy to see why he felt such enthusiasm. We were the very height of attention, with no shortage of pretty young women and strapping young sparks taking their turn to come over and share some insipid thought. As Mr. Ellershaw basked in his success, it was no difficult thing for me to excuse myself, alluding only to a great fatigue.

I immediately went home to change into something plainer and less conspicuous. Then I once more made my way outside and to a hackney—this time to near Bloomsbury Square, where Elias made his home.

Since Cobb had made Elias's fate dependent on my behavior, I had not risked a visit, but as Elias was now working for Ellershaw as well, I believed a single trip of this nature was an acceptable risk. And I wished, to whatever extent I could, to resolve all remaining questions this night.

I was met at the door by his very kind and attentive landlady Mrs. Henry, who welcomed me inside and offered me a seat and a glass of wine. My hostess was a very attractive woman of perhaps forty years or more, and I knew that Elias maintained a special, if not amorous, friendship with her. The two of us rarely shared an adventure, at least an adventure of the nonribald variety, that he did not repeat to her. I feared then that she would hold some sort of grudge against me for having so troubled Elias with my difficulties, but if there was anger in her heart, she showed none of it.

"Your offer is very kind, madam," I said with a bow, "but I fear I haven't the time for pleasantries. There are matters to which Mr. Gordon and I must attend, and if you would be so good as to fetch him, I would be most indebted."

"I am not entirely certain that fetching him is convenient," she told me.

"Oh, I should be very happy to go abovestairs myself, Mrs. Henry. You hardly need trouble yourself, if you have some other matter—"

I stopped because I observed that Mrs. Henry's ears had turned the color of ripe strawberries. When she saw that I saw, she coughed delicately into her hand. "Perhaps you would care to share a glass of wine," she tried again.

I attempted a gentle smile, one that would not suggest I was immune to the scandalous nature of Elias's conduct but rather that his nonsense surprised me no longer. "Madam," I said, "though it may not be comfortable for you to disturb him, I can assure you he will take no umbrage if I fetch him myself."

"I am not entirely sure he will take it kindly," Mrs. Henry said softly.

"Oh, you may depend upon his taking it most unkindly, but it must be done for all that." I bowed once more and ascended to Elias's rooms.

Once I was at the top of the stairs, I pressed my ear against the door—not to satisfy any prurient curiosity, you must understand, but because if I were to interrupt I should hate to do so at the wrong moment. I heard nothing that would tell me one way or the other if this was a good time. So I knocked on the door, firmly enough so that my friend would know this was an urgent matter, but not so firmly that he would throw on a pair of breeches and a shirt and climb out his window—a maneuver he had deployed on at least two occasions to my knowledge when attempting to elude some pesky creditors.

For a moment nothing, and then shuffling noises and a creaking of hinges. The door opened just a crack, and one of Elias's wary brown eyes peered out from the gloom of the chamber. "What is it?" he asked me.

"What is it?" I repeated in disbelief. "*What it is* is that we have much to do. You know I hate to interrupt your dalliance, but the sooner we put all this business behind us, the better off we shall all be."

"Oh, no doubt, no doubt at all," he said. "But tomorrow is much the better day for me."

I let out a snort. "Really, Elias, I understand your need to pursue your pleasure, but you must understand that now is the time to set those needs aside. We must act tonight. Cobb will be laying new demands on me tomorrow, you may depend on it, and I've already told him far more than I would wish. We must see what we can learn of Absalom Pepper and his connection to this Teaser fellow—"

"Hush!" It came out as a bark. "You need not speak of it here. I know all their names. Very well, Weaver, if it is of such urgency to you, go wait at the Rusted Chain just around the corner. I'll be there in one half of an hour."

I snorted once more. Elias's half hours, when he was breaking free of an amour, had been known to stretch for two hours or more. It was not that he was irresponsible, of course, merely that he was inclined to be forgetful.

Elias and I had been friends for some years, and I knew his ways well. He would not bring a whore back to his room, for fear of offending Mrs. Henry (who, over time, had become increasingly less shocked by Elias's behavior), but neither would he bring a woman of any stature—

284 | DAVID LISS

who would find his rooms disagreeable and the openness of their amour compromising. So, in his bed right now would be some actress or tavern girl or tradesman's daughter, a woman of enough standing that Elias could walk with her down the street without attracting hoots, but not so much that she would refuse to walk with him at all.

Knowing all this as I did, I therefore took a bold if not entirely unprecedented step. I shoved myself against the door, knocking Elias backward. Not hard, mind you, but merely with the intention of jarring him out of his refusal.

Elias was, to my surprise, fully dressed, not even having removed his waistcoat. I must have shoved harder against the door than I'd intended, because he stumbled backward and fell on his arse.

"Have you lost your senses?" he cried out. "You must get out of here at once!"

"Sorry to shove you so hard," I said, hardly able to contain my grin. This would take more than the usual pot of ale and chophouse meal to mollify, I saw, but there was nothing for it. Undaunted, I turned toward the bedroom, but circumstances required I take no steps in that direction. The lady resided not therein but rather in one of his comfortable sitting chairs, her delicate fingers around the stem of a goblet.

Her fingers trembled ever so slightly, as did her lips. I saw, even in the diminished light, that she struggled to appear unaffected by the scene, but something had overcome her, though I knew not if it were shame, fear, or anger.

"I would offer you a seat," she said, "but it is not my place to play the hostess."

I could neither move nor speak but only gape like an idiot, for sitting upon that chair was Celia Glade.

—

CHAPTER TWENTY-FIVE

I FROZE IN MY TRACKS.

Celia Glade looked up at me with her beautiful eyes and smiled with such evident sadness that my heart doubled its pace. "You have me at a disadvantage, Mr. Weaver," she said.

I spun around and walked as quickly as I could to the door. To Elias, who was just now rising from his unflattering position, I merely said that I would await him downstairs.

This affair ended so badly for so many that I should spare no sympathy for those who were only moderately inconvenienced, but I have never quite forgiven myself for my rude treatment of Mrs. Henry, as I sat downstairs gloomily, clutching my goblet of wine so hard I feared it would crack—and all while she made awkward efforts to converse with me.

I did not see Celia leave the house—I presume Elias led her out the back way—but a quarter of an hour after our encounter, he came downstairs to signal his readiness to depart. We went to the Rusted Chain and ordered pots. After that we sat in silence for some time.

"I'm very sorry if this is awkward for you, Weaver," he began, "but you never in any way indicated that you should prefer—"

I slammed my hand down upon the table hard enough that nearly every patron in the place now looked over. It mattered little to me. My only goal was to get Elias to cease his blather before I felt I had no choice but to pummel him.

"You knew full well how I felt," I said. "This is outrageous."

"How so?" he asked. "She was yours if you wanted her. You chose not to take her."

"By the devil, Elias, I can't believe you would behave so foolishly. Do you honestly think she pursued you because of your charm?"

"There's no need to insult me, you know."

"No doubt." Angry as I was, I would not end the friendship over this. "But whatever the allure of your charms, you must know that she wanted to learn only what you knew, nothing more."

"Of course. And I wanted what she had. It was something of a battle, I suppose, to see who would give up their goods and who would keep them. As it happened, she learned nothing from me and I received nothing from her."

"And did you have your eye upon her every minute she was in your rooms?"

"Not every minute. A man doesn't wish to use the pot before a lady."

"And do you still have your notes on our current inquiry upon your desk?"

"My hand is very difficult to read for those not acquainted to it," he said quickly, but I could hear his voice wavering. He had his doubts.

I did not have doubts. "While I was at your door, I mentioned the names Absalom Pepper and Teaser."

"Then perhaps you should have been more careful."

I said nothing, because he was, in that regard, quite right. I stared ahead while Elias intermittently bit his lip and sipped at his ale.

"You know," he said, "I never meant to injure you. Perhaps you should have made your feelings for her clearer to me. Perhaps I should have given your feelings more consideration, but I was too busy trying to bed a beautiful willing woman. It's a poor excuse, perhaps, but there it is. And it is entirely possible she had no intention of letting me bed her. We shall never know, of course; she merely accepted the invitation back to my rooms. There had been no intimacy—"

"Enough," I barked. "It's done. She knows too much and we have too little time as it is. That means we must make haste."

"Haste in what?"

"It is time to find Mr. Teaser. He was to fund Pepper's project, so he will know what the project is. And that is the key to this whole affair. I can only hope we find him before she does."

—

THOUGH NEITHER OF US was in a companionable mood, I did my best to put our difficulties behind us, and Elias did as well.

"Do you know the area?" I asked.

"Not well, but enough to know that it is most unsavory and I should much prefer to avoid it than visit it. Still, it must be done, I suppose."

We therefore headed out to Holborn and were not two blocks from the location where Mrs. Pepper had mentioned that I might find Teaser when we saw dark shadows step forth from an alley before us. I tensed at once and put a hand on my hanger. Elias took a step backward, intending to use me as a shield. There were some six or seven men in front of us, and I should have been quite uneasy about the odds, except that I perceived at once they held themselves without the confidence of men prone to violence. Their stance appeared to me uneasy and unpracticed, almost as though they were afraid we should hurt them.

"What have we here?" one of the men shouted.

"It appears we have a pair of sodomites," another answered. "Fear not, sinners, for a night in the compter shall have a most beneficent effect on you, and perhaps, with sufficient time to seek the Lord's forgiveness, you may yet save your soul."

I doubted the soul-saving qualities of the compter, for a sodomite sent to spend the night in that fetid prison could well expect endless hours of abuse. In such places, the time-honored tradition required that the most hardened criminals force the sodomites to consume large quantities of human waste.

"Hold there," I said. "You've no business with me nor I with you. Get ye gone."

"I'll not get gone," one of them cried, the one who had called us sodomites, I believed. "For I am the Lord's servant, sir, and he worketh by my hand." His voice wavered like a street-corner preacher.

"I very much doubt it," I answered, for I knew at once that these were men of the Society for the Reformation of Manners or, at the very least, one of the many organizations in its vein that had sprung up in recent years. These men prowled the streets at night, looking for anyone who might be involved in activities that were in violation of both the laws of God and the kingdom, though not those involved in crimes of violence, since these religious men were hardly equal to such prey. For the very worst of reasons, the constables and the magistrates had allowed these men to act as their proxies, so a group of religiously inflamed and determined citizens could grab a man for no greater crime than drunkenness or seeking a whore's company and arrange to have him locked away for a hellish night. I mentioned that sodomites fared badly in the compter, but it was only the most determined sort of brute who escaped without a severe beating and humiliation.

"'Tis such a thing as a curfew in this town," the Reformation man said to me.

"I have heard that," I answered, "but I've never met a soul who cared a jot for it but zealots like yourself. My friend and I did no more than walk down the street, and I shan't be troubled for it."

"We saw you do nothing but walk down the street, but I know well that you intend to engage in the most bestial acts, crimes that are an abomination to God and nature."

"I'll have none of it," I said, and drew my hanger.

The men gasped, as though they had never conceived that a man going about on his own business would resist these reprehensible accusations.

"I am no sodomite and on no criminal activity," I announced, "but I am a man trained in the fighting arts, so I ask which of you will give me the lie?"

I heard the sound of their breathing, but no more response than that.

"I thought as much. Now be off," I called, and waved my blade about ceremoniously. It did the trick, for the religious ruffians scattered, and Elias and I continued along our path for another block or so until we reached the location Mrs. Pepper had bespoken.

Elias looked around. "Oh, rabbit it!" he said.

"What is it?"

"I begin to perceive why the Reformation men construed our business so falsely. Unless I miss my guess, this Mr. Teaser is to be found at Mother Clap's home."

"Mother Clap?" I cried. "Can that be the name of a real bawd? It sounds more improbable than a friend named Teaser."

"I believe them to be part of the same phenomenon, for I have it on very good authority that Mother Clap's is the most celebrated molly house in the metropolis."

I had no desire to enter a molly house and came close to voicing my objection. But even as I nearly spoke the words, I though it very odd that a man such as myself, who has been forced to face all manner of danger, should be so squeamish in the face of behaviors that offered no direct harm. I might dislike how some men chose to conduct themselves—just as I might dislike cowards—but their existence did not threaten mine.

I glanced at Elias. "You go knock upon the door," I said. "You have a better chance of earning their trust."

I thought he should rage at me for my jest, but he only laughed. "At last I have found something to fill Benjamin Weaver with fear," he said, "and perhaps some way to earn back your goodwill."

Elias knocked hard on the door, and in an instant his efforts were answered. The door opened to reveal a creature in a serving girl's attire, but this was no girl at all. Here was a man, and no small one either, dressed as a girl and wearing a wig, with a prim little bonnet atop. This should have been absurd enough, but the fellow's face was dark with emerging beard, and though he curtsied and conducted himself with all seriousness, the effect was both comic and grotesque.

"Can I help you gentlemen?" the servant asked in a voice that was softened but not emasculated. It was clear to me that this man did not wish to convince anyone he was a woman. No, for all the world he wanted to appear as a man dressed as a woman, and it was a damnably curious and uneasy thing.

Elias cleared his throat. "Yes, we seek a man who uses the name Teaser."

"What's your business with him, then?" the man asked, his voice losing some of its softness. I also observed that his accent was of the lower sort, a kind of Hockley in the Hole accent if I placed it right, and that surprised me. I had always believed sodomy to be the crime of the decadently wealthy, but here was a man of the lower orders. I wondered if he was indeed sodomitically inclined or if this was merely a position he took out of necessity. And then a darker thought crossed my mind, that this low fellow was held against his will. I told myself I would remain vigilant against signs of such horrors.

290 | DAVID LISS

I stepped forward. "Our business with him is our own. Pray inform him he has visitors, and we shall answer for the rest."

"I'm afraid I cannot do that, sir. Perhaps you would like to leave your card, and Mr. Teaser—if there is such a person—will call upon you if he so desires."

I observed that the servant had not denied the presence of the man at first, but now he brought into question his very existence. "He shall not know who we are, but the business is of the greatest urgency. I mean no harm to him or your—your associates, but I must speak with him at once." I handed the servant my card.

"This ain't your home, and you don't command here. I'll leave your card as you wish or no, but be off with you."

Were he a mere serving man I should have, at this point in our impasse, pushed past him. The truth was I had no desire to touch a being of his stamp, so I continued to depend upon words. "I'll not be off. You may let us in of your own volition, or you may attempt to stop us. The choice is yours, sir."

"Call me *madam,* if you please," he said.

"I care not what you call yourself, but stand aside."

At that moment another figure appeared at the door, this one a woman in body as well as in spirit. She was a plump woman of some advanced years, though with large blue eyes that radiated an indulgent kindness. Her clothes were simple yet well-made, and she looked nothing so much as a respectable and generous matron. "Be off with ye. I'll brook no more church palaver from hypocrites such as you. Go tell it to the devil. You've more in common with him than you have with us."

The rant left me puzzled for a moment as to the best way to proceed. Elias, fortunately, ever the diplomat, bowed slightly, and led the way.

"Madam, as we've tried to explain to your servant, we mean no harm, but we have the most urgent business with Mr. Teaser. Allow me to assure you that you have very likely never had two gentlemen upon your stoop less likely to engage in church palaver. My associate is a Hebrew and I am a libertine—one inclined toward women, you understand."

This woman now peered at the card I had handed the servant and then looked up at me. "You're Benjamin Weaver, the thieftaker."

Despite my ill ease, I offered a bow.

"The man you ask about ain't done nothing. I wouldn't think you sunk so low as to be seeking to earn your coin by prosecuting mollies."

"You misunderstand me," I assured her. "My business with the gentleman is to obtain information about an acquaintance of his. I have no interest in bothering you or your friends."

"You swear it?" she asked.

"You have my word of honor. I want only to inquire of him a few significant matters, and then I shall be gone."

"Very well," she said. "Come in, then. We can't have the door open all night, can we?"

This woman, I had no doubt, was the infamous Mother Clap, and she now led us through her home with a sense of wary proprietorship. The place had the cast of a fine home from the previous century, but all was now disheveled and tattered. The building smelled of mold and dust, and I had no doubt that, were I to stamp upon the rug, a cloud of filth should arise.

We wound our way through the house, following our Virgil as she took us through surprisingly tasteful halls and well-appointed chambers. The people inhabiting these spaces, however, were another matter entirely. We came into a large room in which a ball of sorts was under way. Tables had been set up for revelers to sit and drink and talk, and three fiddlers played while six or seven couples crossed an old warped wooden floor. Some two dozen or so men stood on the edges of the floor, engaged in conversation. I observed that, among the dancers, each couple contained one ordinary-looking man and one man much like the servant who had opened the door, dressed unconvincingly as a woman.

Mother Clap led us to a parlor in the back of the house, where a fire burned pleasingly. She invited us to sit and poured us both a glass of port from a decanter, though I observed that she took none herself.

"I've sent Mary to fetch Teaser. He might be indisposed, however."

I shuddered to think what might indispose him. I believe Mother Clap must have read my expression, because she gazed at me rather unkindly. "You do not approve of us here, Mr. Weaver?"

"It is not for me to approve or disapprove," I answered, "but you must acknowledge that the men who spend their time here engage in most unnatural acts."

"Aye, it is unnatural. It is unnatural too for a man to see clearly at night, but that does not prevent you from lighting your way with a candle or lantern, does it?"

"But is it not so," Elias chimed in, with an eagerness I knew represented more the pleasure of exercising his intellect than because he felt passion for the issue, "that the holy writings forbid sodomy? They do not forbid illumination."

Mother Clap gave Elias an appraising look. "They do, indeed, forbid sodomy. And they also forbid fornication with the ladies, do they not, Mr. Libertine? I wonder, my good sir, if you are as quick to raise the objections of the holy scriptures on that score as well."

"I am not," he agreed.

"And did not our Savior," she asked me, "command that we raise up the powerless and wretched, take in and give comfort to those whom the powerful and privileged shun?"

"You must direct all inquiries regarding the Savior to Mr. Gordon," I said.

Elias inclined his head in a seated bow. "I believe you have the best of us, madam. We are creatures shaped by the morals of our society. It may well be, as you propose, that our society's objections are the arbitrary products of our time and place and nothing more."

"One may be inclined to be the product of his time and place," she said, "but is not the virtuous man obligated to make the effort to be more?"

"You most certainly have the right of it," I said, by way of surrender, for though I could not master my feelings on the subject, I knew well that her words were just. As there appeared to be nothing more she could add to illuminate her feelings, and as we inquired no more, we sat now in silence, listening to the crackle of the fire, until, some minutes later, the door opened and a rather ordinary-looking fellow, plainly dressed like a merchant, entered the room. He was perhaps seven or eight and thirty, with an even, boyish face, marred by both freckles and irregular blotching of the skin of the sort more generally associated with much younger men.

"I believe you have asked to see me," he said quietly.

"These gentlemen are Mr. Benjamin Weaver and his associate, Elias Gordon," Mother Clap informed him, making it clear she intended to remain for the interview.

Elias and I both rose to offer our bows. "You are, I believe, Mr. Teaser?"

"That is the name I use here, yes," he said.

He took his seat, and so we did the same.

"May I inquire your true name?" I asked.

He shook his head. "I prefer to keep that private. You must understand that I have a wife and family, and they should be very troubled to know of my dealings here."

I had no doubt he was entirely correct on that score. "You are familiar, I believe, with a Mr. Absalom Pepper."

Teaser shook his head. "I have never heard of any such man."

I felt a pang of despair, but then it occurred to me that Teaser was not his real name, and there was no reason to believe that Pepper would be any more forthcoming. "A man with an interest in silk weaving," I said. "One who carried a book and made notes upon the subject."

"Oh, yes," said Teaser, who now perked up with interest and even agitation. "Miss Owl. Do you know of her? Where is she?"

"Owl," Mother Clap said. "Why, it's been some months since we've had word of her. I've been concerned, I have."

"What news of her?" Teaser asked. "Did she send you to find me? I have been so concerned. She one day merely stopped attending, and I feared the worst. I feared that her family must have discovered our secret, for why else would she abandon me so? Still, surely she could have sent me a note. Oh, why did she not?"

Elias and I exchanged a glance. I looked at the floor for a moment while I gathered the courage to meet Teaser's eye. "You must prepare yourself for unhappy news. Owl, as you style him, is no more."

"What?" Mother Clap demanded. "Dead? How?"

Teaser sat stunned, his eyes wide and wet, and then he slumped over in his chair, one hand pressed to his head in an attitude of theatrical despair. However, I had no doubt that he felt it quite sincerely. "How can she be dead?"

The confusion of gender began to wear at me. "It is a rather complex affair," I said. "There is much of this I myself don't entirely understand, but there are those who believe the East India Company may have been behind the mischief."

"The East India Company," Teaser said, with an affecting mix of anger and misery. "Oh, I warned her about crossing them, but she would not listen. No, she would not. Owl always had to have things her own way."

Given that the worthy of whom we spoke, at the time of his death, was married to at least three women as well as consorting with sodomites, I could not find any reason to challenge this assessment. "I know this must be a terrible shock to you," I said, "but I must nevertheless beg you to answer some of our questions at the moment."

"Why?" he asked, face cradled in hands. "Why should I help you?"

"Because we have been asked to find out who did this terrible thing and bring those responsible to justice. Can you not tell me why you believed the East India Company would wish him dead?"

"By whom have you been hired?" he asked. "Who wants to see justice served?"

I understood I was at a crossroads. There could be no turning back, and in truth I was tired of half lies and deceptions. I was tired of conducting half an inquiry, and I wanted things brought to a head. And so I told him. "A man named Cobb hired me."

"Cobb?" Teaser said. "Why would he care?"

My reader can imagine how I had to contain the urge to jump from my seat. No one in London's business or social circles had ever heard of Cobb, but here a sodomite once involved with a man with three other wives spoke the name as though it were common as dust. And yet I knew that if he were to trust me, I needed to maintain authority and withhold my surprise.

I therefore shook my head. "As to that I cannot say," I told him, as though the matter were nothing to me. "Cobb is but the man who hired me. His motives are his own. Though it is an interesting question. Perhaps you might speculate."

Teaser rose from his chair so quickly, it was nearly a leap. "I must go. I must lie down. I—I want to help you, Mr. Weaver. I want to see justice done, I promise you. But I cannot speak of it this instant. Give me a moment to lie down, to weep, to collect my thoughts."

"Of course," I said, casting a glance at Mother Clap, for I did not wish to impose on her hospitality. She nodded her assent.

Teaser left the room quickly, and the three of us were left in awkward silence.

"You made no great effort to soften the blow," Mother Clap said. "Perhaps you don't believe that mollies feel love as you do."

"Of course not," I said, now feeling somewhat irritated. Mother Clap seemed to feel that my insensitivity toward sodomites was at the root of all the world's evils. "When it comes to delivering unpleasant news, it is my experience that no way is kind or sensitive or gentle. The news is what it is, and far better it should be out, that it might be dealt with."

"I see you do not understand the situation. Owl was not merely Teaser's friend, or merely his lover. Owl was his wife."

"His wife," I said, making a great effort to keep my voice even.

"Perhaps not in the eyes of the law but surely in the eyes of God. Indeed, the ceremony was performed by an Anglican priest, a man who moves through the world as effortlessly and as free of taint as you do, Mr. Weaver."

Evidently, she knew little of my life, but I let that pass. "The men here marry one another?"

"Oh, yes. One assumes the role of a wife, who is forever referred to as *she* from that point on, and their match is as serious and unbreakable as that between man and woman."

"And in the case of Mr. Teaser and Owl," Elias asked, "was this an unbreakable match?"

"On the part of Teaser, certainly," Mother Clap said, with a certain amount of sadness, "but I fear Owl may have been more varied in her interests."

"Among the other men?" I asked.

"And, if you must know, among the ladies as well. Many men who come here would never, if they had their way, gaze upon female flesh again, but others have developed the taste and cannot move away from it. Owl was such a one."

"If I may be so bold as to say so," I told her, "I am not surprised by your intelligence."

"Because you think all men must lust after female flesh?"

"Not for that reason, no. For the reason that Mr. Absalom Pepper, whom you call Owl, was married to at least three women simultaneously. He was a bigamist, madam, and I believe a shameless opportunist as well. It is my belief that Pepper wished to use Mr. Teaser for some means of his own. To that end, he must have seduced the poor fellow to make his heart soft and his purse open."

"A man," Mother Clap observed, "is always trying to open one sort of purse or another."

She opened her mouth to elaborate but was interrupted by a loud crashing noise from outside our room. This was followed by several shouts, some rugged and manly, others in the falsetto of a man imitating a woman. I heard the sound of heavy objects toppling and more shouts, these low and with the air of authority.

"Dear Lord!" Mother Clap sprang from her chair with a surprising amount of agility for a woman her age. Her skin had grown white, her eyes wide, her lips pale. "It's a raid! I knew this day must come."

She opened the door and threw herself out. I heard a somber voice cry out that someone must stop in the name of the king, and another cried out that someone must stop in the name of God. I found it difficult to credit that anyone out there was acting with the authority of either.

"The Reformation of Manners men," Elias said. "That's why they were out here; they were coordinating a raid with the constables. We've got to get to Teaser. If they arrest him, we may never be able to get him back."

He didn't need to finish the thought. If Teaser were arrested and jailed, there was a strong possibility he would be dead before we could get to him, for the other prisoners would bludgeon a sodomite to death rather than share space with him.

I pulled my hanger from its scabbard and lunged toward the window, where I made short work of the curtain lining. I handed one strip of the linen to Elias while I proceeded to tie another around my face, concealing everything below my eyes.

"Are we planning on robbing the constables?" Elias asked me.

"Do you wish to be recognized? You may have a hard time convincing the gentlemen of London to permit you to administer an emetic once you've been smoked as a molly."

He required no further argument. The crude mask—not unlike the sort I would, on occasion, resort to during my youthful days on the highway—was around his face in an instant, and together we rushed out into the fray.

Two masked men brandishing weapons must always attract attention, and here it was no different. Indeed, the constables and the mollies regarded us with equal dread. We pushed through the crowds of men engaged in the unfathomable dance of arrest and resistance, looking for our man but seeing no sign of him.

In the main hall, where once had been dancing, all was now in chaos. Some men cowered in corners while others fought mightily, brandishing candlesticks and pieces of broken furniture. Everywhere tables and chairs lay strewn in disorder; broken glass covered the floor, making islands in the pools of spilled wine and punch. There were some two dozen constables—or roughs who had been hired to act as such—and along with them, another dozen or so men of the Society for the Reformation of Manners. I could not help but reflect that men with such an interest in manners ought to act better than these. I saw a pair of constables holding a molly down on the ground while a Reformation man kicked at him. A group of three or four mollies tried to leave the room, but they were struck down by constables while the Reformation men cheered from a safe distance. The constables were bullies and ruffians, and the Reformation men were cowards. It is ever thus that the cause of righteousness is advanced.

"Teaser!" I called out to the panicked mollies. "Who has seen Teaser?"

No one heard or minded me. These unfortunates had their own difficulties, and the constables were attempting to ascertain if they should try to apprehend us or let us pass. No one moved to detain us, for there were certainly much less robust fish to be hooked. The Society for the Reformation of Manners men—they were the easiest to spy, for these were the ones who cowered and moaned if we even turned our eyes in their direction—demonstrated another attribute of those who would hide their cruelty behind the guise of religion. With such a fervent belief in their Lord, they were ever reluctant to risk being sent to meet him.

"Teaser!" I shouted again. "I must find Teaser. I will get him away from here."

At last one man called to me. A pair of constables had him by either arm, and blood dripped in a pathetic trickle from his nose. His wig hung askew, but still on his head. One of the men who held him was in the process of showing his fellow how disgusting these mollies were— he demonstrated this by grabbing the prisoner's arse and squeezing, as though it belonged to a succulent whore.

This poor fellow's face was twisted in pain and humiliation, but when he saw us, he somehow understood we were not with his enemies, and some expression of sympathy in my eyes may have prompted him to speak. "Teaser's escaped," he called to me. "He's gone out the front with the big blackie."

I began to move toward the front of the house. A pair of constables moved forward to block my path, but I barreled against them with my shoulder, and they fell away easily enough, making room for me and Elias—cowering close behind me—to pass.

Once we pushed through the main room, we were mostly out of the fray. A trio of constables chased after us, but not very hard, mostly for form's sake, so they could explain later that their efforts to apprehend us failed. No one paid these men enough to risk their lives. Arresting a pack of mollies was easy enough work, but best to leave masked bandits for the soldiers.

At the door, a pair of Reformation men stood keeping watch, but when they saw us come charging they quickly moved aside. One moved so fast he lost his balance and fell in my way, and I had to leap over him to keep from stumbling. Outside on the street a crowd had begun to gather, and they hardly knew what to make of us, but our appearance was met mostly with drunken cheers.

Fortunately the stoop was fairly well raised and gave me a sufficient view of the surrounding areas. I looked back and forth, and then I saw them. It was Teaser—I recognized him in an instant, despite the gloom of the street—and he was being pulled along by a very large and surprisingly graceful man. It was dark and I could not see his face, but I had no doubt that Teaser's abductor was none other than Aadil.

CHAPTER TWENTY-SIX

—

*H*OLBORN IS FULL OF COUNTLESS LITTLE STREETS AND DARK ALLEYS, so it might, at first glance, seem the ideal place to make one's escape, but many of these alleys are dead ends, and even a tough like Aadil, I reasoned, would not want to face two pursuers and manage a prisoner while pinned in a corner. I was therefore not very surprised when I saw that he ran down Cow Lane and toward the sheep pens. Perhaps he meant to lose us among the animals.

Elias and I both stripped our masks from our faces and dashed after Teaser and his abductor. Rain had begun to fall—not hard, but enough to turn the snow to slush and make the encrusted ice dangerously slick. We barreled forward as best we could upon so dangerous a surface, but it soon became apparent that we no longer had Aadil and Teaser in our sights. Elias began to slow down in defeat, but I would not have it. "To the docks," I said. "He'll try and take his prisoner across the water."

Elias nodded, no doubt disappointed that our running was not yet at an end. But, tired though he may have been, he followed me as we wound our way through the dark streets only to emerge under the open sky of night near the docks. I heard now the chorus of human life: the oyster girls and meat-pie men calling their wares, the cackling of whores, the laughing of drunkards, and, of course, the endless cries of the watermen. "Scholars, will you have whores?" they called, an ancient pun on *scullers* and *oars*. The quip was as old as the city itself, perhaps, but never lost its spice for this easily entertained lot.

We stopped now on the docks, thick with rich and poor alike, all making their way off or onto boats. Then we heard the shouts upon the water. In accordance with another hoary custom, no respect for rank and class was afforded to those who dared to step foot in a boat, and so low men might call what lascivious words they had to high-born ladies or wealthy gentlemen. The king himself, if he deigned to cross the river by boat, would be afforded no deference, though I doubted he knew enough English to understand what insults might be lobbed at him.

Elias was breathing heavily, looking with unfocused eyes at the countless bodies that surrounded us. I gazed out upon the river, illuminated by a hundred lanterns of a hundred boatmen, a mirror of the starry dome of sky above us. There, not fifteen feet from shore, sat an enormous man, his back to us, and Teaser, facing forward. Between them the boatman rowed. Teaser could not have made his escape, for it would be certain death to plunge into those cold waters, even if he could swim. He was held now on a floating prison.

I grabbed Elias by the arm, dragged him down the dock stairs, and pushed him onto the first empty boat we found. I climbed in after him.

"Ho-ho," the boatman said. He was a young fellow, his shoulders thick with muscles. "A couple of young sparks out for a quiet ride, is it?"

"Shut up," I snapped, and jutted out a finger toward Aadil. "See you that boat? There's extra coin in it if you can overtake them."

He gave me a sideways glance but hopped in all the same and shoved off. He might have been a saucy fellow, but for all that, he knew how to put some grit into his labors, and we were soon pushing through the waves. The water here smelled half of the sea, half of sewage, and it lapped furiously against the sides of the boat.

"What is it now?" the boatman asked. "That spark made off with your catamite?"

"Do shut your mouth, fellow," Elias snapped.

"Fellow, is it? I shall fellow you with this here oar, and say it was the first time a whore ever touched your fundament."

"Saying it shan't make it so," Elias groused.

"Don't bother," I told him. "These boatmen will tell you up is down, only to see if doing so will agitate you."

"Up *is* down, my spark," the rower said. "All but fools know that, for it is only the great who tell us which is which, and if we care to look for ourselves we shall find out different."

We were making some significant progress, I must say, and we closed the gap between ourselves and Aadil's boat. At least I thought it was Aadil, for in the dark of the water, with only our lanterns to light our way, it was not always easy to tell which boat was which. Nevertheless, I felt reasonably certain. When I saw a figure in the boat we pursued turn around, and then urge his boatman to row faster, I knew we still hunted our true quarry.

"They've seen us," I told the boatman. "Faster."

"It don't get any faster than this," he answered, no longer having the wind for banter.

In the boat, the silhouette of Aadil turned again, snapped something at the boatman, and when he didn't get what he wished, I observed him shoving the boatman aside. He began to row himself.

Somehow my own boatman caught sight of this, and once more found the strength within to run his mouth. "What's this?" he shouted over to the other boatman. "You let that spark steal your whore?"

"I'll get it back," he called over, "and you'll find it soon enough lodged in your sweet-smelling shitter."

"No doubt," our boatman called, "for it is but a shitten stick you wield, and it seeks the fundament the way a baby or a whoremonger seeks your mother's bubbies."

"Your mother has no bubbies," the other called back, "for she was naught but a hairy he-bear who conceived you after being swived in the arse by a libertine hunter who knew neither arse from cunny—such a man being your father, or perhaps an ape of Africk; who can tell the one from the other?"

"And your father," our boatman returned, "was the whoreson bum-firking daughter—"

"Quiet!" I cried, loud enough to be heard not just by our boatman but by the other as well.

In that instant, I heard the other's oars quiet and when I looked over, even in the dark I could see them lifting out of the water. From the boat I heard a strange and yet familiar voice shout, "Weaver, is that you?" The voice contained hope and humor—and nothing at all unpleasant.

"Who is that?" I answered back.

" 'Tis Aadil," he said. And then he let out an enormous laugh. "Here I have been exhausting myself, fleeing as though there were someone dangerous after us, and all along it was only you?"

I could not but note his speech. Every time I had heard him open his mouth, he had grunted his words like a beastly savage. Now, though he spoke in the same musical accent he had always used, his speech was refined, grammatically proper, and on an equal footing to anyone born here.

I hardly knew what to say. "What is this?" was the best I could manage.

He let out another rich laugh. "I think," he called over to us, "it is time we talked to each other in somewhat more frank terms. Let's meet at the docks, and we'll find someplace to tell each other our stories."

MERCIFULLY, OUR BOATMEN seemed to understand that something most unexpected had passed between us, and they remained quiet for the remainder of our journey. Elias gave me searching looks, but I hardly knew how to answer his unspoken questions. I merely pulled my coat around me, for it suddenly seemed to grow much colder as the light, steady rain fell upon us.

Their boat landed first, and I did not entirely believe that Aadil's offer to treat with us was not a clever trick—not until he stepped out and waited patiently as we docked and climbed out as well. This side of the river was as crowded and noisy and lively as the other, and it was a very strange place for us to talk, but Aadil merely smiled at us and then offered us a deep bow.

"I have not been entirely honest with you about myself. Of course, you have not been entirely honest with me either, or anyone else at Craven House, but that is no matter. I've since concluded you mean me no harm and, indeed, your presence has been a most interesting catalyst." He looked at the sky. "Sir, this rain continues apace, and if I have learned anything of your English weather, it shall get more unpleasant before it clears. Shall we find some warm and dry shelter?"

I ignored the pleasantries, though I too was anxious to get out of the rain. "Who the devil are you?"

He let out another of his thick laughs. It sounded as though it echoed about his chest before being set free. "My name is, indeed, Aadil. I am Aadil Wajid Ali Baghat, and, though unworthy, I must endure the unbearable honor of being a contemptible servant of his most glorious majesty, the Emperor Muhammad Shah Nasir ad Dîn, *shah an shah,* king of kings, Mogul of India."

"Rabbit it!" Elias whispered. "The filthy bugger's an India spy."

"Hardly filthy, but a spy all the same. Yes, I am an agent of the Mogul. I have been sent here to deal a blow that will, I hope, curb the power of the East India Company. Would you like to hear more?"

Elias appeared as dumbstruck as I felt, yet I managed a few words. "I am not certain I wish to deal any blows against the Company. I have no love of the men of Craven House, I promise you, but I'm not sure its destruction is my affair."

"Perhaps," Aadil said, "you hardly know your affair, or the faces of your enemies, or the nature of their malice."

"No," I agreed. "I don't."

"Then come with me to a nearby tavern if you wish to find out. I shall increase the offer of warmth and dryness with food and drink."

"Now that," Elias said, "is the offer you should have made in the first place."

AS A JEW AMONG ENGLISHMEN, I have ever felt out of place in my own native city, but I soon learned that to be a Jew is a very easy thing compared to being an East Indian. We could hardly walk three feet without someone calling to Aadil or stopping him. Children called him *blackbird* with the meanest contempt or else ran up to him to rub his dark skin and see if it would come off. Men moved out of his way, holding their noses, though he smelled far cleaner, and indeed more floral, than any of their lot could hope. Whores called out to him, telling him they gave special prices to Africans or else that they had never a black privy member and wished to gaze upon one.

I believed I should go mad with rage or simply distracted with chatter were I asked to live his life, but it was clear that Aadil had long since grown familiar to such usage, and he took no note. Nevertheless, I soon discovered that there was one way in which Jew and East Indian were very much alike: the merchant, no matter what prejudices he might hold in his heart, regards the silver of all nations equally. We found our way to a crowded tavern, and though the publican gave Aadil an unwelcoming look, he changed his mind soon enough when the East Indian

304 | DAVID LISS

offered an unwarranted measure of silver for a private room, food, and drink.

Aadil must have known his taverns well, for it was a comfortably appointed room, with two unboarded windows, ample sconces for light, and a handsomely laid table. The food was set before us, though Aadil would have none of it. The meats, he said, were not prepared in accordance with his religion. The same faith, he explained, forbade the consumption of spirituous liquors.

"No liquors, quotha!" Elias cried out. "By the devil, Weaver, I've finally discovered a more unappealing religion than yours." He would not allow our host's abstinence to slow his progress, however, and quickly poured himself a glass of wine and began to inflict serious harm on a plate of cold chicken.

Through all of this, our friend Mr. Teaser sat quietly, hands in his lap. He shook his head when offered food and drink. I though it not entirely surprising. After all, he had heard terrible news and witnessed some remarkable events that day. Nevertheless, I could not understand his passivity in the hands of this black-skinned giant. There was naught to conclude but that Teaser had enjoyed dealings with Aadil Wajid Ali Baghat before and had been given cause to trust the Indian spy.

This supposition was borne out in the sequel, for though Mr. Teaser sat in utter dejected silence, Aadil nevertheless poured a healthy portion of wine into a pewter cup and handed it over to the unfortunate. "Drink it, sir. I know you English find it restoring."

Teaser took the cup in his hands, but he made no motion to drink. "I can't believe she's dead," Teaser intoned. "And poor Mother Clap and my friends—what will become of them? We must go back to help them."

I own I had not expected such brave sentiments from a man who would marry another man, but the night was already full-freighted with surprises and would, I was now certain, yet contain many more.

"We cannot go back, and there's nothing to be done for them," I said. "I am sorry to put it to you so, but it is the truth. With the constables and Reformation men there, it is out of our hands, and from their behavior I gathered they were in the service of some other power, one with money to make certain the business was done. We can only hope that when their dark purpose is fulfilled, they will lose interest in the prosecution of your friends."

"And who do you believe to be that hidden power?" Aadil asked.

I could tell from his tone of voice that he knew himself and only wanted to hear me say it. I could think of no reason to refuse. "Unless I am very much mistaken, the East India Company. I suppose I should say, a faction within the Company, but if it is Ellershaw's or Forester's or some other hand that moves these pieces, I cannot say."

Aadil nodded slowly. "I think you may be right, but I have perhaps a better sense of which faction is behind this. I shall tell you what I know and why I am here. I understand some little bit of your predicament, Mr. Weaver, and I know you are not acting of your own free will. It is my greatest hope that once you hear what I have to say, you will understand that mine is the cause of justice, and you will be willing to aid me in the completion of my tasks."

"The cause of justice," I spat. "Was it in the cause of justice that you murdered Carmichael in the service of Forester?"

He shook his head. "You mustn't think it, for I was fond of Carmichael and his good humor, and I would not harm him. I own I allowed you to believe otherwise, for it helped me to flush you out, which was my greatest concern at the time. I was working in the service of Forester that night—or leading him to believe I worked in his service, I ought to say—and I can inform you that neither he nor I had anything to do with that crime."

"It is convenient for you to say so. And what exactly have you been doing for Mr. Forester all this time?"

Aadil grinned. "As for that, I care not to provide too much detail at the moment. Suffice to say that, like so many men of the East India Company, he has been in search of the mysterious textile engine, and he has used me as his servant in that regard. I, however, have not been entirely the servant of the Company that he believes me to be."

"So you admit your deception."

"No one here," he told me, "is guiltless when it comes to the crime of deceiving the East India Company. But think not that I would harm an innocent like Mr. Carmichael. Not for any cause."

"It does make sense," Elias offered. "Just as Mr. Baghat pretended to be ignorant and hostile, he pretended to have killed Carmichael. That he possesses a generous spirit, and is no true enemy of yours, has been demonstrated tonight."

"What has also been demonstrated tonight is that Mr. Baghat is a skilled dissembler, and we believe him at our own hazard." The words came out hard and fast, and as I spoke them I wondered if I remained truly suspicious or if I resented having been so soundly fooled. Or, it occurred to me, that I find it difficult to change my opinion of a man in the blink of an eye. Recognizing that I could not entirely trust my feelings in this, I softened my stance and rose briefly to bow in Aadil's direction. "Nevertheless, it would be the wisest course to hear all you have to say and give credit to your words where I can."

Aadil returned the bow, showing he had learned British customs as well as speech. "I appreciate your generosity."

"It may be as much curiosity as generosity," I said, without harshness. "Perhaps you can begin by informing me of your connection with Mr. Teaser here, and how it is that you came to his rescue so fortuitously."

Teaser nodded gravely, as though to indicate that I had indeed chosen the right point to enter into these matters.

"It is for this gentleman here and Absalom Pepper that I came to your island in the first place. You must forgive me, sir," Aadil said, turning to Teaser, "for I know you are kindly disposed to Mr. Pepper, and for me to say what I know I must speak ill of him."

Teaser looked down. "It has become all too apparent to me that Owl was not the person I believed. Say what you must. I shall be no less stung for your keeping quiet."

Aadil nodded. "Not two years ago, a low-level clerk working for his most imperial majesty, the Emperor Muhammad Shah Nasir ad Dîn, may he and his sons reign forever, received a very intriguing letter from Mr. Pepper, a letter he thought worthy of showing to his superiors, and they to theirs, and so it went until it reached the eyes of the Mogul's top advisers. In this letter, Mr. Pepper announced that he had invented a remarkable engine, one that would enable ordinary Europeans to produce Indian-like calicoes from cottons farmed in the Americas. He had, in short, invented an engine that could damage one of my nation's principal industries by providing it with a genuine rival."

"So Forester was not wrong," Elias said.

"He was not wrong to believe it could be done, though he was wrong about much else. Needless to say, the Mogul took a great interest in this project, but he believed it would be wiser to observe these matters from afar. As you know, the East India Company may well be a private trading concern, but it is so close to the British government as nearly to be a very part of it. To involve ourselves too directly might bring us dangerously close to war, and with an important trading partner too. So, instead, the Mogul dispatched agents, and to Mr. Pepper we delivered only silence."

Elias was nodding. "So, having heard nothing from the Mogul, Pepper began to pursue matters on his own."

"That is precisely what happened, sir. When he contacted us, he had only the plans for his engine. He had hoped we would pay handsomely to suppress this invention, but when we did not comply he began to pursue the manufacturing of a working model."

"And to that end, Pepper needed capital," I said. "And so he began to ply his charms and pursue a series of marriages, each with a dowry he might apply toward building his engine."

"That was part of how he did it, yes," Aadil agreed. "Pepper might have been a clever man, but he was not a schooled one. He had always made his way in the world by using his charm and becoming appearance, and old habits are not so easily banished, so it occurred to him to seek out such financial men as he could win over with his familiar tricks, which is to say, men who have a passion for other men."

"And so it is he discovered me," Teaser said, breaking his silence. "I have long worked upon Exchange Alley, brokering investments and investing for myself. Owl, whom you call Pepper, made me believe he felt a tenderness for me, and I could refuse him nothing. I gave him more than three hundred pounds."

"And did he create his engine?" Elias asked.

"Perhaps he might have if he had gone to our friend here first," Aadil said, "but, as with many foul schemes, Pepper's began to take a great deal of effort to maintain. He had eleven households for which to provide, and he dared not abandon his wives, lest they come in search of him, discover his trickery, and see him hanged for his crimes. So it was that in his last days all the money he could raise went toward the maintenance of lies already told. For all that, he was too clever and too ambitious to content himself with this financial purgatory. In the end, he discovered, through his dealings with one broker, that there may be better ways to gain wealth than through marriage or amorous attachments. So Pepper began to seek out other investors. And it was in this way he met someone with whom I believe you have an acquaintance."

"Cobb," I said, feeling that all had begun to turn clear. Sadly for me, I could not have been more mistaken. I still understood nothing.

Aadil shook his head. "Not Mr. Cobb, though we shall come to him and his role soon enough. No, the man you know who helped to fund his scheme was a merchant of your own nation, a Mr. Moses Franco."

A LONG SILENCE descended upon the room. Perhaps it was not so long. It may have been only a matter of a few seconds, but to my mind it stretched on unendingly. Teaser showed the puzzled expression of a man out of the know, and Aadil appeared to await my response, but Elias studied the rough wooden floor. He knew what I knew—that something was terribly wrong within my own camp, and a man I had believed to be an unwavering ally might be something entirely different.

But was he? A hundred thoughts raced through my mind. I had never spoken to Mr. Franco about Pepper, never mentioned his name. And he, for his part, had never concealed that he'd had dealings that involved the East India Company. Indeed, he'd told me that his dealings had been unfriendly, and that the Company had always viewed his interventions with a hostile eye. And why should they not, I wondered, if he had been endeavoring to support an invention that would shut down the better part of their trade? It troubled me that Franco had never mentioned this project to me, but then he might not have thought it relevant to my inquiry. Or, and perhaps more likely, he wished to protect his secret, at least for as long as he might do so without bringing harm to himself or me.

It was from these thoughts that I was suddenly jarred by the crash of glass and an explosion of light and heat. No, not heat, but hotness. Flame.

What had happened? I felt myself reacting before I even knew, for the room was ablaze. I was up and pulling Elias away from the heart of the flame while some distant corner of my consciousness told me what I had seen. A barrel, alight and clearly laden with lamp oil or some other flammable liquid, had come crashing in through the window. Elias was now moving toward the open window to escape, but I pulled him back.

"No," I shouted. "Whoever wished to burn us is surely still out there, hoping to flush us out. We must flee with the rest of the patrons and lose ourselves in the crowd."

"Agreed," Aadil said, pulling Teaser by the arm.

I opened the door to our chamber, began to flee, but checked my pace. It became clear at once that ours was not the only room to have been so assaulted. For an instant I harbored the obscenely flattering idea that the attack had not been set upon us but that we had been hapless victims of circumstance, unfortunate bystanders to an unrelated conflict, but I knew this was a foolish hope. There were great powers at work against us, and there could be no denying that we were meant to burn to death.

Elias, who never claimed bravery—indeed, who nursed his cowardice the way other men nursed virtue—was out the door before me, and the instant I stepped through, another barrel came surging into our room, crashing against the wall in the only portion of the closet not yet ablaze. The flames spread in an instant, cutting off my view and access to Teaser and Aadil.

I paused, torn between safety and duty. Elias suffered no such conflict, and was already gone, mixed with the crowd, heading toward the nearest exit.

"Mr. Baghat!" I cried. "Are you unharmed?"

"Thus far," he called back. "If you've a clear path, take it. I cannot make it out that way. My companion and I must take our chances with the window."

"Use caution," I began.

"Tend to yourself," he shouted. "Go now, and we shall talk later."

There was no arguing with such sound advice. I pushed my way into the mass of bodies now struggling to escape the tavern. There were shouts and cries and the sounds of cracking wood and breaking pottery. Thick smoke now filled the rooms, obscuring my view so that I could not see my best course. I had to trust that the people in front of me had some animal sense of safety that would lead us through the inferno. It was a terrible thing to have to trust strangers, but I did not see that I had much choice, so I moved forward, keeping my head down against the smoke, my shoulders hunched against the tongues of flame.

At last we poured out of doors. Already the constables were on hand, as well as neighbors come to fight the fire, passing bucket after bucket of water in order to splash them upon the building. I observed, even in my fear and relief, that they managed the situation as well as they could. There was no hope of saving the tavern—it was already as good as burned to ash—but the surrounding structures could be saved. We were fortunate in the weather, for the rain had picked up since we'd entered, and all around us, over the shouts of terror and the crackle of wood, came the sizzle of water against the advance of flame.

I wondered briefly if whoever had attempted to kill us would have tried a different method had it not been raining. Even a man who might murder without regret may find it harder to burn down half the city with as free a mind. There was no ease about this, however. I could see already that at least half a dozen people had been burned badly. They lay upon the dirt, screaming for aid.

Thus it was that I found Elias. He may have been no lionheart, but now that the danger had passed, he did not hesitate to lend his skills to the needy. He was kneeling over a young man, hardly more than a boy, really, whose arms had been badly scorched.

"Gather some of that snow," he shouted to a woman standing nearby, one of the barmaids, I thought. "Press it upon his arm and don't let him take it off for a full quarter hour."

As he disengaged himself from this patient to see who was next most in need of his services—limited though they were, he would be the first to admit, for burns were terrible injuries—he suddenly went slack and pointed toward the building.

I saw at once what he had seen, though I might have wished I hadn't. Stumbling from the flames like a man emerging from his own grave came Aadil. His clothes and skin had been scorched, and most of his stockings had been quite burned off. Horrible red burns covered his legs, and his face was a mass of soot darker even than his skin. But what troubled me most was the blood. It was on his face, his arms, his legs, but mostly his chest, and it was bubbling forth.

Elias and I both ran forward and caught him as he toppled over. It took nearly all our combined strength to keep him from falling to the ground. Once we set him down, Elias tore open his shirt. "He's been shot," he said. "At very close range, from the look of the powder burns on his clothes."

"What can you do?"

He said nothing and looked away. I understood there was nothing to say.

"Teaser is dead," Aadil gasped.

"Save your strength," Elias told him.

He managed the briefest of laughs. "For what? I go to Paradise, and I have no fear of death, so you need not trouble yourself to comfort me." He paused here so he could cough out mucousy blood.

"You did what you could," I said. "Who shot you, Mr. Baghat? Did you see?"

"I tried to save him, but I could not get to him in time."

"Who shot you, Mr. Baghat?" I said again. "Who did this to you so we might avenge you?"

He looked away and his eyes closed. I thought he was already dead, but it happened that he had one more utterance in him. He said: "Get help. Celia Glade."

Having uttered these words, he breathed his last.

—

CHAPTER TWENTY-SEVEN

*W*E MEANT NO DISRESPECT TO OUR NEWFOUND AND QUICKLY LOST associate, but Elias and I recognized that we would do well to avoid any notice that might fall upon ourselves, and we certainly had no wish to fall in with any constables who might show their faces. I knew too well that a visit before a judge, no matter what one's degree of guilt or innocence, could easily end in a lengthy stay in prison, and I was in no mood to attempt to explain myself even before that most mythical of creatures, the honest magistrate.

Unwilling to face the chaos of another boat crossing, we found a hackney to take us across the bridge. Elias wrung his hands and bit at his lip, but I could tell he had control over his emotions and conducted himself with philosophy. It is a hard thing, even for one such as myself who has chosen a life often filled with violence, to see one man die before your eyes and to be in the same room with another and then learn he has, moments later, burned to death. As a surgeon, Elias was often confronted with injury and often had to inflict hurt himself, but it is quite another thing to witness violence visited upon the innocent, and he took it hard.

"What did it mean?" he said at last. "His last words about Miss Glade?"

Discovering Elias's congress with her seemed now to be a lifetime ago, and I had no energy to spare to think of it then. The betrayal had been insignificant in the light of all that had happened, and I meant to treat it accordingly. "It could mean either of two things: that we must seek her help, or we must seek protection from her."

In the dark of the hackney, I could see him nod methodically. "And which do you think?"

"I know nothing but that we must see Mr. Franco at once. I must learn what he knows of this Teaser fellow and Pepper's invention."

"He is supposed to be your friend," Elias said. "Can it be that he serves the Company?"

I shook my head. "I don't think so. I think it more likely that he has made some investments, perhaps knows more than he realizes, and that he was selected as Cobb's first victim as much for Cobb's convenience as my consternation."

"To keep him from realizing a connection and revealing it?"

"That is my guess. Baghat and Teaser suggested he had some investment in the engine, and the engine is at the very heart of this madness. If there is a way to get our hands on the designs for the cotton-weaving device, we must get it to Ellershaw, and we must do so before midday tomorrow."

"What?" Elias barked. "Give it to the Company? Have you not understood how monstrous it is?"

"Of course I do, but these companies are born to be monstrous. We cannot ask them not to be what they are. Ellershaw once said that government is not the solution to the problems of business, it *is* the problem of business. In that he was wrong. The company is a monster, and it is for Parliament to decide the size and shape of its cage. I shall not quarrel with Company men for seeking to make their profit, so there is great harm neither in keeping the plans from Ellershaw nor giving them up."

"Then why do it?"

"Because the one thing I know about Cobb, the one thing of which I can be certain, is that he knows of the plans for Pepper's engine and he is desperate to possess them. And so the plans must be found. We shall see who threatens whom if I dangle the plans over a fire or promise to deliver them to Craven House. It is time for us to drive this coach. My uncle is dead. Mr. Franco rots in jail. The men I seek to guide me end up murdered. It is foolishness to believe that we will fare much better unless we make new rules for this game."

"Cobb now threatens only us and your aunt," Elias said. "If we choose to ignore the threat, to elude whatever bailiffs he sends after us, he cannot stop us. As to your aunt, I have no doubt that the good lady will endure any temporary inconvenience, no matter how distressing, if you can use it to strike back at your enemies."

Though he could not see it, I offered him a smile. It had been a terrible night for him, and for our friendship, but I knew full well what he had just said to me. He would risk Cobb's wrath and stand by me. And I knew he risked far more than his freedom. Elias was a surgeon with a fine reputation; he had men and women of station to visit. He would risk it all to stand by my side and fight my enemies.

"I thank you," I said. "With luck, this shall be resolved soon. We'll know more after we speak with Mr. Franco."

"Do you then propose that we simply go to sleep and await the opening of the Fleet Prison?"

I let out a humorless laugh. "No, I am in no mind to wait. We'll go to the Fleet now."

"They won't let you visit a prisoner in the middle of the night."

"Anything may be got at any time for silver," I told him. "You know that."

"Indeed," he said. It was hard not to hear the bitterness in his voice. "Has not this whole affair been in defense of that view?"

THE COACHMAN APPEARED skeptical about taking us within the Rules of the Fleet, fearing we would refuse to pay him, and because of the peculiarities of that neighborhood, he would have no legal recourse. Paying him in advance quelled that anxiety, though he still appeared uneasy about a pair of men seeking to gain entrance to the Fleet at night. Nevertheless, he agreed to take us and await our return, though neither Elias nor I expressed much surprise when we heard his coach retreating the moment our backs were turned.

It was now well after midnight, so when I pounded upon the prison gates it took several minutes before anyone arrived to slide back the viewing latch and see who we were and what we wished for.

"I have great need to visit with a prisoner," I said. "One Moses Franco. I must speak with him at once."

"And I must be the king of Prussia," the guard returned. "No visitors at night, and if you weren't a miscreant out about nefarious work, you'd know that." He sniffed a few times like an eager dog. "You smell like a chimney sweep."

I ignored this observation, which I had no doubt was true enough. "Let us dispense with the games. How much to view the prisoner right now?"

The guard did not even pause. "Two shillings."

I handed him the coins. "'Twere better if you, like a public inn, would post a slate with the day's prices and save your customers the trouble of games."

"Mayhap I like the games," he answered. "Now wait here while I fetch your prisoner."

We pressed ourselves close against the slick stones of the building, for the rain had not let up, and though it had been good news not an hour earlier, now we were cold and wet and miserable. The guard was gone for what felt like an eternity, but he finally returned, close to half an hour later. "I can't help you," he told me. "The prisoner has been released. He's gone."

"Gone?" I shouted. "How could he be gone?"

"It were a strange thing that was related to me, and I'd have been back sooner had I not paused to hear the whole story, but thinking you would wish to hear it too, I stayed to learn of it. Now, having checked the slate with the day's prices, I find that interesting stories relating to released prisoners also cost two shillings, so hand over your silver and be glad the prison ain't charging this week for fruitless fetchings."

I slid the coins through the slat. The guard snatched them up. "Now, here's what I heard. A gentleman showed up and offered to discharge the prisoner of his debts and his prison fees. Nothing unusual about that. It happens all the time, of course, but in this case the story made the rounds, for it seems that the very same fellow who come to pay the piper is the one who committed the prisoner in the first place—fellow by the name of Cobb. And what was more interesting than that was that the prisoner didn't wish to be released to go with this fellow. Said he'd rather stay in prison. But we ain't in the business of running an inn, despite what you might have to say, even though it took a couple of turnkeys to force the reluctant and liberated Mr. Franco into his liberator's coach."

A knot of fear and outrage gripped me. It had not been very long since Elias and I reasoned that Cobb could threaten me now with nothing for which I was not prepared, but it seemed he had anticipated this position. No longer content to let Mr. Franco rot in prison, he now took hold of the man himself. I was ever more determined to strike back and strike back hard, and I was now, more than ever, without any idea of how to do so.

THE NEXT MORNING, now but two days before the meeting of the Court of Proprietors, Elias met me at my rooms, as I had asked, and as early as I asked—clear signs that he was every bit as concerned as I was.

"Ought you not to be at Craven House?" he asked me, "managing affairs from there?"

"There's nothing to manage," I said. "If I cannot find the plans for Pepper's engine, there is nothing to be done. I should very much like to find them prior to the meeting of the Court of Proprietors, since allowing Ellershaw to triumph can only rankle Cobb. But before that we're going to have to rescue Franco."

"And how do we do that?"

"I have some ideas, but first we must speak with Celia Glade."

I saw him turn pale and then redden. "Are you certain that's a sound idea? After all, Mr. Baghat might well have been warning us to stay away from her."

"He might have been, but he might have been advising us to seek her out. I should hate to fail to do that which he struggled to tell us with his dying words."

"And what if he meant those dying words as a warning? Should you not also hate to deliver us into danger?"

"I would indeed hate that. However, facing danger is preferable to doing nothing. If she is the enemy, we shall have an opportunity to confront her."

"I advise against it until we know more."

"I presumed you would," I told him, "as your conduct with her must make you wish to avoid her, and the more so in my presence. Thus I took the liberty of sending her a note this morning, asking her to call upon me if she had anything of moment to say."

Elias, who clearly had nothing of moment to say, turned away.

We spent the next several hours in conversation about how we might retrieve Mr. Franco from Cobb's clutches, and I believed we had struck upon some very good ideas. It was nearly noon when my land-lady knocked upon my door to tell me that a lady was outside in a carriage and she would very much like me to attend her.

Elias and I exchanged looks, but we wasted little time before heading out to the street and approaching a handsome silver and black equipage. Looking out the window was the most marvelously dressed lady, a rare beauty in her silk finery, and no doubt a very wealthy and distinguished figure in the beau monde. At least that was my first thought. My second thought was that this creature was Celia Glade.

"Ah, gentlemen, I'm so glad you could attend. I see I'm not the only one who found little reason to return to Craven House just now. If you two would be so kind as to join me in my equipage, we may drive about the town and speak in private. I'm sure we have much to say to one another."

Elias shook his head, almost imperceptibly, but I saw him clearly enough. I also understood him. It seemed to me that his fear of Celia Glade could not be based on Aadil's warning alone. No, I thought it far more likely that he now confused fear with guilt and that he wished to avoid her because her presence reminded him of his rather unamiable behavior toward me. This struck me as a poor basis for dictating strategy.

"Why should we trust a double-dealer like yourself?" I asked, more to please Elias than because I believed she would have an illuminating answer.

"I have every reason to believe," she answered, "that when you enter my equipage you will know why." She looked to me directly, meeting my eyes. "You may not wish to trust me, sir, but you do nevertheless, so let us not waste time upon foolishness."

I stepped forward and opened the door. Inside, Miss Glade sat in the most gorgeous gown of verdant silk, trimmed with ivory lace. She wore delicate calfskin gloves upon her hands, and a very handsome bonnet sat upon her head. But as wondrous as her clothes might have been, what made her glow was the impish smile she wore upon her face, the look of delighted triumph. And I could not blame her for her feelings, for she had clearly triumphed quite nicely.

Sitting next to her, with his hands bound before him, his legs bound at the ankles—both with thick rope nearly the ivory of Miss Glade's lace—was none other than Mr. Jerome Cobb himself.

She laughed as though we shared a joke. "Now do you wish to hear more?"

"You have my full attention," I said. We took our seats, and the footman closed the door behind us.

THE EQUIPAGE BEGAN to bump along. Miss Glade sat with her hands prettily in her lap and wore upon her face the most devilishly seductive smile. Elias hardly knew where to look, but I looked at Cobb. He sat with his head and shoulders bent forward, looking more like a prisoner of war than—well, I hardly knew what he was.

Astonishingly, it was he who broke the silence. "Weaver," he said. "You must help me. Talk to this madwoman and vouch for me. She has threatened torture and imprisonment and hanging. I cannot endure it. I understand you may take issue with my actions, but I have been kind, have I not?"

I would not give him the satisfaction he desired. He had been more polite to me than had his nephew—that much was certain—but he had been my taskmaster. Instead, I asked, "How is it that this woman was able to make you her prisoner?"

"Let us not concern ourselves with the particulars," Miss Glade said. "For now I should hope you'd be happy that I brought you the villain who has so plagued you."

"And do I not get to learn who you are?" I asked.

She smiled again, and may I be damned if my heart did not melt. "You may know what you wish, but I should prefer not to speak before Mr. Cobb. For now, you may ask him what you like, and later we'll speak privately."

I turned to Cobb. "What Miss Glade says sounds reasonable. Tell me now who you are and what you want. I wish to know why you have done as you have to me. And I want to know where Mr. Franco is."

"Gad, Weaver, can you not see the woman is a monster?"

"I am not yet certain if she be angel or devil, but there is no doubt in my mind about you, sir. Now speak, or I'll give you incentive to do so."

"What, you would put me to the torture, after all I've done for you?"

"I should gladly put you to the torture, and more so because of these claims you make. What have you done for me that I should be so glad of your assistance? You have used me, sir, made me into your puppet and plaything, and you have kept me in the dark all the while. You have abused my friends, and because of your schemes three men lie dead: Mr. Carmichael; Mr. Aadil Baghat, the Mogul's man; and one of Pepper's former associates, called Teaser."

I heard a sharp intake of breath. It was Miss Glade, who now had one delicate glove to her mouth. "Baghat is dead?" Her voice was soft and small. "I had not heard it."

I almost thought to say that it was a relief to me that she did not know everything, but I could see the news was hard for her and I refrained from caustic comments. "It was last night," I told her. "At a tavern in Southwark. We were attempting to rescue this Teaser, though that is not his real name. He was—"

"I know who he was," Miss Glade said. "He was Pepper's lover. One of them."

"Yes. We were attempting to learn what we could from him, and we were attacked. Mr. Baghat died trying to save Teaser's life. He had always pretended to me to be a brute and a monster, but in a very short time I learned his true nature." I turned to Cobb. "I despise you for your bringing about the death of such a man. I care not whether you fired the pistol, ordered it done, or if this was a mere consequence of your other mischief. I shall hold you accountable."

"His country has lost a great servant," Miss Glade said, without trace of irony or falseness. "And so, for that matter, has this one. He was a friend to the Crown."

I looked at her. Could she mean what she said? I had long believed her to be an enemy to the Crown. Could I have been so mistaken?

"Who are you, Cobb?" I asked. "Who are you that you have wrought all this death, and for what purpose?"

"I am only a servant," he said, "with little more power in all this than you. I have been manipulated just as you have been. Oh, have mercy on me, sir, I never meant to harm anyone."

"Who are you?" I demanded once more.

Elias spoke. "Oh, enough." It was the first time he'd spoken since we entered the carriage. "Who is he, Celia?"

I observed his informal use of her name but worked hard to keep my face from registering the disappointment.

"He is an agent of the French Crown," she said. "He's a spy, working against King George and the East India Company."

"A French spy?" Elias blurted. "But that's what we thought *you* were."

Something like amusement flashed across her face. "I shall very much like to know how you reached that conclusion, but that is for later, and Cobb is for now. Go on, tell them," she said to him. "And tell them anything else they wish to know."

"It is only partially true, Mr. Weaver. I do work for the French, though it is not out of any loyalty to them. You see, they bought me in much the way we did you. Through my debts. Only in my case, it was not my family that was threatened, but my own person, and while I have little doubt you would have regarded such dangers to yourself with contempt, I have never been the man you are."

"Perhaps," Elias suggested, "because he chooses to flatter you, you will refrain from breaking his fingers."

"He would be wise not to depend upon it," I said. "Tell me why the French Crown would wish to employ me against Ellershaw."

"I don't know," Cobb told me. "They do not inform me of their reasons, just their desires."

"It's rather obvious, I think," Elias said. "You recall my mentioning that the French are starting to develop their own designs upon the East Indies. To no small degree, our East India Company is viewed as an adjunct to the British Crown, for its wealth increases the wealth of the kingdom, and it is involved in a sort of mercantile conquest. Anything the French can do to harm the East India Company harms the wealth of the British nation."

"Just so," Miss Glade agreed. "And though I doubt our friend here has Mr. Gordon's keen mind, I suspect he knows at least that much. Which suggests that he is not being forthcoming, and that perhaps this finger-breaking you discussed might not be out of order. I have promised to deliver this wretch, but I have made no promises as to his condition."

"Deliver him to whom?" I asked.

"Why, the Tower, of course. He is to be a prisoner of the kingdom."

"Not before he releases Franco from his minions," I said.

"I assure you," Cobb stammered, "he is in no danger. It is not in my power to release him, but you need not fear that any harm will come to him."

"Not in your power?" I asked. "Is he not being held in your house?"

"He is there, yes, but Mr. Hammond has him."

"Your nephew?"

"He is not truly my nephew," Cobb said.

And, at last, I understood. "And neither is he your subordinate either. Mr. Hammond is a high-ranking French agent, one who has worked his way into the highest levels of the British customs, and you are but his plaything. You present yourself as being the man who gives the orders only because it provides a further level of protection for Hammond, is that not so?"

Cobb said nothing, and his silence confirmed my suspicions.

"Does Mr. Cobb have another name, one he uses among the French?" I asked.

Miss Glade nodded. "He is called by them Pierre Simon."

It was as I suspected, and it cleared up one remaining question. "So," I said to Cobb, "you sought not only to serve your masters but yourself? You and Hammond and Edgar, using your French noms de guerre, purchased insurance policies upon my life. Clearly you intended, once you were done with me, to kill me and to profit from doing so."

"It was but business," Cobb said, his voice hardly more than a whisper.

"What shall become of Mr. Franco once Hammond learns that Cobb has been arrested?" Elias asked.

"He won't learn," Miss Glade told us. "We discovered Cobb about to leave the country, sailing for Calais on what appears to be official business for his masters. He shan't be missed for a week or more. Hammond has no idea what's happened to his toadeater."

The equipage then came to a stop. I looked out the window and observed we were hard by the Tower. In a moment a quartet of dour-faced soldiers appeared.

"One moment," Miss Glade said to them. And to me, "Have you further questions for Mr. Cobb? I suspect he shan't be made available again."

"How do I get Mr. Franco out of Hammond's home?"

"You can't," he said. "And I would not try if I were you. Leave it alone, Weaver. You are dealing with men who are far more powerful than you can imagine, and Mr. Franco shan't be harmed if you just leave it alone."

"What does Hammond want with him? Does he hope to keep me in line by holding my friend in his clutches?"

"Hammond only discusses his plans with me when he cannot avoid doing so. If you must have answers, I fear you will have to pose those questions to him directly."

"I assure you," I said, "I shall do just that."

"SO," I BEGAN, "WHO ARE YOU?"

We rode now in her equipage, one fewer with Cobb having been led to his doom at the Tower, safely in the hands of soldiers. Surely there would be pain and torture ahead for him, but Miss Glade showed no sign of distress. She appeared, as always, calm and composed.

"Have you not guessed?"

"Not an agent for the French Crown, as I once supposed, but for the British?" I proposed.

"Just so," she agreed. "We have been aware for some time of the danger to the East India Company on two fronts. First, the French wished to infiltrate that they might steal secrets and, if possible, do damage. As you have no doubt supposed, we could not permit such a thing to happen. To that end, we have been cooperating with the Indian Mogul, who may be uneasy about British presence but is wise enough to want to keep his country from becoming a battleground of European powers. Thus I was working in at least some degree of concert with Aadil Baghat. I don't pretend to believe he was entirely forthcoming with me any more than I was with him, but I knew him to be a good man, and I am genuinely grieved to learn of his death. These French are devils who will stop at nothing." Something like grief passed across her face, but it was gone in an instant.

"You said there were two goals the French wished to accomplish."

"Yes," she said. "The second is Mr. Pepper's engine. If the plans for this device should fall into the wrong hands, it could do great harm to the East India Company. Tea and spices may provide revenue, but it is the textile trade that makes it great. Without that trade, it is but a commercial concern."

"And what is it now?" Elias asked.

"The new face of empire, of course," she answered. "Imagine the possibilities. The British Crown may place its stamp, wield its power, see its will done in nations all about the earth, and never have to deploy its military or naval might, never have to convince its own citizens to leave their homes and move to a foreign and inhospitable land. The East India Company has shown us the way with its mercantile conquest. They fund their own expansions, pay for their own armies, establish their own governors. And all the while, British markets expand, British influence grows, and British power swells. Can you truly wonder why we would wish to protect the Company at nearly any cost?"

"So you wish to crush the fruit of British ingenuity in order to promote British empire?" Elias asked.

"Oh, let us not be so uneasy about it, Mr. Gordon. Mr. Pepper is, after all, dead, and he can gain nothing by the promotion of his engine."

"What of his widow?" I said, immediately regretting the question.

"Which one? Do you think any of those unfortunates would ever see a penny, even if the Pepper engine were to be developed? The rights to the inheritance would be caught up in the courts for years, and the lawyers themselves would contrive to steal every penny of it."

"If one man might invent it," I proposed, "might not another?"

"It is possible and may even be inevitable, but it need not be now. The world will not know that such a thing was ever invented, and as possibility is the breeding ground for creativity, no one will think to try to make it anew. If the notion of turning colonial cotton into India-like calico never occurs to anyone, no one will invent it. The task of the Parliament is to keep textiles cheap and easily accessible so that no one needs to go about inventing and altering the system. There are many who believe Parliament made a terrible mistake in the 1721 legislation, and I am one of them. Still, what is done can be undone."

"Are we not forgetting something?" I asked. "Mr. Pepper was killed—murdered—by the East India Company. I cannot believe it is in the government's interests to condone such diabolical lawlessness."

"Mr. Pepper's fate is unclear," she answered. "It may not have been the Company that harmed him at all. He had other enemies—his wives, for example—and any one of them might have decided that he had overstayed his welcome. It may be the French killed him in a misplaced effort to obtain his plans. Right now we cannot say which of these possibilities is most likely."

And there was another possibility, one I dared not speak aloud—

324 | DAVID LISS

that it was not the East India Company but the government itself that had decided it could not risk Pepper's continued works. "As a thief-taker," I said, "it may well be worth my while to inquire into the death of Mr. Pepper and discover who brought about his end. If I can bring the murderer to justice, I should receive a handsome bounty from the state, after all."

"I fear, sir, you will not have time to do that. You will be working for someone else."

"And who is that?"

"Why, me, of course." Her grin, open and joyous and confident all at once, nearly unmanned me. "I am hiring you, sir, for the very generous fee of twenty pounds, to perform a few services on behalf of your king."

I looked away, having no wish to be drawn in by her beauty. "I'll not be anyone's puppet. Not any longer. Hammond's days are quite clearly numbered, and I must believe that his ability to threaten me and my friends must come to an end."

"The ability to threaten, yes, but there are still the debts. You may depend on a generous government ordering those matters to your satisfaction. And there is another matter, sir. The business of the late election involved you in all manners of mischief. You had a private meeting with this nation's greatest enemy, a man who would overthrow our government by force. Perhaps you believe that your dealings with the Pretender are unknown to the ministry, but I promise you they are known in the highest circles of Whitehall. By entertaining his conversation and by not reporting his activities, you committed treason—a capital crime, as you must know."

Elias spoke up before I had the opportunity. "Damme, but you know little of Weaver. If you think to put this gentleman in thrall with your threats to his person, you are far more foolish than I could have supposed."

She smiled at him—so pretty and knowing. "I make no threats, I promise you." She turned to me. "There is no threat, for the danger is past. I mention the incident, sir, not to make you uneasy but to tell you of a component of which you have until now been ignorant. After your meeting with the Pretender, your enemies at Whitehall argued that you were too dangerous, the rebels would one day or another win you to their side, and you must be punished as an example. I tell you this not to aggrandize myself, but so you will know I was your benefactor before we even met. I convinced Mr. Walpole, First Lord of the Treasury, whose influence reigns supreme, to leave you be, arguing that a man of your skills and integrity would yet serve his kingdom."

"You interceded on my behalf?" I asked. "Why?"

She shrugged. "Maybe because I believed this day might come. Maybe because I believed it to be the right thing to do. Maybe because I knew you were no traitor, but a man caught between impossible choices, and though you did not act to harm the Pretender, you did not join with him either."

I shook my head. "I hardly know how to answer this."

"You need not, except to listen to my request. Your king calls upon you to serve, Mr. Weaver. Will you do so? I cannot think but that your own sense of rectitude must lead you to join our cause, particularly when you learn what we wish of you."

"And what is that?"

"We wish you to break into Hammond's house and liberate your friend, Mr. Franco. It shan't be too hard, particularly with Cobb gone. They can ill afford to have servants disturbing their affairs, so there are but two men there besides your friend. Liberate him, sir, and in exchange for this service, we shall pay you the twenty-pound bounty mentioned before and return order to the financial mayhem wrought against you and your friends."

"A munificent offer," I noted, "particularly since you offer to pay me for what you know I would do willingly."

"There is, however, one more aspect to your task. Did you not wonder what was so important that Mr. Cobb would abandon his work here and fly to France? We found in his care a book of code which he confessed contained a copy of Pepper's plans for the calico engine. It has since been destroyed, but we now know that the original and only extant copy of the plans is being held by Mr. Hammond. It is a small calf-skin book, containing all manner of diagrams and drawings. It must be under protection in that house. Go rescue your friend, and while you are at it, find the plans and return them to us."

"Why should I incur such an additional risk?" I asked. "I care only for Franco, and not a jot for the East India Company."

She smiled. "Even if you were to ignore the debt you owe to your kingdom, I do not believe you would remain content to leave the plans for the engine in the care of those who have harmed your friends. The French are behind all this mischief. They have desired those plans more than anything else in the world, and now they have them. Would it not be sweet to take them away?"

I nodded. "You're right," I said. "You know me well enough to understand I can neither ignore the debt I owe you nor endure such a victory on their part. I will get the plans."

"When you deliver them, you'll receive your bounty," she said.

I made no reply, for I knew already that I would have to content myself to doing without twenty pounds. I did not know who deserved the plans, but I already had an inkling of the person to whom I would deliver them. If Miss Glade knew what I planned, I have no doubt she would have done her utmost to stop me.

—

CHAPTER TWENTY-EIGHT

*E*LIAS SAT IN MY FRONT ROOM, HANDILY FINISHING OFF A BOTTLE of port I'd opened only that morning. He was well settled in my most comfortable chair, with his feet up, resting upon the very table I used for most of my meals.

"I'm rather unhappy about all of this," he told me.

"I don't doubt it," I answered. I emerged at that moment wearing dark breeches and a dark shirt to match. I slipped into an equally dark coat—not quite a greatcoat since it was lighter than perhaps the weather demanded and clung more to my form. I could endure the cold, but I could not endure a cumbersome garment that would snag or hold me back.

"I hardly think you would want to go," I told him. "Not that you would know how to conduct yourself if you did come along. And though you might like the sense of the adventure, you must understand there is always the risk of being caught, and I should very much doubt you would like to be sent off to prison."

He put his feet back on the floor. "You may have a point," he admitted, "but there are some rather nasty fellows about. What am I to do with myself until your return?"

"You may wait here if you like."

"But I've finished your port," he explained urgently.

"I do have more than one bottle."

"Oh. Then I shall stay."

—

IT HAD BEEN BITTERLY cold all day, but surprisingly nightfall brought a slight warming, and though I was dressed with less protection than I would like, I was nevertheless able to endure the chill. The sky was dark and heavy with clouds, and an intermittent sprinkling of wet snow dampened my hat and face and turned the filth of the London streets into a slick pool of kennel. Under less pressing circumstances, I might have walked carefully to avoid the streaks of mud and waste and decaying carcasses; that night I cared for nothing but keeping my step and my determination steady.

I silently prayed for luck. The meeting of the Court of Proprietors was the next day, and if I could not free Mr. Franco and take charge of Pepper's engine plans before that, I did not know if afterward I'd be able to make matters right. In order to accomplish my goals, I would need to gain entrance to the house Cobb and Hammond had used. I had broken into my share of houses in the past, but never a fortress run by French spies. I had to believe that precautions, perhaps even traps, had been laid for intruders, and I should hate to take such chances. I would therefore have to gain the help of those who had already cracked the code.

After turning onto Sparrow Street, I stopped and surveyed the scene about me. Anyone who knew my face would be unlikely to know me at that moment. I leaned against a building, my hat pulled down to hide myself in the shadows; no hard trick when all was shadow. It was not yet ten o'clock, and some light spilled into the streets from windows or from lanterns upon passing coaches, but it was dark, make no mistake. And though the streets were far from deserted, an occasional pedestrian or coachman would prove small deterrent. That, at least, was what I hoped.

I removed from my pocket a purse and dropped it upon the ground, making sure to find an exposed stone with no filth or snow upon it. I hit my mark, and a few pennies spilled out, making the shimmering music upon which I had been depending.

In an instant I was surrounded by more than a dozen dark figures.

"Step away from your purse, you old nitty, unless you want to taste my boot."

"I'll step away with all my heart," I answered, "and all the more so because it's not my purse but yours. I am giving it to you, after all." I raised my chin and looked full into the face of the urchin called Crooked Luke.

"Damme," another one said. "Ain't that the spark what took that posture-moll Edgar down a notch or two?"

"It's him," Crooked Luke said. He eyed me carefully, as though I might be a gift of food from an enemy with a history of using poison. "What's this then? The clink of coin on stone was meant to draw us out, weren't it?"

"It was," I admitted. "I have a desire to speak with you. You may say or do as you like, you may help me or no, but the purse is yours."

Crooked Luke nodded at one of his fellows, a small child with a running nose who appeared to be no more than seven or eight—but when he grew close, I could see he was older, though stunted in stature. He dashed forward, grabbed the purse, and retreated.

"You want us for something?" Luke said.

"I do. After our first meeting, I inquired of your friend Edgar the manservant why he harbored such dislike for you. He told me that you were housebreakers, that you had a way in and out of the house without getting caught."

The boys laughed, none more so than Crooked Luke. "He don't like it," Luke agreed. "It drives him terrible angry."

"They are particularly jealous of the security of their house," I said, in as leading a way as I might.

Luke nodded sagely. "That's it. We've nabbed a thing or two, I won't deny it, but it's more the fun of the game. We ain't never taken too much since they're always at home, and as like to fire a musket into us as not. But a few raids, savage-Indian-like, is the way, and they ain't figured our means."

"I wish to get in," I said, "and I would know your secret."

"It's our secret though, ain't it?"

"It is, but I have a secret or two myself, and perhaps an exchange might be in order."

"And what secret is that?"

I smiled, because I knew I had his interest now. "Mr. Cobb is gone. Mr. Hammond will soon be gone. I have no doubt that within a day of Mr. Hammond's disappearance, the creditors will come in and take charge. If, however, some clever young fellows knew precisely when to strike, they might move through the house taking what they liked with impunity."

Luke exchanged looks with a couple of his fellows. "You ain't lying, are you?"

I handed Luke a card. "If I am, come calling upon me. I will give you five pounds if I tell you false. I have come to your aid, young sir, and I hope you won't abuse my generosity with doubt."

He nodded. "I know a thing or two about you," he said. "I ain't got no cause to think you'd tell me false, and if you've made an honest mistake you promise to make good, so I can take your bargain." He turned to look at his companions, who nodded in solemn assent. I did not flatter myself that they nodded in agreement with Luke's assessment of my character, but with the anticipation of claiming the valuables of so fine a house.

"Now you will show me?" I asked.

"Aye, I will. But I hope you haven't too much of a fondness for those clothes upon your back, for they won't be worth much soon."

A MAN WHO, LIKE MYSELF, has broken out of the most notorious prison in London will hardly wince at the thought of a nail snagging his breeches or some soot staining his sleeve. My greatest fear was that some secret passage sufficient for boys should prove a sad obstacle for a man, but this was not the case. Luke took me to a small house around the corner from where Cobb had lived. I could see at once it was a boardinghouse, clean and respectable—not the sort of place generally open to rascals like my friend Luke.

"Now listen good, sir, for this is our freak, and I'll not look kind if you ruin it for us. We have made this work for some months now because the man what owns this house ain't never heard so much as a squeak from us. So you'll tread careful?"

"You may depend upon it."

"And for the clearing of the house?"

"By sundown tomorrow," I said, "if all goes as I anticipate, Mr. Hammond, Edgar, and anyone else associated with that house will be in hiding, afraid to return. Assuming," I added, "they do not get in my way tonight."

"What if all don't go as you anticipate?" Luke asked.

"Then I will make conditions more to my liking. It will only take a word or two whispered about their secret nature to destroy them."

"You mean their being French spies?" Luke said.

I stared at him. "How could you know?"

"I've been in the house, you might remember, and I've heard and seen things. I have me letters, you know."

The boardinghouse had a door leading to the basement. I should have been able to pick the lock, but it was old and easily manipulated, and I let Luke work it for me as a means of showing I respected his command of the terrain. With that, Luke gave me surprisingly clear and concise directions. Once it was open, he bid me farewell, and the boys fled.

Inside the basement. I shut the door and, in accordance with Luke's preference, I locked it again, lest the owners happen upon it. Then I sat upon the stairs, and remained there for ten minutes waiting for my eyes to adjust as well as I could hope. There was little light that came in through the door, but there was enough to give me a fair concept of the layout of the space, and I could find the markers Luke had so well described.

I therefore descended the stairs and carefully moved along the dirt floor of the cellar. In the far corner of the room I found, as I was told I would, an old and decrepit bookshelf with nothing upon it but some equally old and decrepit masonry jars. I removed the jars and slowly slid the bookshelf forward as instructed. Behind it was the hole in the wall Luke had spoken of, covered by a soft sheet of wood.

I had been in fear of a tiny crawl space, but what I found was a smooth cool tunnel, tall enough to walk in with only a slight slouch, wide enough that I would have been able to avoid the walls entirely if I had a light, which I lacked. I could not imagine how such a passage came to be, and it was not until many years later, while entertaining a group of friends with the tale, that a gentleman who was something of a historian of the city's geography was able to inform me. It would seem that the large house that Hammond and Cobb leased had been built by a man whose wife's jealousy and ill temper were matched only by her rudeness in having her separate property settled upon her. This gentleman set up his mistress in the house that now served as the boardinghouse, and the two moved about freely in the late hours of the night, when the wife was asleep. She would ask the servants if her husband had left the house, and in all innocence they could say that he had not.

I was certain that when this gentleman traveled through the tunnel he had the good sense to bring a light, but I had not. In those originary days, too, I could only suspect the walls were still somewhat clean, and perhaps even regularly cleaned. Now they had suffered much neglect, and Luke had been quite right in warning me of my clothes. Every time I bumped against the wall, I felt some new filth splatter me. I heard the scattering of rats, and I felt the sticky tangle of spiderwebs. But it was only filth, and one does not live in so great a city without growing accustomed to such things. I was determined not to let it bother me.

It took some ten minutes to travel the passage, though I don't doubt it would have taken but a minute or two with light. I walked with one hand forward, and at last I came upon another piece of soft wood which, in accordance with Luke's directions, I slid sideways, for this one was on a rail and moved quite easily. I then stepped forward and slid it back. I could not see how it fit, but I heard a satisfying click and had no doubt that Luke's words were true; if you did not know it was a door, you should never suspect it.

My guides had informed me that I would be emerging within the pantry. And so, even more careful to avoid upsetting anything, I made my way to the door, opened it, and stepped out into a poorly lit kitchen.

It was a peculiarity of the house that the kitchen was in the cellar, but it fit the original owner's needs. It hardly mattered to me. I oriented myself, and—after taking a moment to dust some of the more disturbing filth from my clothes—I began to climb the stairs.

Prior to entering the tunnel, I'd heard the watchman call the eleventh hour, so it was indeed reasonable to suppose that most of the house was asleep. But I could not even suspect what most of the house might consist of. How, after all, could Hammond and Edgar keep Mr. Franco against his will? On the other hand, I knew perfectly well it might not be physical bonds that held my friend. I, after all, had been made to do Cobb's bidding without any palpable threat that a stranger might observe. That was, indeed, what I hoped to be the case. If it were but the two of them, I would be able to accomplish what I desired, and do so without bloodshed. If, on the other hand, there were armed men here, servants of the French Crown, things could get violent very quickly, and my chances of success were diminished. There was, however, only one way to learn. I climbed the stairs, and with a gentle twist of the doorknob I made my way into the main portion of the house.

IT WAS A LARGE HOUSE, and though Miss Glade had explained that the French agents could not risk servants, I remained skeptical that there would be no butler, no scullery maid, no laundry girl, no cook. Nevertheless, I found no one. Upon the first floor, I did as rapid a survey as I dared, measuring each step, avoiding every creak of the floor where I could. No one was awake, no one moved, and I heard nothing from abovestairs.

In what I would have earlier imagined to be Cobb's study, I conducted as thorough a search as I could for the plans Miss Glade had described but saw no sign of the little octavo volume of the sort Pepper had been inclined to use. Indeed, it was clear that the space had been put in order, and I could find no signs that there were any private documents. Of course, having just entered the house through a private passage, I could not feel any certainty that there were no means of hiding the book that would escape my notice, but there was only so much I could accomplish in the dark of night with the necessity of quiet. Once I had Hammond in my power, I felt certain I could convince him to give me the book.

With the first floor effectively searched, I proceeded upward, wondering where it was that Edgar slept. A servant, after all, ought not to have his rooms abovestairs. I could, however, speculate on two reasons to explain the anomaly. First of all, because Edgar was the only servant, he would need to be close in case his masters—now master—had any needs in the night. The other possibility, and the one I was more inclined to accept, was that Edgar was no servant, at least not of the sort he pretended. He was, in other words, an agent of the French Crown like his masters. If that were the case, I should have to be most cautious of him.

Climbing the stairs took an inordinate amount of time, but I reached the top safely. I believed there to be three suites of rooms on the floor, and I moved to my left, following the wall carefully until I came to the first door. I slowly turned the knob, and despite my best efforts it squeaked—just a tiny gasp of metal upon metal, though to me it might as well have been cannon fire.

Prepared for the worst, I opened the door and peered inside. It was a front room—inhabited, as best as I could tell, for there were books, a half-empty cup of wine, papers upon the desk. I pushed on, therefore, and opened the next door, with slightly more luck than the first. It was quiet and I entered the room and approached the bed, inhabited by what appeared to me to be nothing more than a lump. I risked the candle, and the figure turned and moved but did not awaken, and I let out a breath of relief. It was Mr. Franco.

I closed the door that we might have more privacy. I regretted that I had to awaken my friend in a most inhospitable manner, but there was no help for it; I placed a hand over his mouth. Though I was prepared to shake him, no such effort was required. His eyes went wide.

I did not know how well he could see me, so I hastened to whisper words of comfort. "Do not cry out, Mr. Franco. It's Weaver. Nod if you understand."

He nodded, and so I removed my hand.

"I am sorry to have had to frighten you so," I said, as quietly as I could manage. "I dared not risk another course."

"I understand," he said, as he sat up. "But what do you here?"

"Things are coming to a head," I said. "After tomorrow these men will present no danger. Already they present no danger, but they do not know it. Yet if we are to defeat them, I must escape with something precious to them."

"The plans for the engine," Franco said.

"You know of it?"

He nodded. "They have made no secret of what they wanted. I feared it meant they intended to kill me when they had accomplished all they wished, so you can well imagine how pleased I am to see you."

"Why have they kept you here?"

"Do you know who these men are?"

"French spies," I said. "I have only just learned."

"Yes. They wanted nothing more than to keep it a secret, but Hammond seemed to know the secret was in danger. He feared that once you discovered it, you would be able to involve the King's Messengers or some other branch of the British government to offer me protection. Hammond is afraid of you, sir. He is afraid the matter is now out of his control, and he had nothing to keep you from destroying him, so he took me hostage."

"But how does he keep you here?"

"He has threatened my daughter, sir. He claims to have agents in Salonica, capable of doing her harm. I dared not risk Gabriella, so instead I was forced to risk you. I pray you will forgive me."

I put a hand upon his shoulder. "Do not be absurd. Your daughter is but one more innocent, and I could not have endured your jeopardizing her safety for my sake. You are here because of me—no, stay your words. I do not take responsibility for what these men have done, nor do I blame myself. You have been caught in my wake, and it has become my responsibility."

"You are here, so you have acquitted your responsibility with much skill."

"When we are all back in Duke's Place and these scoundrels are dead or in the Tower, we may speak of that. As for now, I must get the plans for the engine and get you free. Have you any knowledge of who is in the house and where they rest?"

He nodded. "I believe that Mr. Hammond is sufficiently unimpressed with me that he does not take the necessary cautions in hiding things. I have heard him speak to his servant, Edgar, that he keeps the plans, written in an octavo volume, about his person at all times. That, I imagine, presents certain difficulties for you."

"It does, but it also makes things easier as well. It means I do not have to waste my time in fruitless search. Now, besides ourselves, Hammond and Edgar, who is in the house?"

"No one. It is just the two of them."

"Where do they sleep?"

"Edgar sleeps in the next set of rooms." He pointed to my left. "I suppose it makes them believe that I feel more under their watchful eye, but that is clearly not the case. Hammond sleeps in the large bedroom on the third floor. Climb the stairs and turn right. That door will lead to a sitting room, and the door beyond that is to his bedroom. During the day, Hammond keeps the octavo in his waistcoat pocket. I do not know where he keeps it at night."

"That shan't concern me," I said. "He will know, and that will be enough. Do you believe you can make your way from this house silently?"

"Yes," he said, but there was something in his voice, some hesitation.

"You fear I might fail," I said. "You fear that they will best me and then, if you are gone, they will take out their revenge upon your daughter."

He nodded.

"Then stay here," I said. "You may as well hear what transpires. I only ask that you remain hidden until I come to get you. I can well understand your desire to protect your daughter, and I am confident you can understand my desire to protect you."

He nodded once more.

I shook his hand, this man who had stood with me in the way I had always wished my own father would have but never did. He stood by my family when my uncle died, when I lost the man who had become more like a father than any I had known. He was no warrior, and perhaps even wanting in the area of bravery, but I respected him no less for it. He was the man he was, not built for such struggles as had been visited upon him, and he dealt with them with fortitude. He fretted not about his own difficulties but worried only for his daughter. He expended far more energy in the preservation of my feelings than his own. How could I not respect him?

We embraced, and I left his rooms, determined to finish my business in this house forever.

WITH MR. FRANCO SECURED, I moved on to Edgar's room. I opened the door very slowly and moved through his sitting room. The space was neat and spare, hardly lived in at all. At the next door I turned the handle with excruciating slowness and proceeded into the dark.

As with his sitting room, the bedroom was spare and largely unused. I stepped forward toward the bed, prepared to grab Edgar in much the same way I had grabbed Mr. Franco, though with less gentleness. But I did not grab him, for there was no one to grab. The bed was unmade but empty, and that could mean but one thing: Edgar knew I was in the house.

I turned to rush back to Franco's room. Despite his concerns for his daughter, I saw now that my main task was to get him out of the house unharmed. There would be no time for these French agents to pursue petty revenge. They would be captured or fleeing. Gabriella could come to no harm.

When I turned, however, I found myself facing a dark figure I recognized at once as Edgar. He stood with his legs planted firmly apart, one hand raised with a pistol, the other holding a dagger of some sort.

"You idiot Jew," he said. "I heard you come blundering in. A bear could have made less noise."

"A large bear or a small bear?" I asked.

"Do you think to quip your way out of this predicament?"

I shrugged. "It had occurred to me to attempt to do so."

"That has ever been your problem," he said. "You have been so impressed with your own cleverness, you refuse to believe anyone might be clever but yourself. Now, tell me why you've come here. Did you come for the plans?"

"I came for you," I said. "After visiting Mother Clap's house, I realized that certain inclinations I possessed could no longer be denied."

"You cannot hope to confuse me with your nonsense. I know you are here for the engine plans. You think I care for Franco? He may hide or escape as he wishes, though he should be far better off if he escapes. The question is, who sent you? How much do the British agents know? Has Cobb been taken, or did he escape? You can either tell me now, or I'll take you upstairs. Once we awaken Hammond, he will not hesitate to make you tell him precisely what he wishes to know."

I could not speak as to Mr. Hammond's ability to extract information. I could, however, rejoice that Edgar had just now told me precisely what I wished to know: Hammond was still asleep.

"Has anyone ever observed," I asked, "that you look remarkably like a duck? The truth of the matter is, I have always been kindly disposed toward ducks. When I was a boy, a good-hearted relative brought me one as a present. And now, years later, I meet you, the very image of that duck, and I cannot help but think that we ought to be friends. Come, let us set down our weapons and go find ourselves a pond where I may eat bread and cheese by the shore and you may paddle upon the waters. I shall be happy to toss you bits of crust."

"Shut your foul mouth," he snapped. "Hammond will be able to question you just as effectively if you have a lead ball in your leg."

I did not doubt it. "One moment. There are three facts about the life of the duck that I consider to be of great importance to the matters at hand. First, the female duck makes for a particularly tender and caring parent. Second," I began, but the truth was I did not have a second point. One point sufficed, for I deployed the advice of Mr. Blackburn, who had instructed me upon the rhetorical device of the series. Having informed Edgar that there would be three points, I knew he would remain in expectation of the remaining items. Thus I had the opportunity to surprise him with something else.

In this case, I surprised Edgar the servant and French spy with a powerful blow to his stomach. In my fanciful thoughts, a blow to the nose or mouth, one likely to produce blood and flying teeth, would have been more satisfying, but a blow to the stomach produces the reflex of doubling over. And that meant that even if he managed to fire his pistol, he would be firing down rather than forward.

As it happened, he did not fire, and though he did not let the pistol fall from his grasp, I had it out of his hand before he had even reached the ground. I slipped it into my pocket and, just as Edgar began to push himself upward, I leveled a kick, this time to his ribs. He slid a few inches along the floor and dropped his dagger, which I collected and quickly used to cut several lengths of rope from his bed canopy. These were used, as my practical-minded reader might guess, to bind Edgar's feet and hands. During this process I leveled a few more blows to his abdomen, not out of cruelty or malice, but because I wished to keep him unable to call out until I was able to gag him.

At last I cut a swath of cloth, which I used to do just that. When he was fully incapacitated, I stood up and towered over him. "The ironic thing," I said, "was that you originally observed that I would not be able to quip my way out of my predicament. Now, as for your fate, I see no need to do much at all with you. You perhaps wonder if I will inform the King's Messengers that you are here. The answer is, I shall not. Crooked Luke and the rest of the boys will be having their way with this house at some point tomorrow, and I shall leave them to deal with you."

Edgar grunted and struggled against his bonds, but I affected no interest as I left him.

ONE FLOOR UP and into the bedroom. Events went quickly and smoothly. As promised, Hammond was asleep, and it took no great effort to overpower him. I held his chin in one hand and pressed the tip of Edgar's blade into his chest with the other. It was deep enough to draw blood and to hurt, quite badly from the look upon Hammond's face, but no more than that.

"Give me the plans," I said.

"Never." His voice remained calm and even.

I shook my head. "Hammond, you chose to employ me. You knew who I was when you brought me into your scheme. That means you know what I am willing to do. I will cut off fingers, gouge out eyes, extract teeth. I don't believe you are made of stuff to endure these torments. I shall count to five, and then we will find out."

And so we would have, and he must have known it, because he did not even wait for me to begin my count. "Under my pillow," he said. "It hardly matters if you have the original. A fair copy is already out of the country and, with it, the power to destroy the English East India Company's textile trade."

I chose not to tell him that his copy had been intercepted and that he now surrendered the last hope of his mission succeeding. Instead, I set the blade down, kept a cruel grip on his face, and reached under the pillow to retrieve the rough calfskin volume—an octavo much like the one I had already seen. It was, according to one of his widows, the sort of book that Pepper favored, and a quick flip through, to observe the many schemes and intricate details, told me this was precisely the thing for which I had been searching.

Hammond, however, showed an unexpected display of strength. He quickly maneuvered away from me and then darted to the other end of the room. I slipped the book into my pocket and removed a pistol, but in the dark I could not guarantee much in the way of aim. The fact distressed me but also offered me some comfort if it was a pistol that he himself was after.

I moved forward and caught a better look at my adversary. He stood in the darkness, his night clothes draped around him loosely like the ethereal nimbus of a spirit, and his eyes were wide with terror. He raised his arm and for a moment I thought he brought forward a pistol. Indeed, I nearly fired before I saw it was no weapon but only a small glass vial.

"You may shoot me if you like," he said, "but it will answer little. I have already died, you see." The vial fell to the ground. I suspect he should have liked a dramatic shattering of glass, but instead there was only a weak bounce.

I have been called a cynical man in my life, and perhaps it was un- kind of me to wonder if he merely pretended to have swallowed poison. I would certainly take no chances on that score.

"Is there anything you wish to tell me before you meet your maker?" I asked.

"You blockhead," he spat. "Can you not discern that I have taken this poison so that I can't be made to tell you anything?"

"Of course," I said. "I ought to have considered that myself. Perhaps, in your remaining time, you would like to offer an apology? An encomium upon my virtues?"

"Weaver, you are the devil himself. What sort of monster mocks a dying man?"

"I have little else to do," I said, keeping the pistol trained on him. "I cannot take the chance that you are tricking me and have taken no poison at all, and I can hardly engage in cold-blooded murder and shoot you. I am forced to wait and watch, and I thought perhaps you might wish to use your final moment to converse."

He shook his head and sank to the floor. "I am told it works quickly," he said. "I don't know how much time there is for conversation. I will tell you nothing of our plans, what we have hoped to accomplish or what we have already done. I may be a coward, but I will not betray my country."

"Your country or the new French East India Company?"

"Hah," he said. "You have the right of it. The days of serving one's king with honor are done. Now we must serve his chartered companies. But if I cannot tell you of my nation, I can tell you of yours, and how you have been played for a fool."

"And how is that?" I asked.

Mr. Hammond, however, was unable to respond, for he was already dead.

chapter twenty-nine

—

_T_HERE WAS NOW, I BELIEVED, LITTLE REASON TO FEAR FOR MR. FRANCO. Much trickery and scheming still abounded—I had no doubt of that—but the French were finished for the moment, so Mr. Franco need no longer fear for himself or his daughter. Still, Elias, my aunt, or myself might yet be tossed into debtor's prison.

Mr. Franco was free to travel home by coach, though I declined to join him. It was late, I was exhausted in both body and spirit, and the next day would tax me even further, but I had one stop to make before I could retire. Everything would be resolved within a day's time, but to ensure that it was resolved to my liking I would have to order things with particular care.

I therefore took a coach to Ratcliff Highway and, in the darkness of the quiet morning, when even the cries of London were reduced to whines and whimpers, I entered the very tavern where the clerk Mr. Blackburn had told me so much of value. Indeed, it was only in recent hours that I had come to understand the full extent of his information.

I found the tavern keeper, whom I recollected to be Blackburn's brother-in-law, and, he recollecting me, I was able to overwhelm his natural caution and persuade him to inform me where I might find his relation. It was never his custom, he explained, to reveal a man's home without his permission, but he saw no harm in revealing his place of business, and so he explained that the good clerk had taken a temporary position with a brewer of some note who wanted his books to be set right. Mr. Blackburn, I was told, was most eager to perform his task speedily and well, and could be found in the offices as early as seven o'clock.

I took my breakfast with the good man, partaking of some still-hot bread procured from a nearby baker and a bowlful of raisins and nuts, washed down with a crisp small beer. Then I made my way to New Queen Street, where I found the good Mr. Blackburn in a small windowless closet, surrounded by a pile of innumerable accounting and ledger books and appearing as happy a man as ever I've seen.

"Why, it's Mr. Weaver," he said. He rose and bowed at me from as comfortable a distance as he could manage. "As you can see I have landed upon my feet, sir, in the manner of a cat. The Company may attempt to smear my name, but the truth will out, and I believe the good people I now serve will tell the truth."

"He's a marvelous good clerk," one of his fellows shouted, with evident humor.

"Our books have never been so well ordered," called another.

I knew at once that Blackburn had found employment where both his services and his peculiarities could be enjoyed, and so I felt less uneasy on the score of his losing his former place. "I am relieved to hear you are so happy."

"Prodigious happy," he assured me. "These books, sir, are a disaster. It is as though a hurricane of numbers and errors has struck them, but they shall be made right. It is something of a pleasure, I must say, to find that the difficulties here are no more than mistake and ignorance—"

"Woeful ignorance," called one of his fellows.

"—and not malice," Blackburn finished, in a far quieter voice. "There are no cozening deceptions here, no secret expenditures and tricks meant to disguise any manner of mischief."

"It is on that score I've come to see you," I told him. "I have a question about a matter to which you once referred. Do you recollect that you spoke of a time when my patron asked you to disguise the loss of a certain sum from the books, and when you refused, you found the sum taken all the same?"

"I recall it well," he said. "Though for some reason I do not recollect telling you."

I chose not to dwell on that point. "Can you tell me the sum?"

He considered the request briefly. "I suppose they can do me no more harm than they have already."

So he told me what I wished to know, and it was at that moment that my suspicions were confirmed and I believed I understood everything. Yet there was one more theory to test. The day would prove if I had the better of my enemies, or whether they were far more clever than I could even now perceive.

NEXT, I MADE MY way to Spitalfields, where I knocked repeatedly upon a door until it was, at last, answered by a meek creature whose nature I could not identify as servant, daughter, or wife. I explained that my business was of the most urgent sort and could not wait. She explained that men such as he needed their rest, and I retorted that what I brought was better than any night's sleep. At last my will proved stronger than her defenses, and she invited me in. I sat in a dimly lit and dingy parlor, without refreshment, and attempted to resist the urge to sleep.

At last Devout Hale appeared in the door. He wore a dressing gown and cap, and though the poor light did much to blunt the effect of his scrofula, the cruelty of being awakened at this hour was plainly visible.

"By Jesus, Weaver, what can possibly bring you here at this hour? If you don't have the king himself in tow, I don't want to hear it."

"Not a king," I said, "but a king's ransom. Sit down and I will tell you as little as you need to know to understand."

He sat across from me, hunched over, apparently having some difficulty breathing. Nevertheless, he was soon enough wide awake and listening to my tale as I informed him of things I had previously held secret. I told him how Pepper had been far cleverer than any of them had suspected and invented a cotton weaving engine that would have rendered the East India Company's trade routes worthless, and how French, British, and even Indian agents had been doing all in their power to recover it—each to protect the interests of his own nation.

"I have been told," I explained, "that I must return these plans to the British Crown, for it is in this country's best interest that the East India Company remain strong. I believe myself to be a patriot, Hale, but the heart of what I love in this kingdom is found in its people, its constitution, its liberties and opportunities, not in its companies. I take great pleasure in having helped to thwart the schemes of the French, but that does not mean I cannot see with my own eyes the dangers in handing the reins to the kingdom over to men who value nothing but money and profit."

"Then what shall you do with the plans?" Hale asked.

"I will give them to the men and women who serve this kingdom not with their schemes but with their labor." I reached into my pocket, pulled out Pepper's octavo, and handed it to Hale. "I give it to the silk weavers."

Hale said nothing. He pulled the oil lamp closer and began to examine the pages in the book. "You know I can't read."

"You will have to depend on those who can, and I suspect it will take some time to understand the contents. Yet you and your men will puzzle it out, and when you do, you will be in a position to dictate terms to those you wish. I ask only that you share the wealth with your fellow workers and not become the thing you despise. That book contains the promise of great riches to be endured over generations, and I hope you will give me your word that you will administer its possibilities with generosity rather than greed."

He nodded. "Aye," he said, somewhat breathlessly. "Aye, that can be done, Weaver. It may not yield wealth at all in my lifetime, but I shall manage it as best I can. But tell me, don't you want any of that wealth for your own keeping?"

I laughed. "Should you become rich and wish to make me a gift, we can discuss it at that time, but no. I shall not form a joint stock company with you. I asked you to do me a favor, you may recall, to help me in an endeavor that, though I despised it, I needed to complete. You did, and you asked me for something in return, something I have been unable to grant. I give you this in lieu of what I could not deliver, and I hope you will consider my debt to you paid."

"I accept it on those terms," he said, "and God bless you."

I WOULD NOT HAVE many hours to sleep before my next appointment, but I was determined to take what I could. I sent a note to Elias, asking him to come meet me at my rooms at eleven that morning, which should provide us with ample time to arrive at the meeting of the Court of Proprietors at noon. What I would say to Miss Glade when she demanded the book, I did not know. Perhaps I would tell her the truth. I should, even then, have liked more than anything to give her what she desired, to see if in that moment I might find some place in her that was not designing or scheming.

Indeed, she arrived at my rooms at half past ten. I was fortunately awake—after but an hour's sleep—and dressed, and, though not at my most alert, still able to face whatever she might wish to say to me.

"You broke open the house?" she asked.

I smiled at her. It was my finest approximation of her own smile. "I was able to liberate Mr. Franco, but I could not find the book of plans. Edgar knew nothing, and Hammond took his own life. I searched the rooms, even the house as best as I could, but I could find no sign of it."

She rose quickly, and her skirts fluttered about like leaves on a windy autumn day.

"You could not find it," she repeated, not without skepticism.

"I could not."

She stood and stared at me, hands on her hips. She may have been making an effort to appear angry—she may, for all I know, have been making no effort at all—but she seemed to me so astonishingly beautiful that I felt myself tempted to confess all. I resisted the temptation.

"You," she pronounced, "are not being honest with me."

I stood up to meet her eyes. "Madam, I resent you for forcing me to reply with so trite an expression, but in this case I must observe that what is sauce for the goose must be sauce for the gander. You accuse me of concealing the truth from you? On what occasion have you not concealed the truth from me? When have you not told me falsehoods?"

Her expression softened somewhat. "I have endeavored to be honest with you."

"Are you even a Jewess?" I demanded.

"Of course I am." She let out a sigh. "Do you believe I would make up such a thing merely to disarm you?"

"The thought has crossed my mind. If you are who you say," I asked, "why do you speak, when unguarded, with the accent of a French-woman?"

Here her lips curled into a half smile. Perhaps she did not like to be so exposed, but I knew she could not but approve of my skill in having detected her ruse.

"All I told you of my family is true," she said, "but I never claimed to have told you every detail of my life. As it happens, I spent my first twelve years in Marseilles—a place, I might add, where Jews of my sort were no better loved by Jews of your sort than they are here. In any event, what signifies such a small detail?"

"It might have signified nothing, had you not hidden it from me."

She shook her head. "I hid it from you," she said, "because I knew there was French mischief about, and I did not wish you to suspect I might be part of it. Because I could not tell you all, I wished to hide from you that which I believed must give you a false idea."

"And in the hiding, you merely impressed upon me the need to be suspicious."

"It is an irony, is it not?"

Through an unspoken mutual understanding, we took our seats.

"And your early history?" I asked. "Your father's death and debts, and your—protector?"

"Also true. I neglected to mention, however, that this protector was a man of some influence in the ministry and has risen to even greater influence. It was he who recognized my talents and asked me to serve my country."

"By doing such things as seducing my friends?"

She looked down. "Do you honestly think I would have had to surrender to Mr. Gordon in order to obtain the information I wished? He may be a good friend and a stalwart companion, but he is not well equipped to resist the requests of women. I may have taken advantage of his interest, but my regard for you is such that I would not have created difficulties in the friendship by surrendering myself to him."

"Which friendship?" I asked. "That with Elias or that with you?"

She grinned quite broadly. "Why, either, of course. And now that we have clarified matters, I hope we can discuss the book you perhaps found after all."

I felt myself waver, but even if I believed her story, as I was inclined to, it did not mean I wished for the East India Company to have the book. She might believe herself to be in the right, and her sense of politics gave her every reason to wish to obtain Pepper's plans, but my sense of justice could not deliver it.

"I must repeat that I could not find the plans."

She closed her eyes. "You seem unconcerned that the French may have the engine."

"I am concerned, and I should prefer that they fail miserably in their schemes, but I am a patriot, madam, not a servant of the East

India Company. I do not believe it is the government's concern to protect a company from the creative genius of invention."

"I would not have thought you capable of this treachery," she said. Her beauty, while not precisely gone, was hidden now under a mask of crimson anger. We discussed not some project in which she happened to be involved. Miss Glade, I saw, was a true devotee of her cause. That the British government and the British government alone should have sway over the plans mattered to her profoundly, and I had no doubt she understood my role in preventing that outcome.

"It is no treachery," I said softly. "It is justice, madam, and if you were not so partisan in your views, you would see it."

"It is you who are partisan, Mr. Weaver," she said, somewhat more softly. I flattered myself that while she despised my actions, she understood I took them out of a belief in their rectitude. "I would have thought you might have come to trust me, to trust that I do what is best. I see that you will take guidance from no one. More the pity, for I see you understand nothing of this modern world."

"And you understand nothing of me," I said, "if you think that because I wish to please you I must also wish to please the East India Company. I have suffered before, madam, and I have learned it is better to suffer for what is right than to be given a sweetmeat as reward for what is wrong. You may continue to hunt down and kill inventors if you like—I cannot prevent it—but you must never make the mistake of thinking I will join the cause willingly."

A smirk crossed her lips. "You served Cobb and there was no will there, sir. That is what your king's servants understand of you—that you will fight and fight mightily too for a cause you don't believe in to protect the people for whom you care. Don't think we'll forget it."

"And while you are recalling what I will do while under duress, I beg you to recall that Cobb is now imprisoned and Mr. Hammond is dead. Those who would twist my will to their own ends have not fared so well as they would like."

She smiled again, this time more broadly, then shook her head. "The sad truth of it is, Mr. Weaver, that I have always liked you very much. I believe things might have been very different if you had liked me. Not desired me, sir, the way a man may desire a whore whose name he never cares to learn, but harbored for me those feelings I was inclined to harbor for you."

And so it was that she left me. With a glorious swish of her skirts she departed on that note of finality, so well suited to close a tragic stage play. She delivered her line with such strength that I believed indeed it was the last time I should have dealings with her, and I was inclined to think on my words, if not my conduct, with much regret. As it happened, however, this interview was not the last time I was to see Miss Celia Glade. Indeed, it was not even the last time I would see her that day.

ELIAS ARRIVED WITHIN half an hour of the time he had promised, which I considered very amiable for him. Indeed, I did not mind his lateness, for it gave me some time to regain my composure and to attempt to set aside the sadness I felt after Miss Glade's visit.

I did not allow Elias to linger long, and we soon took a hackney to Craven House.

"How is it," he asked me, "that we will be able to enter at will a meeting of the Court of Proprietors? Will they not turn us away at the door?"

I laughed. "Who would attempt to attend such a meeting without business? The very idea is absurd. There could be nothing more tedious and of less interest to the general public than a meeting of the East India Company."

My understanding of those meetings was quite right, though in recent years we have seen that these meetings have become the subject of much public interest, theatrical rancor, and coverage by the papers. In 1722, however, even the most desperate paragraph writer would choose to fish optimistically in the most unfashionable Covent Garden coffeehouse rather than seek out news in so dull a place as a Craven House Court of Proprietors meeting. Had one such paragraph writer been there that day, however, he would have found his optimism well rewarded.

As I predicted, no one thought to question that we belonged there. We were both dressed in gentlemanly attire, so we fit in with the other hundred and fifty or so dark-suited types who filled the meeting hall. We were conspicuous only in being younger and less portly than the majority.

The meeting was held in a room that had been constructed for the specific purpose of these quarterly events. I had been in the room before, and it had struck me as having the sad emptiness of a deserted theater, but now it was full of life—sluggish, torpid life though it might be. Few of the members of the Court appeared particularly interested in the proceedings. They milled about, gossiping with one another. More than a few had fallen asleep in their seats. One man, among the few younger than myself, appeared to occupy himself by memorizing Latin verse. Some ate food they had brought with them, and one intrepid sextet had actually carried in a few bottles of wine and pewter tankards.

There was an elevated platform at the front and, upon it, a podium. When we entered the room a member of the Court of Proprietors was busy holding forth on the merits of a particular colonial governor whose worth had been questioned. As it turned out, this governor was also the nephew of one of the principal shareholders, and opinions ran, if not exactly hot, then at least toward the lukewarm.

Elias and I took seats in the back, and he immediately slouched into his chair and pulled his hat low. "I rather hate an anticlimax," he said. "Please be so good as to wake me if anything happens."

"You may leave if you like," I told him, "but if you stay, you must stay awake. I need someone to entertain me."

"Or you shall surely fall asleep yourself, I suppose. Tell me, Weaver, what do you expect to happen?"

"I'm not entirely certain. Perhaps our actions will have no perceptible consequences, but there has been much coming to a head. And, most importantly, Mr. Ellershaw's fate hangs in the balance today. Forester will make a case against him, and even if the hand of Celia Glade is not visible in the outcome, even if the business with Cobb turns out to be irrelevant, I wish to see for myself how it plays out."

"And for this I must stay awake?" he asked. "That's not what I call friendship."

"Neither is attempting to bed the woman I like," I noted.

"I say, Weaver, I thought we had agreed not to speak of that anymore."

"Except when I am attempting to manipulate you into behaving as I wish. Then I shall bring it up."

"It's rather rotten of you. How long do you plan to play me so?"

"For the rest of your life, Elias. If I don't make light of it, it shall surely turn sour."

He nodded. "I cannot argue with that. But I notice you say the rest of my life, not the rest of yours. Have you some secret of longevity I have not learned?"

"Yes. Not attempting to bed women desired by one's friends. You must try it sometime."

He was about to answer when I held up my hand.

"Hold," I said. "I would hear this."

One member of the Court of Proprietors, whose task it appeared to be to act as a sort of formal master of ceremonies, was in the process of informing the room that Mr. Forester, of the Court of Committees, needed to address the room on a matter of rather urgent business.

I suspected that when a gentleman wished to address the length of nails used in crates it was described as a matter of urgent business, for no one took particular notice. The sleepers dozed, the diners dined, the chatters chatted, and the scholar studied. My attention, however, was firmly upon the podium.

"Gentlemen," Forester began, "I am afraid that there are two matters of urgent business upon which I am to speak today. One bodes well for the future of the Company, should we manage it well. The other is rather more unpleasant, and though I am loath to mention it at all, I fear it is my duty. But let us attend to productive things first."

Forester signaled to a servant I had not seen before, who dashed over with a decorative lacquered box, swirling with gold and red and black, surely a product of the Orient. Upon the top was a handle in the shape of an elephant, and Forester lifted it and handed the top back to the servant. From the box itself he took out a compact roll of cloth. With this in hand, he returned the remainder of the box to the servant, who dashed off. Clearly there had been no need for the box at all, but I saw that Forester was a man who liked his drama, and I began to sense we would now observe a rather fascinating performance.

"I hold in my hand the future of the East India Company," Forester announced. "As I need not tell you, it was one of the most disappointing moments in our organization's history when Parliament passed the legislation making the domestic sale of India cloth so problematic. We are but weeks away from being forced to bar access to the cloth in our warehouses to our own citizens. Though there have been efforts to expand the markets for the few remaining cloths we may sell, the truth is that our Company failed to mount a proportionate counterattack to the wool interest, and now we may soon find ourselves with declining revenues. I will speak more of that later."

I had no doubt, for Forester wished to lay the blame squarely upon Ellershaw's shoulders, and unless Ellershaw could credibly promise a repeal of the legislation, his days were surely numbered.

"What has happened in Parliament is surely terrible," he said, "and there have been rumors of more terrible developments to come. We have all heard it. There is a new engine, it is said, one capable of turning American cotton into an exact replica of India cloth—every bit as light and comfortable and elegant. Certainly the domestic dyeing industry has been perfecting its trade for years, and much of the India cloth enjoyed in this kingdom has been dyed here, so that if this American cotton could be spun in the mythic engine and then dyed here, it would be impossible for the consumer to tell the difference. I have no doubt that the experts of Craven House could find the slight variances, but not the consumers. Such an engine could mean the end of our cloth trade with the East."

At this the crowd became far more energetic. Hisses and cries of *nay* filled the hall. Indeed, Elias, who had been feigning boredom, was now fully alert. "He knew of it all the time," he whispered.

"I am here to tell you two things, gentlemen. First of all, the engine is real. I have seen its works." The cries drowned him out, and he had to wait several moments before the Court was quiet enough to proceed. At last he did, though the din of the room made it difficult to hear. "Yes, it is true. The engine is real. But the second thing I must tell you is that this is not a moment of defeat but one of triumph. The engine has always been viewed as an enemy of the Company, but not if we own it. If it is ours, if we can use it as we like, for our profit—that, my friends, means riches beyond our imagination."

He had the full attention of the Court. "Think of it. We continue to trade with India. We have our infrastructure there, and all of Europe craves India cloth. But we cease expansion in India and invest instead in North American cotton production. We obtain the cotton from the Americas, have it spun here on engines owned by Craven House itself, arrange for the dyeing, and then sell it domestically. Instead of being at odds with domestic textile production, we are woven into it, if you will excuse the play on words. Yes, the men of the wool interest will continue to give us trouble, but they will no longer be able to argue that we take bread from the mouths of domestic workers. Indeed, we will provide new employment and we shall become the idols of those who seek work. And since we will own the engines, their ability to dictate wages to us will be limited. With these new engines, we shall have absolute power over the textile industry, gentlemen: Indian cloth and foreign markets, American cotton and the home market."

The room turned into an excited mass of voices. Men were standing and pointing, waving their hands about, nodding or shaking their heads. But most, from what I could divine, were excited about the notion.

For my part, I hardly knew how to understand it all. Everything I had done had been for nothing. The Company already had the engine; it would profit from it and turn the London laborer into its drudge. I could only take some pleasure in the fact that this revelation meant that not only had Cobb's French masters lost out on their bid to control the engine but so had Celia Glade and her British masters. The Company had beat them all.

After some minutes of chaos in which Forester tried, unsuccessfully, to regain mastery of the room, I heard a loud call for attention.

"Hold!" the voice shouted. "Hold, let us hold!" It was Ellershaw. He entered the room with a confidence I had never seen in him before. His suit was new and clean and neat, and his bearing was still shambling, but it contained an authority I would have called almost regal.

Ellershaw strode onto the elevated platform and toward the podium. "You must hold," Forester said to him. "I have not yielded the floor."

"Yes, you have," Ellershaw said. "What you discuss is too important to allow the rules of procedure to silence conversation."

"That may be so," Forester sneered, "but the conversation will not be assumed by a madman whose brain is universally known to be disordered from exposure to a scandalous disease."

A great gasp emerged from the crowd, and I observed so many nods and secret whispers that I understood the rumors of his having been rendered mad from the French pox were widely distributed. So it was that I began to have an inkling of Ellershaw's malicious genius.

"Universally known, is it? It is not so known by me, or by any medical man who has taken the time to examine me, rather than a foolish knave who spreads malice. Why, I see in this very hall a surgeon who has examined me. You, sir!" He pointed to Elias. "Stand and tell the gathering if you believe me to have any affliction that could lead to a distemper of the brain."

Elias was reluctant to stand, but Ellershaw continued to urge, and the rumblings of the crowd began to sound menacing.

"You had better do it," I said.

Elias rose and cleared his throat. "I have examined the gentleman," he announced. "I have found no evidence of the disease mentioned, nor any other that can result in delirium."

Murmurs once more spread through the crowd, and Ellershaw only regained command by pounding upon the podium with a thick quarto that slammed down like a gavel.

"You see!" he cried. "Rumors accepted without basis. Now, if we may tend to the matter at hand, I would discuss this machine-produced calico Forester speaks of." He turned to that gentleman. "At the very least, you must allow us to examine this cloth. You say it is as good as India textile, but we have only your word that it is not rough, heavy stuff the public will reject. There have been numerous new engines that have been predicted as our doom, but none of them yet have been worth a fig."

Forester tried to block Ellershaw, but the big man pushed forward and took the roll of cloth directly into his big hands. He examined it, rubbed his hand along it, held it up to the light, even smelled it. He then paused and appeared lost in thoughtful reflection.

"Even you, sir, who have stood in my way, must admit that this is the very thing," Forester said, his voice nearly cracking with triumph. "Can you find a thing wrong with it?"

Ellershaw shook his head. "No, sir, I cannot," he said.

I knew, however, that there was more to come, for there was no concession in his voice. If anything, Ellershaw masked a smile, and he spoke loud enough for the room to hear. These were words not privately exchanged but performed upon a stage.

"I cannot find a thing wrong with it," he said, "because this *is* India cloth, you blockhead. You have wasted our time with this nonsense."

The room was now alight again, but Forester tried to stop the chaos. "If it is so like the original that even a man like Ellershaw finds it hard to tell the difference, does it not prove the cloth's value?"

Now Ellershaw did laugh, a loud, resonating boom. "You have been duped, sir. Someone has tricked you. I tell you this is India cloth, and if you were a true Craven House man—if you'd served your time in India as I have—you would know it." He unrolled two feet or so of the cloth and held it before the room. "Gentlemen, without even touching it, can you not observe that Forester is mistaken?"

The room went silent for a moment as they studied the cloth. What was it they were supposed to see? I had no idea. But then one voice called out, "Why, that's been dyed in India. I know that pattern."

"Yes, yes," another called. "There's not a dyer on this island that can replicate that. It's India cloth."

The room now went mad. They could all see it, or the ones that could not pretended to. They pointed and laughed. They hooted.

This time, however, Ellershaw was able to bring the room to relative quiet in short order. Somehow the enormity of what had just happened allowed for a return to orderly behavior. Though Forester remained upon the platform, he appeared disordered and confused. Red in the face and shaking in the limbs, I supposed he wanted nothing more than to flee this humiliation, but somehow fleeing would be more humiliating than enduring.

How had such a thing come to pass? I recalled Aadil, the Indian spy, who pretended to serve Forester. Clearly he had helped to orchestrate this downfall. Forester sought the engine, which would have hurt Indian trade. The Indian spy had struck back by sabotaging Forester's plans, pretending to acquire domestically produced textiles while instead providing Indian textiles, knowing this moment of exposure must come.

"Friends, friends," Ellershaw said, "let us come to order. This affair is not comic but, rather, cautionary. Mr. Forester is quite right that we have heard rumors of these new engines, and he was right to be vigilant. Can he be blamed because some unscrupulous scoundrels, no doubt out to make a profit from his ignorance, deceived him? Mr. Forester has reminded us to remain on our guard, and for that we must thank him."

I was struck by how quickly Ellershaw had taken charge of this chaos. The room burst into cheers and applause, and Forester was, much to my astonishment, able to retreat with something like honor. I supposed he would be forced to resign from the Court, but at least he could walk out of the room with the illusion of dignity.

Once Forester was gone, Ellershaw returned to the podium once more. "I know that it is not my time to talk, but as I am up here already, may I say a few words?"

The man who had introduced Forester nodded vigorously. Ellershaw was now a hero. Had he asked for permission to light the room on fire, surely it would have been granted.

"Gentlemen, I spoke the truth when I said we must be vigilant against these new engines, but I may also have been guilty of praising myself. You see, I have been vigilant. The rumors are all too true. There are indeed plans for such an engine, not one capable of producing textiles identical to India cloth but a step in that direction. And I believed it was in this company's best interest to suppress this machine, lest it lead to the refining of further engines that could, someday, challenge our markets. It is for that reason that I have gone to considerable lengths to obtain the only extant copy of the plans for this machine." He then reached into his coat pocket and removed a small octavo volume.

Even from the distance at which I sat I knew there could be no doubt of it. It was the very volume I had delivered to Devout Hale that morning.

"Now, I know there has been some dissatisfaction with my performance here of late," Ellershaw continued. "There are some voices who claim I could have done more to thwart the wool interest and prevent the imminent legislation, which will certainly prove a challenge to us in years ahead. I do not think it is true. I have never ceased to work for the repeal of that legislation, but there is only so much we can do, and the wool interest has a long and deep connection to the Parliament dating back to time immemorial. I have no doubt that we will regain our lost ground, but in the end there is much to do to expand the markets that remain open and to guard our rights and privileges fiercely. In having stopped this engine, I believe I have proved my worth."

The crowd apparently agreed with him, for it exploded in cheers and huzzahs. Ellershaw basked in the glow, and at last, when the room was quiet once more, he prepared to conclude his business.

"I do not wish to suggest that I have done all this on my own. I have had a great deal of help, and I wish now to acknowledge those who have assisted me. Our Company has a new advocate, a man who has come over from the wool interest to pursue our cause in Parliament. I should like all of you to welcome into our circle Mr. Samuel Thurmond. He has long served the wool interest, but for the past session he has been covertly working for our company, and he has vowed to use all his influence to repeal the odious legislation."

The old man rose and waved his hat for a moment, a cheerful grin upon his face. Here was not the dour man under Ellershaw's threats, or the tentative schemer who met secretly with Forester. Here, I saw, was a clever man, into the final portion of his life, who wished to secure some comfort for himself and perhaps the son Ellershaw had mentioned. The scheme with the pretended textiles had been perpetrated against Forester with Thurmond's aid. The threats against the old man, the confrontation in Sadler's Wells had been staged, I now perceived, for my benefit and for Forester's. Indeed, I understood at last that my very presence in Craven House had been for Forester's benefit—to make him believe his schemes were threatened by an outside inquiry— so that he might focus his suspicions upon me rather than Thurmond. It was to make him feel that a scheme was afoot, and to spur him on to strike that he might fail and, in his failing, set the stage upon which Ellershaw might climb for his triumph.

The room was now a scene of glad mayhem, with Ellershaw shaking hands, and members of the Court slapping Thurmond on the back, welcoming him to their project as though he were a hero. It seemed to me a most curious thing, since he had obtained this status by betraying his longtime allies. What, I wondered, would prevent him from betraying the schemers of Craven House? Perhaps, I thought, it signified nothing. Ellershaw had made it clear, after all, that these were men who lived from one quarter to the next, one Court meeting to another. What mattered a future betrayal when measured against an immediate success?

I felt myself mightily disgusted by these displays, and I thought to tell Elias that I would endure no more of it, but when I looked up I observed Thurmond shaking hands with a most unexpected attendee. It was none other than Moses Franco.

A thousand thoughts passed through my mind as I attempted to understand why Franco would be here and why he would be upon such friendly terms with Thurmond and several other of the Company men. Then I observed that he excused himself and maneuvered his way toward the main entrance leading to the bulk of Craven House. He opened the main doors and quickly closed them behind himself, but not so quickly that I did not see that someone awaited him outside, and from the look of clothes and body language I guessed that person to be Celia Glade.

I EXCUSED MYSELF TO ELIAS, saying nothing more than that I would return, and then pushed my way through the crowd. As I did so, Eller-shaw grabbed on to my shoulder and met my startled expression with a grin, far more secure and competent than any look I had previously seen upon his face.

"Think not, because I neglected to thank you publicly, that I consider your contribution any smaller than Mr. Thurmond's," he said.

I ignored this barb and pushed my way forward. At length, I separated myself from the room and studied the open space of the house. Luckily, I saw the pair I sought making their way down the hallway to a small closet I knew to have been recently vacated. They must have either expected no intrusion or minded none, for they did not close the door, and upon my arrival at the threshold, I observed Miss Glade handing Mr. Franco a purse.

"What betrayal is this?" I asked, my voice booming loud enough to startle them both.

"Mr. Weaver," Franco said cheerily, though now entirely without the accent he had affected in my presence. "I am so glad to see you, now that this is all over. There are going to be some recriminations—I know it cannot be helped—but let me say now that I am in your debt, sir, and have nothing but esteem and honor for you."

My expression must have presented to him some intelligence he did not desire, for he turned to Miss Glade. "He has already been informed of this particular, has he not?"

The lady blushed. "I'm afraid I have not yet had an opportunity to tell him."

"You are a spy?" I boomed.

Miss Glade put a hand upon my arm. "Take not your anger out upon him. If you are to blame anyone, you may blame me."

"And you may depend upon my doing so. How dare you make so free with my feelings and loyalties? Have you no idea of how I tormented myself with guilt over this man's incarceration? And now I find he was a spy in your service?"

Franco held up his hands to me as if in surrender, an effect not a little marred by his newly got purse, clutched in one hand. Nevertheless, more than trembling with fear, he turned red with mortification, and I sensed that he did indeed regret his deception. The earnestness of this evident regret so disarmed me that I stood still, having no notion of what I should say or do.

Miss Glade chose to take pity on my uncertainty. "Blame not this man," she said. "He was but an unfortunate as you were, forced against his will into Cobb's service."

"Upon my arrival in London, I'm afraid I made some rather poor choices with my money, including an investment in Mr. Pepper's engine—a scheme that brought me to the attention of Cobb. He contrived to acquire my debts as he did with you and your friends, and he then demanded of me that I form a connection with your family."

"Your daughter was a spy too?" I asked, the disgust in my voice undisguised.

"No," he said. "Alas, I could not depend upon so sweet a creature to deceive you, so I dissimulated with her as well. Allow me to say, however, that had the two of you found each other more agreeable, I should have had no objection to a match."

"You do me too much kindness," I said with bitterness.

He shook his head. "When I observed that the two of you would not form a match, I sent her to Salonica, that she might be well away from this madness. I am sorry, sir, very sorry, to have been made to deceive you. I can only hope, when you hear all, that you will not regard me with so much distaste."

"Rather than nursing your indignation toward Mr. Franco," Miss Glade said, "you may discover you wish to thank him. It was out of regard for you that he contacted the ministry and chose to turn coat and join with us."

"It is true," Franco said. "I knew Cobb to be a villain, and you to be a man of honor, and so—with my daughter safely abroad—I risked my safety in order to work for, rather than against, my new home. Sadly, one condition of my service was that you could know nothing of all this."

"And why?"

Miss Glade laughed. "Is it not evident that you are too nice in convictions to be trusted in a matter such as this, when what is right and what is wrong is a matter of some ambiguity? We knew you would never willingly serve the French and that you must rally, if given the choice, to your own kingdom. We were less certain that you could be depended on if there was a conflict between your notion of what was best for the kingdom and ours."

I snorted with disgust. "And so you played me like a puppet."

"We had no wish to," Franco said most pitiably.

"Mr. Weaver, you have been a man in this world long enough to know that we cannot always be used as we wish, and at times we must sacrifice our own inclinations for the good of something greater. If I were to learn my government had deceived me to such an end, I should not object. I should always choose they do so rather than be the loser for it."

"And that is your choice," I said. "Not mine. I know better than to believe the government makes a good bargain by supporting this Company. Two great powers can never live well together, and the time will come when the one must seek to crush the other."

"The day may come," Miss Glade told me, "when the ministry will be at odds with Craven House, but right now we are at odds with the French, and the French wish to destroy the East India Company as a means of destroying our power abroad. Politics cannot always be about what is moral and right and good for all men and for all time. It must be about what is expedient now, and what is the lesser evil."

"That is a wretched way to manage a nation. You are no better than the Company men, thinking only from one quarter to the next."

"It is the only way to manage a nation," she said. "Any other method is doomed to failure."

After a pause, she turned to Franco.

"I believe you have presented your case as well as you might," Miss Glade said to him. "May I suggest you leave us that we may exchange a word in private?"

He did so, bowing once more and rushing from the room. Miss Glade then closed the door and turned to me, her mouth wide, showing me an enchanting grin of white teeth.

"So," she said. "You are angry with me?"

"You speak to me as though we have some connection in which my anger might disturb you. You are nothing to me but a betrayer and a manipulator."

She shook her head. "I won't believe it. You are angry with me, but you do not consider me those things. Your pride is hurt because I have had the advantage over you for these three weeks, but I think when you consider the matter at greater length, you will come to see me in a kinder light. Assuming, of course, you do not already. I think you rather like me more than you will admit."

I did not answer, for I neither wished to confess nor to lie. Instead, I said, "Tell me this. You suggest the French killed Baghat. Did they kill Carmichael? And what of Pepper?"

"As for Carmichael, we have uncovered information that leads us to suspect that one of Ellershaw's men had it done."

"What?" I demanded. "You will let him get away with such a thing?"

"You must understand what the risks are here. This is a struggle of nations for world power, for an empire the likes of which has never before been seen. Such a prize is to be desired, yes, but even more so, that our enemy may obtain it must be fought at all costs. Do you wish for France to dominate Europe and the world? Have you considered how well our people do under English rule—here and in the colonies? Shall I tell you about life in the Catholic countries on the continent?"

"I am aware of those matters," I said.

"I have nothing but hatred for Ellershaw, and I, like you, wish he could be punished for his crimes, but this is a war—a war as real and with as great, if not greater, consequences as the kind fought by great armies upon battlefields. If we must endure a rascal like Ellershaw, then we must endure him—just as kings must endure monsters who sometimes make for remarkable commanders in the field."

"So he is not punished?"

"He cannot be. Even if we had proof, which we lack, it would be unwise to move against him." Here she smirked at me. "And none of your rough justice, if you please. Should any unfortunate accidents befall Mr. Ellershaw, I don't believe the ministry would let the matter rest, and I would not be in a position to protect you. You must seek retribution in your other way."

I could not know what she meant by those words, but I suspected she knew more of my mind than I would like. I turned away from her, crossing my hands behind my back. "And what of Absalom Pepper? Who killed him, and shall that person face justice?"

"I notice you turn away from me when you ask that question," she said. "You do not trust yourself?"

Anxiety and admiration filled me in equal measures, but I could not ignore the challenge. I therefore turned to her. "Who killed him?"

"I think you know the answer," she said, with the little smile that I had come to find both infuriating and irresistible.

"If I knew, would I not visit justice accordingly?"

"I believe you will."

"And you will not stop me?"

She shook her head. "No."

"Can the ministry approve?"

"The ministry will not know."

I studied her very narrowly, wondering if she planned some sort of ambuscade upon me. "Yet you will not attempt to stop me?"

"You must not think me blind in my loyalty. I would do anything to keep France from gaining the power Britain seeks, but that does not mean I am unable to envision what these companies represent. You are right to wonder what happens when they grow too powerful, and I am in agreement with you that it is better that their power be curtailed while we possess a weapon with which to strike. And so you may do as you wish, and I shall, in every official capacity, take no notice of it. In a more private setting, however, I believe you will know of my approbation."

My surprise was complete. "It appears, Miss Glade, that you and I may share more of a sense of justice than I had originally conceived."

"Can you have doubted it? I know you act as you think best, and because I am not in disagreement, I shall aid you as I can. As for the debts harbored against you and your friends, you may depend upon that matter being resolved by the ministry. I cannot, however, pay you the twenty pounds discussed." She looked remarkably saucy as she mentioned the last point.

"I shall endeavor to endure the loss."

"It shall be greater than you think, for I expect you to buy me a rather nice trinket in demonstration of your appreciation. And affection," she said, taking my hand.

I did not wish to appear—or to be—prudish, but I had not yet come to trust this lady, and I did not know with any certainty that she would still not betray me. It was for that reason I did not react more strongly to her advances, which were, I must say, most welcome.

She could not but sense my hesitation. "Come now, Mr. Weaver. Will you only court women like Mrs. Melbury, whose sense of propriety leads them to reject you? I should think you must be delighted to have met a woman not only of your nation but of your inclinations as well."

"You are very bold," I said. Despite my best wishes, I felt myself grinning as well.

"If it is boldness to speak the truth when alone with a like soul, then I confess the crime. I know what has passed between us may have given you a poor account of me," she said, now in a softer tone. She took my hand with a gentleness I found both startling and thrilling. "Perhaps you will call upon me when you are feeling less wounded and we may start anew."

"Perhaps I shall do that."

"Good," she said. "But do not take too long, or I shall be forced to come looking for you. Indeed, I may be asked to come look for you in a less personal capacity, for I can assure you the ministry has had every reason to applaud my earlier intercession on your behalf, and now all the talk is of Weaver and how he can be made to serve the king."

I took my hand away. "I do not believe I should like serving the king in such a capacity. As you observed, I am not inclined to bend my sense of rectitude for expedience."

"There may come a time when the kingdom requires a favor that presents no conflict. I hope you will not close your mind to it."

"And if I have no interest, then shall I call upon you all the same?"

"I beg of you that you do not delay," she answered.

Had we been in a private room, I know not where this conversation might have led, but an empty closet in Craven House during a meeting of the Court of Proprietors seemed to me hardly the most fitting temple in which to worship Venus. With the understanding that we should not be long from each other's company we therefore parted, she no doubt certain that she had begun our relations with a triumph. I departed to seek out Elias and tell him what I had learned, and I walked with a verve to my step.

—

CHAPTER THIRTY

*I*N THE HACKNEY, ELIAS CONTINUED TO SHAKE HIS HEAD. "HOW COULD you not tell Franco was a spy?"

"He gave me no reason to suspect him. Indeed, I believe most of his actions were sincere and as he would choose to behave, so in no way did he seem like a man dissimulating."

"And where to now?"

"There is a last bit of business," I said, "if only for my own satisfaction."

We went to the Throwers Arms tavern, where Devout Hale sat with his boys, drinking quite amiably. I should have thought he might have fled, might have been concerned that I would come looking for him, but he only smiled at me when I entered. He sent his companions away, and we sat at his table. I then introduced Elias, and the two men made some talk about scrofula. Elias plied the older gentleman with his wisdom until I could endure no more of the congeniality.

"Enough of this," I said, slapping my hand upon the table. "Did you think I would learn nothing of your ruse?"

"Of what?" Hale asked most unconvincingly.

"Let me speak plain, then. You betrayed me and your own men. I gave you a book that would bring the East India Company to its knees, and you handed it to Ellershaw. Why would you do that?"

He looked down, unable to hide his shame. "Judge me not too harshly. It is my sickness that led me astray. I told you I was desperate for a cure, and I traded the book for that. I approached the men of the

Company, and they assured me I would get a private audience with the king. It was but a book, Weaver, a nothing to me who cannot read. Surely you cannot blame a sick man for trading something he cannot use or understand for something that can save his life."

"No, I suppose I cannot blame a man who does such a thing. Your decision seems to me flawed but understandable." I sipped at my beer. "Except for one thing. How would you know to give the book to the very man who most wanted it? There are many men, many directors at the East India Company. Why Ellershaw?"

He shrugged. "I don't know. A coincidence, I suppose."

"No, it wasn't a coincidence," I said. "You have been working with Ellershaw for some time now, haven't you?"

"Of course not. That is absurd."

"Is it? I did not make sense of it at first, but when I learned that the East India Company had some silk workers in its employ, I should have known you would make yourself available, for you made it clear that you were so desperate for a cure you would do anything, take any risk. When today, at the Court of Proprietors meeting, Ellershaw held up that book, I knew you had quite made him. He did not need it to destroy his rival, but it was a nice success to play out before the Court. You betrayed the future of your cause for the gratification of an East India man."

"Keep your voice down," he hissed at me.

"What?" Elias asked. "Your men know nothing of your living upon Company silver?"

"Of course," he said, rather quickly. "They don't turn their backs on money, no matter if it come from the East India or elsewhere. It is an uncomfortable arrangement, but it is one they have come to accept."

I rose to my feet. "I beg you to listen, men of the silk trade. Is it true that you know Mr. Hale is in the pay of the East India Company?"

All eyes were upon me. I believe I would have been damned for a blackguard liar had not Hale risen to his feet and hurried to the door as quickly as his sickened condition would permit him. A half dozen of his men followed him. I doubted that Hale would get very far, and the only question was what they would do to him once they caught him. He was a sad man and a sick man, and he had sold out his boys for a false hope of a magic cure. There would be rough music, I had no doubt of it, but I also had no doubt that Hale would live to accept his reward of the king's touch and to discover the falseness of the hope.

ELIAS AND I THOUGHT it best to move to another tavern and found one not too far away, where we sat with our pots and our contemplation.

"I approve your cleverness in discovering Hale's treachery," he said, "but the truth is, Weaver, I find it to be too little and too late. I cannot help but feel that we have been here before."

I raised one eyebrow. "What do you say?"

"Well, this isn't the first time this has happened," he said. "You become involved in some inquiry, and it is clear that there are great forces out there trying to manipulate you, and despite your best efforts in the end you are manipulated. Maybe some of the more reprehensible people are punished, but those with power get precisely what they want. Does that not bother you?"

"Of course it bothers me."

"Is there no way to be more vigilant?" he asked. "You know—to prevent this sort of thing from happening so regularly?"

"I suppose there is."

"Then why have you not availed yourself of it?"

I looked up at him and grinned. "Who says I haven't?" I finished my pot and set it down. "With so many spies and so much manipulation involved, I could not but be aware that there were those who would turn it to their advantage if I let my guard down for a moment. As ever when dealing with men of such power, there is only so much one can accomplish, but I believe I have done my best to thwart them."

"But how so?" he asked.

"Finish your pot, and you will find out."

WE TOOK A COACH to Durham Yard, where we once more knocked on the door and were greeted by Bridget Pepper, Ellershaw's wife's daughter. She was chief, I now believed, among those I had styled the Pepper widows. Elias and I were shown inside, where we waited but briefly before the good woman entered the parlor.

"Good afternoon, madam," I said. "Is your husband home?"

"What cruel joke is this?" she asked. "You know quite well that he is dead."

"I thought I knew that quite well," I explained to Elias, but with the intention that she listen as well. "It was one of the few basic truths I was given by Cobb, but then I began to wonder. With so much deception about, how did I know Pepper really was dead? What if Cobb lied to me, or what if Cobb had been lied to? Given that we know he had a traitor in his midst, I now believe it to be the latter."

"So Pepper is not dead?"

"No. It was part of the agreement he reached with the East India Company. He would give up the plans—plans they knew he would never be able to duplicate on his own because, as one of his other wives explained, he lost ideas the moment he wrote them down. In exchange for this sacrifice, he would be permitted to remain married to this young lady here. And perhaps something else: a new life abroad, I suspect. You must truly love him, to remain by his side despite his—shall we say—excesses."

"I know not why you should defame his memory and torment me so," she said. "He's dead. He's dead."

"I wonder," I said. I removed something from my pocket and showed it to her. "I wonder if this is the sort of thing that might bring him back from the grave."

With my warmest smile, I showed the young lady the octavo containing the plans for Pepper's engine.

"WHAT DID ELLERSHAW HAVE?" Elias asked me, as we walked to the back of the house.

"The first book I received from the lady in Twickenham," I said. "It appeared remarkably similar in form and content, and there was no way to tell the plans it contained were abortive. Indeed, it looked to me so much like the true plans, that had there not been a slight imperfection on the calfskin of the other, a mark in the shape of a *P*, I would not have been able to tell them apart."

In the back of the house, Mr. Pepper sat with a book and a glass of wine. He rose to greet me. "I must admit," he said, "I had some vague hope this was a possibility, but it was never more than a vague hope. You are indeed an impressive man."

But it was not I who was impressive. There was in fact something about Pepper that radiated more warmth, more kindness, more contentment than any other man I'd ever met. He was indeed handsome, but the world is full of handsome men. No, he had something else, and though I knew it was false, it was still remarkable and undeniable, like a bolt of lightning that one fears but that still produces awe.

I handed him the book. "I suggest you remove yourselves to some other part of the kingdom. The East India Company may not take well to your attempting to realize these plans."

"No. As you deduced, that was the agreement. My death should be widely reported in order to keep me safe from the French. The ministry went to a great deal of trouble to make sure that French spies intercepted letters telling how the Company had murdered me."

"And," I guessed, "Mr. Ellershaw brokered this deal, providing you with a handsome dowry, allowing you to live happily with his stepdaughter, and ignoring your other—shall we say—*entanglements,* in exchange for surrendering the plans."

Mrs. Pepper put a hand upon her husband's shoulder. "You need not dance about the matter," she said. "I know the somewhat circuitous path my Absalom walked before we came together. I do not resent him for doing what he had to, and now that we are joined I am content to forget his past."

"But then," I proposed, "Ellershaw had second thoughts. He could not risk your continued existence and wished to have you removed. It was then Mrs. Ellershaw who protected you and hid you away. That is why she thought I sought out information about her daughter on her husband's behalf. I don't know if she understood the truth of Mr. Pepper's other attachments, but if she did, it could hardly matter more to her than it did to her daughter."

Pepper patted his wife's hand and grinned at me, a look both winning and lascivious. "Actually I must point out—for I am rather proud of it—that this good woman delivered unto me *two* handsome dowries. The bargain we struck was that Mrs. Ellershaw was to believe her husband violently disapproved of the match. She provided the dowry, and then Mr. Ellershaw matched it. A rather handsome scheme, I believe."

He did not wait for my approbation, but instead began to look through the book. "Oh, yes. Very clever. Very clever indeed. I do have my moments. At times I think myself the very best of men." He paused and looked up at me. "You must tell me why you do not keep the plans for yourself. This cannot yield fruit for some many years, and thus I can offer you no reward."

"I don't want the plans, and I don't want the reward," I said. "I could never understand your designs, and bringing them to any useful state should be far more work than I desire. I shall be honest with you, Mr. Pepper. Though we have never met, I have followed your trail all over the metropolis and have found you to be a most reprehensible man. You take what you will and care nothing for the feelings of those you harm."

"That's rather harsh," he said good-naturedly. "And you'll find that there are many who disagree with you."

"Be that as it may," I said, "I cannot claim to like you, but I believe that the man who invented the engine ought to benefit from it, even if that man is a rogue. To take the plans for myself would be theft of the highest order. I also believe that in the end you will do much less harm in the world if you are financially comfortable. And, finally, my aim here is that the East India Company be dealt with as it ought, and I believe you are enough of a contriver to see these plans brought to reality."

"It is very honorable of you."

"No, it is wicked," I said. "I want them to know their efforts failed. All this energy expended in keeping a man from improving technology, in preventing people from having more control over the commodities they wish to buy. They think they own mankind when they only own their company. I have been very badly abused, Mr. Pepper, and the greatest satisfaction I can have is doing what I can to make certain that those who abused me are brought low. I do not think that it will happen soon, but I can content myself with knowing that I have planted a seed that favors the future."

He grinned and slipped the book in his pocket. "Then many thanks to you," he said. "I'll use it in good health."

Back in the hackney, Elias let out a laugh. "He truly is a foul man."

"They're all foul. We're all of us foul, each of us in our own way. We excuse it in ourselves, and perhaps in those we love, but we delight to condemn it in others."

"That is very philosophical of you."

"I am of a philosophical bent today."

"Then here is something to ponder," he said. "It is a very strange thing that when dealing with these companies the man who acts out of spite and revenge, as you have now, comes across as the most moral. That, I suppose, is the warping power of greed."

I had no doubt that he supposed correctly. I struck a blow against greed that day—I would not take the satisfaction away from myself by denying it—but I knew it was like striking a blow against a storm. If a man had a delicate enough instrument, he might be able to measure the effect, but the storm would still rage according to its inclination; it would do its damage, and the world would never know that someone had exerted his will, perhaps all of his will, in the effort to lessen its force.

THE DEVIL'S
COMPANY

A Novel

DAVID LISS

A READER'S GUIDE

I first met David Liss in northern Italy at a crime-fiction-and-blues festival. Mr. Liss, hiding behind stylish prescription glasses, comes across as a man lost in his own world . . . until he begins to speak. From that point on, you find yourself in the company of a man of excellent humor, keen intelligence, and razor wit. This author of six critically acclaimed bestselling novels (and the recipient of an Edgar Award) is probably best known for his character Benjamin Weaver, the early eighteenth-century ex-pugilist and "thief-taker," whose exploits lay bare the early traumas and extremes of modern capitalism while taking the reader on a thrill ride through the underbelly of London. *The Devil's Company* continues his story.

This interview was conducted in our homes in Budapest, Hungary, and San Antonio, Texas, a world away from Benjamin Weaver's London.

—Olen Steinhauer, *New York Times* bestselling author of *The Tourist*

Olen Steinhauer: How did you get started writing fiction?

David Liss: Corny though it might sound, I've always wanted to write fiction. I have a very clear memory of writing a short story in the second grade. I believe it involved spaceships. After I graduated from college, I tried writing a novel, but I wasn't sufficiently prepared for how *hard* it would be to put a real book together, and I gave up, concluding that my ambitions of being a writer were misguided. However, I never really stopped thinking about it, and several years later, when I was in graduate school, I decided I would try again. This time I was able to apply the analytical and critical thinking skills I'd gained in a punishing doctoral program to figuring out how a novel actually worked and where I'd gone wrong before. Those efforts turned into my first published novel, *A Conspiracy of Paper*.

OS: In 2008, you were named an Artist for Integrity by the United Nations Office on Drugs and Crime. Can you tell us something about how that came about, and how I can get one?

DL: That was, admittedly, something I never expected. I was invited to participate in a UN anti-corruption convention in Bali along with a series of other artists—a director, an actress, and a couple of musicians. I never really understood why they selected me, but it involved a free trip to Bali, so I wasn't complaining.

OS: One thing that really impresses in *The Devil's Company* is the way you use language to evoke the period without it ever feeling stuffy, static, or imitative. Which is to say, it reads like a historic text imbued with modern pacing. How did you achieve this? Did you read a lot of primary texts from the time, or did you simply let your imagination roam?

DL: Historical fiction is always a tricky balancing act. I want to maintain the illusion of bringing the reader into the past, but at the same time, a contemporary audience wants pacing and language to be absorbing and comfortable. When I was in graduate school studying eighteenth-century British literature, I read countless eighteenth-century documents, and I feel like I got a pretty good sense of the rhythm and feel of the language. When I write a novel set in that period, I try to invoke that rhythm and pepper what is essentially modern prose with eighteenth-century vocabulary, idioms, and, occasionally, syntax. When I first tried doing this, I had no idea if it would work, but now I feel relatively comfortable with the middle ground I've staked out.

OS: There's a school of thought that posits that historical fiction is, in essence, fantasy fiction, because none of us were around to know the visceral reality of those times. Do you hold to this view?

DL: I think this is essentially true. Historical fiction often fulfills the same escapist role as fantasy fiction, though the reader has the advantage of learning actual history along the way. Not that the history of orcs is without interest. . . . Much of the pleasure of reading—and writing—historical fiction is the re-creation of an alien world. The historical novelist takes many of the details of that world from the actual historical record, but there is always a lot of guesswork, connecting the dots, and speculation involved, even in historical fiction that follows the script of history fairly closely. I try and re-create the past as faithfully and as accurately as I can, but I also know that it is my interpretation with my biases and conceptions.

OS: You've recently entered the world of comics, writing for Marvel. Has that had any effect on the way you write novels?

DL: I'm not sure it's had a direct effect, but the experience has been an incredible challenge for me as a storyteller, and an opportunity to grow. Writing a comic book script is an entirely different way of telling a story than is writing a novel, and I think any time a writer gets to re-think the mechanics of narrative, it's a good thing. I would never write fiction the way I write comics, but I think my experience in one medium affects and informs the way I approach another. And I also think that the core elements of what makes a story successful—tone, character, narrative energy—are all the same in just about every storytelling medium, be it fiction, comics, television, or film. The difference is how the medium permits the execution of these elements.

OS: *The Devil's Company* shines a fascinating light on the relationship between Jews and Christians in early eighteenth-century England. Ellershaw, for example, constantly gives Weaver backhanded compliments that belittle his race. How did London compare to other European capitals in regard to anti-Semitism?

DL: In the early eighteenth century, London was probably the most desirable city in Europe for Jews to live. The novel depicts what to contemporary readers must seem like pure anti-Semitism, and of course it is, but it has to be seen within the context of English culture at the time. The English, in general, disliked Jews, but they also disliked

Catholics, the French, Germans, the Dutch, the Italians, and just about everyone else, and they were not shy about saying so. There was very little violent anti-Semitism in eighteenth-century Britain, and Jews were never in any real danger of being expelled or having their property arbitrarily seized, so as distasteful as much of the English attitude seems, it is a far cry from most of Europe at the time, and certainly most of Europe in centuries past.

OS: Benjamin Weaver is a "thief-taker," essentially a hired gun (or fist), a mercenary. How prevalent was this profession in England at the time, and was there a specific thief-taker you used as a model?

DL: Thief-taking was very real. There was no police force, such as we understand it, in eighteenth-century Europe, and law enforcement was largely a privatized business. Thief-takers received a fairly hefty bounty for bringing in felons who were later convicted, and that was supposed to promote freelance law enforcement. Often it simply promoted schemes by which poor and helpless victims were framed by thief-takers conspiring to find a patsy and share the bounty.

Benjamin Weaver is, in many ways, inspired by Daniel Mendoza, who lived much later in the century. He was a much celebrated Jewish boxer, and later, when he was too old to fight, he earned his living by accepting thief-taking commissions. Like Weaver, he was generally an honorable fellow, but thief-takers of this sort were likely in the minority.

OS: In an interview with *January Magazine,* you talked about Benjamin Weaver's love interest, Miriam, who makes only a brief appearance in this book. You said that you'd gotten rid of her because you "felt like the character was done." What did you mean by that, and does this mean that you can see a point where Weaver himself will be "done"?

DL: I think that when you write about a character over multiple books, you have to be careful not to repeat the same personal narratives over and over again. I don't believe in resetting the clock.

I felt the character was done because the emotional muck I'd dragged them through must have consequences, and I could not realistically see them as continuing to have feelings for each other after everything that had come before. As for Weaver himself, I don't need to write a certain number of novels with this character. I've gone back to him twice when I've had ideas for the character I wanted to work with and stories I wanted to tell. I have no plans to write another Weaver novel at this moment, but I reserve the right to change my mind tomorrow. I do think that at some point I ought to write at least one more to put a kind of period on his narrative.

OS: The namesake of this novel is the East India Company, and its level of brutality and cynicism is often shocking. Yet at the same time, to a jaded reader from the early twenty-first century, it's never unbelievable. How many of the company's shenanigans did you take from real life?

DL: I did not set out to write a historical novel in which the East India Company is an allegory for the modern corporation. Rather, in my research, I was astonished to discover just how many modern corporate practices were already in play in the early eighteenth century. The main plot of murder and deception is, of course, fiction, but the business practices I portray are all historically accurate. If anything, corporations were much more brutal in the past than they are now because certain kinds of human life (non-British, the very poor, etc.) were held cheaply, and there was no one to prosecute abuses of what we today would call human rights.

OS: One of the many lively scenes occurs in Mother Clap's, a boarding-house/club catering to homosexual men. Clearly, such an establishment was illegal in London at the time, yet Weaver and others know of its existence. How common were such places in eighteenth-century England, and how did they exist alongside the law?

DL: There were several such "molly houses" in eighteenth-century England, though Mother Clap's is certainly the most famous. And yes, they were illegal, as was homosexuality, but there was no clear means of regulating such activity. Prostitution was illegal as well, but prostitutes operated nearly everywhere and in the open, and almost always without fear of the law. Eighteenth-century London was a society caught in the throes of a strengthening, unregulated capitalist system, while older, more ideological systems of regulation (a uniform, mono-lithic religious structure, the monarchy, the class system) were weak-ening. At this point, if something was making money, and not interfering with public order (or a more powerful entity's ability to make money), it was generally left alone. The most seriously and con-sistently punished crimes in this period were crimes against property.

OS: The London you describe sounds in ways like a libertarian ideal, where the free market is untethered by government regulation—yet no one would call it utopia. In another of your novels, *The Whiskey Rebels*, wild libertarians in the West try to bring down the federal govern-ment's financial system. In *The Ethical Assassin*, the title character uses fierce—and very compelling—social critiques to argue for his vegan lifestyle.

All this is just to say that your books are rife with thought-provoking social observations and criticisms. Do you see this as a primary func-tion of the novelist? (I ask this of a United Nations Artist for Integrity, remember.) And how much effect can novelists have in the video-and-Internet age?

DL: I think my primary function as a novelist is to entertain readers. Once we get too self-important and forget that very basic role, we pro-duce far less effective novels. That said, I believe that if I am lucky enough to have readers, I ought to write something worth reading, and to that end, I do often write about issues I think are important. In other words, I see writing about important issues as my secondary function as a novelist.

Can we have much effect? Honestly, I don't know. It's the rare novel (I can think of *Uncle Tom's Cabin*, but not any others) that radically af-fects a major cultural movement. On the other hand, it's better to con-tribute to an important social conversation than to opt out because you don't believe you can dominate it.

1. At the beginning of *The Devil's Company*, Benjamin Weaver states he is able to "adopt the most plastic of morals . . . when the circumstances dictate." How does disguise help and hinder him in this endeavor? Does this mentality hold true for Weaver throughout the novel? When does "acting as something he is not" conflict with doing what he believes is right? What does he do? Does he "preserve [his] soul"?

2. After Jerome Cobb first meets with Weaver and outlines the terms of his "plan" and demands Weaver's cooperation, Weaver leaves thinking he has a choice, though he later realizes "I had no choice." How does Cobb secure his control over Weaver? Consider the role and manipulation of choice and freedom in the novel.

3. Benjamin Weaver's uncle, a fellow victim of Cobb's machinations, suggests to Weaver, "You cannot fight him if you don't know who he is or why he would work so diligently to render you toothless. In revealing to you what he has in mind, he may also reveal to you the secret of how to defeat him." How does Weaver use this advice to his advantage and what does he discover to be the secret to unraveling Jerome Cobb?

4. Jerome Cobb's nephew, Hammond, believes that "darkness holds far greater terrors than any monstrosity, no matter how terrible, revealed in the light." Do you think this is true? Does Weaver? How is disguise used in the novel to engender fear and/or power?

5. How does Weaver gain entry into the East India Company "fortress" and Ambrose Ellershaw's trust and confidence?

6. Does Benjamin Weaver have a weakness? Why can he not "content [himself] with a state of ignorance" as Cobb suggests?

7. How do the challenges facing the "Devil's Company" and their competitors—greed, globalization, competition, capitalism, corruption, innovation—resonate today? How have these challenges evolved?

8. Ellershaw explains to Weaver that "no arsenal and no weapon in the arsenals of the world is so formidable as the will and moral courage of free men." Do you agree? Does Weaver? How is this statement ironic, given Ellershaw's role in the East India Company and *The Devil's Company*?

9. Discuss the anti-Semitism Weaver is confronted with throughout the novel.

10. When Weaver inquires after the insurance policies taken out on his life, he is asked, "How can it be diabolical when it is the law?" Consider the "oceans of absurdity" that this question invokes for Benjamin Weaver.

11. What would the executives of the East India Company argue drives commerce, need or desire? How do they—and the capitalist framework—manipulate these two factors?

12. How does Ellershaw defend the "Honorable Company" and why does Thurmond suggest they instead call themselves the "Devil's Company"? How do the "Company men" view the "Government

men" and vice versa? Do they have any of the same interests? What does the legislation of 1721 symbolize in their different spheres? How do both sides attempt to rectify their positions? Discuss how their positions relate to freedom, diplomacy, "the wealth of the nation," and "the natural evolution of things."

Read on for an excerpt from

David Liss's

THE WHISKEY REBELS

Ethan Saunders

It was rainy and cold outside, miserable weather, and though I had not left my boardinghouse determined to die, things were now different. After consuming far more than my share of that frontier delicacy Monongahela rye, a calm resolution had come over me. A very angry man named Nathan Dorland was looking for me, asking for me at every inn, chophouse, and tavern in the city and making no secret of his intention to murder me. Perhaps he would find me tonight and, if not, tomorrow or the next day. Not any later than that. It was inevitable only because I was determined not to fight against the tide of popular opinion—which is to say, that I ought to be killed. It was my decision to submit, and I have long believed in keeping true to a plan once it has been cast in earnest.

It is a principle I cultivated during the war—indeed, one I learned from observing General Washington himself. This was in the early days of the Revolution, when His Excellency still believed he might defeat the British in pitched battle, Continental style, with our ill-disciplined and badly equipped militias set against the might of British regulars. It was the decisive military victory he wanted; indeed, in those early days it was the only sort he believed worth having. He would invite the officers to dine with him, and we would drink claret and eat roast chicken and sip our turtle soup and he would tell us how we were going to drive the Redcoats back at Brooklyn, and the unfortunate affair would be over before winter.

That was during the war. Now it was early in 1792, and I sat at the bar of the Lion and Bell in that part of Philadelphia euphemistically called Helltown. In that unsavory scene, I drank my whiskey with hot water while I waited for death to find me. I kept my back to the door, having no wish to see my enemy coming and because the Lion and Bell was as unlovely a place as Helltown offered—and those were mighty unlovely. The air was thick with smoke from pipes plugged full of cheap tobacco, and the floor, naught but dirt, had turned to mud with the icy rain outside and the spills and spitting and tobacco juice. The benches lay lopsided in the newly made hummocks and ruts of the ground, and the drunken patrons would, from time to time, topple over and tumble like felled timber into the muck. Perhaps a drinker might take the trouble to roll a friend over to keep him from drowning, though there could be no certainty. Helltown friends were none the best.

It was a curious mix there: the poor, the whores, the desperate, the servants run off for the night or the month or forever. And alongside them, throwing dice upon uneven surfaces or hunched over a hand of cards spread across ripped velvet, were the gentlemen in their fine woolen suits and white stockings and shimmering silver buckles. They'd come to gawk and to rub elbows with the colorful filth, and most of all they'd come to game. It was the spirit of the city, now that Alexander Hamilton, that astonishing buffoon, had launched his great project, the Bank of the United States. As Secretary of the Treasury, he had singlehandedly transformed the country from a republican beacon for mankind into a paradise for speculators. Ten years earlier, with a single stroke, he had transformed me from patriot to outcast.

I removed from my pocket a watch, currently my only possession of value if one did not account my slave, Leonidas. I had, despite the decisions that had prevailed among the wise drafters of our Constitution, never quite learned to think of Leonidas as property. He was a man, and as good a man as any I'd known. It sat ill with me to keep a slave, particularly in a city like Philadelphia, whose small population of owned blacks numbered in the dozens, and one could find fifty free blacks for each bondsman. I could never sell Leonidas, no matter how dire my need, because I did not think it right to buy and sell men. On the other hand, though it was no fault of his, Leonidas would fetch at auction as much as fifty or sixty pounds' worth of dollars, and it had always seemed to me madness to emancipate such a sum.

So the timepiece, in practical terms, was currently my only thing of worth—a sad fact, given that I had removed it from its rightful owner only a few hours earlier. Its glittering face told me it was now half past eight. Dorland would have eaten his fashionably late dinner well over two hours ago, giving him ample time to collect his friends and come in search of me. It could be any minute now.

I slid back into my pocket the timepiece I'd taken on Chestnut Street. The owner had been a fat jackanapes, a self-important merchant. He'd been talking to another fat jackanapes and had paid no mind while I brushed past him. I'd not planned to take the watch, nor did I make a habit of such things as common theft, but it had been so tempting, and there seemed to be no reason not to claim it and then disappear in that crowded street, clacking with the walking sticks of bankers and brokers and merchants. I saw the watch, saw it might be taken, and saw how I might take it.

Even then, if that had been all, I would have let it go, but then I heard the man speak. It was his words, not my need, that drove me to take what was not mine. This man, this lump of a man, who resembled a great and corpulent bottom-heavy bear, forced into a crushed-velvet blue suit, had been invited to a gathering the next week at the house of Mr. William Bingham. That was all I knew of him, that he, a mere maker of money, nothing more than a glorified storekeeper, had been invited to partake of the finest society in Philadelphia—indeed, in the nation. I, who had sacrificed all for the Revolution, a man who had risked life in return for less than nothing, was little more than a beggar. So I took his watch, and I defy anyone to blame me.

Now that it was mine, I examined the painting in the inside cover, a young lady of not twenty, plump of face, like the watch's owner, with a bundle of yellow hair and eyes far apart and open wide, as though she'd been in perpetual astonishment while she sat for the portrait. A daughter? A wife? It hardly mattered. I had taken from a stranger a thing he loved, and now Nathan Dorland was coming to avenge such wrongs, too innumerable to catalogue.

"Handsome timepiece," said Owen, standing behind the bar. He was a tall man with a head long and narrow, shaped like one of the pewter mugs into which he poured his ales, with wheat-colored hair that curled up like foam. "Timepiece like that might go a way toward paying a debt." He held out one of his meaty hands, covered with oil and filth and blood from a fresh cut on his palm to which he paid no mind.

I shrugged. "With all my heart, but you must know the watch is newly thieved."

He withdrew the hand and wiped it on his filthy apron. "Don't need the trouble, but I ought to send you to fence it now, before you lose it at game."

"Should I turn the watch to ready, I would not use it for something so ephemeral as a tavern debt." I pushed my empty mug toward him. "Another, if you please, my good man."

Owen stared for a moment, his tankard of a face collapsed in purse-lipped indecision. He was a young man, not two-and-twenty, and he had a profound, nearly religious reverence for those who had fought in the war. Living, as he did, in such a place as Helltown, and moving through indifferent social circles, he had never heard how my military career had met its conclusion, and I saw no advantage in sharing information that would lead to his disillusionment.

Instead, I favored other details. Owen's father died in the fighting at Brooklyn Heights, and more than once had I treated Owen to the tale of how I had met his father that bloody day, when I was captain of a New York regiment, before my true skills were discovered and I was no longer to be found upon the battlefield. That day I led men, and when I told Owen the tale, my voice grew thick with cannon fire and death screams and the wet crunch of British bayonet against patriot flesh. I would recount how I had given Owen's honored father powder during the chaos of the ignominious retreat. With blood and limbs and musket balls flying about us, the air acrid with smoke, the British slaughtering us with imperial fury, I had taken the time to aid a militia volunteer, for we had shared a moment of revolutionary comradeship that defied our differences in rank and station. The tale kept the drinks flowing.

Owen took my mug, poured in some whiskey from an unstoppered bottle and hot water from a pitcher near the stove. He set it down before me with a considerable thud.

"Some would say you've had your fill," he told me.

"Some would," I agreed.

"Some would say you're abusing my generosity."

"Impertinent bastards."

Owen turned away and I opened the watch once more, setting it upon the counter, where I might stare at the tick of its hands and the girl who had meant so much to the merchant. To my right sat an animated skeleton of a man in a ragged coat that covered remarkably unclean linen. His face was unshaved, and his nasty eyes, lodged between the thinning brown hair of his crown and the thickening brown hair of his cheeks, stole glances at my prize. I'd seen him come in an hour earlier and slide a few coins across the bar to Owen, who had, in exchange, handed a small parchment sack to the ragged man. Owen did a brisk trade in that greenish powder called Spanish fly, though this man, his magic dust in hand, seemed content to sit at the bar and cast glances at me and my timepiece.

"I say, fellow, you are looking upon my watch."

He shook his head. "Wasn't."

"Why, I saw it, fellow. I saw you setting larcenous eyes upon my watch. This very one."

"Ain't," he said, looking closely at his drink.

"Don't you speechify at me, fellow. You were coveting my timepiece."

I held it up by the chain. "Take it if you have the courage. Take it from my hands while I observe you rather than skulking in the dark like a sneak thief."

He continued to gaze inside his pewter mug as though it were a seeing crystal and he a wizard. Owen whispered a word or two to him, and the skinny gawker moved farther down the bar, leaving me alone. It was what I liked best.

The hands of the watch moved. It was strange how a man could find himself in so morose a state. Only a few days before I had considered Dorland's pursuit of revenge as a vague amusement. Now I was content to let him kill me. What had changed? I could point to so many things, so many disappointments and failures and struggles, but I knew better. It was that morning, coming from my rooms and seeing the back of a woman half a block ahead of me, walking quickly away. From a great distance, through the tangle of pedestrians, I had seen a honey-brown coat and, above it, a mass of golden-blond hair upon which sat a prim if impractical wide-brimmed hat. For a moment, from nothing more than the color of her hair, from the way her coat hung upon her frame, from the way her feet struck the stones, I had convinced myself that it was Cynthia. I believed, if only for an instant, that after so many years and married though she was to a man of great consequence, Cynthia Pearson knew I now lived in Philadelphia, knew *where* I lived, and had come to see me. Perhaps, at the last moment, recognizing the impropriety, she lost her courage and scurried away, but she had wanted to see me. She still longed for me the way I longed for her.

It lasted but an instant, this utter, unassailable conviction that it was Cynthia, and then disappointment and humiliation struck me just as hard and just as quickly. Of course it had not been she. Of course Cynthia Pearson had not come to knock upon my door. The idea was absurd, and that I should, after ten years, be so quick to believe otherwise testified to how empty was my sad existence.

When Owen returned, I closed the watch and put it away, and then I drained my drink. "Be so good as to pour another."

Owen hovered before me, shaking his head, his mug handle of a nose blurring in the light of the oil lamps. "You can hardly keep yourself sitting. Go home, Captain Saunders."

"Another. I am to die tonight, and I wish to do it good and drunk."

"I daresay he is already quite drunk," said a voice from behind me, "but give him another if he likes."

It was Nathan Dorland. I needn't look, for I knew the voice.

Owen's eyes narrowed with contempt, for Dorland was not an imposing figure. Not tall, not broad, not confident or commanding. "Unless you're a friend of Captain Saunders, and from the look of you, I'm guessing you ain't, I'd say this is none of your concern."

"It's my concern, because when this wretch is done with his drink, I mean to take him outside and introduce him to a concept called *justice,* with which he has been all too unfamiliar."

"And yet," I said, "I am familiar with *injustice.* Such irony."

"I don't know your complaint," said Owen, "and I know the captain well enough to trust you've got your cause. Even so, you'll not harm him. Not here. If you've a grievance with him, you must challenge him to a duel, like a gentleman."

"I have done so, and he has refused my challenge," Dorland said, sounding very much like a whining child.

"Duels are fought so early in the morning," I said to Owen. "It's barbarous."

Owen looked over at Dorland. "You've heard it. He has no interest in fighting you, and you must respect that. This man is a hero of the Revolution, and I owe him a debt for my father's sake. I'll defend his right to fight or not fight whom he wishes."

"Hero indeed!" Dorland barked. "I suppose when he is spinning tales of his time with Washington, he may have neglected to tell you the one in which he is cast out of the army for treason. Haven't heard that one? Ask him if you doubt it. Captain Saunders's career ended in disgrace, and as to the matter of your father, be assured he tells every tavern keeper in Philadelphia that he fought with his father or brother or uncle or son. Our friend here has given so many doomed men powder, he is like the angel of death."

Owen's eyes glistened in the light of the fireplace, and I shrugged, for I had been caught. I would not shy away from an untruth, but it seemed a contemptible thing to lie about a lie.

"I *was* at Brooklyn Heights," I said. "I might have seen your father.

And no matter what you may hear said of me, I can promise you I was never a traitor. Never."

My words only served to make Owen more teary. He looked over at Dorland. "Leave now. I don't want trouble, and nor do you."

"What does he owe?" I heard the ease of wealth in Dorland's voice. "I'll pay his debt."

Owen said nothing, so I spoke. "'Tis near eleven dollars." It wasn't true. I owed less than six, but if Dorland was going to pay for my death, at least Owen should profit from it.

I heard behind me the music of metal on metal, and then a purse landed hard upon the bar. "There's three pounds of British in it," said Dorland. "Near fifteen dollars. Now Saunders comes with me."

I nodded at Owen. "'Tis my time. Thanks for the drinks, lad."

I pushed myself off the rough wooden stool, and the room turned to a wild and topsy-turvy thing, with the floor leaping up toward me and bar stools taking flight like startled birds. I reflected on the danger of drinking so long without rising—that it is often hard to say precisely how drunken one has become if there is no new movement against which to test oneself. And then I believe I lost consciousness.

PHOTO: © TRISH SIMONITE

DAVID LISS is the author of *The Whiskey Rebels*, *The Ethical Assassin*, *A Spectacle of Corruption*, *The Coffee Trader*, and *A Conspiracy of Paper*, winner of the 2000 Edgar Award for Best First Novel. He lives in San Antonio with his wife and daughter and can be reached via his website, www.davidliss.com.